Stuart Neville has been a musician, a composer, a teacher, a salesman, a film extra, a baker and a hand double for a well-known Irish comedian. His debut novel *The Twelve* was published to great acclaim in 2009 and was awarded the *Los Angeles Times* Book Prize in the mystery/thriller category.

Visit the author's website at:
www.stuartneville.com

COLLUSION

Former paramilitary killer Gerry Fegan wanders New York City, hiding from a past he escaped at terrible cost. But he made a fatal mistake: he spared the life of Bull O'Kane, a ruthless man who wants revenge. Too many witnesses survived a bloody battle at his border farm, and now he wants them silenced, whether man, woman or child. O'Kane calls the Traveller, an assassin without pity or remorse. Back in Belfast, Detective Inspector Jack Lennon, father of one of the witnesses, is caught up in a web of official secrets and lies as he tries to uncover the whereabouts of his daughter. The closer he gets to the truth about the events on O'Kane's farm, the more his superiors instruct him to back off.

Books by Stuart Neville
Published by The House of Ulverscroft:

THE TWELVE

STUART NEVILLE

COLLUSION

Complete and Unabridged

CHARNWOOD
Leicester

First published in Great Britain in 2010 by
Harvill Secker
The Random House Group Limited
London

First Charnwood Edition
published 2011
by arrangement with
The Random House Group Limited
London

British Library CIP Data

Neville, Stuart, *1972 –*
Collusion.
1. Paramilitary forces- -Northern Ireland- -Fiction.
2. Political violence- -Northern Ireland- -Fiction.
3. Revenge- -Fiction. 4. Missing persons- -
Investigation- -Northern Ireland- -Fiction.
5. Northern Ireland- -Politics and government- -
1994 – - -Fiction. 6. Suspense fiction.
7. Large type books.
I. Title
823.9'2–dc22

ISBN 978–1–4448–0679–3

Published by
F. A. Thorpe (Publishing)
Anstey, Leicestershire

Set by Words & Graphics Ltd.
Anstey, Leicestershire
Printed and bound in Great Britain by
T. J. International Ltd., Padstow, Cornwall

This book is printed on acid-free paper

For Nat Sobel, who changed my life

1

'We're being followed,' Eugene McSorley said. The Ford Focus crested the rise, weightless for a moment, and thudded hard back onto the tarmac. Its eight-year-old suspension did little to cushion the impact. McSorley kept his eyes on the rear-view mirror, the silver Skoda Octavia lost behind the hill he'd just sped over. It had been tailing them along the narrow country road since they crossed the border into the North.

Comiskey twisted in the passenger seat. 'I don't see anyone,' he said. 'No, wait. Fuck. Is that the peelers?'

'Aye,' McSorley said. The Skoda reappeared in his mirror, its windows tinted dark green. He couldn't make out the occupants, but they were cops all right. The tarmac darkened under the growing drizzle, the sky a blank, heavy sheet of grey above the green fields.

'Jesus,' Hughes moaned from the back seat. 'Are we going to get pulled?'

'Looks like it,' Comiskey said. 'Fuck.'

Hedgerows streaked past the Focus. McSorley checked his speed, staying just below sixty. 'Doesn't matter,' he said. 'We've nothing on us. Not unless you boys have any blow in your pockets.'

'Shit,' Hughes said.

'What?'

'I've an eighth on me.'

1

McSorley shot a look back over his shoulder. 'Arsehole. Chuck it.'

McSorley hit the switch to roll down the rear window and pulled close to the hedgerow so the cops wouldn't see. He watched his side mirror as Hughes's hand flicked a small brown cube into the greenery. 'Arsehole,' he repeated.

Comiskey peered between the seats. 'They're not getting any closer,' he said. 'Maybe they won't pull us.'

McSorley said nothing. He raised the rear window again. The car rounded a bend onto a long straight, the road falling away in a shallow descent before rising to meet the skyline half a mile ahead. He flicked the wipers on. They left wet smears across the windscreen, barely shifting the water. He'd meant to replace them a year ago. McSorley cursed and squinted through the raindrops.

A white van sat idling at a side road. It had all the time in the world to ease out and be on its way. It didn't. Instead it inched forward to the junction, the driver holding it on the clutch. McSorley wet his lips. He felt the accelerator beneath the sole of his shoe. The Focus had a decent engine, but the suspension was shot. Once the road started to twist, he wouldn't have a chance. He eased off the pedal. The van drew closer. Two men in the cabin, watching.

McSorley's stomach flipped between light and heavy, heavy and light, while adrenalin rippled out to his fingers and toes. He fought the heaving in his chest.

'Christ,' he said out loud, without meaning to.

'Nothing to worry about. They're only cops. They're going to pull us, that's all.'

The Focus neared the white van, and McSorley saw the men's faces. They stared back as he passed. His eyes went to the mirror. The Skoda's reflection swelled. Blue lights flickered behind the grille, and its siren whooped. The van edged a foot or two out of the junction.

The Skoda accelerated, disappeared from the mirror, and reappeared alongside the Focus. McSorley saw white shirts and dark epaulettes. The woman cop in the passenger seat signalled to the side of the road.

'Fuck,' McSorley said. He gently squeezed the brake and shifted down. The Skoda slipped past as he let the Focus mount the grass verge. It skidded on the wet grass and mud. The Skoda stopped a few yards ahead. Its reversing lights glared, and it rolled back to stop just feet from the Focus's bonnet.

'Keep your mouths shut, boys,' McSorley said. 'Answer them when they talk to you, but don't give them any lip. Don't give them any excuses. Right?'

'Right,' Hughes said from the back.

'Right?' McSorley said to Comiskey.

Comiskey gave him a quivering smile. 'Aye, no worries.'

Two cops got out of the car, donning hats and bright reflective jackets. The woman wasn't bad looking, light brown hair swept up under her cap. The man was tall and in good shape. His rich tan looked alien beneath the grey sky. They approached the Focus, the man leading.

3

The wipers scraped across the windscreen, the rubber-on-glass creak in counterpoint to McSorley's heartbeat. He put his finger on the button, ready to lower the window when the cop asked. Instead, the cop grabbed the handle and opened the door. Rain leaked in. It had been raining for nearly three months solid. All day, every day, no let-up. McSorley blinked as a heavy drop splashed on his cheek.

'Afternoon,' the cop said. He had an English accent, hard and clipped. 'Shut your engine off, please, sir.'

McSorley turned the key. The engine died, freezing the wipers in mid-sweep.

'Just keep your hands where I can see them, there's a good chap,' the cop said.

That accent, McSorley thought. Officer class. It spoke of parade grounds and stiff salutes, not traffic patrols and police checkpoints.

The cop ducked his head down. 'You too, gentlemen.'

Comiskey put his hands on the dashboard; Hughes placed his on the back of the passenger seat. McSorley gripped the steering wheel and studied the cop's face. His skin was a deep brown, not the shallow tan of a week at the beach. His lips were shiny from balm applied to the cracks, as if they'd been baked in some arid place. A vision of this cop crawling across a desert flashed in McSorley's mind. The image terrified him, and he couldn't think why.

The cop's hands stayed out of view until he reached in and took the key from the ignition. A black leather glove, expensive looking.

4

'What do you want?' McSorley asked. His voice bubbled in his throat.

The cop straightened and looked back down the road. 'You're not wearing your seat belt. Any reason?'

'I forgot,' McSorley said. He looked to the rear-view mirror, knowing what he'd see. The van pulled out of the junction, turning towards them.

The woman cop walked to the passenger side. She leaned down and peered in, first at Comiskey, then at Hughes. Comiskey gave her a weak smile. She did not return it.

'Well, that won't do,' the tanned cop said. 'You don't want points on your licence, do you?'

The van filled the rear-view mirror. The woman cop waved, and it pulled alongside the Focus. The tanned cop reached in and hit the button to open the boot. It would have sprung up a good six inches when the car was new, but now it just loosened itself from the seal. The woman cop went to the back of the Focus, and the boot lid whined as she opened it fully. Cold, damp air kissed the back of McSorley's neck. The smell of manure from the fields around them mixed with the bitter sting of his own sweat.

The two men stayed in the van's cabin, but McSorley heard heavy feet moving inside, and then its rear doors opening. He went to crane his head around, but the tanned cop hunkered down beside him, smiling.

McSorley studied the peeler's face and all at once knew every tale the lines and cracks told.

He had been in a dry and barren place, crawling in the dirt, hunting his prey. Iraq, maybe Afghanistan. Maybe somewhere the Yanks and the Brits would never admit to. And now he was here, not far from the Irish border, his sun-scorched face blank and unyielding. Just another job.

'You're not a peeler,' McSorley said.

The cop's hard smile didn't even flicker. 'Where are you headed today, sir?'

'I said, you're no peeler. What do you want?'

Footsteps scuffled behind the two vehicles. Something screeched and groaned as it was dragged along the floor of the van. Voices issued orders, hissed and strained. The cop's eyes never left McSorley's.

A voice said, 'On three. One, two, three — hup!'

The Focus lurched and leaned back on its rear axle as something monstrously heavy was dumped in the boot.

'What the fuck was that?' Comiskey asked.

Hughes turned in the seat, but the parcel shelf blocked his vision. McSorley watched shifts in the light in his rear-view mirror. He wanted to weep, but smothered the urge. He heard more scuffling, then the thudding of feet clambering back into the van. The car's boot lid slammed down, and McSorley saw the woman cop through the back window, along with a heavy-set man. The parcel shelf didn't quite find home; something pushed it up from beneath.

The woman cop carried a long sports bag. The heavy-set man raised an automatic rifle. It

6

looked like the Heckler & Koch G3 McSorley had fired behind a Newry pub years before. The man approached from the driver's side, keeping the rifle on McSorley.

McSorley felt the heat of tears rising behind his eyes. Fuck if he'd cry. He swallowed them. The rear passenger side door opened. He looked back over his shoulder.

The woman cop reached in and dropped something metallic. Its weight thudded on the carpet between Hughes's feet.

'Oh, fuck,' Hughes said. He scuttled sideways, behind McSorley, away from whatever lay there.

She tossed something else in. It clanked against the first object.

'Oh, Jesus,' Hughes said, his voice rising into a breathy whine.

The woman drew a pair of long cylinders from the bag. McSorley stared at them for a moment, his brain struggling to catch up with what he saw, before he recognised the twin barrels of a shotgun. She placed it butt-first into the footwell, letting the long barrels fall across Hughes's thigh.

'Fuck me, they're guns,' Hughes said as the door swung shut. 'What's going on, Eugene?'

McSorley looked back to the tanned cop. The cop smiled, winked, and closed the driver's door. He held up the car key, showed it to McSorley, and thumbed it twice. The locks whirred and clunked. The cop placed the key on the bonnet, just beneath the glass.

'Christ,' McSorley said.

'What are they doing, Eugene?' Comiskey asked.

7

'Oh, sweet Jesus.' McSorley crossed himself. His bladder screamed for release. He fought it.

The two cops, who McSorley knew were not cops at all, got back into the Skoda and pulled away. The van eased in front of the Focus. The man with the rifle grinned at McSorley. He kept the gun trained on him as he climbed into the open back.

Comiskey tried the handle. 'Open the locks,' he said.

'Can't,' McSorley said. Tears warmed his cheeks. 'The bastard double-locked it. You need the key to open it.'

The van moved off, picking up speed. The man with the rifle waved. McSorley's bladder gave out.

'Oh, God,' McSorley said. 'Jesus, boys.'

Comiskey slammed the window with his elbow. He tried it again. Hughes lifted the shotgun and rammed the butt against the rear window.

McSorley knew it was pointless. 'Oh, Christ, boys.'

Hughes hit the window once more, and it shattered. He lurched to the opening. Comiskey scrambled to climb back and follow.

Waves of rainwater smeared the windscreen as the van grew smaller in the distance. Hughes roared as he forced his shoulders through the gap.

'Jesus,' McSorley whispered. 'Jesus, boys, they killed us.'

He barely registered the detonator's POP! before God's fist slammed him into nothing.

2

Detective Inspector Jack Lennon knew it was shit work, but the choice had been made clear: keep an eye on Dandy Andy Rankin and Rodney Crozier as they met in a greasy spoon café on Sandy Row, or spend the rest of the week typing up notes for the Public Prosecution Service. His buttocks still ached from the stint of PPS donkey work they'd dumped on him last year. He didn't fancy another taste.

The information had been passed along from C3, or Special Branch as most people knew them. Rankin and Crozier, two of Belfast's leading Loyalists, were to meet at Sylvia's to try to settle an argument that had so far put five men in hospital. One had lost an eye, another was breathing through a tube in his throat, but no one had died yet. The plan was to keep it that way.

Spats between the Loyalists were a constant nuisance. Every few weeks a thug or two would turn up with his head broken over some quarrel or other. But sometimes the spats boiled over and people got killed. No one on the force cared too much if the odd drug dealer got taken out, but it would rile the politicians and the press, not to mention the paperwork it would generate. So it was best to keep tabs on things, try to head off trouble at the pass. That's what Chief Inspector Uprichard had said when he assigned Lennon the job. Lennon had been at a loose end since he'd lost his place on the Major Investigation Team, so this sort of busywork was the best he could hope for. Observe and report, see who's talking to whom, judge if the exchanges are friendly or heated, make sure it's not something that could escalate.

Lennon watched the café from a van with Water Board markings. He'd parked up in a side street across the way, put a lunch box and a flask on the dashboard, and opened a copy of the *Belfast Telegraph*. He had spread the pages across the steering wheel fifteen minutes ago and settled in.

Rankin and Crozier sat by the window. Lennon could see them clear as day, but could only imagine their conversation. There was no money in the pot for bugging the place. The pair were only of mild interest to Special Branch, so did not merit the budget. This was strictly eyeball duty, nothing more. Yep, Lennon thought, shit work. Part of him wondered if they just wanted to get him out of the office.

The targets huddled together, their proximity suggesting soft voices, even if the expressions on their faces did not. Crozier wore a Glasgow Rangers football top, his tattoos blurring on his thick forearms. Rankin sported a grey suit with a pink shirt, open at the collar to display his heavy gold chain. His teeth looked unnaturally white against his orange tan. Sylvia Burrows, the café's proprietor since it had opened in the early Seventies, placed two steaming mugs between the men. She did not linger to make chitchat.

The men barely acknowledged her.

Lennon scribbled on the pad in his lap and looked at his watch. Twenty minutes now since he'd pulled up, ten since Crozier had arrived, no more than five since Rankin had joined him. Lennon yawned and stretched. Maybe the PPS paperwork wouldn't have been so bad.

Just a few weeks ago he'd been on a Major Investigation Team, second to DCI Jim Thompson. Good work, proper police graft befitting his rank. He'd pissed it away over a bloody speeding penalty he'd tried to get quashed for that piece of shit Roscoe Patterson. The traffic cop, Constable Joseph Moore, had come over all self-righteous when Lennon tackled him.

It wasn't the sixty quid, Lennon had explained, money wasn't the issue. Roscoe had plenty of money. Lennon might have said that last part twice, he couldn't quite remember. The issue was the three points Roscoe couldn't afford on his licence. Things got heated when Moore, one of the newer Catholic recruits filling up the ranks since the Patten reforms, questioned why Lennon would stick his neck out for a Hun bastard like Roland 'Roscoe' Patterson. Lennon knew he shouldn't have grabbed Moore's throat and pushed him against the wall, and he apologised the next day. He didn't know, however, that Moore had gone to CI Uprichard and claimed Lennon had tried to pass on an offer of a bribe from a known Loyalist paramilitary.

Thus Lennon found himself in front of Uprichard's desk being offered the choice of unpaid leave or a full disciplinary hearing. Without his old friend DCI Dan Hewitt's intervention, the latter would have been the only option. Uprichard reminded Lennon that his record was not unblemished, and a hearing would be unlikely to do him any good, even if the allegation couldn't be proven.

Lennon chose leave. He sat at home for three days before boredom got the better of him. On the fourth day he boarded a flight to Barcelona. The hotel was a pit. George Orwell was supposed to have stayed there during the Spanish Civil War. From the looks of it, he'd picked the wallpaper. But the room had a balcony overlooking Las Ramblas, and the weather allowed him to sit out in the evenings with a can of San Miguel, watching the tourists and the locals avoid each other's eyes on the street below. When midnight came, he toured the tapas bars, looking for American or English women he could charm with his accent. Most nights, he succeeded.

He returned from Barcelona only to feel like a spare wheel, no real use to anybody, so every crappy meaningless job came his way. Including this one.

Rankin and Crozier's hands became more animated. Fingers stabbed at the tabletop as points were made. The mugs shook. Lennon blinked and focused, shifted in the driver's seat, leaned forward.

Crozier held up his hands, palms out, maybe trying to placate the other man. Rankin didn't look like he was having any of it. His forefinger wagged in Crozier's face. Crozier sat back, his shoulders slumping in exasperation.

Lennon glanced down to his pad and noted the change in tone. When he looked up, Crozier was on his feet, turning to leave.

Good, Lennon thought. If it was over, he could get the fuck out of there and type up the notes. That done, he could wait around for some more shit work.

Rankin tugged at Crozier's sleeve. Crozier slapped his hand away. Rankin stood, his chair tipping over.

'Jesus,' Lennon said to the empty van. 'This is getting a bit tasty.'

Rankin pulled a knife from his pocket and buried the blade between Crozier's ribs.

Lennon blinked, tried to make sense of what he'd just seen. 'Fuck,' he said.

Rankin withdrew the blade. Crozier didn't go down. He stared at the other man, his mouth slack. Rankin drove the blade home again.

'Christ,' Lennon said. He reached for the radio, hit the emergency button. It would send a signal out to every receiver on the network, saying an officer needed assistance, pinpointing his position.

Crozier swung a fist, throwing Rankin back, still clutching the knife. Rankin tumbled over the chair, disappeared from view. Crozier put a big hand to his side, pulled it away, examined the bright red on his fingers. He staggered back until he met the wall.

Lennon opened the glovebox and grabbed the Glock 17 and the wallet with his ID. He threw the door open and stepped out. He shoved the wallet down into his pocket and pressed the Glock against his thigh. He ducked into the traffic, his gaze fixed on the window, adrenalin crackling through him, sending sparks to his fingertips.

Rankin reappeared, clambered over the chair towards Crozier. The bigger man put his hands up, but too slow. The blade punctured his neck.

A car horn blared and tyres squealed as Lennon crossed the road. A woman screamed inside the café. Lennon raised the Glock. Crozier slid down the tiled wall, Rankin over him, the knife ready to come down again.

Lennon hit the door shoulder first, raised the Glock and aimed to where Crozier lay bleeding. No Rankin. The woman screamed again. Lennon wheeled the gun around, saw Rankin seize Sylvia's hair, bring the blade to her throat. Sylvia gasped, eyes wide behind thick glasses. Rankin held her close.

Lennon pulled his wallet and flipped it open. He showed Rankin the ID and tucked the wallet away again. He levelled the pistol, left hand supporting the right, shoulders set for the recoil.

'Let her go, Andy,' Lennon said.

Rankin back-pedalled, dragging Sylvia with him by her hair. He glanced over his shoulder and guided her behind the counter towards the rear door.

'Don't, Andy,' Lennon said as he followed. 'The alley's closed off. There's walls at either end. You can't go anywhere.'

Rankin pulled Sylvia tight to him, the blade up

14

under her chin. Lennon saw red on her skin. He couldn't tell if it was Crozier's blood or hers.

'Oh Jesus help me,' Sylvia said.

'You're all right, Sylvia,' Lennon said as he reached the counter. He gave her the easiest smile he could manage. 'Andy's not going to hurt you. Everyone round here likes you too much. Where'd they go for their fish and chips if anything happened to you, eh? No more pasties, no more sausage suppers. Everyone knows Sylvia does the best feed in town, right? Right?'

Sylvia didn't answer as Rankin backed towards the door.

'How's that going to go down around here if Andy hurts you, eh? He won't be able to show his face. Come on, Andy, let her go. We can sort it out. Crozier's still breathing. Don't make it worse.'

Lennon searched for some sign of doubt or panic on Rankin's face, found nothing but dead eyes set in his tanned skin.

'I'll cut this old bitch open,' Rankin said, his lips moving against her dyed hair. 'Don't think I won't.'

'No,' Lennon said, taking a step closer. 'You're not that stupid. Everyone knows how smart you are, right? You can't get away. Even if you could, where would you run to? This isn't the Dandy Andy we all know.'

'Don't call me that.' Rankin pointed the blade at Lennon. 'Nobody calls me that to my face.'

'Sorry,' Lennon said. He raised his hands, the Glock aimed at the ceiling, in apology. 'I didn't think. I'm not a thinker like you. You're the

15

smart one in your crew, that's how you got where you are today, right?'

Rankin brought the blade back to Sylvia's throat. 'Don't come any closer.'

Lennon stopped. 'You know you can't go anywhere. You know you can't hurt Sylvia. You're too smart to do that. It's time to think, Andy. What's the best thing to do? What's the smart thing to do?'

'Christ,' Rankin said. The death slipped from his eyes. Fear replaced it, childish panic, reason about to flee.

'Easy, Andy,' Lennon said. He held his hands out to his sides, the Glock aimed towards the hotplates and fryers at the back of the open kitchen. 'Take a few breaths, all right? Let's be calm about this. Let's be smart.'

Rankin gulped air, and the sanity returned to his face. 'All right,' he said. 'How do we get out of this?'

'Let Sylvia go for a start,' Lennon said. 'Then put the knife down.'

Streets away, a siren wailed.

'They'll be here soon,' Lennon said. 'Best if we're all calm by then, eh? You and me just sitting at a table waiting for them, right? 'Cause if they come storming in with you and me facing off like this, it could get tricky. Right?'

Rankin looked to the windows at the front of the café. His mouth curled as the panic threatened to take him again. Dead calm overcame it.

'Right,' he said.

'Good man,' Lennon said. 'Now, just let go — '

16

Rankin shoved Sylvia at Lennon. The top of her head cracked against his chin. They both tumbled backwards. Lennon grabbed the counter with one hand, reclaimed his balance, cradled Sylvia with the other arm. A cool draught washed around them from the open door as Rankin vanished through it.

Lennon gathered Sylvia to him. 'You all right?'

She gawped at him through her crooked glasses, her mouth opening and closing.

'Sit down,' he said, forgetting Rankin for a moment. Even if the prick got out of the alley, he'd be lifted in no time. Sylvia was more important right now. He lowered her to the floor, her back against the rear of the counter. 'Deep breaths. You're all right.'

Lennon went to rise, but she clutched at his shoulders. He crouched beside her, wrapped his arms around her shoulders, and kissed the top of her head.

'You're safe,' he said.

He stood, looked at Crozier's bloodied form propped against the wall. The Loyalist's shoulders rose and fell as he moaned. He'll live, Lennon thought. He went for the door and the alley beyond, Glock up and forward.

Rankin clung to the wall at the northern end of the alley, grunting as he tried to haul himself up.

'You should've used the wheelie bin,' Lennon called.

Rankin dropped the two or three feet to the ground and turned.

'It's right here,' Lennon said, indicating the

17

plastic bin by the door. 'You could've put it up against the wall, climbed on top, and you'd have been away.'

Rankin pressed his back against the brickwork. His breath came in hard rasps, his eyes bulging. He still held the knife in his right hand.

'Why'd you have to scare poor Sylvia like that?' Lennon asked. He stopped a few feet from Rankin. 'You can knife shit-bags like Rodney Crozier all day long for all I care, but putting the frighteners on a nice lady like Sylvia? That's not on.'

Rankin raised the knife. Sweat beaded on his forehead. 'You keep away from me.'

'Or what?'

The siren drew close, another not far behind it.

'Stay back,' Rankin said. He grimaced and hissed through his teeth. His face reddened.

'Or what, Andy?'

'Or . . . ' Rankin dropped the knife and clutched his left arm with his right hand. He went down on one knee. His hands went to his sternum as if trying to hold his heart in place. His jaw muscles bunched and bulged as his face went from red to purple. 'Fuck me,' he said between gritted teeth.

He hit the ground face first.

'Jesus,' Lennon said.

3

The Traveller followed Orla O'Kane along the wide corridor. She had thick ankles. Her blocky heels made dull thuds on the carpet. A property developer by profession, she buried her father's money in houses, hotels and office blocks. Most likely some of it went into this building, a mansion outside Drogheda, the former home to a British landowner, now converted to a private convalescent home.

He couldn't help but be impressed when he drove up the gravel driveway, cutting between lawns and landscaped gardens, the house standing three storeys high up ahead. The River Boyne ran behind it, the tall pylon of the new cable-stayed bridge carrying motorway traffic across the water visible above the treetops perhaps half a mile away.

The rest of the building had been cleared; all the rooms were empty. He'd seen one cleaner and one nurse in the grand entrance hall. A few men loitered around the grounds and in the corridors, but they certainly weren't medical staff, with their watchful eyes and bulges in their jackets.

'Does he pay a lot of medical insurance, your da?' the Traveller asked.

She stopped, clicking her heels together. Christ, she had a big arse on her. Broad across the shoulders, too. Her business suit did its best

19

for her, but she was a big lass, there was no hiding it. Not a bad face, though.

'He values his privacy,' she said over her shoulder. She had the hard consonants of a woman used to being listened to, not questioned.

The Traveller smiled at her. If she'd been anyone else's daughter, he might have had a crack at her. She'd be a good ride, he could tell, the hard-nosed ones always were. But this one was too dangerous.

He followed her along a first floor hall in the east wing. She walked to the second-last door on the left. A grunt from inside the room greeted her knock. She opened the door and waved the Traveller through.

Bull O'Kane sat in the corner, tall sash windows on either side of him. A neat lawn edged by copses led to a high wall perhaps forty yards beyond the glass. The river flowed on the other side.

The daughter cleared her throat. 'I'll be outside if you need me, Da.'

O'Kane smiled. 'All right, love.'

A draught cooled the Traveller's back as the door swished closed.

'She's a good girl,' O'Kane said. 'Smart as a whip. Can't keep a man, though. Always goes for gobshites.'

The Traveller walked to one of the windows. 'Quite a view,' he said. A heron waded in the shallows across the rain-swollen river. 'Good fishing here, I bet. Salmon, trout. I should've brought my rod.'

'You don't look like a knacker,' O'Kane said.

The Traveller turned to face him. 'And you don't look like you could afford a room in this place, let alone the whole lot of it.'

O'Kane sat with his feet up on a stool, a blanket covering his lap down to his ankles. He had a faecal smell about him. The Traveller had heard the old man took a shot to the knee and another to his belly, damaging his bowel. O'Kane wore a bag now, and would do for the rest of his days. He was thinner than the Traveller had imagined, frailer than a photograph he'd seen. Age was catching up with him, spurred on by his injuries, but his eyes still burned hard.

'Someone told me your real name's Oliver Turley,' O'Kane said. 'Is that right?'

The Traveller sat on the edge of the bed. 'Might be. Might not. I've been called lots of things. Smith, Murphy, Tomalty, Meehan, Gorman, Maher, I could go on.' He leaned forward and whispered, 'There's some people say I'm not even really a Pavee.'

A dead mask covered O'Kane's face. 'Don't get smart with me, son. I'm a serious man. Don't forget that. I'll only warn you the once.'

The Traveller leaned back and nodded. 'Fair enough. But I'm a serious man too, and I don't like answering questions. You'll know as much about me as I want you to know.'

O'Kane studied him for a moment. 'Fair enough. I don't care if you're a gypsy, a traveller, a knacker, a tinker, or whatever the fuck you lot call yourselves these days. All I care about is the job I need doing. Are you the boy for it?'

'I'd have thought a man like you has plenty of

boys to do his dirty work for him.'

O'Kane shook his head. 'Not this job. I can't have anyone connected to me involved. And it needs done right. Quiet, like. No fuss, no bother.'

'All right,' the Traveller said. 'So, what is it?'

O'Kane's face darkened. 'Only a handful of people know what I'm going to tell you. You do this job right, it'll be just you and me knows the whole story. You'll be paid well to keep quiet once it's done. Big money. But if I ever hear a whisper of it down the line . . . ' O'Kane smiled. 'Well, I won't be looking for a refund. Understand?'

'I understand,' the Traveller said.

O'Kane pointed to a file on the bedside locker. The Traveller reached for it. He removed loose sheets of paper, photocopies, computer print-outs. Some pages had photographs, others blocks of text.

'I don't read,' the Traveller said.

O'Kane eyed him. 'Don't or can't?'

The Traveller spread the pages on the bed beside him. 'A couple of people thought that made me stupid,' he said. 'They don't think much of anything nowadays.'

O'Kane clicked his tongue against his lower lip three times. He started talking. He talked about the madman Gerry Fegan, how he'd been driven by figments of his drink-addled imagination to kill Michael McKenna, Vincie Caffola, a crooked cop, and O'Kane's cousin, Father Eammon Coulter. He talked about the politician Paul McGinty's botched attempts to contain it, how

22

they'd made things worse, costing more lives, including McGinty's own. It had ended in a bloodbath at an old farm near Middletown, O'Kane's son dead, shot by a traitorous ex-soldier called Davy Campbell, and the old man injured.

Fegan got away clean, taking Marie McKenna and her child with him. They had vanished into thin air, it seemed. Aside from O'Kane, two survivors from the scene remained: McGinty's driver, and Kevin Malloy, one of O'Kane's boys. Malloy was hit in the gut and the chest. The driver Quigley had taken O'Kane and Malloy to a hospital in Dundalk, saving both their lives.

'This needs to go away,' O'Kane said. 'The Brits, Dublin, the boys in Belfast; they all want it cleaned up.'

'They said it was a feud,' the Traveller said. 'On the news. They said those three dissidents ambushed McGinty at the farm.'

'The Brits put that together,' O'Kane said. 'They got McSorley and his boys at the border. They planted the guns in the car, made it look like they'd blown themselves up with their own bomb. Lovely job, it was.'

The Traveller nodded. He couldn't deny he was impressed. 'But that's not all, is it?' he asked. 'There's too many people in the know.'

'Quigley and Malloy,' O'Kane said. 'I want them gone, and so do the Brits. And there's a lawyer, Patsy Toner. Get rid of him, too. The Brits will turn a blind eye. They'll make sure the investigation turns nothing up. They've as much to lose as anyone.'

The Traveller folded his arms across his chest. 'But any arsehole could do those three. That's not why you need me.'

'I want Fegan,' O'Kane said. 'I want him brought to me alive.' He pointed a thick finger to emphasise the point. 'Alive. He's no good to me if he's not breathing, you understand? Nobody knows where he went. You'll have to draw him out.'

'How?'

'Marie McKenna and her child. The cops have them hidden, but there's been a bit of luck.'

'Oh? What's that, then?'

'Marie McKenna's father had a stroke last week. He's lucky to be alive, or maybe unlucky, depending how you look at it. He's in a bad way. I'm told there's a good chance he'll have another one before he recovers, and it'll probably do for him.'

'So you reckon she'll come out of hiding to go and see him,' the Traveller said. 'Her and the kid'll show themselves.'

O'Kane tilted his head. 'I'm told you've no problems doing women and children. Is that right?'

The Traveller shrugged. 'Depends on the money,' he said.

4

'I don't trust him,' Orla said to her father after one of the men had escorted the Traveller out. 'Them gypsies are all the same. They'd thieve the breath from you if you let them.'

'Trust's got nothing to do with it,' the Bull said.

The visitor gone, he shrank back into the chair, grew somehow smaller.

It still tore at her. He'd seemed a giant when she was a child, whether his hard hands were gathering her to him or slapping her around the ears. While other men seemed to diminish in size as she grew up, her father remained as big. It wasn't just the height and breadth of him, though they were impressive. His size came from within; he was a giant of the soul, the boss of everything. But now he was smaller, like someone had sucked the giant out of him and left only the skin and bones behind.

That someone was Gerry Fegan, and even to think his name forced hate to swell in her breast. But she was a practical woman, always had been. While her brothers pissed away their youth living off their father's name, she had strived to make herself worthy of it.

'Do you want back into bed?' she asked.

'Aye, love,' he said. 'I'm tired.'

Orla went to him, slipped her arms under his. He linked his hands behind her neck, and they

25

grunted together as she hoisted him up.

'Easy, now,' she said as he lowered his damaged leg, the blanket spilling away. He hissed as his foot settled on the floor.

Only a few months before, the very idea of lifting him would have been absurd, even as broad and strong as she was. But with the giant hollowed out of him, she could manage it, barely.

Orla back-pedalled, letting him take tiny baby steps as he followed her momentum. She felt the edge of the bed against her thighs and turned him. He sagged onto the mattress, and the bed groaned. She scooped up his legs and swung them up and over the blankets. He gasped and cursed.

'There, now,' she said. 'Lie back.'

He did as he was told and settled into the mound of pillows. Sweat glistened on his blotched forehead. She fetched a cup of water and held it to his lips, then dabbed at the dribbles on his chin with a tissue. The softness of the flesh made tears climb up from her throat. She swallowed them.

'I don't like him,' she said.

'He's the best,' her father said. 'Doesn't matter if you like him or not. I'm paying him to do a job, not to be your friend.'

'You don't need him for Toner and the rest of them.' She dropped the cup and the tissue into the wastepaper bin. 'Any fucker could do them.'

'Don't swear, love,' the Bull said. 'It doesn't suit a girl to swear.'

She took his big hand in hers. 'Oh, don't be such an old nag. Point is, you could get anyone

26

who knows how to do the job to go after them boys.'

Her father sighed, the breath leaking out of him until his massive chest seemed to sink back into itself. 'It's not them I need him for. It's Fegan.'

Orla studied the broken veins criss-crossing his face, the tufts of his eyebrows, the dark circles beneath them. 'You could let Fegan go. No one's heard of him since. He'll stay away. He's no reason to come back.'

His hand loosened in hers. 'I'm sick of talking about this. You'll not turn me.'

'The dreams won't stop if you kill him,' she said, renewing her grip on his thick fingers. 'You think you'll be well again if he's dead, but you won't. There's no — '

'Go on, now, love.' He pulled his hand away from hers. 'I'm tired.'

'All right,' she said. She leaned in and placed a kiss on his damp forehead, holding her lips there until he turned his head away.

The door closed softly behind Orla as she let herself out into the corridor. She sat in the chair facing her father's room. Fat ugly sobs bubbled up from her middle as she buried her face in her hands. Once again she imagined putting a pillow over the old man's face and saving him from whatever it was that festered inside his mind.

5

Sylvia Burrows dabbed at her nose with a balled-up tissue. Her thick glasses magnified her tearful eyes. She sniffed long and hard, then slumped as she let the air out. Lennon sat across the interview room table from her, a pad covered with his spidery scrawl lying between them. He'd type the statement up in the afternoon and call her back to sign it in the morning.

'I seen three men shot dead in my café over the years,' Sylvia said. 'One of them in the late Seventies, another in 1981 during the hunger strikes, and the third one just before the ceasefire. I knew every one of them, called them by their names when I held their hands. I'll never forget that feeling, the trembling in their fingers. Then it stops and they go cold.'

She laid her hands flat on the graffiti-strewn table, spreading her fingers wide. Old burns scarred the loose skin, a blue plaster wrapped around the ring finger of her left. She stared down at them. 'Jesus, I'm getting old,' she said.

Lennon placed his hands on top of hers. She clasped his fingers, squeezed them.

'You're a good young fella,' she said.

He fought the urge to pull his hands away, to tell her there was little good about him.

'Handsome,' Sylvia said. She lifted his hands, turned them, studied the shape of them. 'I never married, you know. There was plenty chased me,

28

but I could never settle. Too many handsome boys to pick from. That was my soft spot, the handsome boys.'

Lennon returned her smile. 'Thank you for talking to me. I hope you'll testify, if it gets to court.'

'I never testified before.' She returned his hands to the tabletop. 'Two of them, I saw their faces when they shot those men in my café. I could've drawn pictures of them. I can still see them now. But I got the phone calls late at night, the bullets in the post. I never went to court. But I will this time.'

She squeezed Lennon's wrists.

'Thank you,' he said. 'You'll be safe, I promise. There's no need to be afraid.'

'Afraid's got nothing to do with it,' she said, her face hardening. 'People should stick by their own. My God, trying to kill someone the same sort as you. If you can't trust your own kind, who can you trust, hmm?'

Lennon forced a smile and slid his hands from beneath hers. 'I'm glad you feel that way.'

A knock at the door broke the moment. Chief Inspector Uprichard leaned in.

'Can I have a minute?' he asked.

★ ★ ★

DCI Dan Hewitt sat to the side of Uprichard's desk, watching Lennon. Hewitt and Lennon had come through Garnerville together. Hewitt had progressed higher in the ranks, despite being a year younger than Lennon at thirty-six. He was smart, always playing the angles, and well suited to the covert work of C3 Intelligence Branch. While Lennon struggled his way into C2 Serious Crime, Hewitt eased into the shiny new replacement for Special Branch. In the reborn police force, cleaned and polished for the post-ceasefire Northern Ireland, there was no longer any need for the cops to have their very own secret service.

Except everyone knew that's exactly what C3 was, and many continued to call them Special Branch, unless they were filling out a form or talking to the press. The officers of C3 still worked in sealed rooms, locked away from their colleagues, protected by a wall of silence and number pads on the doors. Only ten years ago, Special Branch saved countless lives by running informants, mounting surveillance operations, and making life difficult for the paramilitaries. But they played dirty, as did MI5 and the army's Fourteen Intelligence Company. Every agency ran its own operations, sometimes co-operating, more often not. All of them worked in the cracks between the law and the necessary, and all of them had blood on their hands. Some felt the peace process rendered the likes of Special Branch at best obsolete, at worst a dangerous relic of the quasi-military role the police had played in this place for thirty-odd years. Others felt the force-within-a-force still had a vital job to do while the paramilitaries remained on the streets. Lennon wasn't sure which side of the argument he came down on. It depended on whom he was most pissed off with at any given time: C3 or their enemies.

Uprichard rocked his chair back and forth. The creaking gnawed at Lennon's nerves.

'What?' he asked.

Uprichard fidgeted.

Hewitt scratched his chin.

'What?' Lennon asked again.

Uprichard looked at Hewitt. 'You wanted to see him, not me.'

Hewitt sighed. 'How solid is it?'

Lennon looked from one man to the other. 'How solid is what?'

'The case against Rankin.'

Lennon laughed. Hewitt's frown deepened. The laugh died in Lennon's throat. 'You're serious?'

Hewitt raised his eyebrows and waited.

'I have a witness who saw him knife Crozier and is willing to testify to it. I've got a victim who can identify him when he's fit. I've got a weapon with Crozier's blood and Rankin's prints on it. I've got the blood on his clothes. Do I need to go on?'

Hewitt's face reddened. 'Fuck,' he said. 'There's no way to spin it?'

Lennon sat forward. 'Spin it? Nothing short of a time machine is going to keep Dandy Andy Rankin out of Maghaberry. Unless I've missed something, I'd have thought putting Rankin away was, you know, good.'

'Not for everyone,' Hewitt said. 'Look, do you have to put attempted murder to the PPS? What about GBH? A fight that got out of hand. No intent to kill.'

Lennon swallowed anger. 'Go over to the City Hospital and take a look at the hole in Crozier's throat. Tell me Rankin didn't try to kill him. He's lucky he didn't hit the — '

'It couldn't have been self-defence? There was a lot of confusion at the scene. Did you identify yourself properly as a police officer?'

'I identified myself. Jesus, he had poor Sylvia Burrows with a knife to her throat.'

'Fuck,' Hewitt said.

Lennon sat back. 'Can someone explain to me how bagging a piece of shit like Rankin could possibly be a bad thing?'

Uprichard coughed. 'Well, Jack, you know our colleagues in C3 move in mysterious ways. They often have information that us ordinary officers don't. There may be wider implications to this, other operations that might be comp — '

'Rankin exercises a huge amount of control over his patch of Belfast,' Hewitt said, ignoring the look of annoyance on Uprichard's face. 'He keeps everyone in line, keeps the dealers away from kids, stops the local boys from cutting each other's throats. He may be a piece of shit, I won't disagree with you there, but he's a useful piece of shit.'

'Is he an informant?'

Hewitt tilted his head. 'You know better than to ask me that, Jack.'

'Is he? Is he a tout?'

'That's none of your concern. Listen, Rankin keeps discipline among his boys, something the Loyalists have always lacked. It's the same on your side of the fence. When McKenna and

McGinty got killed, the whole Republican movement could have torn itself apart, but the leadership clamped down, kept them in check.'

'What the fuck do you mean, my side of the fence?'

'Now, Jack,' Uprichard said, his tone ominous.

'I just mean you're a Catholic, you're from that community,' Hewitt said, showing his palms.

Lennon went to rise from his chair, with no idea what he'd do next, but Uprichard said, 'Jack, please, let the man finish.'

Lennon sat down and locked his fingers together.

Hewitt smiled. 'You know how tight a ship the Republicans run. The Loyalists aren't like that. They'd kill each other's grannies to get ahead. We take a stabilising force like Rankin out of the community, Christ knows what might happen.'

Lennon stared hard at Hewitt. 'Is this you talking, or the Northern Ireland Office?'

'Inflicting grievous bodily harm, Jack. GBH. He'll do time, even if he pleads, which I guarantee he will. You'll put Rankin away. It'll be on record as your arrest, your case. It'll look good for you, how you performed under pressure, how you carried out first aid on Rankin and Crozier, how you stopped that old dear getting cut up. There could be a commendation in it for you. You can interview Rankin at the hospital when the doctors say he's fit, see if he'll give you any dirt you can follow up on. I wouldn't be surprised if you got back on a Major Investigation Team.'

Lennon kept staring. 'GBH with intent.'

'No,' Hewitt said. 'That could be a life sentence if he gets the wrong judge.'

'He'll only get five with GBH, probably less if he cooperates. That means two and a half at most if he behaves himself inside. He'll do a chunk of that on remand.'

Hewitt stared back. 'I'll make sure the PPS push for the maximum.'

'Will you shite,' Lennon said.

Uprichard said, 'DCI Gordon has a space coming up on his MIT. Charlie Stinson is going to South Africa for a year on placement. I'm sure Gordon could use you.'

Lennon's mind lingered on that idea. DCI Gordon led the best Major Investigation Team in the city.

'You were the smartest one out of the lot of us back at Garnerville,' Hewitt said. 'Smarter than me, even. Don't cause yourself grief over a shit-pile like Rankin. Besides, you can't claim any moral high ground given your recent history. You got off light with that Patterson business. You owe me a favour.'

Lennon buried his face in his hands.

'Fuck,' he said.

6

Sometimes dreams followed Gerry Fegan into waking. He knew the border between his mind and the world beyond was solid, but the dreams had a way of crossing over. Just a few months ago, he drowned his terrors with whiskey every night. Now that he was sober they flourished, swelled, grew until they rubbed against his daylight hours.

But still, anything was better than before, when the shadows of the dead followed him through Belfast's backstreets and alleyways.

He threw the blankets aside and let the damp air jerk him awake. Even as his consciousness flickered to life the dream-figures climbed the walls. He blinked and rubbed them away. The heels of his calloused hands scoured his eyelids as the city's early rumbles and screeches seeped through his single window. He hoisted himself upright and dropped his legs over the side of the cot.

The scarring on Fegan's left shoulder itched, a shiny pink sun surrounded by the slashes of amateur stitches. He rubbed them with his palm, the layers of hard, cracked skin scraping the irritation away. Aches of fatigue rippled through his shoulders and arms as he stretched.

Last night, just before knocking off, Tommy Sheehy had given him a message from the Doyles. They wanted to see Fegan at the site this morning. The summons had been gnawing at his gut ever since. He knew about the Doyle twins, both round-faced, cheery men. They were forever slapping their workers' backs, making jokes, sometimes slipping a little cash in their pockets, winking, saying, 'Get yourself a drink, son, you're a good grafter.'

And the workers would smile, nod, say thank you, and never look the Doyle brothers in the eye. The boys on the site talked over sandwiches and flasks of coffee. Fegan didn't join in the conversations much, everyone knew he was a quiet one, but he listened. They said Packie Doyle fed a man's liver to his dog. They said Frankie Doyle made another man cut off his wife's little finger in front of their children. Fegan knew enough of hard men to know the stories were most likely just that: stories. The truth would be much uglier.

He knew a killer when he met one. Packie Doyle stank of it, Frankie more so. They wanted to see Fegan at nine. The radio alarm clicked on. He slapped it quiet. Car horns and shouts rose up from the street, echoing between the high buildings.

Fegan got to his feet, crossed his one room, and raised the blind. He pulled the window up, ignoring its creaking protest. September warmth flowed around him. The air in this old building was always colder and wetter than outside.

Just two months he'd been here, and he loved New York. Never mind the miserable room he shared with mice and cockroaches. This city had no memory. No one cared who he was, what he'd done. He could walk through the crowds, as clean as the next man, his guilt buried. Until last night. Until the Doyles sent for him.

★　★　★

'You're Gerry Fegan from Belfast,' Packie Doyle said.

'*The* Gerry Fegan,' Frankie Doyle said.

'You've got me wrong,' he said.

The Doyles each grinned the same grin back at him, Frankie from behind the big mahogany desk, Packie from his perch on the window-sill overlooking the alley behind the bar. Plastic sheeting covered every surface to protect it from plaster and sawdust.

'Oh, yeah,' Packie said.

'We've got you wrong,' Frankie said.

'My name's Paddy Feeney,' Fegan said. 'I'm from Donegal. I showed your foreman my passport.'

The foreman had no qualms hiring an illegal immigrant for the renovations. Most of the boys were illegals from one place or another. He'd given Fegan a day to prove his carpentry skills. He didn't look too hard at the passport.

'If you're not Gerry Fegan from Belfast,' Frankie said, 'you'll not be bothered that someone's looking for a man of that name.'

Packie said, 'Someone's willing to pay good money for the whereabouts of a Gerry Fegan from Belfast. They even sent out a photo.'

Frankie placed a computer printout on the desk. It showed a man in his mid-to-late

37

twenties, sharp, hollow features. The picture was at least two decades old, a police mug shot.

'It's not me,' Fegan said.

'Looks like you,' Frankie said.

'A lot like you,' Packie said.

Fegan looked at the young man in the picture. It made him ache at his centre. 'It's not me,' he said.

'We did some asking around,' Frankie said.

'Called some boys in Belfast,' Packie said.

'They said Gerry Fegan's a mad bastard.'

'Said he was hard as they come.'

'Dangerous.'

'A killer.'

Both men had round heads like light bulbs, and thick bodies. If you were stupid, you'd think them fat and slow. Fegan knew different.

Packie got off the windowsill, came around the desk, and sat on its edge. Cheap aftershave scratched at Fegan's nasal passages.

'I saw you take on that big Russian fella,' Packie said. 'He was twice the size of you, and you flattened him.'

Fegan knew he'd regret that. Andrei wasn't Russian, he was Ukrainian, and he had a big mouth. He'd been needling Fegan all day. He said something ugly about Fegan's mother. Fegan hadn't lost his temper, his pulse had barely risen. 'I just wanted him to leave me alone,' Fegan said.

'Fuck, he left you alone, all right,' Packie said. 'He didn't even come back for his pay.'

Frankie sat quiet, now, letting his brother talk. He met Fegan's gaze and smiled.

'It won't happen again,' Fegan said. 'I'm not a fighter.'

'Paddy Feeney may not be a fighter,' Packie said, 'but Gerry Fegan sure as fuck is.'

'I told you, I'm not this Fegan.' He got to his feet. 'I'm Paddy Feeney, and that's all there is to it. If you don't believe me, there's nothing I can do for you. I've work to be getting on with.'

He turned to the door.

'Sit the fuck down,' Frankie said.

Fegan turned back to the brothers. He'd thought he was done with taking orders from men like these. Hard men, men with a hollow place inside that allowed them to profit from the suffering of others. Fegan had known many such men. He'd killed some, but that was another world and another life. He sat down.

Frankie smiled. 'So, you're Paddy Feeney from Donegal. Do you have a good life here, Paddy?'

'It's all right,' Fegan said.

'You making a few bucks?'

'A bit,' Fegan said.

'You're good with your hands,' Frankie said.

Fegan didn't like the way Frankie licked his lips. 'I can cut straight. That's all this job needs.'

'But you've more skills than that,' Frankie said.

Fegan looked at his feet.

'Do you want to earn a little more money?'

'I earn enough,' Fegan said.

'No such thing as enough,' Frankie said. 'Just a small job here and there, nothing too strenuous. Good money for a man with good hands.'

39

'I don't need more money,' Fegan said.

'Maybe you don't, but that's not really the point, is it?' Frankie said. 'Let's say we take your word for it. Let's say we believe you're Paddy Feeney from Donegal, not Gerry Fegan from Belfast. We don't get in touch with the man who's looking for this Gerry Fegan and tell him we might know of his whereabouts. There's nobody by that name works for us. How much is that worth?'

Fegan looked from Frankie to Packie. 'I need to get back to work. I've the handrails for the staircase to finish.'

'Sure, you take a day or two to think about it,' Packie said.

'Talk to us in a couple of days,' Frankie said.

Fegan stood and went to the door.

'One thing, Gerry,' Packie said.

Fegan stopped.

'He meant to say Paddy,' Frankie said.

'Don't be going anywhere,' Packie said. 'Some friends of ours will be keeping an eye on you. You won't see them, least not all the time, but they'll see you.'

Fegan didn't look back. 'Those handrails need doing,' he said. He closed the door behind him.

7

The doormen at Lavery's nodded as Lennon entered. The bar looked cleaner these days, lighter. The smoking ban might not have helped turnover, but it certainly sweetened the air. Belfast's traditional student haunt seemed to draw an older crowd, now. No tang of cannabis tickled Lennon's nose, the haircuts were less exotic, the dress code not quite so grungy. He allowed himself a small ripple of nostalgia as he took a stool at the bar, thinking of his student days when he and his friends blew their grants on cider.

Lennon had studied psychology at Queen's, managed a decent degree. He might have got that MSc, maybe even gone after a doctorate, if things had been different. As it turned out, he didn't even attend his own graduation ceremony. His mother had bought a new dress for it, gone all the way from her home in Middletown, near the border, to Marks & Spencer's in Belfast. She had borrowed money from the Credit Union to pay for it.

He remembered her parading up and down the living room of the old house, asking again and again if it was a good fit, did the hem hang properly, was it slimming on her. Lennon and his elder brother Liam exchanged weary looks as they told her once more it was beautiful on her. 'But the money,' she said, chewing her lip in

41

worry. 'I wouldn't spend the money if it's not right.' She wagged a finger at them in turn. 'Don't you dare tell me it's right if it's not.'

'It's lovely on you, Ma,' Liam said as he rose. His big shoulders stretched the fabric of his shirt tight. He still sported a black eye from the hurling match a few days before when he'd caught a stray swipe from a teammate's stick. At least that's what he'd told his mother. 'Stop fretting about it. It's only money.'

'Only money,' she said, her eyes narrowing. 'Listen to him. Wait till you're raising wee 'uns and tell me it's only money. Sure, it cost me every penny I had, and every penny I hadn't, to put that one through university. And he spent the lot on beer and cider and chasing after women.'

She pronounced it *wee*-men.

Lennon feigned offence. 'It was the rent,' he said. 'The grant hardly covered it.'

'My arse,' she said, the closest she ever came to swearing.

A little more than a week later, a day before she was due to wear it to the graduation ceremony, she took the dress back to Marks & Spencer's. She exchanged it for a black one so that she could bury what was left of Liam.

Lennon remembered carrying his brother's coffin. It weighed hardly anything. Sixteen years ago, and the silence of the mourners still came to him when he least expected it.

He pushed the memory away, and scoped the bar. Early yet, plenty of room for improvement. He'd spent an hour at the station's small gym, gone home to shower, blasted a ready-meal in the microwave, and then headed out. He had reason to celebrate. A meeting with DCI Gordon had been arranged for the morning, and he had a good chance of being back on an MIT before the end of the week. He ignored the sick bubbling at the pit of his stomach when he thought of Dandy Andy Rankin getting off with GBH. But he could live with it, drown out his own conscience, if it meant getting back into an MIT.

No tourists in Lavery's tonight, only midweek drinkers trying to recapture their student days. He caught the barmaid's attention, a thin wisp of a girl with dyed black hair.

'Pint of Stella,' he said, dropping a fiver on the bar.

A duo tuned guitars in the corner; a woman one-two'd into a microphone. She was tall, looked almost as tall as Lennon, with a mass of blonde curls. The blackboard outside had said 'Nina Armstrong'. He sized her up, and the followers that gathered around her. Too many men vying for her attention, too much work. Pity. She looked good in a hippie kind of way.

They started to play. She could sing, her voice clear and sinuous, and the guitarist wasn't bad. More punters drifted in, pairs and larger groups. The Stella burned his tongue. He studied the women, found their weaknesses.

★   ★   ★

A hacking smoker's cough woke Lennon. Hard fingers of sunlight found his headache. He forced his eyes open, squinted at her, as the queasy pain pulsed inside his skull. She stood in a camisole and thong, a lighter in one hand, a cigarette in the other. He wondered what she intended to use as an ashtray for a moment before he noticed the half-full wine glass on the bedside locker, three butts already doused in it.

'Fuck, look at the state of you,' she said. A chesty laugh turned into a barking cough.

He scrambled for a name. Something Irish. She wasn't a Prod. Siobhan? Sinead? Seana? He rubbed his eyes, willing it to come. All he could remember clearly from last night was her shouting in his ear, telling him she was a nurse at the Royal, while he stared down her top.

'Morning,' he said.

Jesus, rough as biscuits, she was. I must be losing my touch, he thought. The idea frightened him. He reached out. 'Give us a drag.'

'I thought you didn't smoke.'

'I don't.' He clicked his fingers at her.

'Just one, right? I've only a couple of fags left.'

She approached the bed and placed the filter between his lips. He sucked, inhaled, felt the heat, coughed, let it charge his brain. 'Fuck,' he croaked.

She laughed, her breasts jiggling inside her camisole. She had a Celtic knot tattooed on the left one. He saw it through watering eyes, smelled tobacco and sex. He wondered if he could muster another go, but decided against it. He craned his head so he could see the clock past her hip. It had gone eight. He was supposed to be in DCI Gordon's office at nine.

'Fuck,' he said, throwing back the quilt. 'I need to get moving.'

'You can run me home, can't you?'

'Where?' The wooden floorboards chilled the soles of his feet, clearing a little of the fog behind his eyes.

'Did you not listen to a word I said last night?' She pointed to her chest. 'Or were you too interested in these?'

He sighed. 'Where?'

'Beechmount Parade. Off the Falls.'

'No. I've to be at work for nine or I'm in shit. I can't get all the way over there and back again.'

'At work?' She stood with one arm across her stomach, her other hand pointing the cigarette at him. 'You told me you were an airline pilot.'

'Did I?'

'Yeah, you fucking did.'

'Jesus,' he said.

'So, what are you? You're hardly answering phones in the call centres if you can afford this place.' She walked to the window and pulled back the blind. 'River view and everything. Fucking nice. What *do* you do?'

'Look, take a taxi.' He pointed to his jeans, bundled on the floor. 'Take the money out of my wallet.'

'Fucking typical.' She scooped up the jeans and dug for the wallet. 'All big talk. Get your end away, everything's all right, never mind me. Fucking arsehole.'

She found the wallet, opened it, and smiled. The smile turned to a frown. She turned the wallet face out to him, showing him the photograph. 'Who's this?'

'My daughter,' he said.

The smile flickered and returned. He could tell she begrudged it. 'How old?' she asked. 'A year?'

'Five,' he said. 'Coming six.'

'Jesus, could you not take a newer picture?'

He thought about answering the question, that he'd take a newer picture if only Ellen's mother would allow him to know his daughter, that she never would because it was how she punished him for what he'd done, that they'd moved away months ago, that he'd been trying to find out where they'd gone since then.

Instead, he said, 'Ten quid ought to do you.'

'All right, big spender,' she said as she looked for the money. 'I get the message. I'll be out of your way in — '

She stopped talking.

'There's bound to be a ten in there,' he said.

She stared at him, and he understood.

He raised his hands, said, 'Look, I — '

'A fucking cop?'

'I — '

'You're a fucking peeler?'

She threw the wallet. It slapped against his chest and fell to the floor. She looked down at it. She stooped, picked it up, pulled out two ten-pound notes, threw it again. This time he caught it. He tossed it on the bed beside him.

'Jesus, if anyone knew I'd gone home with a cop,' she said. 'Fuck me, I'd be burnt out of my house.'

Lennon smiled. 'Then tell them I'm an airline pilot.'

'Arsehole,' she said, gathering bits and pieces of clothing. 'Jesus, I knew peelers made decent money, but a place like this?' She pulled her jeans from the chair in the corner, disturbing the jacket underneath. 'How much is your mortgage? Or do you rent? Must be a fucking — '

Something heavy dropped to the floor. She stared down at the leather pouch.

'Is that what I think it is?'

He shrugged and nodded.

She kept her eyes on it as she slipped her jeans on and tucked the money into her pocket. She picked it up. She turned it in her hands, slid the pistol from its sheath. 'What make is it?' she asked.

'A Glock,' he said. He watched her drop the holster to the floor. She had chips in her nail varnish.

'You ever shoot anyone?' she asked.

'No,' he said. The lie was well practised.

'That scar on your shoulder. You said you got it in a car crash.'

'That's right.'

'I don't believe you.'

He didn't answer.

She traced the Glock's lines, brought it to her nose, smelled it. Her tongue brushed her upper lip. 'It's heavy,' she said. 'Is it loaded?'

'Of course,' he said.

'Shouldn't you tell me to be careful? Shouldn't you take it off me?'

'Maybe,' he said.

'There's a safety catch or something, right?'

'No,' he said. He made a gun with his fingers and aimed at her. 'You just point it and pull the trigger. Simple as that.'

She looked up from the Glock. Her eyes couldn't hold his. She walked slowly to the dressing table, cradling the pistol like it was made of tissue, and set it down. It hardly made a noise against the wood.

She said, 'I should go.'

8

The Traveller eased back onto the bed and pulled the sheet up around him. 'Going away for a while,' he said.

Sofia kept her naked back to him, the late afternoon light pooling in the valleys of her flesh. A scar, pale against her tan, spread across the small of her back. He'd never asked how she got it, but he had a good idea. 'What for?' she asked.

'Business,' the Traveller said.

She stretched as she rolled onto her back, her skin brushing against his, the stubble of her underarm scratching at his shoulder. 'When will you be back?' she asked.

'Depends,' he said. 'Not long, maybe.'

'Maybe,' she echoed. 'You said that last time.'

'Then get yourself someone else to play with. Won't bother me. Just make sure he wears a johnny. Don't want to catch nothing off some dirty bastard.'

'Pig,' she said as she rolled away.

He reached under the sheet and squeezed a fleshy buttock. She slapped his hand away. The sound of it reverberated around the high-ceilinged bedroom. It was made up to look like some grand old place, with cornices and an elaborate rose above the light, but the house couldn't have been standing more than five or six years. New money trying to look like old, the Traveller thought. Sofia had inherited the place from her dead husband, along with half a dozen other properties, a fat investment portfolio, and a luxury-car dealership. Did she know he was the one that did the husband in? He reckoned so, but she'd never let on. That scar on her back wasn't the only one. The first time he'd bedded her there had been something close to gratitude in her eyes.

Not that she'd bought the hit. That had been a rival businessman the husband had shafted on a deal. When the Traveller had been watching the doomed man's comings and goings, figuring out the job, he'd seen Sofia driving the big Range Rover away from the massive house. He'd followed her to some young lad's place where she drew the curtains and emerged two hours later with her skirt crooked and her hair messed up. He'd made a mental note then to call on her once the job was done.

Two years ago, that was, and he visited her at least once every few weeks. He'd even taken her to Benidorm. She got drunk and tearful on cheap sangria and talked about her only regret: the husband hadn't given her a baby. He sometimes wondered why she didn't just quit the pill and not tell him about it, get pregnant and say goodbye. Maybe she had an honest streak in her. He laughed out loud.

'What's so fucking funny?' she asked.

'Nothing,' he said. He turned onto his side and slipped his arm around her waist, pulled her in close to him. She took his hand and placed it on her plump breast.

'Fancy another?' he asked.

'Already?'

He squeezed. 'Me? Sure I'm always raring to go.'

'Bastard,' she said.

★　★　★

It took an hour and a half to drive north through Ardee, Carrickmacross, and Castleblaney before hitting the outskirts of Monaghan town a few miles south of the border. The Traveller had bought a ten-year-old Mercedes from a dealer he knew near Drogheda. It was a big, wallowing estate with 200,000 miles on it. An automatic with plenty of room in the back if he needed to stash anything or anybody.

The Bull had described the place well, even drawn a map. The Traveller stopped at junctions as he got nearer, traced the shape of the words on the map with his finger, and matched them to the road signs.

He remembered the word 'alexia' as a shadow, how a doctor explained it to him in broken English fifteen years ago. Another name for it was acquired dyslexia. Something about the piece of Kevlar they dug out of his head, how it fucked up something in his brain, made written words turn into a jumble of criss-crossing lines.

The doctor had told him he'd never read anything again. That didn't bother the Traveller at first; he'd never been one for books. But when he re-entered the living world, the lack of words became an obstacle. So he had trained himself to memorise the letters as shapes, all twenty-six of them. He could study a word, judge each letter in turn, and decipher its meaning if he tried hard enough. But more than one or two words, and it might as well be Chinese. It suited him to let the likes of Bull O'Kane think he was illiterate. No one ever suffered for being underestimated.

Another thirty minutes and he found Malloy's place, just as it was getting dark. An old cottage set back a hundred yards from the road with a single-track lane running up to the small garden.

He stopped the car halfway along the lane, far enough so the Merc couldn't be seen from the road, and not too close to the cottage. He pulled the IMI Desert Eagle from under the seat. People said a Glock or a SIG was a better combat pistol, and they were probably right, but the Desert Eagle was a big bastard that scared the shite out of anyone he pulled it on. It was noisy, too. If you needed to take someone's head off in a crowded pub without worrying about heroes, it was the one. It sounded like the end of the world, and it could stop anything with its .44 load.

Lights glowed behind drawn curtains up ahead. He got out of the Merc and walked towards them. If the Traveller lived in a place like this, he'd have a dog. A big, mean one. He kept to the grass verge to silence his footsteps and listened for growling as he approached.

Kevin Malloy had a wife, the Bull had said. She might or might not be in the cottage. Malloy was still bedridden from his injuries. It was a simple job, really. Get in, do anyone inside, grab any money, wreck the place, get out. The cottage stood black against the hills behind. Just twenty yards now. The wind changed direction.

There, a low rumble as a dog caught his scent. The Traveller froze, listened, waited. The Eagle's heft felt good. Solid, like the power of God in his hand. He started towards the house again.

The rumble turned to a growl punctuated by gasps. He could hear the animal's excitement and fear. No sign of it in the shadows yet. He listened for another sound: the high jangle of a chain. No one would leave a big dog loose out here, but he wanted to be sure.

It launched into a clamour of barking, then, the low bass vowels of a deep-chested animal. The Bull said Malloy was an arsehole. If he was an arsehole he'd have a dog he thought made him look hard. Something stupid and brutal, maybe a Rottweiler or some kind of mastiff, rather than a smart guardian like a German shepherd or a Dobermann.

The braying grew louder and the Traveller heard heavy paws crunching on gravel. Then a gallop, the jangle of chain, and a yelp as it snapped taut. That was all he needed to know.

He reached into his pocket and took out the Vater earplugs. Drummers used them to protect their hearing. The little beehive-shaped pieces of rubber blocked out the dangerous frequencies but let through the detail of the environment. They blocked out the worst of a gunshot, but you could still hear a mouse fart. He pressed the two earpieces, joined by a twelve-inch plastic string, into place. He worked his jaw open and closed, swallowed, and walked.

There it was, some sort of mastiff cross. A low wall surrounded the cottage. The dog stood just inside the open gate. It stopped its barking and watched the Traveller approach. There was enough light yet to see the glow of its eyes. He pulled back the Eagle's slide to chamber a round and thumbed the safety off. The dog's legs quivered and its chest rumbled.

The Traveller raised the Eagle in a two-handed grip, his wrists firm so his shoulders would take the brunt of the recoil, and squeezed the trigger until he felt resistance. Sometimes he forgot which was his right hand, and which was his left. Something else that came out of his brain along with that piece of Kevlar. Not that it mattered much; he had trained one hand to be about as strong as the other.

He lined the sights between the dog's eyes. It lunged. He blew its skull apart.

The boom rolled across the hills. The Traveller watched the house for movement. No surprises now, just get in and do it. He marched to the old wooden door and booted it below the handle. He kicked it again, and it swung inward. He went in gun first, ready to take down anything that moved.

The tiny open-plan kitchen and living room was empty. Old bottles and beer cans crowded around the sink. The remains of a Chinese takeaway littered the dining table. The place reeked of stale cigarettes and alcohol, damp and rotten food. Only two doors led from this room. One of them stood open, revealing a dirty bathtub and toilet. He went to the other, the

Eagle at shoulder level.

The Traveller threw it open, and the door frame exploded around him. He fired blind into the room three times, the recoil throwing him backwards against the table. His wrist shrieked; splinters and plaster dust stung his face.

'Bastard,' he said. He wiped his sleeve across his eyes. Hot pain seared the right. He shook his head, tried to dislodge whatever burned there.

'Jesus,' he said. He rubbed the heel of his left hand against the eye. It came away wet and red. 'Dirty fucker.'

He calmed his breathing and listened. Moaning and sobbing came from the room. The Traveller crossed to it, both hands supporting the Eagle.

Kevin Malloy lay on the floor between the bed and an open wardrobe, his legs tangled in sheets, a shotgun by his side. A ragged hole was torn in his shoulder.

The Traveller lifted the shotgun and admired the polished wooden stock and steel barrel. 'Fuck, that's a beauty,' he said, putting it on the bed. He recognised the stag's head logo. 'Browning. Very nice. Think I'll have that. You got more shells?'

Malloy lay there shaking. His blood soaked the carpet. It squelched under the Traveller's feet. He kicked Malloy's shoulder. Malloy screamed.

'I asked you a question,' the Traveller said. 'You got more shells for that?'

Malloy turned his head. 'In . . . in there.'

The Traveller stepped over him and found three boxes of 20-gauge cartridges in the bottom

55

of the wardrobe. He threw them on the bed beside the Browning.

'Anyone else here?' he asked.

Malloy shook his head.

'Where's your missus?'

Malloy cried.

The Traveller kicked him again. When Malloy's screaming died down, the Traveller said, 'Where is she?'

'In town,' Malloy said. 'Please don't kill me.'

'When'll she be back?'

'I don't know. Please don't kill me. I've money. You can have my cash card and my PIN. There, in my wallet.'

The Traveller went to the dressing table and put the wallet in his pocket. It would help make it look like a robbery, but he'd dump it somewhere on the road. No way he'd use the card.

He rubbed his right eye on his sleeve, hissed at the sting. 'You might've fucking blinded me, you know.'

'I'm sorry,' Malloy said. 'Please don't kill me.'

The Traveller flicked the Eagle's safety on and tucked it into his waistband. He went to the bed and lifted the Browning. He turned it in his hands, tested its heft. It was compact and light. 'Fucking lovely,' he said. He pulled back the slide to eject the spent cartridge and pushed it forward to load the next. The action was smooth and easy. 'That's a beauty,' he said, running his fingers over the smooth walnut stock. He wedged the butt against his shoulder and lined up Malloy's head.

'Jesus,' Malloy said.

The Traveller took three steps back. He didn't want to get covered in the splatter.

Malloy wept and prayed.

The Traveller blinked blood away from his right eye. He sniffed and swallowed. He shifted his weight onto his leading foot, braced for the recoil, and pulled the trigger.

It didn't make too bad a mess of Malloy, considering. The recoil gave the Traveller a solid kick to the shoulder, but it was a controllable piece. He held the Browning out to admire it again. 'Nice,' he said.

He pulled the earplugs out by the plastic string and put them in his pocket. He opened and closed his jaw to clear the pressure. His eye stung pretty bad, now. He walked back to the kitchen and turned on the tap. A scoop of cold water eased the burning a little.

He wondered if there were any old plastic bags under the sink in which to carry the boxes of cartridges back to the car. He opened the cupboard doors.

A woman lay trembling on her side in there, squeezed beneath the plumbing. She covered her head with her hands, her knees drawn up to her chin. She smelled of gin.

'Ah, fuck,' the Traveller said.

He reached for the earplugs.

9

Fegan knew he was being followed. The tall, broad man had been ten paces behind him when he entered Grand Street station. It was almost six, still dark above ground, when Fegan boarded the D Train. He watched the other man pass the car. Fegan guessed the follower would choose the next car along, probably glancing out at every stop to see if his quarry left the train.

He'd be wasting his time. Fegan would ride the train all the way to Columbus Circle so he could walk in the park as the sun came up. Sleep had barely touched him last night. The Doyle brothers' oily words and knowing grins kept him from slipping under, so he rose early and headed out.

Fegan took a seat and opened his book. It was slim, a little over a hundred pages, and he'd found it not long after arriving in New York. He'd been walking along Bleecker Street, mouth and eyes agape, the city seeming to roar through him. He passed a small shop, stopped, and turned back. A memory drew him towards the door. The sign above the entrance said Greenwich Judaica. He walked in.

He couldn't recall the title of the book Marie McKenna told him about just a few months ago while he sat terrified beside her, but he could hear the sadness in her voice as she told him how her dead uncle, the man he had killed, forced her

58

to tear it up. After some explaining, the young man in the shop found a copy of *Yosl Rakover Talks to God* in a box of used books. Fegan had read it twice so far, picking over the words in the same slow and deliberate way he had when he was at the Christian Brothers School back in Belfast. He hadn't been much of a reader then, and he wasn't now. He caught himself moving his lips as he grappled with the text, and brought a hand to his mouth.

Fegan liked to read on the subway. His cold, damp room was too quiet. Outside was too noisy. The subway's rattle and thrum was just right. Besides, you needed somewhere to put your eyes. He'd found it strange his first few days here, people seeming to fall asleep the instant they took a seat, or even clinging to the poles. But then he started doing it too.

Victor Gonzalvez, an electrician from Brazil with wide, hairy shoulders, called it New York Narcolepsy. Rather than constantly avoiding other passengers' eyes, it was easier to close your own and drift. But then the dreams would creep in behind Fegan's eyelids, refugee visions from the night. So he preferred to read.

The train slowed, its brakes singing, causing his weight to shift on the seat. A flat voice announced 59th Street — Columbus Circle. Fegan stuffed the book down into his pocket, left the car, and made his way up towards ground level. He still crackled with that childish excitement as a fleet breeze ferried the noises and smells of the city down the stairwells to swirl about him.

Fegan didn't care about the footsteps behind. The Doyles thought he'd flee the city, and he would, but not yet. He needed time to think, to plan. He wouldn't let them panic him into running before he knew where to go. When he was ready, he would slip out of the city regardless of who followed. Perhaps back to Boston — he'd spent a month there before coming to New York — or maybe Philadelphia.

It was past six-thirty, now, and the first hints of light glowed behind the towers to the east of Central Park. The glass palace of the Time Warner Center reflected the weak dawn. Fegan had gone in just the once and felt poor as he wandered between the boutiques full of hard-faced women and stiff-backed salesmen. He had no desire to return. Countless yellow taxis rumbled around the Circle, carrying workers getting an early start. Fegan waited for a break in the traffic before crossing over to the massive Maine Monument and the park entrance beyond. He resisted the urge to glance behind.

He took the path that ran under the westerly wall's shadow and hesitated as the trees darkened the way. Yellows and reds peppered the leaves, but autumn had not yet set them to balding. The follower was still behind him somewhere, Fegan sensed him there, but his footsteps were lost in the morning bustle. He scolded himself and kept walking. If he hurried he could be at Umpire Rock in time to watch the sun rise over the grand buildings of Park Avenue. He would keep to the wide paths.

Quick footsteps came from behind, and Fegan

braced himself. As they approached, he heard them veer to his right. He turned his head to see an early jogger pass, giving him a wide berth. Fegan allowed himself a glance over his shoulder. The darkness concealed all but the vague silhouette of the big man. He kept walking, his hands buried in his pockets, but curled into fists all the same. He couldn't —

Oh God she's burning the child's burning oh no please no make it stop she's burning —

Fegan staggered, barely held his balance, his stomach hurling bile up to his throat. He coughed, choked, wrapped his arms around his middle as the shock of the vision pounded his chest and stomach. Another jogger coming towards him slowed, thought about —

Jesus sweet Jesus no don't let her burn please stop it she's drowning in the smoke she's burning —

Fegan's legs betrayed him, and he pitched forward. His left shoulder hit the ground first and the pavement scraped his cheek. He vomited, hot foulness stinging his throat and nostrils. The jogger stopped for a moment, hopped from foot to foot, then sprinted to him.

'Sir?' he said as he crouched. 'Sir, do you need help?'

'She's burning,' Fegan said.

The jogger called to someone beyond Fegan's vision. 'Excuse me! Sir! This man needs help. Do you have a phone?'

The follower came into view, his heavy shoulders twitching as he looked around, confused.

'Do you have a cell?' the jogger asked. 'I don't carry mine when I'm running.'

'Uh,' the follower said. He looked back to the park's entrance.

'Sir,' the jogger said. 'This man needs help. Do you have a cellphone to call an ambulance?'

The follower patted his pockets as he looked in every direction but down. 'I, uh, don't know if I, uh . . . '

'Do you have one or not?'

'I guess not,' the follower said.

'Will you stay with him while I get help?'

The follower sighed and nodded.

'We need to get him into the recovery position,' the jogger said. 'Help me out, here.'

The follower bent down to grab Fegan's legs while the jogger slipped a hand underneath his neck. Fegan felt his body turn, his head supported by the —

She's burning the fire it's eating her up the child oh no not her —

Fegan's right foot lashed out and connected with the follower's knee. The follower screamed as Fegan felt something buckle. Then he was up, his shoulder ramming into the jogger's chest. Fegan ran as the jogger went tumbling, each breath scorching his throat, his eyes streaming. He ran until his legs and lungs could carry him no further.

10

The elevator doors slid open and Lennon stepped inside. Susan, the divorcee from upstairs, stood there with her daughter Lucy huddling against her.

Susan's face brightened. 'And how's you this morning?' she asked, reaching out to stroke his upper arm.

'Not bad,' Lennon said, returning the smile.

Susan had flirted with him from the moment she moved in a year ago. She was attractive, he couldn't deny it, but he'd never responded. It took him six months to figure out why: she was a good woman bringing up a child on her own. A child around the same age as the daughter he'd abandoned. She didn't need a bastard like him to mess her around. Susan deserved a decent man who'd treat her well, who'd look after her and Lucy. Lennon knew that wasn't him. He'd only let her down.

Sometimes, when she'd lean her shoulder against his in the lift, or when she'd brush her hand against his as he held a door for her, he thought about telling her so. He considered telling her he was no good, that she should stop the flirting, it could only lead to hurt for her and her daughter.

But what was the point?

'You look thoughtful,' she said. 'Busy day today?'

'Something like that. A big interview.'

She nodded and smiled. He'd never told her he was a cop. The elevator door swished open. He stepped aside to let her out first. Her hand ran down his sleeve and glanced off his fingers.

'See you,' she said.

He smiled in return. Outside the lift, he stooped to fiddle with his shoelace so that she could get some distance on him. Distance would be best for all concerned.

★   ★   ★

'You have friends in high places, Dandy,' Lennon said.

Rankin crossed one slippered foot over the other and stared at Lennon from the hospital bed. 'Don't call me that,' he said. 'Anyone calls me that to my face, and anyone I hear of calling me that behind my back, they get sorted. Right?'

'Sorted,' Lennon echoed, a laugh thinning the word as he spoke it. He took a plastic cup from the stack on the bedside locker and opened the bottle of Lucozade that stood beside them. 'You don't mind, do you?'

He didn't wait for an answer before filling the cup. Three swallows drained it of the fizzing orange liquid, and he filled it again. He'd headed out again last night, and the late hours had started to catch up on him. A boost to his blood sugar wouldn't go amiss.

Dandy Andy Rankin looked resplendent in his silk pyjamas and dressing gown. No hospital duds for him. If not for the wires snaking out from beneath his pyjama top, connecting him to the beeping monitor at his bedside, he'd have looked like an aristocratic gentleman enjoying a late morning. Albeit with a Red Hand of Ulster tattoo peeking out from between the buttons on his chest. The graze on his cheek from when he'd hit the ground behind Sylvia's café had started to scab over. A cut on his lip suggested that Crozier at least got a decent punch in before Rankin knifed him.

Lennon took another swig of Lucozade and went to the window. They'd given Rankin a nice quiet private room, the kind of room only those with the best medical insurance could afford, while the rest of Belfast's sick and injured had to make do with the NHS. Being a scumbag had its perks. The only downside was a police guard on your door.

'Like I was saying,' Lennon continued, 'friends in high places. I'm told you're going to cooperate, which is awful good of you. If it'd been up to me, you'd be facing two counts of attempted murder. I'd have plenty to make it stick. But your pals have persuaded me to put GBH to the Public Prosecution Service. Aren't you the lucky boy?'

'Luck's got nothing to do with it, son,' Rankin said, a slight lisp lending his speech a greasy effeminacy. 'It pays to befriend the right people.'

'You're not their friend,' Lennon said, turning from the window. 'You're a tout. You're a commodity. They'll shit on you the second you're no more use to them.'

'That's another name I don't like.'

'I don't give a flying fuck what you like,' Lennon said. He put the cup on the windowsill and dragged the vinyl-covered armchair from the corner to face Rankin's bed. It wheezed displaced air as Lennon sat down, an odour of stale urine coming with it. 'You tout for Special Branch. That's why they stepped in for you, asked me to soften the blow. That's what got you off the hook.'

'I'm not off any hook,' Rankin said. 'I'm still going to do time, aren't I?'

'Not the sort of time you should be doing,' Lennon said. 'You're getting off easy, and you know it. I agreed to the GBH against my better judgement. Now what are you going to do for me?'

'Sweet fuck all,' Rankin said, smiling, his eyebrow arched. 'Special Branch tells the likes of you to jump, you jump. Don't make out you're doing me any favours, son. You're just doing what you're told.'

'Maybe, maybe not. I haven't sent the file to the PPS yet. A lot can change between now and then.'

Rankin turned his face to the window. 'Fuck yourself.'

Lennon leaned forward. 'Course, I have my own contacts among your boys. And Crozier's. I might say the wrong thing to one of them. I might let something slip. And I know how you boys talk amongst yourselves. Rumours spread like crabs in a whorehouse. Next thing you know you've got a gun in your — '

'Don't threaten me,' Rankin said. He turned

his gaze back to Lennon, his eyes blank like a cadaver's. 'Don't do it. You can't scare me. You're not the only one with contacts. I know all sorts of boys in all sorts of places, some of them on the other side. Some of them aren't on ceasefire. Some of them would love to have a crack at a peeler, score a goal for their fucking lost cause. You get me, son?'

Lennon didn't reply.

Rankin's eyes came back to life. 'Right, now we've shown each other how big our cocks are, let's try being a wee bit civil about it, eh? You want to ask me some questions, go on ahead. Maybe I'll answer them, maybe I won't. Fair enough?'

Lennon held his stare for a few more seconds. 'Fair enough,' he said. 'What was the aggro between you and Crozier about? Off the record. You're not under caution.'

'That cunt's been doing business with the Lithuanians.'

'We know that already,' Lennon said. 'Everyone knows that. You've been doing business with them too.'

'Not like this.' Rankin shook his head. 'I buy and sell with them, the usual trade, move girls about, sometimes get the odd bit of blow off them. They're useful now and then, but that's all. But we keep them out of our areas, them and the rest of the foreigners. Let the taigs have them for neighbours if they want, but keep them off *my* streets.'

Too late, Lennon tried to hide his anger at the word. It had been a while since anyone had called him 'taig' to his face.

Rankin paused, registering the offence. 'What, you're the other side of the house, are you?'

'That's neither here nor there,' Lennon said.

'Best cop I ever knew was a taig,' Rankin said. 'Put away a lot of people, that boy, including me. Twice.'

Lennon ignored Rankin's clumsy attempt at prettying up his bigotry. 'You were telling me about Crozier and the Lithuanians.'

'Aye, right. Rodney Crozier wasn't just doing a bit of trading with the Liths, he was getting into bed with them in a big way. See, when Michael McKenna got his brains blown out a few months back, that left a big gap.' Rankin stopped talking and tilted his head. 'What?'

Lennon's jaw had tightened at McKenna's name. 'Nothing,' he said.

Rankin studied him for a moment before continuing. 'Anyway, the Liths started moving in to his old places on the Lower Falls, the apartments he'd been running girls out of, but they needed muscle on the street.'

'Not Republican muscle?'

'No, see, McKenna's higher-ups wouldn't let their boys take up the slack. They're too busy pretending to be politicians these days, they don't want to get their hands dirty. They don't want any of McKenna's old shit sticking to them when it's election time, you understand?'

Lennon nodded. 'I understand.'

'Now, the Liths can't go too deep into that part of Belfast, but those places around Broadway are wide open for them. So they've got

Crozier's boys doing the donkey work, and he's getting a big slice for his trouble. He's raking it in, and I'm left swinging.'

'Surely there's plenty to go around,' Lennon said.

'But he's getting all the traffic off the motorway. All the punters from Lisburn, Craigavon, Lurgan, Dungannon, they just turn off at the roundabout and they've got all the action they want.'

'So what was the meet with Crozier about?'

'To see if I could talk sense to him,' Rankin said. 'Fuck knows why I thought he'd listen. He always was a thick cunt. All mouth, the big man so long as he had his boys to back him up. I thought if I got him on his own, just the two of us, we could be reasonable about it.'

'Didn't work out that way,' Lennon said.

Rankin clucked, smiled, and raised his hands. 'Didn't, did it? I had to try something, though. I even went to my handlers a while back to see if you lot would do something. I told them I'd do anything they wanted to get Crozier shut down, give them any dirt on him I could find. They said no, there wasn't enough men or money to go after him like that. If I didn't know better, I'd say Rodney Crozier was touting as well.' Rankin fixed Lennon with a long hard stare. 'Is he?' he asked.

'I wouldn't know,' Lennon said. 'You know as well as I do C3 tell us sweet fuck all.'

'C3? That's a fucking stupid name. Makes them sound like a car. They're still Special Branch, same as before. So if you can't tell me

69

about Rodney Crozier, then tell me something else.'

'What?'

'Why'd you flinch when I said Michael McKenna's name?'

'I didn't.'

A smile crawled along Rankin's lips. 'Yes you did. Don't bullshit a bullshitter, son.'

Lennon stood. 'I think that's all for now.'

'Hang on,' Rankin said, raising a finger at Lennon, his eyes narrowing. 'You're the cop that took up with McKenna's niece, aren't you? She had a child to you, didn't she? That fairly stirred the shit among his boys. I heard they were ready for doing her, only McKenna wouldn't have it.'

Lennon leaned over Rankin until he could smell the stale remains of his aftershave. 'Keep your mouth off that,' he said.

'I wasn't surprised when I heard she fucked off out of it,' Rankin said. 'Took the child with her, too.'

Lennon straightened. 'What do you know about that?'

'Only what I heard. Like I said, I know boys on the other side. They talk.'

'What did they say?'

Rankin grinned. 'I've said too much already, son. Best I shut my mouth now.'

Lennon leaned on the bed, his face inches from Rankin's. 'What did they say?'

Rankin mimed zipping his mouth shut, his eyes twinkling.

Lennon grabbed the lapels of his dressing

70

gown and pulled him close so their noses almost touched. 'What did they say?'

'Easy, son,' Rankin said, smiling. He put a hand on Lennon's shoulder. 'I'm only winding you up. They didn't say much, it was all a bit confused, like.'

Lennon released the lapels and let Rankin sit back. 'Go on.'

'Everyone thought she just got the frighteners when her uncle got hit, and that whole feud kicked off. But then I heard some other stuff, just rumours, you know?'

'Like what?'

'Like it wasn't a feud,' Rankin said. He smoothed his dressing gown over his chest. 'Nobody could say for sure what it was, but it wasn't a feud. Them three dissidents that blew themselves up had nothing to do with it, for one thing. What I heard, and don't quote me, it was just the one man done it. Some fella just went clean buck mental and went after McKenna and McGinty and the lot of them.'

'Bullshit,' Lennon said. 'There was an inquiry.'

Rankin laughed. 'Since when did an inquiry prove anything? Anyway, that's what I heard. Might be true, might not. But that's not all.'

Lennon sighed. 'Christ, just tell me.'

'I heard the woman was mixed up in it, her and the wee girl. *Your* wee girl. Jesus, don't tell me you didn't know all this? Them Special Branch boys really don't tell you fuck all, do they?'

Lennon's heart fluttered. 'Is that it?'

'It's all I heard,' Rankin said.

Lennon backed towards the door, almost stumbled over the chair.

'A thank-you would be nice,' Rankin called after Lennon as he retreated from the room.

11

'Thomas McDonnell,' the doctor called. A long streak of piss with a miserable face, he hovered in the waiting-room doorway.

'That's me,' the Traveller said.

The doctor nodded and walked away. The Traveller followed him. He'd used the Community Hospital in Armagh before, and the name Thomas McDonnell. They had a man of that moniker in the system somewhere, and health care was free up here, so the Traveller had no compunction about using it.

Except the Accident and Emergency doctors were always so fucking miserable. He'd had a broken right hand treated in the A&E at Craigavon once. A boxer's fracture, they called it. He swore blind he hadn't got it by punching some poor bastard's face in, but they didn't believe him. He could see the contempt on every single person who treated him that night. All except that little auxiliary nurse. The night hadn't been a total loss in the end.

This doctor was no more affable than the rest of them as he examined the Traveller's eye. It had streamed all last night, keeping him awake as he lay in the back of the Mercedes, and he couldn't stop squinting and blinking as he drove north this morning.

'What happened?' the doctor asked.

'Got something in my eye,' the Traveller said. 'Hurts like fuck.'

73

The doctor bristled. The Traveller noticed the little pin in the shape of a fish on the doctor's lapel. Jesus, he was a God-botherer.

'How did it get there?' the doctor asked.

'Don't know,' the Traveller said.

The doctor sighed. 'Head back.'

Before the Traveller knew what was happening, the doctor squeezed some orange stuff out of a little tube into his eye.

'Fuck's sake,' the Traveller said, blinking.

The doctor sighed again. 'It's just to help me see better. Let's have a look.'

He pushed back the Traveller's upper eyelid and shone a light in. 'Hmm,' the doctor said. The mint on his breath masked something sourer.

'What?' the Traveller asked.

'There's a foreign body under the upper lid, looks like a little fragment of wood, and you've a minor corneal abrasion. The nurse will irrigate the eye to remove the object and apply some antibiotic ointment.'

'Nurse?' the Traveller asked.

'Mm-hmm,' the doctor said.

'No, you do it,' the Traveller said.

The doctor released the Traveller's eyelid. 'No need,' he said. 'It's quite simple. She'll just pour a bit of saline solution into the eye to flush it out and apply an antibiotic ointment to stop any infection. The abrasion will heal in a few days.'

'You do it,' the Traveller repeated. He grimaced as whatever the doctor had put in his eye found its way to the back of his throat.

'Really, there's no need. It'll only take a — '

'You're the doctor, you fucking do it,' the

Traveller said. 'It's my fucking eye. It needs a doctor. I'm not having some blade just out of school poking at it. You do it.'

The doctor did his best to look authoritative. 'Please moderate your language, Mr McDonnell. Nurse Barnes is a skilled and experienced A&E nurse. She's done this a thousand times. And I'm not sure she'd appreciate being called a 'blade'.'

The Traveller lowered his feet to the floor. 'You do it,' he said.

'Honestly, there's — '

The Traveller stepped closer, the doctor's ear within biting distance, and whispered, 'You. Fucking. Do it.'

The doctor's voice quivered. 'Mr McDonnell, we won't tolerate abusive behaviour in this — '

The Traveller seized the back of the doctor's scrawny neck in his left hand, and pinched his windpipe between the fingers and thumb of his right.

'Are you going to do it?'

The doctor staggered back, taking the Traveller with him. A swivel chair tipped and fell to the floor. The doctor swiped a pen holder, scattering its contents across his desk. He made choked 'Ack!' noises as his face reddened.

'Are you going to do it?'

A scream came from behind. The Traveller twisted towards the voice, the doctor's throat still in his grip. The nurse in the doorway screamed again.

'Fuck,' the Traveller said.

He kicked the doctor's feet from under him and ran.

12

'I need a favour,' Lennon said into his phone as he waited for the lights to change at the junction of the Lisburn Road and Sandy Row.

'What sort of favour?' Dan Hewitt asked.

'I want to see some files,' Lennon said. He held the phone between his ear and his shoulder as the lights changed and he released the handbrake. 'Whatever you've got on the McKenna feud.'

'No chance,' Hewitt said. 'You've no reason to see them. Not unless you've got a live investigation, and that mess was wrapped up months ago. What do you want them for?'

'It's something Andy Rankin said.'

'What's the feud got to do with him?'

'Nothing, it was just something he mentioned. A rumour he'd heard. I want to check it out. Come on, you know I'm doing you a big favour settling for that GBH.'

'And you're getting back on an MIT in return,' Hewitt said. 'I think that makes us square.'

Lennon struggled to concentrate on the road as he wove through side streets to get back to Donegall Pass. 'I need to see them, Dan.'

'No you don't,' Hewitt said. 'You *want* to see them. Not the same thing at all. I couldn't let you have them even if I wanted to. I have to show a live investigation before I can pull the files.'

'Shit,' Lennon said. 'There must be some way.'

'If you want files on Rankin, I can maybe do something for you, within reason.'

'How about if you cross-reference Rankin and McKenna? If there's any match-up, can you give me the files? Crozier too. Rankin told me Crozier's been taking over McKenna's turf since he died. That ties it to my case.'

Lennon listened to silence for long seconds until Hewitt sighed and said, 'All right, I'll see what I can do. A lot of it'll be redacted, though. You'll be looking at more blacked-out lines than anything else.'

'Okay,' Lennon said, 'whatever you can get me.'

'Give me an hour,' Hewitt said.

★   ★   ★

The thin file landed on Lennon's desk ninety minutes later. He flicked through the photocopied pages, less than twenty of them. True to Hewitt's word, most of it had been blacked out by thick lines drawn with marker pen. But not all of them were redacted in the original. Some of the pages smelled of solvent, the black lines fresh and slightly damp to the touch.

A Post-it note clung to the inside of the folder. In Dan Hewitt's neat script it said:

Jack,

There's not much, but it's the best I can do for you. Remember, Dandy Andy has done us a lot of good. Like I said, he's a

77

piece of shit, but a useful piece of shit.
Shred these when you're done.
    Dan

Dandy Andy Rankin was indeed a piece of shit. Not only had he been leeching off his own community for years, but he'd also been spoon-feeding information to Special Branch, and more recently their new face, C3 Intelligence Branch. The first three pages were a profile complete with mug shots and a career summary, Dandy Andy's Greatest Hits. Scanning the pages, Lennon could discern at least half a dozen assassinations that had been thwarted, five arms caches that had been discovered, and hundreds of thousands of pounds' worth of Ecstasy, cocaine and cannabis shipments that had been stopped en route to Belfast.

All this came at a price, of course. Rankin had been allowed to operate in relative peace. A single paragraph below the photos outlined his various enterprises. Those suits weren't cheap.

The following pages were the most interesting. Rankin had been passing bits and pieces of information on Rodney Crozier's emerging relationship with Belfast's Lithuanian gangs. The consolidation of the European Union alongside Northern Ireland's stabilisation had drawn prosperity to this part of the world, but the criminals followed close behind.

The South had seen it first, with Dublin's underworld growing more vicious by the day. Gangland killings were now almost as frequent in the Republic as paramilitary killings had been in the North during the Troubles. Up here, the paramilitaries still kept control of the rackets; ordinary decent criminals didn't have a look in, but competition from Eastern Europeans was starting to bite.

The Loyalists had been cooperating with the Lithuanians for some time, now. They put up a front of resisting foreigners in Protestant areas, intimidating the hard-working immigrants who took the jobs no one else would, but behind closed doors they sucked up to the gangsters from Lithuania and elsewhere. Prostitution was one of the biggest earners for them, and the Liths had a good supply of young women from Russia, Romania, Belarus and Ukraine. None of that was news to Lennon, much as it shamed him. He flicked through a series of memos and transcribed messages, reading what hadn't been obscured. Each mentioned McKenna at least once, but nothing substantial. Nothing he could link back to what Rankin had told him at the hospital.

The final section was a transcription of a meeting between Rankin and one of his handlers. Lennon scanned the few readable scraps that had been left.

DATE: 05/09/2007
LOCATION: Car park, Makro Warehouse, Dunmurry, Belfast
INTERVIEWING OFFICER: DI James Maxwell, C3
SUBJECT: Andrew Rankin, a.k.a. Dandy Andy Rankin

Interviewing officer notes that Rankin was visibly agitated throughout the conversation, as evidenced by his fidgeting and chain-smoking.

JM: What have you got for me?
AR: Rodney bloody Crozier. I want him put away.
JM: Jesus, Andy, not this again.
AR: It's this business with the Liths. He's getting too big for his boots. He'll be shitting all over me if it goes on much longer.
JM: We've talked about this before.
AR: And I'm going to keep talking about it till you fuckers get your thumbs out of your arses and do something about it. Ever since Michael McKenna got his stupid brains blown out, Rodney fucking Crozier's been palling up to them, getting his —

McKenna's name scratched at Lennon. Everyone on the force knew Lennon's connection to McKenna, even if it was history. A third of a page was blacked out. Lennon skipped ahead.

— people talk, like. Crozier couldn't have moved into that part of town if McKenna was still around.
JM: And?
AR: And if you lot don't do something about it, I will. Fuck me, I never

80

thought I'd see the day. One of our own running with the Liths, putting money in the other side's pockets. I knew Rodney Crozier's father. He'd turn in his grave if he saw who his son was doing business with.

JM: Listen, our hands are tied. We can't mount an operation of that scale just on your say-so.

AR: Jesus, who runs the cops these days, eh? Who's telling you to turn a blind eye to all this carry-on? That business with McKenna getting bumped off, then all the shit that —

More lines scrawled over with black marker. The feud. The killings in Belfast. The bloodbath on an old farm near the border. The inquiry established that dissidents had ambushed the politician Paul McGinty there, and the investigation was concluded when three of them blew themselves up with their own bomb a few months later. A specialist forensics team had matched the remains of the guns in their car to the scene of the shootout.

When Lennon heard the news of McKenna's death his first thought had been of Marie and Ellen. He'd considered phoning her, even went as far as punching the number into his mobile, but then he realised he didn't have a clue what to say. He could ask to speak to his daughter, but he knew Marie would say no. And anyway, what do you say to a child who doesn't know you?

It wasn't for lack of trying on his part. For more than two years after Ellen was born he'd tried to initiate some kind of contact. He'd left her mother while she carried their child. He couldn't forgive himself for that sin, so had no expectation of anyone else offering absolution, but Ellen was still his child. Marie refused every attempt, every approach. It was nothing more than punishment for his crime, and he knew he deserved it, but Ellen didn't. He considered going through the courts, forcing Marie to give him access, but he'd seen how the system drove more families apart than it pulled together. Parents used their children as weapons against each other. He wanted no part of that. Eventually he decided it would be better to let the child grow up oblivious to him than make her the centre of a battle that wasn't of her making.

Lennon's own father had abandoned his family, leaving only vague memories of a man who would roar with laughter one minute and strike out in anger the next. He'd gone to America, Lennon's mother had said, and when he had enough money he would send for his wife and children. Years later, she still had that spark of hope in her eyes every time the postman shoved paper through their door. The letter never came.

For Lennon, family did not mean warmth and comfort. It meant pain and regret. His family had cut him off for joining the cops; Marie's family had done the same to her for taking up with him. Blood bonds were so easily severed, surely his child would be happier never having been tied to him in the first place.

But he never forgot.

Up until she moved away he had parked once or twice a week on Eglantine Avenue and watched Marie and Ellen come and go. Ellen looked like her mother, at least from a distance. He imagined getting out of his car, approaching them, hunkering down to see Ellen eye to eye, holding her small hand in his.

But what good could come of that? It would only confuse the child, and Marie would whisk her away from him. She kept that hardness in her well hidden. He'd touched it more than once when they'd been together. It felt like the bones beneath her skin, but colder and sharper. She knew keeping his daughter from him was the only way to punish him for what he'd done. Even if he did go to court and demand access, put Ellen through that circus, what kind of father could he make? No better than his own, certainly.

He shook the thought away and started reading again.

— all over the fucking place. Every-body knows there was more to all that. But it was forgotten about bloody quick.

JM: Jesus, you boys must gossip like a bunch of auld dolls at the bingo. None of that's anything to do with you.

AR: Nothing to do with me? I'm losing a fucking fortune 'cause Michael McKenna went and got himself —

Half a page missing this time. Lennon scanned down.

— irl. And she's not been seen since.

He stopped there, his mouth dry. He traced the blacked-out lines with his finger, looking for any sign of the letters they concealed. That last word, was it girl? He tried to find some moisture in his mouth to wet his lips, but his tongue rasped against the roof of his mouth.

Lennon pushed the papers aside and checked his watch. Almost lunchtime. He lifted the phone and dialled the C3 office. He asked for Hewitt.

'You fancy some lunch?' he asked when Hewitt answered.

'With you?'

'Yes,' Lennon said. 'With me.'

'I gave you the files, Jack. That's more than I should've done.'

'Come on, for old times' sake.'

'Christ,' Hewitt said. 'What are you after?'

'Just a couple of questions. And a bacon sandwich.'

Hewitt sighed. 'All right, canteen in ten minutes.'

* * *

Hewitt picked over a salad while Lennon chewed cold bacon. The folder lay on the table between them. A squad of boys from the Tactical Support Group sat on the other side of the canteen, shouting and guffawing over their chips and

84

beans. There must have been a raid planned for the afternoon, some house with reinforced doors and heated rooms for the cannabis plants, or a corner shop with smuggled cigarettes stashed in the back.

'You weren't joking about the redactions,' Lennon said. 'Most of it was blacked out.'

Hewitt took a sip of mineral water. 'What did you expect? You're lucky you saw any of it.'

Lennon spooned sugar into his tea. 'I know. There's only the one bit I'm curious about.'

'Don't even bother asking,' Hewitt said.

'Just this one bit.' Lennon took a swig of lukewarm tea. 'About that business with Michael McKenna, the feud, McGinty getting ambushed near Middletown.'

'What about it? Everything was made public after the inquiry. McGinty's faction fought amongst themselves, and the dissidents got involved. It was a bloody mess, but it's all over with.'

Lennon struggled with the bacon. Hewitt waited patiently. Eventually, Lennon swallowed and asked, 'Then why's it all blacked out? Why the secrecy if it's all in the public domain anyway?'

Hewitt put down his fork and wiped his lips with a napkin, even though his mouth was clean. 'Look, Jack, I let you see those notes as a favour. I'd be in trouble if anyone knew I'd let you get anywhere near them. Don't push your luck.'

'You heard about Kevin Malloy? What happened to him night before last?' Lennon asked. 'He was one of Bull O'Kane's crew. Bull

O'Kane owns the farm where McGinty got killed.'

'That Malloy thing was a robbery gone wrong,' Hewitt said. 'Besides, it's nothing to do with us. It was on the other side of the border. The Guards can take care of that one. You're fishing. What for?'

Lennon took a chance. 'What do the notes say about Marie McKenna?'

Hewitt paled.

'In the Rankin interview,' Lennon continued, not giving Hewitt a chance to sidestep. 'Right at the end, he mentions her.'

'No he doesn't,' Hewitt said with a weak laugh. He picked up his fork and stabbed at soggy lettuce leaves.

'He does,' Lennon said. 'Right at the end.'

Hewitt dropped the fork and reached for the folder. He pulled out loose pages and flipped through them. He found the Rankin interview and traced the lines with his fingertip. After a few seconds of page turning, Hewitt said, 'It doesn't mention Marie McKenna anywhere.'

'Nope,' Lennon said. 'Made you look, though, didn't I?'

Hewitt stared hard across the table at him, his cheeks flushed, before stuffing the pages back in the folder. 'I'll hang on to these,' he said, 'make sure they're properly disposed of.'

'Was Marie involved in any of that?' Lennon asked.

Hewitt stood. 'I'm not having this discussion with you, Jack.'

'I drive by her street sometimes,' Lennon said.

'Not in a dodgy way, you understand, just if I'm passing. Her windows have been boarded up for a while now. I asked around, at her work, places like that. They said she'd moved away, they didn't know where. She went in a hurry.'

Hewitt moved around the table to Lennon's side. 'Jack, if you want any more information from our files, you can make an official request.'

'She moved away with my daughter,' Lennon said. 'You know my family disowned me when I joined up. Personnel have my next of kin down as a cousin I only talk to once a year, for Christ's sake. Ellen's the only mark I made on the world. The only family I've got, and she doesn't know who I am. I just want to know where she is.'

'All right.' Hewitt placed a hand on Lennon's shoulder. 'I'll tell you this as an old friend. I shouldn't discuss it at all, but I'll make an exception for you.' He leaned in close to Lennon's ear. 'These papers say absolutely nothing about Marie McKenna or her child. Fair enough?'

Lennon turned his head so their eyes were inches apart. 'Fair enough.'

Hewitt patted his shoulder and walked away, the file tucked under his arm.

'But, Dan?' Lennon called after him.

Hewitt stopped, sighed, and turned around.

'If you're lying to me,' Lennon said.

'You'll what?'

Lennon thought about it for a few seconds before telling the truth. 'I don't know,' he said.

13

Gerry Fegan stood still and closed his eyes when the long Cadillac slowed alongside him. He'd been as careful as he could, getting off the F Train at Delancey Street station instead of East Broadway, and taking the most circuitous route he could find to his building on the corner of Hester and Ludlow Street. He would have fled when he had the chance, only he needed money and his fake passport. He had no choice but to go back to his shabby little room on the Lower East Side.

The brakes whined. 'Doyles want to see you, Gerry Fegan,' a heavily accented voice called.

Fegan opened his eyes and turned to Pyè Préval. He was the only black man the Doyle brothers would have about them. The small and wiry Haitian leaned out of the rear passenger side window. Fegan had met him a few times on the sites he'd worked on. In his strange mix of Haitian Creole and English, Pyè often told Fegan he wanted to visit Ireland. He asked Fegan about the weather and the landscape, the drink, and the 'fi' — the girls. Fegan liked him in a way, but knew a bad man when he met one. Pyè would be handy with a knife, Fegan was sure of it.

Pyè got out of the car and held the door open. 'Zanmi mwen,' he said, his smile as bright as the day. He pointed inside the limo. 'My friend, get in machin nan.'

'Jimmy Stone's going to need surgery on that knee,' Frankie Doyle said. He speared a meatball with his fork and squashed overcooked pasta into it with his knife.

The tourists on Mulberry Street paid no attention to Fegan or the Doyles as they talked at a table outside the restaurant. The brothers didn't offer Fegan any food.

'Tell him I'm sorry about that,' Fegan said.

Packie Doyle snorted and mopped his mouth with a paper napkin. 'Christ, I don't think sorry's going to do it, Gerry.'

Fegan didn't protest at the name. 'Will he be all right?' he asked.

'Eventually,' Frankie said. 'He'll be on crutches for a month or two, and he'll have a limp for a good long while. Some of the boys thought we should do you over for that, Gerry. Do both your knees, see how you like it.'

Fegan said nothing. An image flickered briefly in his mind: breaking a young man's left knee behind McKenna's bar on the Springfield Road. It had been more than two decades ago, and remembrance could do no good. He pushed the memory away.

Packie mopped up sauce with a fistful of bread. 'We don't want a fight with you, Gerry,' he said.

'No fight,' Frankie said. 'Jesus, if we wanted that, we wouldn't be sitting here now. We could just as easy turn you in to the cops, or immigration even, as hand you over to this guy who's looking for you.'

'We could've done that,' Packie said through a mouthful of bread, 'but we didn't.'

'Look at things our way for a minute,' Frankie said. 'Good men are hard to find.'

'You can't get the help these days,' Packie said.

'So along comes a good man,' Frankie said, 'and we want to put some work his way.'

'But he throws it back in our face,' Packie said.

'And we're just trying to do him a good turn,' Frankie said. 'You see where we're coming from, Gerry?'

Fegan clasped his hands together. 'I just want to be left alone.'

'We all want a quiet life,' Packie said.

Frankie nodded. 'What we want and what we get are two different things.'

'You owe us, Gerry,' Packie said. 'And not just for keeping quiet about who and where you are.'

'Jimmy's surgery won't be cheap,' Frankie said.

'Thousands, it'll cost,' Packie said.

'There's no getting round it, Gerry,' Frankie said.

'Everybody pays,' Packie said.

'Sooner or later,' Frankie said.

Fegan eyed the bottle of red wine the brothers shared. He swallowed against the dryness in his throat. 'What do you want me to do?' he asked.

14

Lennon watched Marie McKenna's flat for an hour, his mind working over the documents Hewitt had let him see. The windows were still boarded up, no outward sign that anything had changed since May. He often scolded himself as he sat there, parked wherever the best vantage point lay. This was stalker behaviour, plain and simple, and he hated himself for it.

Worst of all, the one night he could have done any good, he hadn't been there. Just a day before Marie disappeared, Lennon sat in this very parking space and watched a tall thin man call at her door. When she welcomed the stranger in, Lennon had sped off, almost clipping another car. The next day he found out the man was Gerry Fegan, a known killer. Fegan had been arrested for brawling with another thug outside the flat.

Lennon asked CI Uprichard what was going on. Uprichard made a call while Lennon waited, nodded his head and grunted agreement. When Uprichard hung up, he paused, smiled and said, 'Best just leave it.'

But Lennon didn't leave it, at least not for a while. He asked around, begged favours, and leaned on lowlifes. All he could get was that she'd moved away in a hurry, taking the little girl with her.

His little girl.

He had put it to the back of his mind, convinced himself his daughter was lost to him, but still once every week or two he would take a detour by Eglantine Avenue. Like this evening.

The window above Marie's flat lit up. A young man with a roll-up cigarette between his lips appeared for just a moment as he lowered the shabby blinds. An idea presented itself. Lennon pushed it away. The idea resisted. He gave in, knowing it was a mistake.

Lennon climbed out of his Audi, locked it, and walked towards the flat. There were three doorbell buttons. The bottom one, the button for Marie's flat, had no name tag. The middle one said 'Hutchence'. Lennon held his thumb on it for five seconds, then took a step back.

The middle blind on the bay window shot up, followed by the sash pane. The young man leaned out. 'Yeah?'

'Police,' Lennon said. 'I need a word.'

The young man banged his head on the window frame as he ducked back inside. Lennon heard the frantic muttering of at least three voices from above. He guessed it wasn't tobacco the young man was smoking.

The young man's head appeared again. 'Can I see some identification please?' he asked, his voice breaking like a twelve-year-old's.

'If you like,' Lennon said. He pulled his wallet from his hip pocket, opened it, and held it up. 'I doubt if you'll be able to read it from up there, though.'

'I'll be down in a minute,' the young man said, the last word at least an octave higher than the rest.

Lennon scanned the tiny garden as he waited. Marie used to keep it pretty neat. Now litter and dead leaves gathered in the corners, and a summer's worth of weeds had grown up through the cracks in the concrete.

A light appeared in the glass above the front door. Lennon put on his best scary cop face, ready to put the wind up the youngster. The door opened. He held his identification up at the kid's eye level. There was no sound but the flushing of a toilet somewhere upstairs.

Eventually the kid smirked and said, 'John Lennon? Was Ringo busy?'

Lennon gave the boy his hardest stare. 'Detective Inspector John Lennon. My friends call me Jack. You can call me Inspector Lennon. Understood?'

The kid's smirk dropped. 'Understood.'

'Is your name Hutchence?'

'Yes.'

'First name?'

'David.'

'What are you, a student?'

'Yes.'

'At Queen's?'

'Yes.'

'You having a party, David?'

'No!' The young man held his hands up. 'It's just me and my flatmates. We weren't making any noise. We've no music going or anything.'

Lennon leaned forward and sniffed the air

between him and the kid. 'You been smoking anything?'

'Just fags.' The young man forced his shaking hands together as the toilet flushed again.

Lennon stepped into the hall. 'How long have you been here?'

'Just a couple of weeks,' the kid said as he shuffled backwards. 'Term only starts on Monday.'

Lennon walked past the young man and peered up the stairwell. Another kid's head ducked out of sight on the landing above. A flatmate, presumably. 'Who lives on the top floor?' Lennon asked.

'No one yet. The landlord said there's more students moving in next week.'

Lennon pointed to the door in the hallway beyond. It had been six years since he'd left the ground floor flat, and that life, behind. 'What about in there?' he asked.

'It's empty too,' the kid said. 'The landlord said someone rents it, but they're away travelling or something.'

Lennon tried the door handle. It was locked, of course. 'Is there ever anyone around?'

'No, there's . . . oh, wait!' The young man's face lit up like he'd won a prize. 'Someone picked up the post last week. There was a pile sitting there.' He indicated the shelf above the radiator. 'We went out one night, and when we came back, it was gone. Do you want the landlord's number?'

'No,' Lennon said. He'd tackled the landlord not long after the flat had been boarded up and come away with nothing. He handed the kid a card. 'If anyone ever comes around, goes in there, takes anything away, anything at all, you give me a call, all right? And I'll pretend I didn't smell anything funny coming from upstairs.'

The young man gave a weak smile and nodded.

'I'll see myself out,' Lennon said.

15

The Traveller didn't like this one bit. The broad-shouldered man with dirty-fair hair was clearly a cop. The Traveller hadn't noticed him pull up, so he had to assume the cop was watching the flat too. Of course, it was possible the cop wanted something with the kid who answered the door, but the Traveller knew that wasn't so. He knew it in his gut.

Christ, it had been a long day. When he fled the hospital he drove straight to Portadown, constantly checking the mirror with his one good eye. He considered ditching the car, but the risk of stealing another was greater than the chances of his number plate being caught on CCTV in the hospital car park.

Once he'd got to Portadown he'd pulled into the first place he could find. He walked until he found a chemist and bought a little tube of antibiotic eye ointment and a bottle of water. The girl behind the counter stared at the orange streaks around his bad eye made by the stuff the doctor had used. He held his hand out for his change. She put it on the counter and stepped back.

When he returned to the car, he tilted his head back, pulled up his eyelid, and poured the water in. Jesus, it went everywhere, but it seemed to do the trick. He dried his face with his sleeve as best he could, and then put a dollop of the ointment in his eye. He sat there blinded for half an hour before heading for the motorway. It took less than forty minutes to reach Belfast, nudge his way through the traffic on the Lisburn Road, and turn right into Eglantine Avenue. He knew to look out for the church on the corner.

As soon as he parked, he put another dollop of the ointment in his bad eye, hoping it would ease the stinging and itching. Instead, it left him squinting and swearing. Maybe that was when the cop pulled up. The Traveller cursed himself. He and the cop had been sitting yards from each other, watching the same boarded-up flat, for at least an hour. The Traveller always listened to his instincts, that reptilian part of his brain, and right now it was telling him the cop was trouble. He took the mobile phone from his pocket, entered the password, and dialled the only number it held.

'What?' Orla O'Kane barked.

'Who's the cop?'

'What cop?'

'The cop who just went into Marie McKenna's building. The same cop that's been sitting watching it for at least an hour.'

'Jesus,' Orla O'Kane said.

'Jesus what?'

'That wee girl of hers. The father's a cop. Can't remember his name, but I'll find out. What's he look like?'

'Big fella, good shape,' the Traveller said. 'Dark blond hair. His suit looked better than a cop could afford, even with the danger money they get up here. Maybe he's bent.'

'I'll see what I can dig up. I heard about our

friend in Monaghan on the news, by the way. Pity about his wife.'

'Yeah, pity,' the Traveller said.

'I suppose it couldn't be helped.'

'No, couldn't,' the Traveller said.

'Fair enough. What about Quigley?' she asked.

'I'll maybe call and see him a bit later.'

'You do that. I need some progress to — '

'Whisht!' the Traveller hissed, silencing Orla. 'The cop's coming out. I'll maybe follow him, see what I can see.'

'Don't take any chances,' she said, her voice low and serious. 'We're not interested in him. If he's a problem, deal with it, but leave him alone otherwise. Understood?'

'Understood,' the Traveller said. 'Don't worry, I'll just have a wee shufti. Nice talking to you, big lass.'

'Watch your m — '

The Traveller hung up and slipped the phone back into his jacket pocket. The cop crossed the road ten yards ahead and disappeared from view. The Traveller lowered his window a little. He heard a car door opening and closing with a solid thud. Something quality, probably German or Scandinavian, or maybe a late Ford. An engine sparked and caught with an ugly diesel clatter. The Traveller lowered his window a little more so he could lean out. Up ahead, a silver Audi A4 pulled out and accelerated towards the Malone Road.

'Nice motor,' the Traveller whispered to himself. It looked pretty new. Thirty-five thousand euro, maybe forty, depending on the engine size and the options. He didn't know what it would cost in pounds sterling, but it would still be big money for a cop. The Traveller turned the old Merc's key, and the ignition whined until the engine burped and farted into life. He let a Citroën pass so he could keep it between him and the Audi before he pulled out.

The cop turned right on the Malone Road, as did the Citroën, but he surprised the Traveller by immediately turning left into the cluster of churches and old houses that led to Stranmillis. The Citroën stayed on the Malone Road, leaving no buffer between the Audi and the Merc. The Traveller had to be careful. He didn't know the names of these little streets, but he knew Stranmillis Road when the cop turned onto it. The Traveller let two cars pass before he followed, giving him some cover.

The river came into view as they approached the roundabout at the bottom of Stranmillis. Surely the cop didn't live down here? A doctor or a solicitor could just about manage a mortgage around these parts, but surely not a cop.

'Jesus,' the Traveller said when the peeler pulled into a smart apartment block just beyond the roundabout. He didn't dare follow the cop into the car park, so he kept driving, wondering if it was really his place or a girlfriend's. Maybe the peeler was shagging some lady lawyer, or a female executive after a bit of rough.

'Dirty fucker,' the Traveller said. He headed back towards the Lisburn Road hoping one of those fancy new restaurants had pictures on their menus.

16

Lennon sat at his Mexican-style dining table eating microwaved lamb rogan josh. The edge of the Mexican-style chair cut into the backs of his thighs. The set had cost almost five hundred, but he'd got it on finance. He was sure the interest rate would have been scandalous if he'd looked at it. But he hadn't, just signed the form the salesman put in front of him. They delivered the table and six chairs a few days later, and he'd never eaten a comfortable meal while seated here.

He thought back, searching for the last time anyone else had sat at the table. Months ago, he reckoned, and he couldn't remember her name. She drank coffee and he drank tea while they barely looked at each other. He took her number even though they both knew he'd never dial it.

The lamb turned sickly in Lennon's mouth. He swallowed it and pushed the plate away, then washed his palate with a swig of lukewarm tap water. The silence pressed on him with a cold insistence. He could only take his own company for so long, so he cleaned up, changed, and headed into town.

He decided to try the Empire's basement bar. A blues band did their best for an indifferent crowd mostly made up of students getting an early start on the weekend. Lennon scoped the women and felt every day of his thirty-seven years. He wasn't quite old enough to be anyone's father, but maybe a creepy uncle. He ordered a pint of Stella as he wondered where else he could go. The small pang of guilt he'd felt at drawing forty pounds cash on one of his credit cards grew sharper and deeper as he handed a twenty over. His bank account had run dry the day before. Anyone with common sense would wait for pay day rather than spend borrowed money, but common sense and money never occupied the same parts of his mind.

Two girls leaned on the bar beside Lennon. Not young enough to be students, he thought, too well dressed. They both wore the kinds of clothes and jewellery that rich boyfriends or fathers would never buy. They made their own money, probably working in one of the call centres that had sprung up across the city.

'Two Smirnoff Ice,' one of the girls called across the bar.

Lennon held out the ten-pound note he'd just got back in change, forgetting any notion of frugality he might have entertained a few seconds before. 'Allow me,' he said.

The nearest girl looked him up and down. 'If I wanted my dad to buy my drinks, I'd have brought him,' she said. 'Thanks anyway.'

Lennon forced himself to finish his pint before leaving. He phoned Roscoe Patterson to see if he had anything on tonight.

★ ★ ★

Less than thirty minutes took Lennon to the apartment block overlooking Carrickfergus Marina.

Roscoe said nothing when he opened the door to the penthouse flat, and Lennon followed him through the entrance hall to the living room. The shaven-headed, bull-shouldered man took a seat and resumed his computer game. His thick fingers moved over the controller with a curious grace. Uniformed soldiers died under a hail of gunfire on the massive plasma screen, the shiny new Playstation 3 whirring in the cabinet beneath it.

'Sit down,' Roscoe said. 'She's got a punter in. He'll not be long.' His face creased in an absent-minded grin. 'They never are.'

Lennon lowered himself into the leather sofa facing Roscoe. The floor resonated as the surround-sound system's woofer made the most of the game's explosions.

'The neighbours don't complain about the noise?' Lennon asked.

Roscoe winked. 'Just the once,' he said. 'There's only a couple here during the week, anyway. The rest is holiday lets or weekend places.'

Lennon shifted, trying to get comfortable as his jeans slid across the leather.

'I heard you lifted Dandy Andy,' Roscoe said as he blew someone's head off.

'That's right,' Lennon said.

'Good job,' Roscoe said. 'He's a cunt. Will he do time?'

'A little. Not much.'

Roscoe shrugged. 'Better than nothing,' he said.

Lennon watched the blurred tattoos on

Roscoe's forearms flex and ripple as he worked the controller. 'You know what Rankin's gripe with Crozier was?'

'Don't be asking me that,' Roscoe said. 'I'm not touting for you.'

'I heard Crozier was palling up with the Lithuanians,' Lennon said. 'He was filling the gap Michael McKenna left when he got his brains blown out. He was supplying the muscle while they supplied the girls. He was letting them set up their own places on McKenna's old turf.'

'Know nothing about it,' Roscoe said. 'Ah, fuck! Look, I got shot now 'cause of you.'

'So you and your boys are okay with Crozier doing business with the Liths?' Lennon asked. 'You know they pay dues to the Republicans, don't you? Crozier's putting money in their pockets.'

'Dirty business, that,' Patterson said. 'Them Liths are trafficking girls in from all over the fucking place, Russia, Ukraine, all them auld shitty holes. Keeping them doped up so they can have them doing punters for fuck all money. Slaves, like. I don't hold with that. I deal in quality, not quantity. You pay a bit more, but you know the girl's there of her own free will, and she's getting her fair share of the money. And she'll be so clean she'll squeak when you stick it to her.'

'You're a prince among pimps,' Lennon said.

Roscoe grinned. 'I should put that on my business cards. Anyway, so long as I'm turning a pound, Crozier can give the Liths free blowjobs for all I care. And the taigs. No offence, like. Now, either change the subject or fuck off.'

'Fair enough,' Lennon said. 'Who've you got on tonight?'

'Debbie,' Roscoe said.

'Debbie?'

'Edinburgh Uni. She's doing her Master's in commercial law, she tells me. Whatever the fuck that means. I normally just bring her over on weekends, but she's got some bills to pay. Fucking lovely wee thing, she is. You'll like her.'

A door opened in the entrance hall, and Lennon heard the rustling of clothes. The shadow of a man, his head bowed, passed the door.

'Everything all right?' Roscoe called.

'Yes, thank you,' a small voice replied.

'Dead on,' Roscoe said. 'You can let yourself out.'

The apartment door opened and closed.

'Give her a minute to clean up,' Roscoe said.

'You boys talk amongst yourselves,' Lennon said. 'About what's going on. Who's doing what to who, that sort of thing.'

'Aye,' Roscoe said. 'But like I said, I'm not touting for you. You're a good friend to have, Jack, but don't push your luck.'

'Michael McKenna,' Lennon said. 'Paul McGinty, too. What do you reckon to all that? The inquiry said it was a feud, all internal stuff. You ever hear anything different?'

Roscoe smiled. 'That was a good week,' he said. 'My auld da used to say the only good taig was a dead taig. Lot of good taigs that week. No offence, like.'

'None taken,' Lennon said.

Roscoe's mobile phone beeped. He picked it up and thumbed a button. 'She's ready for you,' he said.

Lennon got to his feet and walked to the door.

'There was one weird thing came of it all,' Roscoe said.

Lennon stopped in the doorway. 'What was that?'

'That lawyer, Patsy Toner,' Roscoe said. 'They said he lent that bent cop his car, and the cop wound up getting his head took off. They said it was mistaken identity, said the dissidents meant to get Toner. But then the dissidents blew themselves up, problem solved, everything gets back to normal.'

Lennon walked back to Roscoe. 'And?'

'Patsy Toner's a regular with one of my girls. She says he's in pieces. He still comes to see her, but he can't manage anything. She's tried handjobs, blowjobs, stuck her finger up his arse, everything she can think of. Not a fucking thing.'

'I could've done without that image,' Lennon said.

'Me too,' Roscoe said, his lip curling. 'But you hear worse in my line of work.'

Lennon leaned on the back of Roscoe's chair. 'I'm sure you do, but what's your point?'

Roscoe shrugged. 'Might be nothing, but she told me he turned up pissed off his face one night. He was blathering about how it wasn't over, they wouldn't let it go, it was only a matter of time before they came for him.'

Lennon stood upright. 'Is that right?'

Roscoe smiled. 'Is what right? I didn't tell you nothing.' He turned back to his game. 'I'm not touting for you. Now go and see that wee thing before she gets lonely.'

Lennon patted the other man's muscled shoulder. 'Thanks, Roscoe.'

He went back to the entrance hall. A thin streak of light reached across the carpet from the bedroom door. He rapped the wood with his knuckles, and the door opened. She had shoulder-length brown hair and smelled of strong soap.

'Put a hundred on the dressing table, love,' she said, her Scottish accent easing through her smile. 'Then we'll talk about the options. All right, sweetheart?'

Lennon forced himself to maintain eye contact. 'Roscoe and me have an arrangement.'

She stood on tiptoe and called over his shoulder. 'Roscoe?'

Roscoe's voice came back from the living room. 'Whatever he wants. I'll sort you, don't worry.'

Her face slackened for a moment, whether with contempt or sadness he couldn't tell. Then it brightened, as if a light behind her eyes had switched on, and her lips parted in a smile that could cut glass. 'Whatever you want, darling,' she said.

17

Just a few months ago, Declan Quigley had saved Bull O'Kane's life by dragging his huge bulk into a car and speeding to a hospital in Dundalk. Even so, O'Kane wanted Quigley gone. It wasn't the Traveller's place to question the Bull.

Quigley lived with his mother in a red-brick two-up-two-down off the Lower Ormeau. The Traveller circled the area around the house. He couldn't park up and hope no one noticed him as he did at Marie McKenna's place on Eglantine Avenue. This was a close-knit community. Any stranger would draw attention if they stayed in one place too long.

A gang of fifteen or so youths wandered from street to street, making their way towards the interface with the Loyalist-dominated Donegall Pass. Looking for a fight, the Traveller thought. They'd probably get it. He circled back towards Quigley's street.

The mother was doting, the Bull said, didn't know night from day. There was no need to touch her, even if she saw everything. The Bull had been quite clear on that point, and the Traveller intended to honour his promise.

He tucked the old Merc into a parking bay on the Ormeau Road, next to a fenced-off housing development where the sports ground used to be. It'd be a trek to Quigley's house, but it was the most secluded place he could find to leave the car. He kept his head down as he walked along the main road, avoiding eye contact with the few people he passed.

The Traveller walked as far as the Ormeau Bridge before looping back along the river. He counted side streets as he made his way north. The Bull had told him how many. A police siren wailed somewhere towards Donegall Pass, followed by cheers. The youths had got their fight by the sound of it.

He ducked into the narrow alleyway that cut along the back of Quigley's terrace. Seven houses along from the river end, the Bull had said. The Traveller kept tight to the wall and counted gates. He worked his way through the alley's blackness, careful of his footing. Litter snagged his heels, old plastic bags and cigarette packets. He kicked an empty can and froze. Inside one of the houses, a dog barked at the clatter. When it settled, he started moving again.

A siren screamed along Ormeau Avenue. The Traveller saw a cop car flash past the far end of the alley. A moment later he heard the screeching of tyres and the whoops and laughter of breathless boys. He moved faster, reached Quigley's back gate, pressed against the painted wood and found it open. As he slipped into the yard he kept his eyes on the far end of the alley. Two youths appeared there, their trainers skidding as they rounded the corner.

The Traveller eased back into the yard and pushed the gate closed. It stood as high as the wall, would keep him hidden, but it had no latch. He listened to the hammering of feet as the boys sprinted along the alley.

'Quick, they're coming!' a voice said.

'Fuck's sake, hide!' another said.

The Traveller heard hands slapping on wood as the boys tried the gates. Too late, he went to block Quigley's, and the boys burst through.

He put the first one down with a blow to the temple, and the sound of skull meeting brickwork cut the boy's cry short. The other slipped as he tried to halt his momentum and landed at the Traveller's feet.

The Traveller swooped, threw him on his belly. Before the boy could scream, the Traveller had his throat in the crook of his elbow. The boy didn't struggle long.

The Traveller got to his feet and pressed his back against the gate. Heavy footsteps trudged along the alley, accompanied by deeper voices and radio static.

'No, they're gone,' one of the voices said.

A burst of static replied as the footsteps drew closer.

'Christ knows,' the voice said. 'Balfour Avenue, probably.'

Wood rattled as the cops tried the gates. The Traveller leaned against the flaked paint, braced himself.

'No chance,' the voice said. 'I'm not doing any more running tonight. I'm too old for this shit.'

The gate pushed against the Traveller's back. Static crackled.

'Up your arse,' the voice on the other side of the wall said. 'I'm going back to the car.'

The footsteps receded towards the Ormeau

Road. The Traveller stooped down and checked if the boys were breathing. They both were, but the first one he'd hit was slick with blood. The other would wake before too long with a crushing headache. The Traveller had to get this done. He went to the back door and peered through the glass into the kitchen. An old woman in a dressing gown stood gazing at a biscuit tin, her lips moving as if she were trying to remember the words of a song.

He tried the handle, but the door was locked. The old woman looked up at the sound. She approached the door and turned the key. She opened it and stared at the Traveller for a moment. 'Bobby, love, where've you been?' she asked.

'Away,' the Traveller said.

'Away where?'

'Just away,' the Traveller said. 'Can I come in?'

The old woman stepped back to let him enter. She stroked his arm as he passed. 'You missed your tea, love.'

'I had something when I was out,' the Traveller said.

'What did you have, love?'

'Fish and chips,' the Traveller said. He heard a television in the next room.

She slapped his arm. 'You could've brought some back with you,' she scolded.

'They'd be cold,' the Traveller said. 'Where's Declan?'

'He's watching the telly,' the old woman said.

'Ma?' a slurred voiced called from the next room. 'Ma! Who're you talking to?'

'It's Bobby,' the old woman said. 'He's home. He got fish and chips, but he never brought us any back.'

The Traveller went to the door and stepped through. Declan Quigley froze half out of the armchair facing the television.

'How're ya, Declan,' the Traveller said. 'Better sit down, there's a good fella.'

The old woman followed behind. He turned to her and asked, 'Any danger of a cup of tea?'

'Surely, Bobby, love.'

'Ta very much,' the Traveller said. He watched her shuffle to the kitchen before he turned back to Quigley. 'Who's Bobby?'

Quigley sagged back into the chair. 'My brother,' he said, his voice shaking. A half-empty bottle of vodka and a glass sat on a side table next to him. 'The Brits shot him twenty years ago. She thinks every man she meets is Bobby. Except me. Who are you?'

'Doesn't matter,' the Traveller said, taking a step towards him.

'Jesus, I knew it wasn't over,' Quigley said. 'When them three blew themselves up, then Kevin Malloy the other night. The news said it was a robbery, but I knew it was lies.'

The Traveller reached into his pocket.

'Wait!' Quigley held his hands up. 'Wait a minute. I haven't said a word to anyone. I know what happened, I saw the whole thing, I know all that stuff about a feud was bullshit. I could've gone to the papers and told them the truth. I could've made a fortune. I could've made enough to look after my mother. But I didn't. I kept my mouth shut. There's no call for this.'

The Traveller thought about arguing, explaining the nature of things to this man, but what was the point? He sighed and took the knife from his pocket. The blade opened with barely a sound. Best to do it quiet.

Quigley took a swig of neat vodka from the bottle and coughed. 'There's no call for it,' he said, putting the bottle back on the table. 'It's not fair.'

The old woman's voice shrilled from the kitchen. 'Do you want a biscuit, Bobby, love?'

'You have any Jaffa Cakes?' the Traveller called back.

'No, love. But I've got Penguins.'

'Aye, that'll do.'

Quigley seemed to shrink in the chair. 'Christ, I'm tired,' he said. 'So tired. Maybe I should've run, but who'd look after my mother? So I've been sitting here waiting. I haven't slept in months. I can't eat. I've lost a stone and a half. I should've killed Gerry Fegan, you know. Or tried, anyway.'

The Traveller stopped. 'Why didn't you?'

'I couldn't,' Quigley said. He started to cry. 'I was too scared. He was too . . . big.'

'Big?'

Quigley looked down at his shaking hands. 'Like nothing could hurt him. Like nothing could stop him. Like if he set his mind to killing someone, then they were already dead. I'd never seen anything like it in my life.' He looked up at the Traveller. 'Until now. Promise me you won't touch her.'

'I won't,' the Traveller said.

Quigley stared hard at him. 'Promise me.'

'I won't touch her,' the Traveller said. 'I swear to God.'

Quigley unbuttoned his shirt collar, pulled the fabric away from his throat, and laid his head back. 'Make it quick,' he said.

'No, not the throat,' the Traveller said. 'You'll piss blood everywhere. All over your ma's carpet, up the walls, fucking everywhere. Just close your eyes. I'll make it easy.'

Quigley's head dropped, and he wept. Tears blotched his shirt. 'What a fucking waste,' he said.

'Quiet, now,' the Traveller said. 'It'll be quick, I promise. Close your eyes.'

Quigley squeezed the armrests and closed his eyes. His breath quickened. He whined. The Traveller switched his grip on the knife to underhand and leaned on the chair. Quigley inhaled, held his breath. The Traveller made one, two, three thrusts, burying the blade to the hilt each time before drawing it out again.

Quigley breathed out, his exhalation bubbling as it thinned. He coughed. A small red bloom, about the size of a rose, spread on his chest.

The old woman screamed 'Bobby!' and drove a knitting needle into the Traveller's upper arm.

18

Lennon showered, the water hot as he could stand. He scrubbed himself pink and buried that hard little ball of filth so deep down inside himself he could barely feel it. It was always the same. He'd do it knowing he'd hate himself for it, and afterwards swear he'd never do it again. The burning guilt would last a day or so before he could wash it away and forgive himself.

He turned his mind from the Scottish law student, her sighs and moans and affection as transparent as her underwear. Instead, he thought about Roscoe Patterson's words. Lennon knew Patsy Toner all too well. He'd interviewed many a thug with Patsy Toner in attendance. The slimy little shit called himself a human rights lawyer. The only human right Patsy Toner cared about was the right to get paid.

Lennon hadn't seen Toner around the interview rooms and court hearings for quite some time. Logically, he could put it down to the killing of Brian Anderson. When the bent cop was found dead in Toner's borrowed car, followed by the bloodbath near Middletown, the party moved swiftly to distance itself from the lawyer and the rest of Paul McGinty's lackeys. Toner's human rights work would naturally have dried up, but there were still plenty of petty hoods and lowlifes who needed representation. Party backing or not, Patsy Toner was a seasoned defence solicitor, well used to dealing with the PPS and the courts.

But no, Lennon couldn't remember the last time he'd seen the little lawyer and that stupid moustache of his. He'd make a point of looking him up.

Lennon shut the shower off and stepped out into the steamy bathroom. He towelled himself down and wrapped himself in a dressing gown. The en suite bathroom was small but beautifully appointed. It was one of the main features that sold him on the flat. That and the river view. He stepped into the bedroom, his head shrouded in the towel. The memory came to him as it always did: crying as a child when his mother dried his hair too roughly after bath time.

His mother.

It had been almost a month since he'd last gone to see her in the nursing home. Not that it made much difference to her. Maybe he'd go down to Newry tomorrow evening. Short notice, but the routine would work regardless. He would send a text message to his younger sister Bronagh stating the time he meant to call with their mother. He would receive no reply. If his time clashed with any other family member, they would quietly reschedule. It suited everybody to do it that way.

When Lennon's mother had first heard a whisper that his brother Liam had joined the local boys, had volunteered for the cause, she had begged him to reconsider. She told him he'd wind up in prison, or worse, shot dead by the cops or the Brits.

Liam had smiled as she ranted, then he wrapped his arms around her, told her not to listen to rumours. He had no interest in fighting anyone. Sure, he had a job with a local mechanic, fixing farm machinery. He had a future. Why would he piss it away on such nonsense?

Lennon remembered Liam making eye contact with him over their mother's quivering shoulder, and Lennon knew he was lying.

He also knew Liam was lying when he turned up with that black eye.

Lennon had been home from university a month, earning pennies in a local petrol station. The diesel the station sold was hooky stuff, stripped agricultural fuel from one of the plants that were hidden all over the countryside. Everyone knew Bull O'Kane ran them, but everyone knew to keep their mouths shut, even if their cars wound up with ruined fuel pumps from the bootleg diesel. It might cost a grand or more to fix a knackered engine, but opening your mouth to complain would cost you a lot more. It would signal you as a tout, and touts never came out of it well, if at all.

Liam had been breathless and cheery, but unscathed, when Lennon met him for a pint after the hurling match. But he didn't argue when Liam arrived home in the early hours of the following morning with blood seeping from the welt under his eye and told their mother he'd caught a swipe from a hurling stick at the game.

Later, as birdsong began to drift into the bedroom the two brothers shared, Liam lay

116

staring at the ceiling, his muscled forearms behind his head, his big chest rising and falling. Lennon watched him in the half-light, fear and love and resentment fighting for dominance of his heart. He jerked, startled, when Liam spoke.

'I'm not a tout.'

'What?' Lennon sat up in his bed.

Liam's voice quivered in his throat. 'Whatever happens, whatever you hear, I'm no tout.'

'What the fuck are you talking about?'

Liam paused, then said, 'Someone else is covering their tracks, laying it on me. If anything happens to me, you remember that. Tell Ma and the girls. Don't say nothing to anyone else, though, or you'll wind up in the shite yourself.'

'I won't,' Lennon said. 'But what's going to happen?'

'I don't know,' Liam said. 'Maybe nothing. *Probably* nothing.' He rolled over onto his side, his eyes glinting in the early light as they met Lennon's. 'Look, forget I said anything. I'm just blowing, all right?'

'All right,' Lennon said.

'Listen, we're all proud of you getting your degree. You stick at it, right? Get the master thing, whatever you call it, and the doctorate. You get out of this shit-hole and make something decent for yourself. You hear me?'

'Yeah,' Lennon said, the word drying to a whisper in his throat.

'Right,' Liam said, burrowing down into the bedclothes. 'Get some sleep.'

Lennon lay back on the bed, but sleep did not come. Looking back across those sixteen years, he sometimes imagined he knew at the time it would be his last real conversation with his brother.

Sixteen years since Liam died. The anniversary had been just two months ago. Sixteen years since Lennon had applied to join the then Royal Ulster Constabulary, making an enemy of almost everyone he'd ever known. Sometimes, when the dawn crept across his ceiling like that time back in Middletown, he cursed the choices he'd made.

Some said that when you're on your deathbed, it'd be the things you didn't do that you'd regret. Lennon knew that was a lie.

He rubbed the towel back and forth across his scalp and walked to the open-plan living area.

A stack of letters lay open on the coffee table. On top was a mortgage reminder. He'd pay that tomorrow, phone up and swear it was the bank's mistake to decline the payment. Two or three credit card statements lay beneath that. They could wait another week or two. So long as he kept the mortgage and the car payments on track, he could survive. Particularly if he didn't think about it too much.

Lennon took a beer from the fridge and went back to the sofa. The leather cooled his skin where the shower had scalded it. He prised the cap off and took a swallow. He made calculations in his head: how much he needed for bills, how much for food, how much for diesel for the car. When he couldn't make the figures come out right, he stopped counting.

The phone rang. He answered it.

'Your first day back on MIT starts early,' DCI Gordon said. 'Two dead on the Lower Ormeau. A mess, apparently. I'll be there in twenty minutes. You'd better be waiting for me.'

★　★　★

'You're late,' Gordon barked as Lennon entered the hall. The DCI waited in the doorway to the living room.

'I came as quick as I could,' Lennon said, squeezing past a photographer.

'Not quick enough,' Gordon said. 'You only live along the river a bit. You been drinking?'

'Just the one,' Lennon said. He peered past Gordon's shoulder.

'He's confirmed dead,' Gordon said. 'At least one stab wound to the chest, probably more. We'll let the photographer get some snaps before we go in.'

'You said two. Where's the other one?'

'Out the back,' Gordon said. 'Only a young fella, too. Looks like he busted his head on the wall. It's dark as a coal miner's armpit out there, and the rain's coming on. We'll get a tarpaulin over the yard and get a proper look in the morning. The forensics team will come down from Carrickfergus first thing. I want you here to oversee it.'

Lennon leaned over the threshold and scanned the room. The victim, a man with curly dark hair, sat with his back to the door, his arms hanging limp over the sides of the chair. A side table had been tipped over. A vodka bottle and a

119

glass lay on the floor. It didn't look like the victim's place, though. Old woman's furniture, fussy wallpaper, frilly things and tacky ornaments. 'Anyone else here?' Lennon asked.

'The victim's mother's just gone.' Gordon stepped back to let the photographer through. 'She's on her way to the City Hospital. Looked like she got a belt in the mouth. They had to sedate her, kept screaming 'Bobby did it.' A neighbour says Bobby was her son. A soldier shot him when he drove through a checkpoint twenty years ago.'

'We can cross him off the list, then,' Lennon said. He pointed at the body. 'So who's our friend?'

'Well, that's interesting, as it happens. The deceased is known to us. In fact, he's been a guest of ours on more than one occasion.' Gordon smiled. 'This is — was — Mr Declan Quigley, former driver for the late Paul McGinty.' Gordon looked at Lennon. 'What?'

'Declan Quigley,' Lennon said.

'Yes.'

'Paul McGinty's driver.'

'That's right.'

'It can't be a coincidence,' Lennon said.

'What?'

'Kevin Malloy the other night. He was wrapped up in that feud too.'

Gordon put his hand on Lennon's shoulder. 'Look, that feud business is long over with. Don't go jumping to conclusions or you'll miss something. Declan Quigley was a scumbag. Scumbags know other scumbags, and there's no

120

shortage of them in Belfast. You're no good to me if you're not looking at all the possibilities. Understand?'

'I understand, it's just that — ' Lennon trapped that thought behind his teeth.

'Just what?'

'Nothing,' Lennon said. He would make a point of calling on Marie's landlord tomorrow. The last time Lennon questioned him it turned up nothing, but he'd been subtle, edging around the real questions. This time he'd be a little firmer.

The photographer squeezed past them.

'On my desk in the morning,' Gordon called after him. He nudged Lennon. 'Come on. Take notes. And watch where you put your feet.'

Lennon took a pad and pen from his pocket as he followed Gordon to the centre of the room. They both faced Quigley's body.

'Hmm,' Gordon said. 'Does anything about Mr Quigley look odd to you, Detective Inspector Lennon?'

'Yes it does,' Lennon said.

'Why?'

Lennon hunkered down by the side of the chair. He pointed with his pen. 'No defensive wounds to the hands or the forearms. A stab victim will usually try to shield themselves, even try to grab the blade.'

'So?'

'So either the attacker moved so fast Quigley didn't see it coming, or he just let it happen.'

'And the wound, or indeed wounds?'

Lennon stood up and leaned over the body. A

121

fist-sized red stain sat at the centre of Quigley's chest. 'Very clean. Most fatal stabbings are done in a frenzy, lots of punctures scattered around the torso, the arms, the shoulders, the neck, even the head.'

'Like your friend Mr Rankin did to Mr Crozier,' Gordon said.

'That's right. But this is one, two, maybe three stabs, grouped tight together, directly through the breastbone and into the heart. He probably drowned from the blood filling his chest cavity. Not much mess. The attacker knew what he was doing.'

Something by the upended table caught Lennon's eye. 'Look,' he said, pointing.

Gordon crouched beside him. 'A knitting needle. I do believe that's blood on the tip.'

'Couldn't be the weapon,' Lennon said. 'Knitting needle wounds are tiny. It was definitely a blade that did for our Declan.'

'I'm inclined to agree,' Gordon said. 'Make sure forensics get a sample of that blood off to Birmingham first thing. If we're lucky, it's the murderer's. And if we're double lucky, we'll have him on file.'

19

'Se easy,' Pyè said. 'You just hold him for mwen, yes?'

'Hold him for you?' Fegan asked.

'Wi, yes, what I say?'

'All right,' Fegan said.

Pyè got out of the car. Fegan followed, closing the passenger door behind him. Its alarm system blipped and blinked as Pyè thumbed the key fob. The pawnshop stood in darkness. The Doyles said Murphy lived above it. They said Murphy shafted them on some jewellery deal, that he'd put money in his pocket that should have gone in theirs. Now they wanted that money back. They said Pyè would do the work. Fegan was just for show.

Pyè hammered the shutters. 'Hey, Murphy! You home?'

Fegan watched the windows above for lights. Nothing stirred.

Pyè kicked the shutters. 'Murphy! Mwen know you home!' He kicked three more times, and the shutters rippled with the force of it.

A window across the street opened. 'Shut the fuck up! You know what time it is?'

Fegan and Pyè turned to it. A bald-headed man leaned out of a third-storey window.

'Fuck you!' Pyè shouted. 'Mwen fuck you up, motherfucker.'

'What?' the bald man asked.

'Mwen say fuck you,' Pyè said. 'Mwen show you mwen knife.'

'The fuck you talking about?' the bald man said. 'You going to talk tough, do it in fucking English, you fucking French-talking son of a bitch!'

'French?' Pyè turned to Fegan, waved a hand at the angry man across the street. 'Li say French?'

'What?' Fegan said.

'Li say French,' Pyè said. 'Motherfucker.' He kicked the shutters again. And again.

A light appeared above the shop. Fegan stepped back onto the road and peered up at it. The window opened, and a red-headed man appeared. 'Whoever the fuck's kicking my shutter better have a fucking good reason, I swear to God.'

'Hey, Murphy!' the bald man across the street called. 'You tell your friends not to come round waking people up, you hear me?'

'Aw, fuck off, Cabel!' Murphy shouted. 'Mind your business and go back to bed.'

'When people be kicking the shit out of your shop and waking me up, it *is* my business, you Mick bastard.'

'Fuck you, Cabel,' Murphy said. 'Go back to bed or I'll come over and *put* you to bed, you hear me?'

'Fuck you, Murphy!' The bald man slammed his window closed.

'Asshole,' Murphy said. He looked down. 'Now who the fuck is kicking my shutters?'

'Open, Murphy,' Pyè said. 'Mwen want talk with you.'

'Who's that?'

'Pyè Préval. Come down.'

'Pyè?' Murphy leaned out to see better. 'Why the fuck didn't you call me? Jesus Christ, you scared the shit out of me. Who's that with you?'

'This friend mwen, Gerry,' Pyè said. 'Li cool. Come down. Open the fucking door.'

'Don't tell him my name,' Fegan said.

'What?' Pyè said.

'Don't tell him my name.'

Pyè shrugged. 'Wi, sure, no name.'

They waited until they saw a light through the shutter. It rose with a mechanical groan to stop at eye level. The door beyond opened, and Pyè ducked under the metal. Fegan followed.

'Close it,' Pyè said.

Murphy obliged. He held the button until the shutter sealed them in.

Guitars lined the pawnshop's walls. Fegan walked in a slow circle, remembering the Martin he'd had back in Belfast, the one Ronnie Lennox left to him. He'd meant to learn to play it, but that hadn't worked out.

'So what do you want at this time of night?' Murphy asked. He wore an open dressing gown, revealing a stained undershirt and pyjama bottoms. His slippers didn't match.

'Upstairs,' Pyè said.

'What for?' Murphy asked.

'Parle,' Pyè said. 'Talk.'

'We can talk down here.'

'Non,' Pyè said. 'Upstairs.'

There on the wall, Fegan saw it. The headstock said C.F. Martin. It looked like the guitar Ronnie had given him, the same shape, the same size. The lacquer hadn't taken on the same deep gold of age, but it was still pretty. Fegan reached up and brushed the strings with his fingertips. He'd never got to hear what Ronnie's guitar sounded like. It still sat propped in the corner of his old house on Calcutta Street for all he knew.

'Hey, don't touch that,' Murphy said. 'It's expensive.'

'Non, non, non,' Pyè said. 'You don't say shit to friend mwen Gerry, hear?'

Murphy held his hands up. 'I'm sorry, Pyè,' he said. 'I didn't mean nothing. It's expensive, is all.'

'Don't tell him my name,' Fegan said.

'Wi, sorry,' Pyè said.

'I didn't hear your name,' Murphy said. 'Touch the guitar if you want. Knock yourself out.'

'Upstairs,' Pyè said.

'All right,' Murphy said. 'Come on.'

He led them through a back room to a narrow staircase. 'I wasn't expecting visitors,' he said as he climbed ahead of them. 'I would've cleaned the place up otherwise.'

The door at the top of the stairs opened onto a small apartment and a ripe odour. Old newspapers gathered in piles around the living room. Murphy toured the place, picking up pornographic magazines and empty beer cans. He ducked into the kitchenette and dumped an armful of detritus under the sink.

Fegan and Pyè exchanged a glance and a grimace.

Murphy came back out. 'So what's this about?' he asked.

'Sit,' Pyè said.

'Jesus, Pyè, you're making me nervous. Come on, tell me what this is about.'

Pyè pointed at the one chair clear of litter. 'Sit,' he said.

Murphy did as he was told.

Pyè looked at Fegan and nodded at the space behind the chair. Fegan moved to it. Murphy twisted to follow Fegan with his eyes.

'You're scaring me, boys,' Murphy said. He kept his head turned to Fegan. 'You don't say much, do you? What does he want? Can you talk, Mr No Name? Or are you here just to look mean?'

'Friend mwen Gerry Fegan,' Pyè said. 'Li the meanest motherfucker you ever met. Li a lougawou. Li a bòkò, a bad witch. Li fuck you up big time.'

'Don't tell him my name,' Fegan said.

'Sure,' Pyè said. 'Non worry, Gerry.'

'Pyè, I don't know what you're saying to me.' Murphy turned first to Fegan, then the Haitian. 'And I don't know who the fuck this guy is. Tell me what you want, and I'll give it to you if I can, all right? Just speak English, okay?'

Pyè stepped carefully over his words. 'You bought jewels from Doyles. You say jewels worth sa much. You sell jewels, you say jewels worth sa much.' Pyè held his palms up and open as he stepped closer to Murphy, raising and lowering his hands like scales. 'Sa much, sa much. Big different lajan. You put lajan in pocket, wi?'

'I don't know what the fuck you're talking

127

about,' Murphy said. He turned in the seat. 'Gerry. Gerry, right?'

'No,' Fegan said. 'That's not my name.'

'Gerry, what's he talking about?'

'I'm not Gerry,' Fegan said. 'I'm Paddy. Paddy Feeney.'

'Wi, li Paddy Feeney,' Pyè said. He pointed at Fegan. 'Paddy Feeney, li fuck you up.'

Murphy wrung his hands. 'Gerry, Paddy, whatever the fuck your name is, I don't give a shit, just please tell me what the fuck he's saying to me. What does he want?'

'I'm not sure,' Fegan said. 'Pyè, what are you saying to him?'

'Lajan!' Pyè shouted. 'Doyles want they lajan.'

'What's 'lajan'?' Fegan asked.

'Lajan!' Pyè opened his arms wide. 'Dollar, motherfucker. Dime, quarter, buy stuff, you understand?'

'Money?' Fegan asked.

'Wi, money!' Pyè grabbed his own hair in exasperation. 'Lajan, money. What the fuck I say?'

'Money?' Murphy asked. 'What money?'

'I don't know,' Fegan said. 'What money, Pyè?'

'Doyles' money,' Pyè said. He started to pace. 'You say jewels worth sa much. You buy jewels off Doyles, wi? But you know jewels worth sa much, and you sell them, put lajan in you pocket. Wi?'

'What?' Murphy said.

Fegan leaned down to Murphy. 'I think I know what he's getting at. Did you buy some jewellery off the Doyles?'

'Yeah,' Murphy said. 'They had some stuff to move. They always have stuff to move. I don't ask where it comes from, I just find a buyer for it. So what?'

'I think Pyè reckons you told the Doyles it was worth less than it was,' Fegan said. 'And then you sold it to someone else for what it was really worth, and you kept the difference. Does that sound right?'

Murphy nodded first, then shook his head. 'Yeah, no, that wasn't it. That wasn't it at all. The market, you know, what you call it . . . fluctuates.' He turned back to Pyè. 'The market fluctuates. I paid the Doyles market price, right? When I sold the stuff on, the market was in my favour, that's all.'

'Doyles want they lajan, they money,' Pyè said. He took a knife from his pocket, a big hunter's piece with a serrated blade. 'This knife mwen. Money. Now, motherfucker.'

Murphy turned back to Fegan. 'Gerry, tell him — '

'I'm not Gerry,' Fegan said.

'Whatever the fuck your name is, tell him I paid the Doyles a fair price, and I made a fair profit.'

'I don't think he'll listen to me,' Fegan said.

'I haven't got the money,' Murphy said. He lowered his voice and stretched up to Fegan. 'You know how much the rent is on this place? It's only Jersey, I know, but Christ they charge for it, Gerry. I'm one week away from being put out on the street.'

'That's not my name,' Fegan said. He looked

up at Pyè. 'He says he doesn't have it.'

Pyè raised his eyebrows. 'Non? Okay.'

'Okay?' Fegan asked.

'Okay?' Murphy asked.

'Wi, okay,' Pyè said. He took two steps forward and stuck the blade in Murphy's upper arm.

Murphy screamed.

Fegan stepped back.

'Lajan, blood, no different,' Pyè said. He pulled the blade from Murphy's arm and stabbed him in the thigh.

Murphy screamed.

Fegan said, 'Jesus, Pyè.'

Pyè stood back and said, 'What? Li no got money, li get knife. No different. Doyles happy.'

Murphy wept. 'Listen to me, Pyè, I got no money. Fuck, I'm bleeding. It hurts. Jesus, I need a doctor.'

'Get lajan, mwen get doctor, wi?'

'I got no money,' Murphy said. He pressed one hand against his thigh and the other on his upper arm. 'Jesus, look at the blood.'

Pyè stabbed Murphy's other thigh. 'No lajan, no doctor.'

Murphy screamed again. 'Pyè, you bastard! Fuck!'

Pyè leaned close, his hands on his knees. 'Mwen say last time. No money, no doctor. Konprann? Understand, motherfucker?'

'Oh God,' Murphy said. Sweat mixed with tears on his cheek. 'I got a couple hundred downstairs in the safe. Take any stock you want. Whatever you can carry, all right? Take it all. Just don't cut me no more. Please.'

'That not enough, Murphy.'

'Please, Pyè, I don't got it. Please, no more.'

'Fuck,' Pyè said. He grabbed Murphy's hair, forced his head back to expose the throat. He drew back the knife, ready to open Murphy's jugular.

Murphy said, 'Please don't.'

Pyè put his shoulder behind the blade.

Fegan leaned across the back of the chair and grabbed Pyè's wrist. 'Don't,' he said.

Pyè stared at Fegan. 'What you do, Gerry?'

'Don't,' Fegan said.

Pyè tried to pull his wrist free, but Fegan held firm. Murphy shrunk away from the blade. Pyè tried to prise Fegan's fingers from his wrist. 'Let go,' he said.

'No,' Fegan said. He pushed down and to the side, taking Pyè's balance.

Murphy slid to the floor and crawled away, blood trailing behind him. He craned his neck to watch Pyè and Fegan struggle.

Pyè grabbed Fegan's throat with his free hand, the chair still between them. Fegan kneed the back of it, taking Pyè's feet from under him. The Haitian fell forward and lost his grip on Fegan's throat. Fegan smashed his forearm across Pyè's jaw. Pyè's head rocked to the side, and he blinked. Fegan shifted his weight, taking Pyè's body with him, and the Haitian slumped to the floor, his eyes blank. Fegan took the knife from his fingers.

'Stick him, Gerry,' Murphy hissed. 'Fucking stick him.'

Fegan looked up from the blade.

Murphy lay in his own blood, hate and fear on his face as it dripped out of him. 'Go on, stick that motherfucker.'

'No,' Fegan said.

Pyè moaned and blinked. His eyes focused on Fegan and the knife. He gasped and scrambled backwards.

'Get out of here,' Fegan said. 'Tell the Doyles I won't do their dirty work.'

'They kill you, Gerry.' Pyè wiped blood from his lip.

'Maybe,' Fegan said. 'Go on, get out.'

Pyè got to his feet. He opened and closed his mouth, worked his jaw from side to side. 'For him?' he asked, looking at Murphy. He shook his head. 'Doyles right. You a crazy motherfucker.'

'Go,' Fegan said.

Pyè walked towards the door. He paused at Murphy's side. 'Soon,' he said.

Murphy crawled away from him.

Pyè turned in the doorway. 'See you round, Gerry.'

Fegan stayed silent and watched him leave. In the quiet, he became aware of Murphy's ragged breathing.

'Thank you, Gerry,' Murphy said as he struggled towards the telephone.

'That's not my name,' Fegan said. He crossed to the telephone, lifted it, and placed it on the floor by Murphy's bloodstained hand. 'Call an ambulance,' he said.

He left Murphy alone and bleeding.

20

Lennon stood waiting in the hallway of the terraced house when the forensics team arrived from Carrickfergus at first light. They picked over Quigley's corpse first while the photographer took daylight shots of the boy in the yard. Lennon's eyes were dry and hot as he watched from the kitchen window. He'd gone home for a couple of hours, but sleep had eluded him.

He looked at the boy's body, his face turned up to the sky, the tarpaulin that covered the yard overnight pulled back to let the light in. The acute angle of his neck suggested the blow to his head hadn't killed him. Seventeen or eighteen, nineteen at most. He wore a tracksuit and Nike trainers, most likely fakes bought at a market stall somewhere. Chances were he was from the neighbourhood. He probably made a point of carrying no identification, but they'd know who he was before long. Some mother would find her son's bed had not been slept in, and when the talk of a youth's dead body lying in a yard nearby reached her, she would know. When she came running to Quigley's door, he would deal with her.

The photographer came back into the kitchen. He brought the camera to Lennon and showed him the little screen. 'Look,' he said, scrolling through the images. 'Here.'

The image showed a knife in the boy's hand,

tucked beneath him. Lennon looked out the window again. The body obscured the weapon.

'The killer didn't get far,' the photographer said. 'Looks like he slipped and fell bad.'

'Maybe,' Lennon said. 'He's lying on his left side, but his back and his right's dirty too. Look where his head is. He didn't break his neck and roll over.'

'Who's to say where that dirt came from?' the photographer said.

'We'll let forensics have a look before we jump to any conclusions. Have printouts of those on DCI Gordon's desk as soon as you can.'

'Will do,' the photographer said as he headed for the living room.

Lennon went to the back door and scanned the yard, taking in every piece of litter, every puddle. A layer of scummy green algae covered the concrete, a muddle of footprints just visible on the surface. They could be anybody's from the old woman's to her dead son's, from the boy to the doctor who confirmed him dead. The rain that had fallen before the tarpaulin could be raised dulled them all the more. Useless.

'It's too perfect,' Lennon said to himself.

His mobile rang. He answered it.

'Something interesting just turned up,' DCI Gordon said.

'Same here,' Lennon said.

'You go first,' Gordon said.

Lennon told him about the knife the photographer had spotted.

'Well that's that, then,' Gordon said. 'Almost.'

'Almost?'

'The duty officer at North Queen Street logged a report that two officers broke up a fight between rival gangs at the interface between the Lower Ormeau and Donegall Pass. They chased some of the youths along the Lower Ormeau. The kids split up, and the officers followed two of them into the alley behind Quigley's house. That's where they lost them.'

'Did they get descriptions?' Lennon asked, stepping aside to let one of the forensics team past.

'Vague, but probably enough. Both males, mid-to-late teens, short dark hair, both slender, both wearing tracksuits and trainers. One of them, the taller of the two, wore an Adidas tracksuit and Nike trainers. Sound familiar?'

Lennon looked at the boy's body. 'Yes,' he said.

'Mind you,' Gordon said, 'there are plenty of Adidas and Nike fans in this part of the world. It'd be quite a coincidence, though.'

'A fucking huge one,' Lennon said.

'Language,' Gordon scolded. 'But of course that means — '

Lennon finished the thought. 'There was another kid here.'

'As soon as the body's identified, I want every single person that lad ever knew interviewed. Clear?'

'Clear,' Lennon said.

'Good,' Gordon said. He hung up.

'Inspector?' a voice called from behind.

Lennon turned.

A constable leaned in from the living room.

135

'You'd better come out front.'

Lennon followed him through the living room where most of the forensics team still examined Quigley's body, and out to the hall. It was early yet, and the air outside had an autumn chill. A thin crowd gathered on the street, children and women hoping for a glance at a body.

One woman stood apart, her path blocked by a policeman. She was barefoot with a dressing gown held loose around her. Her hands shook as she stared at Lennon, her mouth open, her eyes full of dread and hope.

Lennon went to her.

'I'm sorry,' he said as she collapsed in his arms.

21

The Traveller lay on his stomach, the sheets bunched at his feet. He couldn't get comfortable. His left hand tingled; his fingers felt distant, like they were attached to someone else's hand. The old bitch had missed any big veins, but the Traveller feared she'd done something to his nerves. He'd heard about that sort of thing, how all the nerves were joined together, and injury to one part of the body could have repercussions for another.

Same thing with that lump of Kevlar they'd taken out of his brain. The Traveller remembered little of the moments leading up to the explosion, only fragments of images, the wires coming into view as he'd pulled the sheets of rusted corrugated iron aside, the idea that he might die. After that, waking up in some dirty foreign hospital, unable to remember his name, unable to speak. He'd spent months there being poked and prodded. They showed him the piece of his helmet that had wound up inside his head. Who would think a little piece of plastic could take so many things away from him? Everything was connected. So, the tingling in his fingers bothered him.

If he'd been able to read, he'd have looked it up on the hotel room's Internet connection. The foreign girl at reception told him he could get the Internet through the telly when he checked in yesterday. That had been before he headed out to see Quigley. She'd watched him when he came back in, doing his best to hide the stiffness in his arm. The Traveller smiled at her as he passed. When he got to the lift, he turned and studied the floor in case he'd left any blood in his trail. None, thank Christ.

He stared at the shaft of light at the centre of the drawn curtains. How come hotel room curtains never closed properly? The light hurt his head, so he screwed his eyes shut. He rolled onto his right side, and the movement caused his left upper arm to flare in distress.

'Fucking old bitch cunt bastard fucking shite-licking arse-fucker,' the Traveller said. He'd thought Mrs Quigley was too soft in the head to be a problem. A fucking knitting needle, for Christ's sake.

The wound hadn't bled that much, really, but it hurt like holy fuck. He wondered for a crazy moment if he should go to another hospital, let them look at it, see if she'd done any real damage. He could give another false name. He'd done it before. But those had been emergencies where one risk outweighed the other. This just hurt.

The Traveller threw his legs over the side of the bed and sat up. No use in lying there, wallowing in the pain and tingling and anger. He twisted his arm to see the wad of toilet paper he'd taped to the small pinhole of a wound. A blotch of dark red was all the paper showed for the pain, but a fucker of a bruise had begun to spread out from it. He'd seen it before, just the once. A stupid bastard called Morgan had got stabbed by his wife with a knitting needle. A peculiar thing, it was. The shape of the needle meant the wound sealed shut almost completely, letting little blood seep out. But the damage was done, the bleeding hidden beneath the skin. Morgan had almost died. The Traveller had finished the job with a screwdriver a week later. The wife's father had paid him well for the job.

He turned the bedside clock so he could see it better. Coming seven forty-five. Traffic noise rose up from University Street. He would have preferred a better class of hotel, maybe a nice little boutique place, or that new Hilton over by the Waterfront theatre, but this one offered more privacy. It was a cheap chain hotel, the kind of place sales reps and those too drunk to drive themselves home would stay in. Normally he would have slept deep and well, but the hole in his arm put an end to that. The Traveller wondered for a moment what he'd do with the early morning. It didn't take long to decide, even if he knew it would cause some annoyance. He picked up the mobile, thumbed in the password, and dialled.

'What?' Orla O'Kane answered.

'It's me,' the Traveller said.

'What the fuck do you want this time of the morning?' she asked. 'I'm not even out of bed yet.'

'Were you asleep?'

'No,' she said. 'I don't sleep too well.'

The Traveller twisted his back, trying to find somewhere for his left arm that didn't hurt like a bastard. 'I know the feeling,' he said.

After a short pause, Orla asked, 'So what do you want?'

'Tell me about Gerry Fegan,' the Traveller said.

'My father told you about him already,' she said. 'You'd find out some more if you could read the fucking files he gave you.'

'Tell me about him,' the Traveller repeated.

'Why?'

'Quigley talked about him last night,' the Traveller said. 'He talked about him like he was something . . . '

'Something what?'

'I don't know.' The Traveller thought hard about his words. 'He talked about him the way my ma used to talk about charms, and spirits, and seventh sons of seventh sons. The old stuff, you know? Quigley had this look on his face when he talked about this Fegan fella. Like he was something else. Something . . . other.'

Orla sounded very tired. 'Listen, if you don't think you're up to the job, tell me now. We'll pay you for what you've done so far and call it quits. We need a solid man on this, not someone who gets the fear because he hears some stories.'

'No,' the Traveller said. 'I'm sound. I just want to know who I'm going after. When we draw him out, when I take him on, I want some notion what he's made of.'

'Fair enough,' she said. 'Gerry Fegan is the only man ever struck my father and lived, and he did that when he was a teenager. He's a killer, just like you. I'll tell you the truth, if you can take it.'

The Traveller stopped picking at the wad of tissue over the wound in his arm. 'Yeah, I can take it.'

'If I tell you this, there's no going back. It's final. You either see this job through or there's a price on *your* head. Do you understand me?'

'I understand,' the Traveller said.

Orla O'Kane sighed. 'All right,' she said. 'I don't know if you can kill Gerry Fegan. I don't know if any man can. You're right, from what my father says, he's something *other*. He watched him walk out of a gunfight that left four men dead and my father gut-shot, and Fegan didn't have a scratch on him. He just walked away. I'll tell you something now, and if you repeat it, I'll find out. And if I find out you repeated it, I'll send every man we've got after you. Are you ready for me to tell you?'

The Traveller said, 'Yes.'

'Gerry Fegan is the only man alive my father is afraid of.'

For a moment the Traveller thought of some glib response, that he wasn't afraid of anyone, even if the Bull was. He thought better of it. 'Yeah?' he said.

'That's right,' Orla said. 'My father made a bargain with him that day. He said he'd leave Fegan and Marie McKenna in peace if Fegan let him live. Do you understand what I'm telling you?'

'What?'

'My father is Bull O'Kane, for Christ's sake. The Bull. The cops, the British Army, the SAS, MI5, the fucking UVF, the UDA, every fucker

141

out there that ever stood against him. He never bowed to any of them. But he begged Gerry Fegan for his life. Like a fucking whining dog, he begged Fegan not to kill him.'

The Traveller sat silent, unsure how to respond to Orla's confession.

'Do you hear me?' she asked.

'Yes,' the Traveller said.

'Do you understand what I'm telling you?'

'No,' the Traveller said, honestly.

'I can't allow a man my father is afraid of to live. It's as simple as that. Now listen to me carefully. I've made a confession to you I've never made to another living soul. I've made that confession because I think you're the only man who stands a chance against Fegan. Your life comes down to a couple of choices. You kill Fegan, or Fegan kills you. That's all that's left for you now. There's no walking away. Not any more.'

The Traveller swallowed and said, 'Don't worry, I'll — '

He stopped talking when he realised the phone was dead.

22

Fegan needed the passport. He wasn't going to flee the country yet, but he had to get out of New York. No question, Pyè would have run straight to the Doyles, and they'd have sent their boys to Fegan's building. But would they be here yet? He had to assume as much.

He clung to the steel slats, his shoulder pressed to the closed shop-front, as he peeked around the corner to Ludlow Street where the building's reinforced door waited for his key. Nothing stirred. The Chinese catering supply businesses stood silent beneath their awnings, graffiti-scarred shutters closed tight. Fegan examined the cars parked nose to tail along the street, looking for silhouetted heads and shoulders, a reflection in a wing mirror, anything. The dark hollows of the doorways revealed nothing. But they could be there, waiting, whether he saw them or not.

Wait, there. What looked like an old BMW, its passenger window cracked open. A wisp of cigarette smoke puffed out. Or was it a trick of his fatigued imagination?

There, a movement, and more smoke.

Fegan cursed. The building had a back entrance, but it was heavily fortified and only opened from the inside. If the Doyles' boys were smart, they'd have it guarded. But unless they were very smart, it would be only one or two men. If Fegan could take them, he might be able to use the fire escape to reach his apartment.

He retreated along Hester Street, past the store and the coffee shop, until he found the alley that cut back to the rear of his building. Corrugated iron gates sealed it shut. The super, Mr Lo, kept his decrepit old Ford Taurus parked behind them. Fegan had never seen it move.

The gates were decorated with a crudely painted Stars and Stripes, with NO PARKING sprayed across the white and red. A metal frame surrounded them with a bar running across the top. Fegan jumped, but he couldn't reach the bar.

A garbage bin stood outside the coffee shop. A chain tied the lid to the shop's shutter frame, so he lifted it off and lowered it to the sidewalk as slow and easy as he could. He tipped the bin over, careful of any rubbish that might clatter as he emptied it onto the ground, then carried it back to the gates. Fegan climbed on top and reached up for the bar. He hauled himself up, threw a leg over the top, and let his weight carry him over. The smell of motor oil reached him as he dropped to the ground.

The car's windscreen reflected the dim orange light that crept in from the street. Fegan squeezed past, wondering how Mr Lo ever opened the doors to get inside. He worked his way towards the back corner and rounded it as darkness swallowed him. His feet picked through litter as he skirted the dumpsters. He moved slow, seeking human forms in the black, breathing shallow to stay —

Oh no God the fire she's burning she's crying the child is burning —

Fegan gasped and fell against the damp wall. The pain burst behind his eyes and swept to the back of his skull before streaming down his spine. His legs quivered with the effort of keeping him upright. He sucked air in, forced himself to breathe, let his heart find its rhythm again.

Footsteps from deeper in the alley, slow, careful, afraid. Fegan flattened himself against the wall and stared hard into the darkness. Someone waited for him. Had they seen him? They'd heard him, all right, and now they approached. Somewhere beyond his vision, they drew closer. Fegan squinted, trying to —

No Jesus no don't let her burn it's eating her the fire it's eating her up don't let it get —

Fegan screamed. He crumpled among the drifts of old newspapers and burger wrappers that lay piled against an upended dumpster. Rats scrambled from beneath him. He pressed his palms to his temples, tried to stop the image escaping from his mind into the real world. The fire abated, leaving only the sound of his lungs tearing at the chilled air. He took one last gulp and held it.

Whispers, now. Two voices in a low staccato. Maybe ten feet away. Fegan curled up tight to the side of the dumpster. He could see nothing more than a few inches away. They would be just as blind. If he could —

The fire the fire oh God the fire no no —

'No!' Fegan hissed through gritted teeth. He

pushed the vision away, swallowed bile, breathed deep, listened.

The alley was silent now, but he could sense them just feet away. Fegan shrunk into the corner between the dumpster and the wall. He watched the dark in front of him, waiting for some disruption in the black.

A can rolled in front of him, rattling along the pavement. A hushed voice cursed. Another shushed it. Fegan got his feet under him, crouched against the dumpster. He pushed one foot back against the wall.

Only darkness before his eyes, no matter how hard he stared into the black. He heard the snick-snick of a round being chambered. Stale sweat wove its way through the alley's scents and odours. Fegan held his breath until it burned for release.

A pinpoint of green light blinked at him from the murk.

It took less than a second to understand what it was: a mobile phone on someone's belt. Another second decided Fegan's next action.

He pushed with the foot against the wall, shoulder first, launching himself at the green light. He roared. He slammed into someone's hip, heard them cry out, felt them buckle. His momentum carried him and his target into another body, and another voice echoed in the alley until all three slammed into the far wall.

A gun boomed, and Fegan's ear numbed for a moment before a high whine followed him to the ground. Feet tangled in his arms, and he reached up and grabbed fabric and skin. A man's weight fell on top of him, and Fegan's hands spidered along a soft torso until they found a tender throat. He slammed the edge of his hand into it and the body on top of his writhed.

A muzzle flashed in the alley, its hard report breaking through the whine in Fegan's ears, and something punched the ground by his head. He hauled the body across his own. The muzzle flashed twice more, and the body convulsed. Fegan ran his hand down the arm until he found the gun clasped in its fingers. He raised it towards where the muzzle flash had been and squeezed the trigger three times. In a fiery strobe, he saw a man raise his arms then fall backwards.

Fegan scrambled from beneath the body, crawled to the far wall, turned and stared back. Nothing moved in the black, but he heard a stuttering gurgle. He aimed the pistol at the sound, ready to fire again.

Had the Doyles' men on Hester Street heard the shots? The enclosed alley might have damped the sound, sent it skyward between the rising storeys, but he couldn't risk it. There was no point trying to mount the fire escape now; stealth was no more use to him. He got to his feet and edged along the wall towards the back door.

Fegan felt in the darkness for the metal among the brick. His hand found it, cold and damp. The broken bulb was just visible above it. Noise was the least of his worries, so he hammered the door with his fist. Mr Lo's shitty little room was just on the other side.

147

Fegan listened. Nothing. He hammered the door again.

'Fuck off!' a muffled voice came from the other side. 'I call the cops already.'

'Mr Lo?' Fegan called.

A pause, then, 'Who that?'

'It's Gerry . . . Paddy. Paddy Feeney.'

'Who?'

'Paddy Feeney from the eighth floor,' Fegan said. 'Let me in.'

'What you do out back? Where your key?'

'I'm in trouble,' Fegan said. 'Let me in, give me five minutes to get my stuff, and I'll be gone.'

'Trouble? I hear gun. No way I let you in. I gonna call the cops. They lock you up.'

'You said you called them already.'

'I lie,' Mr Lo said. 'Now go 'way.'

'Please.' Fegan pressed his ear against the metal door. 'I'm in trouble. I need your help. I gave you six months' rent in advance, didn't I?'

'Yeah,' Mr Lo said. 'So?'

'I'll go tonight,' Fegan said. 'You can keep the rent.'

'Yeah, I keep it,' Mr Lo shouted. 'Lease say you give three month notice.'

'Jesus,' Fegan whispered. Men were coming to kill him, and he was standing in an alley, quibbling over the terms of his lease. 'Fuck the lease,' he said. 'Keep the rest and I'll give you two hundred in your hand.'

'Fuck you,' Mr Lo said. 'I no get shot for two hundred.'

'What, then?'

'Five hundred,' Mr Lo said, his voice like a petulant child's.

Fegan thought about the bundle of notes in a plastic bag, taped beneath the dressing table in his room. Mr Lo was gouging him, but he had no choice. 'All right, five hundred,' Fegan said. 'But you open this fucking door right now.'

Locks snapped, bars rolled back. Mr Lo's eye appeared in the crack of the door.

'Come in,' he said.

23

Lennon sat with his head in his hands, afraid to look at Gordon or Uprichard when he spoke. They thought they had the case wrapped up. Lennon doubted they'd take it well to hear he thought different. He told them anyway.

'I don't think it was the kid.'

'It's too early to think anything,' Gordon said. He'd had an Ulster fry sent up to his office from the canteen. He swished a piece of sausage around in a pool of yellow egg yolk.

From his spot against the radiator, CI Uprichard watched Gordon eat. He'd had a minor heart attack last year, and talk was his wife made him eat muesli for breakfast. 'Wait for the post-mortem,' he said, 'even if you can't wait for forensics to come up with something.'

'We know he wasn't there alone,' Lennon said.

'So there was another kid,' Gordon said through a mouthful of egged sausage. 'Doesn't mean the one we found didn't do it. Doesn't mean he did, either. You jump to conclusions far too quickly, DI Lennon. You should learn to stand back and take in the facts as a whole. Thirty years I've been at this, and one thing I can tell you for certain.' He jabbed his fork in Lennon's direction for emphasis. 'Investigating with an agenda will lead you in circles.'

'Agenda?' Lennon asked.

'That's right,' Gordon said. 'First thing you

said to me when you found out it was Quigley: 'Couldn't be coincidence,' you said. That'll taint everything you do from here on if you're not careful.'

Lennon had to concede the point. 'Fair enough,' he said. 'What now?'

'I suggest you go home and get some rest,' CI Uprichard said. 'You look exhausted. We can't do much until the post-mortem and forensic reports come back.'

Gordon chewed toast, spitting crumbs as he spoke. 'We've got three teams doorstepping the area to see who the kid was friends with. If anything comes up, we'll call you back in.'

'All right,' Lennon said. He got up and headed for the door.

'Don't go chasing things that aren't there,' Gordon called after him. 'You'll end up missing the truth for want of a lie, young Lennon.'

⋆   ⋆   ⋆

Lennon lay on his back for an hour, wishing for sleep. A dull hint of a headache loomed behind his eyes. Making up for the lost hours of the night before would ease it, but he knew the more he wished for the warm darkness the less likely it would come.

The quiet again. Too much silence, and too many thoughts to break it. Most were of Marie and Ellen. He had found out everything he could when they first disappeared, begged favours, pressed anyone he knew for more information. The same story everywhere he turned: Marie felt unsafe after her uncle got his brains blown out, so she made herself scarce. After a while, Lennon eased up. He told himself to let it go. His daughter was lost to him. It didn't matter if she lived in Belfast or somewhere across the sea; he'd never know her anyway.

But then Dandy Andy Rankin talked, and once more every thought formed around Marie and Ellen. Lennon couldn't force his mind to look away. There was only one thing to do. The landlord lived on Wellesley Avenue, two streets north of Eglantine Avenue. He could be there in ten minutes.

★   ★   ★

Jonathan Nesbitt, sixty-seven and retired, blinked at Lennon's ID. 'What can I do for you?' he asked.

'Can I come in?' Lennon asked, putting one foot inside the door.

'I suppose, if you — '

Lennon stepped past him and said, 'Thanks.'

Nesbitt's hall was a little dowdy, but well kept. He had two properties he rented out, houses his wife had inherited from her father before her own death a few years ago. The hall led to a high-ceilinged living room. Cheap prints hung on the walls, cherubic children, dogs playing cards. An old television sat in the corner, Philip Schofield and Fern Britton exchanging banalities in oversaturated colour.

'What's this about?' Nesbitt asked as he followed Lennon in.

152

'Sit down,' Lennon said.

'Oh, thank you,' Nesbitt said with no attempt to veil his sarcasm. He lowered himself into the armchair facing the television.

Lennon sat across from him. 'It's about the house you own on Eglantine Avenue. The ground floor flat, in particular.'

Nesbitt's eyes rolled. 'Miss McKenna,' he said.

'That's right,' Lennon said.

'For the last time, Miss McKenna moved out in a hurry, I was given a year's rent in advance, my son boarded it up for me, and that's that.' Nesbitt tilted his head and narrowed his eyes. 'Hang on, you were here asking about it before. Two or three months ago, wasn't it?'

Lennon nodded. 'Yes,' he said.

'What do you think I'm going to tell you now that I didn't tell you before? Look, I was asked to hold the flat for Miss McKenna, I was given the rent in advance, she moved out, and that's all there is to it.'

'Who asked you to keep the flat?'

Nesbitt shifted in his seat. 'I'm not at liberty to say.'

'I'm a police officer,' Lennon said.

'And I'm a retired civil servant and a landlord,' Nesbitt said.

'You don't follow me.'

'Oh, I follow you all right. But I don't have to tell you anything I don't want to.'

'I can compel you to talk to me,' Lennon said. 'I can formally interview you at a station, on record. And if you still don't want to answer the questions, I can bring you in front of a

153

magistrate, and you'll — '

'Don't waste your breath,' Nesbitt said. 'They told me you'd try that. They said they'd quash any legal action, it'd never see a court.'

'Who said that?' Lennon asked.

Nesbitt coughed. He waved his hand in the air as he searched for the right words. '*They* did,' he said, eventually.

Lennon sat forward. 'Who's 'they'?'

'I'm not at liberty to say,' Nesbitt said. His eyes glittered as he smirked. He clearly enjoyed his power over Lennon.

'Someone picked up Marie's post last week,' Lennon said. 'They must have a key.'

'Nothing to do with me,' Nesbitt said. 'I haven't set foot in that flat since it was boarded up.'

'Who has the key?'

'*They* do,' Nesbitt said. He bit his knuckle to suppress a giggle.

'And who is 'they'?'

'I'm not at — '

'Yeah, I know.' Lennon stood up. There was no use in pressing the landlord. He took a card from his jacket pocket. 'Do me one favour, though. If anyone comes around asking more questions, anyone who isn't, you know . . . *they* . . . give me a shout, okay?'

Nesbitt took the card with a contemptuous sniff, and studied it at arm's length. 'We'll see,' he said.

'Please,' Lennon said. 'Anyone you're not sure of comes around, let me know.'

'Anyone?' Nesbitt set the card on the arm of

154

the chair and stared up at Lennon. 'Anyone like you?'

Lennon said, 'I'll let myself out.'

His mobile rang as he got into his car. 'Yeah?' he answered.

It was Gordon. 'Blood type on the knitting needle matches the kid's, and he has a small puncture wound on his thigh. His prints are on the knife, of course. It'll take a few days for proper DNA matches from Birmingham, but it looks pretty solid. Mrs Quigley stabbed him with the needle, he fled to the yard, lost his footing in the wet, and that's that.'

'What about the other kid?' Lennon asked.

'Haven't turned him up yet,' Gordon said. 'The locals are cooperating for the most part — the paramilitaries told them to — but no sign. We'll find him before too long, don't worry.'

Lennon settled into the driver's seat. 'I don't know,' he said.

'You don't know what?'

'Doesn't it seem a little . . . well . . . easy?'

'You're a more experienced investigator than that, DI Lennon,' Gordon said. 'This was a clumsy, stupid, hasty killing. Clumsy, stupid, hasty killers don't cover their tracks. They're almost always caught within twenty-four hours. Granted, the fact that the killer managed to break his own neck while escaping is a stroke of luck. But nevertheless, pending all reports from our more scientific colleagues, I consider this one wrapped up.'

'You told me it was too early,' Lennon said.

'That was this morning,' Gordon said. 'This is

155

now. Like I told you, don't go chasing things that aren't there. Take the rest of the day off. You did good work at the scene. I won't forget it.'

'Thank you,' Lennon said.

He hung up and put the phone back in his pocket. Nesbitt watched him from his living room window. The old man had a phone to his own ear. Lennon wondered who he was talking to.

24

Orla O'Kane stood alone in her room in the old house's servants' quarters. The small window overlooked the long, sweeping driveway. She flicked the tip of her cigarette against the rim of the ashtray. With her free hand she dialled the mobile she'd given the Traveller.

'What about ya, love?' he answered.

She closed her eyes and took a deep drag on the cigarette.

'Fegan's in New York,' she said. 'We got word from a friend in the NYPD. Some arsehole called Murphy turned up in a hospital, said some Irish fella and a darkie gave him a going over. Said the Irish fella stopped the darkie from killing him. Said the Irish fella's name was Gerry Fegan.'

'You want me to fly to New York?' the Traveller asked.

'No,' she said. 'Stick to the plan. Use the woman and the girl. We're told they'll be out in the open soon. Make him come to you.'

'All right,' the Traveller said.

'Besides, you've got Patsy Toner to take care of yet.'

'True,' the Traveller said.

Orla hung up and dropped the phone on her single bed. She stubbed the cigarette out and checked her watch. Her father's colostomy pouch needed changing, and he didn't like either

157

of the nurses to do it. Instead, Orla had to undo the pouch of faecal matter from the stoma, the surgical opening in her father's belly. Then she would dispose of it and attach a fresh pouch. She'd wept the first few times she'd had to do it. Now she simply ignored the smell and got on with it.

Two flights of narrow stairs took her down to the first floor. She crossed the gallery overlooking the entrance hall and knocked on her father's door.

'Who is it?'

'It's me,' she answered.

'Come in.'

His voice carried an urgency she didn't like. She opened the door and entered, then stopped between the door and the bed.

'Don't just fucking stand there staring,' Bull O'Kane said. 'Come and help me.'

He sat on the edge of the bed, sheets and blankets tangled around his legs. They were stained orange and red. An upturned plastic bowl lay on the floor, a tumbler beside it. The tray rested against the bedside locker.

Orla approached him. 'Jesus, Da, why didn't you call one of the nurses?'

'Because I don't want them fussing round me. Just help me, all right?'

She knelt down, retrieved the tray, and placed the bowl and tumbler upon it. The smell was bad down here, so close to him. She plucked a handful of tissues from the box on the bedside locker and dabbed at the puddles of soup and orange juice on the floor.

158

'You have to let the nurses help you sometimes,' she said. 'That's what we pay them for. I can't always be here to pick up after you.'

'I don't want them near me,' the Bull said. 'If I can't depend on my own daughter, then Jesus, who can I depend on?'

Anger broke free of her, hot and pure, before she could catch it. 'Then be more fucking careful, you — '

The slap knocked her sideways, and she landed on her shoulder. Her ear burned, a high whine sounding somewhere deep inside it. She lay there until her breathing came under control.

The old man gazed into the distance. 'My own daughter, for Christ's sake.'

Orla got to her knees, balled up the tissues, and placed them on the tray. She stood, carried the tray to the door, and left the room. Her ear whined as the tears burned her eyes. She threw the tray at the wall, and watched the last drops of soup and orange juice streak the wallpaper before the plastic clattered to the floor.

25

The Doyles' men had scattered as soon as they heard the sirens coming. Fegan had everything he needed in a sports bag and was walking west along Hester Street when the blue and red lights flickered on the buildings behind him. He'd turned south on Forsyth Street and kept walking until he reached the ferry terminal. He and the commuters making their way home from their night shifts ignored one another as the boat slipped across the bay to Staten Island. He disembarked and kept walking. He collapsed once with visions of child-eating fire and smoke. He screamed at the dawn before picking himself up and moving on, sweat coursing over his body.

Fegan wasn't sure enough to admit it to himself, but somewhere deep in his gut he knew he was going home. The phone in his pocket had dried blood between the keys, its screen was cracked, but it still worked. He often dreamed of it ringing. He was never sure if he felt terror or relief at its clamour, but he had a notion the answer wasn't far off.

26

Lennon parked his Audi on the side street by McKenna's bar. Traffic passed along the Springfield Road just a few yards ahead. He wondered if he dared do this. His hand rested on the door handle for thirty long seconds before he decided. The decision made, he got out, locked the car, and walked to the pub's entrance. The handful of afternoon drinkers fell silent when he entered. This was not the kind of place that welcomed strangers. He returned their stares in turn and walked to the bar.

'Pint of Stella,' he said.

The barman took a glass and filled it with foam. He set it in front of Lennon.

'Big head on that,' Lennon said.

The barman brought the glass back to the tap and topped it up.

Lennon took out his wallet and put a five-pound note on the bar. The beer was cold enough to sting his throat. The barman put the change in front of him.

'You're Tom Mooney,' Lennon said.

'That's right,' Mooney said. 'Who are you?'

Lennon opened his wallet, subtle, shielded by his hands.

Mooney's shoulders slumped. 'What do you want?'

Lennon stowed the wallet away. 'You know Marie McKenna?'

161

'Of course I do,' Mooney said. 'Her father used to own this place.'

'No he didn't,' Lennon said. 'Her uncle owned it. Her father's name was on the licence, but Michael McKenna owned this place.'

'Not any more,' Mooney said.

'No,' Lennon said. 'Funny thing, that, what happened to Michael. Then that business with Paul McGinty on that farm in Middletown.'

'It was a bad doing,' Mooney said.

'Yeah,' Lennon said. 'You ever hear anything of Marie these days?'

'She moved away,' Mooney said. 'That's all I heard.'

'Any idea where she went?'

'Haven't a baldy notion,' Mooney said.

'None at all?' Lennon asked. 'No rumours? No whispers?'

Mooney leaned close. 'I'm hard of hearing,' he said. 'I can't hear whispers.'

Lennon gave Mooney a smile. 'It's personal business,' he said. 'Nothing official. She's not in trouble. I just need to talk to her about something. Did she leave any word where she was going?'

'Not a peep,' Mooney said, his face softening. 'Not even her ma knows where she is. Marie just phoned her up one morning, said she was away, and that was that. You know her father had a stroke a couple of weeks back?'

'No, I didn't.'

'Yep. He's in the Royal now. I went over to see him. Paralysed down one side, his mouth's hanging open, can't talk. Fucking pitiful. Some

162

of Marie's ones were giving off 'cause she didn't come back to see him. If you want my opinion, she got scared over that feud and just packed up and got out. Can't blame her, really.'

'No,' Lennon said. 'Can't blame her.'

'Anything else?' Mooney asked.

'One thing. You were one of the last people saw Michael McKenna alive,' Lennon said. 'He left here with some drunk, dropped him home, and went to the docks to get his brains blown out. The reports say he phoned you from there just before it happened.'

'I cooperated,' Mooney said. 'I gave my statements. It's all on record. If you want to know anything, just look it up. Now drink up and get out.'

Lennon took a swig of gassy beer. 'I want another Stella,' he said.

'You haven't finished that one yet,' Mooney said.

'I'm planning ahead,' Lennon said. 'The inquiry said the Lithuanians got McKenna and that sparked it off. Is that what you think happened?'

'I gave my statements,' Mooney said.

'That's not what I asked.'

'It's all I'm saying.'

'You know about Declan Quigley,' Lennon said.

'Aye,' Mooney said. 'Another bad doing. I heard some kid did it. Is that right?'

Lennon ignored the question, asked one of his own. 'He ever drink here?'

'Sometimes.'

'How'd he been lately?'

163

'How do you mean?' Mooney asked.

'What sort of form was he in? Was he depressed? Nervous? Angry?'

'All three,' Mooney said. 'He got a bad scare when McGinty was killed.'

'Did he ever talk about it?'

'Never,' Mooney said. 'He wouldn't. He was a soft shite, but he did time in the Maze and Maghaberry. Small-time stuff, he could've got off if he'd touted, but he kept quiet and took the sentence. A fella like that doesn't talk. Speaking of which, I've said too much already. I'll leave you to it.'

Mooney turned to go, but Lennon called, 'One more thing.'

Mooney sighed and turned back. 'What?'

'Patsy Toner.'

'What about him?'

'I heard he's been on bad form too,' Lennon said. 'I heard he's been on the bottle.'

'He likes a drink,' Mooney said.

'More than he used to?'

'Maybe.'

'I heard he's been scared about something,' Lennon said. 'I heard he talks when he's drunk. You ever overhear anything?'

Mooney leaned over the bar. 'Like I said, I'm hard of hearing. Now, do you want that second pint or what?'

Lennon drained his glass and suppressed a burp. 'No, I've had enough. But thanks.'

Mooney nodded and walked away.

★　★　★

164

Thirty minutes later, Lennon sat parked on Eglantine Avenue staring at Marie's boarded-up windows. Occasionally, small groups of kids in school uniforms walked past, probably heading for the takeaways on the Lisburn Road. Ellen must have started her second year of primary by now.

Marie only allowed him that one photograph. He hadn't met her since then, and that had been four years ago. It was no more than he deserved. She had sacrificed so much for him, and he had betrayed her.

He hadn't meant to. If anyone had asked him if he was capable of such a thing a week before it happened, he would have said no, absolutely not. He had learned since then never to underestimate a man's weakness.

They'd been living in the flat for a year when it all fell apart. Marie's nesting instinct had gone into overdrive, and every weekend was spent touring shopping centres looking for the perfect cushion cover, or the ideal mirror to go above the fireplace.

They'd been standing in a furniture store off the Boucher Road for an hour, Marie agonising over a pair of bedside lockers while a sales assistant looked on, when Lennon noticed the shape of her in the light. His mind wandered to the times when she'd clambered on him, the soft 'oh' of her mouth at the point of orgasm, the feel of her weight on him. It had been a while. She was saying something and he snapped himself back to the here and now.

'You haven't heard a thing I just said.' Her

165

eyes were cold stone.

'I'm sorry, what?'

'Look, if you can't be bothered listening to me then why did you come?'

The sales assistant looked at his feet.

Lennon smiled, his voice soft. 'I'm sorry, I was just daydreaming. What were you saying?'

'This is important to me.'

'I — '

'This is our home. This is our future together.'

Lennon stopped smiling. 'I know. I'm sorry.'

The sales assistant remembered an important matter that needed his attention elsewhere.

'You're not sorry,' she said. 'You don't care.'

'Of course I do.'

'No you don't, or you'd fucking listen. Why am I bothering to run myself ragged over this when you don't give a shit?'

'Marie, please.'

'Fuck you.'

He stayed ten steps behind her all the way to the car.

The irony was that Wendy Carlisle had been the one who'd introduced Lennon to Marie eighteen months before. She was the media officer at Lennon's station, and a hard-luck girl if ever he'd met one. They became friends, though looking back he couldn't think why.

She stumbled from one bad relationship to another, five of them while he knew her, always ending up hurt and bitter. Lennon had tried his luck, but she said she knew his type, she wouldn't get chewed up and spat out by a user like him. She always smiled when she said it, but

166

anger hid beneath the teasing.

When Wendy passed a request for an interview on to Lennon, he had no idea it would change the course of his life. He saw something in Marie, recognised the separation from her roots as a reflection of his own situation. He hadn't meant to fall in love any more than Marie had. Given her family — she was a McKenna, niece of Michael McKenna, for Christ's sake — he should have gone nowhere near her. Their relationship destroyed what was left of the ties to her kin, and Lennon's colleagues made a point of pulling him up on it every chance they got. He'd been in line for a move to Special Branch, but at the last moment he was switched to CID. They never said why, but he knew. He was a Catholic cop at a time when such a thing was still a rarity, and now he was mixed up with Michael McKenna's niece. He didn't know which was worse: the threats from Republicans, with the Mass cards and bullets that arrived in the post, or the hard stares and silence he met in his workplace.

As soon as they moved in together, Marie started talking about children. Always at night, when they lay together in the dark. Just thinking out loud, she'd say. Just talking. Nothing serious.

Serious or not, it terrified him. It wasn't the idea of sleepless nights or being tied down that frightened him so much. Rather it was the certainty that he would, sooner or later, let the child down. He tried to tell Marie this, to explain it was his own weakness that scared him, but the words never came out right. Every conversation ended with her cold back to him as he silently cursed his clumsy tongue.

After a while, they didn't talk about it any more. The stony grey of her eyes cooled, her lips thinned, her laughter dried until it rasped like sandpaper on wood. They should have ended it then, but neither of them had the courage.

★ ★ ★

Lennon's head jerked up to bounce against the Audi's headrest. Had he been asleep? His head had that sodden feeling, like clay behind his eyes. He looked at his watch. Coming five. When had he last checked the time? An hour, maybe.

'Jesus,' he said.

Lennon fired the Audi's ignition and listened to the diesel clatter and rumble. He blinked the sleep away.

A man approached on the pavement. Mid-thirties, Lennon guessed. A hard face, lined more by life than age. His right eyelid was red and swollen. His left arm hung stiff and long at his side. He nodded at Lennon as he passed.

Lennon watched the man's back in his side mirror. The man disappeared between the parked cars. Lennon opened the Audi's door and climbed out. He looked up and down Eglantine Avenue.

No sign of him.

Lennon settled back into the Audi, his mouth dry. He wanted another pint of Stella, and maybe some company.

27

The Traveller kept walking along the side street, his head down. He chanced one look back over his shoulder. No one followed. His Merc was parked on the next street north, the one tethered to Eglantine Avenue by this side street. He didn't know its name. Belfast was starting to grate on him, with its red-brick houses and cars parked on top of one another. And the people, all smug and smiling now they'd gathered the wit to quit killing each other and start making money instead.

He reached the Merc and got in. He dialled the number.

'For fuck's sake, what now?' Orla asked.

'Jesus, love, don't bite my face off.'

'Don't 'love' me, you gyppo bastard. I'll come up there and cut your balls off. Now what do you want?'

The Traveller sensed it was not an idle threat. Was she on the rag? 'All right,' he said. 'That cop. What did you find out about him?'

'Why?'

''Cause he's sitting outside that McKenna blade's flat again. What's he doing hanging about there? Who is he?'

'That cop's the least of your worries, believe me,' she said. 'He's Jack Lennon, a detective inspector. A smart cop. He should be higher up the ranks, but he's been in some bother. He had

169

a sexual harassment charge hanging over him a few years back, some tramp from the office tried to make a claim against him. The charge didn't stick, but the reputation did. He's in debt up to his eyeballs. He's too friendly with some Loyalists. We're told he might be taking payment in kind from the brothels, and another cop accused him of trying to pass on a bribe. His superiors are wary of him, think he's bent. Don't worry about him.'

'Well, I *am* worried about him,' the Traveller said. 'He's going to get in the way. I should do something about it.'

'No,' Orla said. 'You have a go at a cop, even if he's bent, you'll fuck everything up.'

'I'll do it right,' the Traveller said. 'There'll be nothing to connect him — '

'No, I said. Look, certain people are indulging us by letting you clean up this mess. You tackle a cop, they won't indulge us any more. You understand?'

'Whatever you say, love,' the Traveller said.

Hard silence for a moment, then she said, 'What about Patsy Toner?'

'I'll call with him tonight.'

'Good,' Orla said. 'You're stretching my patience. Just do what we're paying you to do.'

'All right,' the Traveller said.

He hung up and pocketed the phone. 'Grumpy auld pishmire,' he said. He started the Merc and went looking for Patsy Toner.

28

Lennon found him in the Crown Bar of all places. Despite the snugs, the Crown was the last pub in Belfast to drink in if you wanted privacy. Patsy Toner sat at the far end of the bar, staring at the red granite. Lennon could just see him beyond the wood and glass panels that divided the bar up.

The hubbub of locals and tourists combined to make a hearty rumble of laughter and raised voices. Lennon realised this was the perfect place for a frightened man to drink. Patsy Toner was probably safer here than in any bar in the city.

Lennon edged his way through the early evening drinkers towards Toner. Holidaymakers and office workers stood in clusters, the tourists with their pints of Guinness, the locals with their WKD and Magners cider.

He sidled up behind Toner and waved for the barman's attention. 'Stella,' he called over the lawyer's shoulder.

Toner turned his head a little to the side, to see who stood so close. Lennon wondered if he'd be recognised. He had interviewed many of Toner's clients. A good lawyer remembered the names and faces of the cops he met in his work.

Sure enough, Toner's shoulders tensed.

The bartender set the pint on the raised drain tray, letting the foam slop over the rim. Lennon leaned across Toner and put the money in the

171

bartender's hand. He lifted the pint, but stayed pressed against Toner's back.

'How've you been, Patsy?' he asked.

Toner stared ahead. 'Do I know you?'

'We've met in a professional capacity,' Lennon said.

Toner turned his head. 'I don't remember your name.'

'DI Jack Lennon.'

Did Toner flinch? The lawyer looked back to his drink. 'What do you want?'

'A word,' Lennon said.

Toner spread his hands flat on the bar. The fingers of his left looked thin and waxy. His shoulders slumped.

Lennon looked back over his shoulder. 'There's a snug free,' he said. 'Bring your drink.'

They sat at a table walled by ornate wood and stained glass. Lennon closed the snug's door.

A waitress opened it again, pointed to the sign. 'Sir, this snug's reserved.'

Lennon showed her his ID. 'I won't be long.'

'The party should be here any minute,' she said.

'I'll get out when they come,' he said. He smiled. 'Just a minute or two. You'd be doing me a big favour. Please?'

She hesitated, then smiled. 'Okay, I'll — '

Lennon closed the door and sat down. He stared at Toner across the table. Toner's hands shook as he raised his glass.

'How's it going, Patsy?' Lennon asked.

Toner grimaced as he swallowed. His glass clinked on the tabletop. 'What do you want?'

'Just to see how you're doing these days,' Lennon said. He took a sip of Stella and leaned forward. 'I heard you weren't doing so well. I heard you had something on your mind.'

Toner forced a laugh. 'Who told you that?'

'A couple of people,' Lennon said. 'Friends of yours.'

Toner laughed again, this time shrill and jagged. 'Friends? You're talking shite. I don't have any friends. Not any more.'

'No?' Lennon feigned surprise. 'You used to be a popular fella. All sorts of friends in all sorts of places.'

'Used to be,' Toner echoed. He wiped whiskey from his moustache. Two days' stubble lined his jowls. 'Friendship's a funny thing. You think it's solid, for life, but it can blow away just like that.'

Lennon nodded. 'I know what you mean,' he said, truthfully.

Toner stared back at him, something turning behind his eyes for a few seconds before dying away. 'Look, get to the point,' he said. 'You're not here just to pass the time.'

Lennon laced his fingers together on the tabletop. 'I heard you've been acting strange lately, like you're scared. I want to know what you're afraid of.'

Toner sat back and folded his arms. 'Who told you that?'

'People,' Lennon said.

'What did they say?'

'That you've gone downhill since Paul McGinty died. That you're drinking like a fish. That you know more about what happened than

173

you're letting on, and it's ripping you to pieces.'

'No.' Toner shook his head, slow, his eyes unfocused. 'No, that's not . . . It's not . . . Who said that?'

'You've been talking when you're drunk,' Lennon said. 'You said it's not over, they'll come for you, it's only a matter of time.'

Toner's cheeks reddened. 'Who said that?'

'A friend of yours,' Lennon said. He thought about taunting the lawyer with the tales Roscoe had told him, that Toner was so scared he couldn't get it up any more. He decided against it.

'Bollocks,' Toner said. His eyes glittered.

'Maybe I can help,' Lennon said.

'Bollocks.' Toner tried to stand, but his legs couldn't hold him upright.

'I can help,' Lennon repeated. 'We can help. I have contacts in Special Branch. They can protect you.'

Toner snorted. 'Protect me? Jesus, I wouldn't need protecting if it wasn't for them cunts. You're not here on official business, are you? If you'd told anyone you were talking to me they'd have warned you off.'

'Who would?'

'Who do you think?' This time Toner's legs held him. The table shook as his thighs squeezed past it. 'Your fucking bosses. Special Branch and the Brits. You want to know what's happening, talk to them, not me.'

Lennon reached for his wrist. 'Patsy, wait.'

Toner pulled his arm away and opened the door. 'Talk to your own people, see what they'll tell you.'

'Marie McKenna,' Lennon said. 'Her daughter. *My* daughter.'

Toner froze. 'Jesus, that's who you are. You're the cop Marie took up with.'

'That's right,' Lennon said.

The waitress appeared over Toner's shoulder, a group of young professional types behind her. 'I need the snug,' she said.

Toner ignored her. 'You want to know where she is?'

'Yes,' Lennon said.

'I don't know,' Toner said. 'Nobody does. She's better off out of it. So are you. Don't go stirring things up. That's all I'll tell you, and that's too much.'

'Excuse me,' the waitress called.

'Just a second.' Lennon took a card from his pocket and pressed it into Toner's hand. 'If you want to talk.'

'I won't,' Toner said, handing the card back. 'Leave it alone. Will you do that? Leave it alone. It's best for everyone.'

Lennon lifted Toner's lapel and tucked the card into his inside pocket. 'Just in case,' he said.

Toner suddenly looked very old. 'Leave it alone,' he said. He turned and headed towards the exit.

Lennon slipped the waitress a fiver and thanked her. He went for the door, taking his time to let Toner melt away. There was no sign of the lawyer when he shouldered his way out onto Great Victoria Street, taxis and cars and buses blaring horns at one another as they fought for space under the shadow of the Europa Hotel.

He remembered the resolution he'd made last night and checked his watch. It had only just gone six-thirty. He'd forgotten to text his sister, but it would hardly matter. Most likely nobody would bother with visiting his mother on a week-night. If he got a hustle on he could be in Newry before eight, sit with her for an hour, and be back in Belfast by ten.

Lennon walked towards the car park on the Dublin Road, his mind flicking between a frail old woman, a frightened lawyer, and a little girl who didn't know his name.

*　*　*

For the third time in twenty minutes, Lennon told his mother who he was. For the third time, she nodded with only a vague hint of recognition on her face. She fussed with her dressing gown for a moment before looking back up at the wall opposite her bed.

Every visit was like this, a string of bland exchanges punctuated by bouts of confusion. He came anyway, perhaps not as often as he should, but enough to be noticed. It wasn't that he begrudged her the time. Rather it was that he hated to see her like this, even though she'd disowned him years ago. He hated that he'd had to wait for her mind to go before he could see her again. She was little more than a shadow of the woman who had giggled like a girl when he and his brother danced with her at weddings and confirmation parties.

'The evenings are fairly drawing in,' she said,

looking to the growing darkness beyond the window. 'Next thing you know, it'll be Christmas. Who's having Christmas this year?'

'Bronagh,' Lennon said. 'It's always Bronagh.'

Bronagh was the eldest of his three sisters. It was she who had told Lennon to leave and never come back all those years ago.

The day before Liam went in the ground, Phelim Quinn, who sat on Armagh City and District Council, called at Lennon's mother's house. He took the mother aside, expressed his condolences, and reminded her it wouldn't do any good to talk to the police. Sure, they'd do nothing for them anyway. Liam had paid for his mistakes, and it would be best for everyone to just put it behind them, move on. In a very quiet voice, Lennon's mother told Quinn to get out. As Quinn walked down the path to the small garden gate, Lennon caught up with him.

'Liam wasn't a tout,' Lennon said. 'He told me.'

Quinn stopped and turned. 'He told me the same,' he said. 'Doesn't make it so.'

Lennon's throat tightened, his eyes burned. 'He wasn't. He said someone was covering themselves, putting the blame on him.'

Quinn came close to Lennon, the councillor's whiskey breath souring the breeze. 'Watch your mouth, son. Your family's had enough grief. Don't give them any more.'

Tears fought for release. Lennon forced them back. No way he'd cry in front of this bastard. No way. 'You got the wrong man,' he said. 'Just you remember that.'

He turned and went back inside to where his mother and his three sisters huddled together. Still he held the tears back, the sting of them scorching his eyes as they tried to get out. He swallowed them, and he'd never cried a single tear since.

The day after Liam went in the ground, two uniformed cops came. Bronagh kept them on the doorstep for ten minutes before her mother intervened and let them in. Lennon watched the cops from the living room doorway. They spoke in flat tones, their questions bland, their responses perfunctory. They knew they were wasting their time, Lennon could tell by their faces and their postures. Their visit was nothing more than a formality, a T to be crossed so that the case could be filed away with hundreds of others that would never be solved for lack of cooperation from the community.

Lennon stopped them in the hallway.

'Phelim Quinn,' he said.

'What about him?' the sergeant asked.

'He did it. Or he knows who did it.'

The sergeant laughed. 'I know who did it,' the sergeant said. 'Constable McCoy here knows who did it. Every other bloody person on this street knows who did it. The second any one of them will go on record, then we've got a case. Until then, we might as well go after Santa Claus.'

He put his hand on Lennon's shoulder. 'Listen, son, I'd dearly love to be able to put the bastards that killed your brother away. I really would. But you know as well as I do that's never going to happen. Christ, if there was any chance

178

of collaring them, it wouldn't be lumps like us calling to see you, it'd be proper detectives. We make the notes, we fill out the forms, and that's as much as we can do. Best thing you can do is stay out of trouble and look after your ma.'

The sergeant and constable left Lennon in the hall and closed the door behind them.

Over the following weeks, the house seemed frozen, everyone locked in grief, anger and fear, with no way to express it. As Lennon lay awake at night, now alone in the room he and his brother had shared, he considered the implications of his decision. He had filled out the forms, giving the address of his student digs in Belfast. He was back at Queen's, starting his psychology Master's, when the call for the first test came. The relief at getting away from his fractured home was tarnished by the fear of what he had embarked upon. Six months of interviews and physical exams followed while he worked part time as a porter at the Windsor House mental health unit at the City Hospital. All the time, he kept it secret, even from his friends at Queen's.

Lennon spent fewer weekends at home, driving down from the city to the village in the second-hand Seat Ibiza he had inherited from his dead brother. The empty bed in his room seemed like a shrine to Liam, and its presence would allow him no sleep. He asked his mother once if he could remove it. She slapped him hard across the cheek, and he did not ask again. Bronagh began to exert more control over the household, organising meals, doling out chores to her younger sisters, while her mother spent

179

her days staring at air.

A torturous Christmas passed, the meals taken in near silence. By March, the final hurdle loomed: the security checks. Lennon was sure they'd eliminate him because of his brother, and began to quietly wish for the rejection letter to arrive. A part of his mind that was both hopeful and fearful told him that perhaps, just maybe, his brother hadn't been involved long or deeply enough for his name to be associated with any crime. Or perhaps supplying the Belfast address as part of his application would distance him from his family. When the letter arrived instructing him to report to Garnerville Police Training College for induction, he spent an age staring at the words, knowing he meant to attend, knowing his old life would be gone.

He went home one last weekend, chatted to some old school friends over a pint in the local, did messages for his mother, walked the length and breadth of the village. After Sunday Mass, he told his sisters and his mother over the roast dinner Bronagh had prepared. Claire and Noreen said nothing, just gathered their plates from the table, put them in the sink, and left the room while Bronagh sat still.

His mother gazed at the tablecloth, her body trembling. 'You'll be killed,' she said. 'Just like Liam. You'll be killed. I can't lose two sons. I can't. Don't go. You don't have to go. You can change your mind. Stay at university, finish your Master's, get a good job. Don't do this. Don't.'

'It's what I want to do,' he said. 'I need to do it. For Liam.'

Bronagh shook her head, her lip curled in disgust. 'Don't you dare use him to justify this. You know what this'll do to your family. Ma won't be able to show her face. We'll be lucky if we're not burnt out.'

'But it'll never change,' Lennon said. 'How can we complain about the RUC being a Protestant force when we refuse to join? How can we condemn them for not protecting this community when we won't allow them to? I'm doing this for — '

'Just get out,' Bronagh said. She slipped her arm around her mother's shoulders. 'Look what you're doing to her. Get your stuff and get out.'

That evening, Lennon left the home he'd grown up in. With a tattered suitcase and a sports bag carrying his few possessions, he drove back to Belfast. He heard through an old friend that Phelim Quinn once again called on his mother a few weeks later. This time, Quinn told her if her son ever returned to Middletown, he'd be shot. For the second time in a year she told the councillor to get out of her house.

★ ★ ★

Lennon bent down and kissed his mother's forehead. She reached up and stroked his cheek. A crease appeared on her brow.

'Where'd all those lines come from?' she asked. 'You look more like your father every time I see you.'

Lennon doubted she remembered the last time she'd seen him. 'So you keep telling me.'

181

'He'll be back soon,' she said.

'Who? Our da?'

'Aye, who do you think? The Pope? He'll be back soon, and he'll take us all to America with him.'

Lennon could barely recall his father's face. Almost thirty years had passed since he'd seen it. No one had heard tell of him since, but it would do no good to remind Lennon's mother of that. Let her cling to her delusions if they brought her a glimmer of happiness.

'He'll take us all to some fancy place in New York. Me, you, Liam and the girls. All of us together.'

'That's right, Ma,' Lennon said. He kissed her again and left her there.

The exit to the car park opened as he approached it. Bronagh stepped through and froze when she saw him. She stood there for a few seconds, still as a cold morning, before putting her head down and walking past him.

'Bronagh?' he called.

She stopped, her back to him, her gaze fixed on the floor. Her hands formed fists, opening and closing. She wore a smart jacket and skirt. She'd probably come straight from the hotel she managed in the centre of Newry.

'How's she been?' he asked. 'Are they looking after her?'

'I didn't know you'd be here,' she said.

'Sorry, I forgot to text you.'

'Don't do it again,' she said. She walked away without looking at him.

29

The Traveller was sick of waiting. Two and a half hours now, coming three, and no sign of Toner. The little runt of a lawyer had left his wife and kids and moved into a grotty flat off the Springfield Road. The Bull said he was drinking himself to death. The Traveller would be doing Toner a favour, really. Put him out of his misery.

He shifted in the driver's seat. The wound in his arm wouldn't let him settle, and his eye itched and stung. He'd put a dollop of antibiotic ointment in it twenty minutes ago. For conjunctivitis, the chemist had told him. The stuff found its way down to the back of his throat and turned his stomach. He'd opened the window an inch to let the night air at it, but it did little good. Everything was a blur in that eye. The Traveller knew he wasn't at his best. It wouldn't matter with a speck of fly shit like Toner, but anyone harder, he'd have to hold back.

A fresh flutter of stings and itches made the Traveller's eyelid twitch, and a warm drop of something ran down his cheek. 'Fuck,' he said.

He pulled a wad of tissues from the door pocket and mopped his face and eye. The soft paper stuck to something on his eyelid and tore. He blinked, shreds of tissue flapping against his cheek. 'Fuck,' he said. 'Shite bastard fucking whore.'

The Traveller screwed his eyes shut and put his head back. He picked at bits of tissue, feeling them tug at the stickiness on his eyelid. He felt in the door pocket for the bottle of water. He found it with his fingertips, unscrewed the cap. Blinded, he poured some into his palm and splashed it across his eyes. He wiped them with the heel of his hand, then his sleeve. His vision came and went as he blinked. He reached for the interior light switch and flicked it on. His reflection in the rear-view mirror blurred and focused. Jesus, that eye looked bad enough. The lid was red and swollen, the eyeball was streaked red. Maybe he needed more of that ointment. He looked around him to see where he'd dropped it.

He saw Patsy Toner standing on the footpath across the road, outside his building, staring back.

'Fuck,' the Traveller said. He reached between his legs, under the seat, where he'd stowed the Desert Eagle, found only rubbish and damp carpet.

Toner stood frozen for just a second before he turned and ran for his front door. The Traveller explored the darkness beneath him, grazed his knuckles on the metal rails that supported the seat. As his hand flailed in the narrow space, he spared Toner a glance. The lawyer's panicked whines didn't mask the sound of his key scraping at his lock.

The Traveller twisted his torso as he shoved his hand further back. His injured shoulder screamed at the effort, but he was rewarded by

184

the feel of cold pistol in his fingers. He pulled the Eagle free, leapt out of the car, on his feet, chambered a round, aimed.

Toner's door slammed shut.

'Fuck,' the Traveller said. He ran for the door, kicked once, twice. It wouldn't budge. Toner lived on the top floor. The Traveller hit the buzzer for the first floor flat. He hit it again. He stayed close to the door in case the flat's occupant looked down from the window above. He heard footsteps on the stairs inside.

A woman of young middle-age opened it, her face sharpened with anger. 'What do — '

The Traveller crushed her nose with the butt of the gun. She fell back and her head bounced on the polished floorboards. She sighed, coughed blood, and stilled. Her chest rose and fell. The Traveller thought about finishing her, but there was no time. He stepped over her and made for the stairs. He took them two at a time until he reached the top floor.

Toner's door would give with one kick, the Traveller was sure of it. He paused, breathed deep, wiped his sleeve across his eyes. The right blurred, and he blinked until it cleared. He formed a good combat grip on the Eagle, one hand supporting the other, and booted the door below the handle. It slammed back against the wall. A ragged couch faced him in the dimness. Dishes, bottles and the detritus of takeaways littered a coffee table. The Traveller edged into the room. A breeze licked at the dampness on his face.

'Fucking cock-pulling arsehole,' he said.

A door in the corner of the kitchenette stood ajar. It opened onto a metal staircase that descended into the yard two floors down. A fucking fire escape.

The Traveller's eye flickered and blurred and burned. Something warm trickled down his cheek. His left shoulder ached.

'Bastard cunt of a motherfucking whore's son,' he said.

30

Fegan sat in the darkness of a cheap motel room near Newark Airport, breathing hard. Had the phone really rung? He reached for it and thumbed a button.

No calls. He returned it to the bedside locker and lay back down on top of the blankets. The pillow was damp with sweat. He had dreamed of fire, of a little girl swallowed by black smoke as her screams turned to the sound of a phone ringing. Her name was Ellen McKenna and she would be almost six by now. Only months ago, Fegan had carried her past the bodies of men he had killed. She had closed her eyes and pressed her wet face against his neck, just like he told her to. Her skin had been hot against his.

The last time he'd seen her, she waved at him from the back of her mother's car at Dundalk Port. It seemed a lifetime ago. He had told Marie McKenna to call the cheap mobile phone he carried with him if she was ever in danger. That phone had not left his side since. He rubbed his left shoulder with the heel of his right hand. The scar itched, like baby spiders burrowing beneath the shiny pink skin.

Fegan considered the dream. Could dreams break into the waking hours? He had come to understand the thin borders between this place and others. That was why dreams of fire and burning girls terrified him, made his gut tighten

187

and his legs slip from under him.

Ellen's mother never featured in these dreams. Fegan sometimes struggled to remember what Marie McKenna looked like. He remembered her on the dock, warning him to stay away, but her face had dissolved into something unreal. Like a person he had only imagined, who had never actually existed. When his phone rang, which he knew it would, she would be real again. He dreaded the moment.

But if — when — she called, he would go. He had sworn he would make her and Ellen safe. He had spilled so much blood in his life, but his greatest sin had been to drag Marie and Ellen into the violence that always seemed to gravitate to him. He had brought death to their door; he would do anything to prevent it crossing their threshold.

The room shook as a plane passed overhead. The call would come soon, he was sure of that. After that phone call, he would go to the airport and buy a ticket to Belfast. He would fly home to the city he thought he'd never see again and finish what he'd started.

31

'What were you doing at Jonathan Nesbitt's house yesterday?' DCI Gordon asked, his hands folded on top of his desk.

Dan Hewitt stood silent in the corner.

Lennon looked at each of them in turn. 'Just asking a few questions,' he said.

'About what?' Gordon asked.

Lennon scrambled for some reply. Before he could come up with one, Gordon said, 'I sent you home yesterday to get some rest, not to go harassing a decent man like Jonathan Nesbitt.'

'It was only a few questions,' Lennon said.

'Pertaining to what?' Gordon didn't wait for an answer. 'You go knocking on people's doors, flashing your badge, your questions had better be relevant to an investigation I'm supervising. Were they?'

Lennon shifted in his seat. 'Not directly.'

'Not directly.' Gordon pursed his lips. 'Which is another way of saying 'not at all'.'

Hewitt cleared his throat. 'Look, we know why you went to Mr Nesbitt's house, and we know what sort of questions you asked. Mr Nesbitt reported it to his contact in Special Branch yesterday afternoon. My colleagues weren't best pleased. Not for the first time, I had to do some sweet-talking on your behalf.'

'You owe DCI Hewitt your gratitude,' Gordon

said. 'I was ready for dropping you from my team, but he's convinced me to let it go. But you're on thin ice, understand?'

Lennon sighed and nodded.

Gordon leaned forward. 'Understand?'

'Yes, sir,' Lennon said.

Gordon's face softened. 'Look, you're an excellent police officer. You should be a DCI by now, heading up your own MIT. Behave yourself, and you've got a good career ahead of you. Don't get sidetracked by personal agendas.'

Lennon couldn't hold his gaze. 'Yes, sir,' he said.

'Good. Now, go on. Chase up the forensics on our friend Mr Quigley, there's a good fella.'

Lennon stood and went for the door. As he walked down the corridor, Hewitt caught up with him.

'I need a word,' Hewitt said.

Lennon stopped. 'What?'

'Listen, Jack, I did you a big favour today.' Hewitt kept his voice low and even. 'You might never know how big.'

'Well, I owe you,' Lennon said, walking away.

'I'm about to do you another one,' Hewitt called after him.

Lennon turned. 'Yeah? And what's that?'

Hewitt walked past him and opened the door to the copy room. He looked inside, then beckoned Lennon to follow him in.

Lennon entered the room. 'So what's the favour?'

'Me telling you to leave it alone, that's what.'

Lennon smiled in spite of himself. 'Funny,

you're the second person to tell me that since yesterday.'

Hewitt's face fell. 'Who else said it?'

Lennon put his hands in his pockets. 'A little bird.'

'Jesus, Jack, tell me you'll leave it alone, please.' Hewitt took a step closer. 'You know Special Branch doesn't piss about. They'll fuck you over soon as look at you.'

'They? By *they*, you mean *we*. Right?'

'Don't put me in this position, Jack. I stuck my neck out for you today, and it wasn't the first time. I've been a good friend to you, whether you think so or not. I'm being a friend to you now. Leave it alone.'

Lennon's hands made fists inside his pockets. 'For Christ's sake, this is my daughter we're talking about. She's been missing along with her mother for months now. I know Marie was mixed up in that feud, the McGinty business, and no one's seen her since. How do you expect me to leave it?'

Hewitt paced the floor as he considered. He stopped, nodded. 'All right. I'll tell you one thing, and one thing only. But promise me you'll leave it alone.'

Lennon took his hands out of his pockets and flexed his fingers. 'Tell me what?'

'Promise me.'

'I can't.'

Hewitt stared hard at Lennon. 'Promise me.'

Lennon's shoulders slumped and he leaned against the photocopier. 'Fuck,' he said. 'All right.'

Hewitt took a breath. 'You're right, Marie was mixed up in that feud.'

'Jesus,' Lennon said.

Hewitt held his hands up. 'But only on the periphery,' he said. 'Not directly. She moved away just as a precaution. I don't know where she is, but — '

'I don't believe you.'

'Jack, I — '

'You're C3, Special Branch, for Christ's sake, so don't tell me you don't know where she is.'

'She's safe,' Hewitt said. 'Marie McKenna and her little girl — *your* little girl — are safe. That's all I can tell you. They're safe. Okay?'

'Where are they?'

'They're safe,' Hewitt repeated. 'That's all you need to know.'

'Christ,' Lennon said. He went to swipe a stack of paper off the top of the copier, but thought better of it. Instead, he clasped his hands at the back of his neck and inhaled.

Hewitt said, 'There's one more thing.'

Lennon exhaled and his head went light. 'What?'

'It doesn't mean anything.'

'What?'

'I don't want you making something of this. It's just a coincidence.'

Lennon's hands dropped from behind his neck. 'What? Fucking tell me.'

'The lawyer, Patsy Toner.'

Lennon's heart went cold. He let his face go slack, prepared to show no reaction to whatever Hewitt was about to tell him. 'What about him?'

'He has a flat off the Springfield Road. A woman was assaulted in his building around eleven last night. An intruder broke her nose. She doesn't remember anything about it. Toner's door was kicked in. He's missing.'

Lennon wiped his mouth with the back of his hand.

'I know you were asking questions about him,' Hewitt said. 'Tom Mooney at McKenna's bar is an informer. He told one of my colleagues you were asking after Patsy Toner.'

Lennon thought about denying it, knew there was no point. 'That's right.'

Hewitt raised a finger. 'Well, don't go asking after him any more. Whatever happened at his flat has nothing to do with you, and nothing to do with Marie McKenna, understand? Patsy Toner is mixed up with all sorts of bad people. Whatever trouble he's in is his own and no one else's. The only reason I'm telling you this is so you don't find out off someone else and go chasing some bloody conspiracy that isn't there. Now, for God's sake, leave it alone.'

Lennon studied Hewitt's face, his grey eyes, the lines around his mouth. He tried to remember if he'd ever really liked him, even back at Garnerville.

'Tell me you'll leave it alone,' Hewitt said. 'Please.'

Lennon swallowed, nodded. 'All right,' he said. 'I'll leave it alone.'

32

The Traveller took a seat at the bar. There was plenty of choice; he was the only one here. Apart from the barman, Tom Mooney.

Mooney put down his newspaper. 'How're ya?' he said, his head tilted, his eyes taking in every detail.

'I'm grand,' the Traveller said. He gave Mooney a wide smile.

'That's a bad-looking eye you've got there,' Mooney said.

The Traveller's fingers went to the heat above his cheek, stopped just short of touching the inflamed eyelid. 'Infection,' he said. 'Stings like a fucker.'

'You should see a doctor.'

'Probably should. Probably won't.'

Mooney stared for a second or two. 'What can I get you?'

'Pint of Smithwick's,' the Traveller said.

Mooney took a glass to the pump. The beer swirled cream and brown as it poured. He placed the drink on the bar. The Traveller put a ten next to it.

'You've not been in here before,' Mooney said as he wiped the bar with a damp cloth. 'We get mostly regulars here, a pretty tight crowd. Not a lot of passers-by just drop in, if you know what I mean.' He looked up. 'Unless they're after something, that is.'

The Traveller smiled. 'Is that right?'

'That's right,' Mooney said. He didn't drop his gaze when the Traveller returned it. Bit of fight in him, by the look of his stance.

'You think I'm after something?'

Mooney's hands slipped beneath the bar counter, where the Traveller couldn't see them. He wondered what the barman had under there. A baseball bat, most likely.

'Yeah, I sort of got that notion,' Mooney said. 'Tell me straight what you want, and we'll see how we go. I've had enough fucking about to do me for a right while, and I'm not in the mood for any more today. All right?'

The Traveller nodded. 'All right. I'm looking for Patsy Toner. He drinks here sometimes.'

Mooney straightened. He tried to hide his surprise at the Traveller's words, but failed. 'He hasn't been in here for a while.'

'No? Where else does he drink?'

'Different places,' Mooney said.

'There's a lot of different places,' the Traveller said.

'This is the only place I pull pints in,' Mooney said. 'Can't tell you much about anywhere else.'

The Traveller watched a thin film of perspiration form on Mooney's forehead, the tensing of his forearms, the clenching of his jaw. 'I'm not the only one's been asking for him, am I?'

Mooney said nothing, just stared back.

'Was it a cop?' the Traveller asked.

'Drink up,' Mooney said. 'Door's over there.'

'Big broad fella,' the Traveller said, feeling a

195

warm trickle down his cheek. 'Sandy-coloured hair. Nice suit.'

Mooney grimaced. 'Jesus, your eye.'

The Traveller pulled a tissue from the bundle in his jacket pocket. He mopped the wetness from his cheek. It left a mix of pale yellow and red on the paper. He sniffed and something cloying and tangy slipped down the back of his throat. 'Give us some water, will you?'

Mooney hesitated, then filled a tumbler. The Traveller soaked a wad of tissue and dabbed his eye, wincing at the sting. The sodden paper came apart as he worked.

Mooney produced a bar towel from some-where. 'Here,' he said. 'It's clean.'

The Traveller dipped a corner of the towel into the water and again dabbed his eye. 'Thanks,' he said. 'Listen, you seem like a decent sort of a fella. You say you don't know where Patsy Toner is, no problem. But tell me straight: was there a cop in here asking after him?'

'Yeah,' Mooney said. 'And I told him as much as I told you. Fair enough?'

The Traveller folded the towel as he studied the barman. Working in a place like this, he wouldn't, couldn't tell the cops anything substantial, even if Patsy Toner should happen to turn up dead. He must have kept some fierce secrets in his time. 'Fair enough,' the Traveller said. He indicated the towel. 'Can I have this?'

Mooney shrugged.

'And I was never in here, and I never asked you anything about Patsy Toner, right?'

Mooney said, 'Like I told that cop, I hear

nothing, I see nothing. Now, you going to finish that pint or what?'

The Traveller was about to answer when his mobile rang. Instead, he said, 'See you around.'

He left the bar and answered the phone as he walked to his car.

'You made an awful bollocks of things last night,' Orla O'Kane said.

'He got — '

'I'm not interested in why you made a bollocks of it, I just want to know what you're going to do about it.'

The Traveller unlocked the Merc and got in. 'I'm going to kill the hairy-lipped wee fucker, that's what.'

'Make sure you do it today,' Orla said. 'Things are moving along, now. There'll be a development within the next forty-eight hours, and you better be ready to do the needful.'

'What sort of development?' the Traveller asked.

'You'll know soon enough. Now for Christ's sake, sort Patsy Toner out. And just to make life a little easier for you, I'm going to tell you where to find him.'

33

'The Sydenham International,' Patsy Toner said.
'By the City Airport?' Lennon asked.
'That's it,' Toner said.
'Give me half an hour,' Lennon said.

★ ★ ★

The Sydenham International Hotel hadn't aged well. It hadn't been able to keep up with the wave of shiny new establishments that had mushroomed all over Belfast during the last few years, and its days were surely numbered now there were some decent hotels by the airport.

Lennon entered the dowdy reception area. The owners had done their best to spruce the place up, but failed. He peered into the dimly lit bar and saw Toner hunched over a glass in the darkest corner. Lennon took his time, let the lawyer sweat. He got himself a pint of Stella at the bar. The barmaid, who was just a little too old for her exposed bellybutton ring and fake tan, didn't return his smile.

He crossed to Toner's table. The lawyer had dark rings under his eyes and a sour odour about him. 'What's up?' Lennon asked.

'I need a smoke,' Toner said. Lennon followed him out through a pair of patio doors to what passed for a beer garden: a patch of potholed tarmac and a couple of picnic tables with tattered parasols, along with a few buckets of sand for cigarette ends.

Toner placed his drink on a table and sat on the attached bench. He took a packet of Embassy Regal out of his pocket and offered one to Lennon. Lennon rarely smoked, even when he drank, but he took one just to get the lawyer on his side. He sat down opposite.

Toner sparked up with a cheap lighter and did the same for Lennon, smoke clouding the space between them. Lennon noticed Toner's left hand again; waxy and thin, like it had been locked in a cast, the muscles atrophied.

'Someone tried to kill me last night,' the lawyer said.

'I know,' Lennon said.

'At my flat,' Toner said, his hands and voice shaking. 'Someone tried to shoot me.'

'I know,' Lennon said again, but this time it was a lie. He had guessed as much about the attempt from what Hewitt had told him, but he didn't know about any shooting.

'You ever had a gun pointed at you?' Toner asked. 'You ever been shot at?'

'Yes,' Lennon said. 'A few times. But then you should know that, shouldn't you, Patsy?'

'What?'

Lennon inhaled nicotine, let it sizzle through his brain. 'Years ago, I was only a few months on the job, still a probationer.' He exhaled a thin wisp of blue, wishing Toner smoked something heavier, like Marlboros or Camels. 'Before the ceasefires. I was on a patrol in the city centre, just off Royal Avenue. Some of your lot ambushed us. Two of my friends died. I took a bullet in the shoulder, just under the armoured vest.'

'My lot?' Toner smiled under his moustache. 'Nobody's my lot. Not any more.'

'Well, back then they were. Three boys were lifted for it within twenty-four hours. I was there to testify on the first day of the trial, but I never got a chance. You had the case thrown out on a technicality. The searches weren't sound, so that was that. Two decent young men dead, I get a nice big scar to show for it, and three pieces of shit walk free. They probably killed again. How much did you make out of that case?'

'I remember you now,' Toner said. 'You got a commendation or something for that, didn't you? There was another survivor. You saved him.'

'A medal,' Lennon said.

Toner smirked. 'You wear it much?'

'I never collected it.'

'Why not?'

Lennon took another hit of the cigarette, winced at the hot gravel in his throat. 'Didn't feel like it,' he said. 'So tell me about last night.'

Toner told Lennon about walking back to his shitty flat, approaching his front door, seeing the man in the old Mercedes estate dousing his face with water, and just knowing.

'Knowing what?' Lennon asked.

'That he was there to kill me,' Toner said, suddenly looking even smaller. 'So I ran like fuck. Into the building, up the stairs, into my flat, and out the back down the fire escape. I kept thinking, Jesus, if there's another one round the back, I'm fucked. But there wasn't. There was just him.'

'Who was he?'

'I don't know,' Toner said.

'Did you get a look at him?'

Toner shook his head.

'Who do you think sent him?'

Toner sighed as his eyes went distant and watery. 'I'm going to tell you this because I've got to tell somebody before I go off my head. It's been eating away at me for months. I've been scared shitless.' The lawyer's voice rose to a whine. 'I can't eat. I have to drink myself unconscious just so I can get some sleep. I wake up every morning and first thing I do is puke.

'I kept telling myself it was over and done with, all settled, all swept under the carpet. But I knew. I knew someone would come for me. And then I heard about Kevin Malloy, so it was just a matter of when. I knew they wouldn't let me go.'

'Who's they?' Lennon asked.

'They?' Toner gave a short, sharp laugh that choked in his throat. ' 'They' is fucking everyone. The cops, the Brits, the Irish government, the party, fucking Bull O'Kane.'

Lennon eyed Toner, wondered if he *had* lost it. 'That's a lot of people,' he said.

'Collusion,' Toner said, his voice dropping to a low, angry hiss. 'Everyone talks about collusion, how the cops and the Brits and the Loyalists were in it together. To hear some people talk, you'd think the Loyalists couldn't take a shit without MI5 or Special Branch wiping their arses for them.'

Lennon laughed. 'Look, I know about the Loyalists. Everybody knows — '

'Everybody knows it all, but no one says anything. Look, collusion worked all ways, all directions. Between the Brits and the Loyalists, between the Irish government and the Republicans, between the Republicans and the Brits, between the Loyalists and the Republicans.' Toner ran out of breath and his face reddened. He pulled hard on his cigarette and coughed. 'All ways, all directions. We'll never know how far it went. All the small things, all the big things. Loyalists supplying Republicans with fake DVDs and Ecstasy tablets. Republicans wholesaling laundered diesel and bootleg vodka to Loyalists. Feeding off the hate, letting on they're fighting for their fucking causes when all the time they're making each other rich. And the killings. How many of our own did we set up for the Loyalists to take out? How many of their own did the Loyalists set up for us? How many times did I get a taxi to some club or other on the Shankill with a name in an envelope, and two days later, some poor cunt from the Falls gets his head took off?'

'I don't understand,' Lennon said. 'What's all this got to do with someone having a crack at you last night?'

'Paul McGinty,' Toner said. He raised his waxy hand to count on his fingers. 'Michael McKenna, Vincie Caffola, Father Coulter, that cop who got shot in my car.'

Lennon's chest tightened at McKenna's name. He smelled blood, followed the scent. 'The feud.

I read the inquiry report. Some Scottish guy, an ex-soldier, was in the middle of it all. He stabbed the priest. He wound up dead in the shootout near Middletown, along with McGinty.'

'Davy Campbell,' Toner said. 'He was an agent.'

'An agent? How do you know that?'

Toner stared hard at Lennon as he ground his cigarette into the tabletop. 'Because I got him in.'

Lennon felt the heat of his own cigarette as it burned closer to his fingers. 'What, you mean — '

'Yeah, I was a tout. I fed information about McGinty to MI5. They passed it on to Special Branch and Fourteen Intelligence Company, and anyone else they felt like sharing with. Like I said, collusion goes all ways, all directions.'

'All right,' Lennon said. He dropped the cigarette to the ground and crushed it beneath his heel. 'So tell me what really happened.'

Toner let a long sigh out, his small chest deflating. He took another cigarette from the packet, didn't offer one to Lennon, and started talking.

34

The Traveller recognised the cop's Audi in the hotel car park. 'Fuck,' he said.

He steered the big Mercedes around the scruffy quadrangle of potholed tarmac until he found a spot behind a van. It would obscure him from the Audi's position, but he could still see the car park's exit. He'd be able to see the cop leave, and then he could go in after Toner. Room 203, Orla had said.

He lowered the driver's side window a couple of inches. The breeze had started to cool as late afternoon approached. It felt good on his stinging eye. He adjusted his position so his bad shoulder didn't rest against the seat back.

The cop troubled him. Christ knew what that little shite Toner was telling him in there. Had he got a good look at the Traveller the night before? Would Toner be able to give the cop a description? And if he could, would the cop make the connection with the man he'd seen on Eglantine Avenue earlier in the day?

The Traveller made his mind up. He didn't care what Bull O'Kane had to say about it, he would take care of the cop when the job was done. As soon as he'd mopped up O'Kane's unholy fucking mess, he'd indulge himself by breaking the cop's neck.

Yes, that was how he'd do it. The cop was a big fucker, wide through the shoulders where the

Traveller was narrow, but he reckoned if he could get him pinned, get a knee in his broad back — yes, a good grip, a good pull and a twist.

The Traveller ran the tip of his tongue across his upper lip. Suddenly he thought of Sofia, the scent of her, the softness of her buttocks and her belly. He shifted in the seat, his jeans pinching at him. The movement aggravated his shoulder, and he winced. The wince aggravated his eye, and he hissed through his teeth.

Sofia. Jesus, she was a good ride. He'd had his share of women, some he remembered, more he didn't. But she was the best of them. There had never been that heat, that *scalding* heat, with anyone else. It burned his skin where it touched hers when he buried his face between her shoulder and her neck, the two of them shuddering together.

The Traveller decided there and then on another indulgence: after breaking the cop's neck, he'd give Sofia a baby. When he was done here, and everyone who needed killed was dead, he'd go back to Sofia, throw her down on the bed, and tell her he was going to give her the child she'd wanted from her dead husband. After she'd caught pregnant, he'd never see her again. No sense in getting tied to a woman and a kid like that; he'd just give her what she wanted then leave her to get on with it.

So that was that. Break the cop's neck. Give Sofia a baby. Simple, but then the Traveller had never found life complicated. He remembered his mother gathering him to her one day when he was a teenager, kissing the top of his head, saying, 'Ah, son, you'll always land on your feet. Just stumble on through. The devil looks after his own.'

And she was right. Even now, he couldn't fathom why he'd taken a notion one day, left his mother's home, got on a boat and crossed the Irish Sea. He'd wandered around Liverpool for a month, walking from one construction site to another looking for work, like generations of Irishmen had done before him. He'd eked out an existence for thirty days before finding himself in front of an army recruiting office.

He stood on the pavement looking up at the sign, at the posters in the window. He could no longer visualise the words, but he remembered the pictures. Young men in uniforms in exotic places, holding guns, climbing things, fixing things, driving things. The recruiting officer shook his hand, talked to him like a man.

A few months later, when he was still eighteen, he found himself in some fucking miserable place, one of those communist countries that had fallen apart, trying to protect processions of old women and little children as they trudged along mud roads, away from the massacres in their towns and villages. Made all that shit in Northern Ireland look like the kid stuff it was.

He'd had no stomach for the North and all its squabbling since then. Bunch of fucking selfish, childish, spoilt whiners who pissed and moaned and started throwing bricks when they couldn't get their own way. Every time he saw some politician or other on the telly slabbering 'cause the other side got a better deal, the Traveller wished he could drag them by the hair to some village whose name he couldn't pronounce and show them the babies torn in half by shrapnel, or a young mother raped and gutted because she was the wrong sort, her children left screaming at the memory of it for the rest of their miserable lives.

The Traveller would grab the politician by the throat, make the lying bastard look at it, make them see it all, and say, 'There, now that's a conflict. That's a war. That's hatred. That's fear. That's blood. That's brutality. That's killing for the sake of it. Look at it.'

He checked himself in the rear-view mirror. 'Stop it,' he said. 'Just fucking quit it. Save it for Patsy Toner.'

The anger. Yet another symptom of losing a bit of your brain: a quick and violent temper. The Traveller breathed deep and pushed the rage back down to his gut where it belonged. He had to keep it in check, channel it, use it, not let it use him. There had been times, years ago, when he let it get the better of him. His vision would turn to a long red funnel, and some poor bastard's brains would be spilled across a pavement, or their throat would be ripped open by a shard of glass. Not any more. He had learned to control it, keep it in his belly like a battery stores power. When he needed it, he could switch it on, just for a moment, just long enough to do the awful things that paid so well.

After a while it felt like nothing, as if taking a life was like taking a breath. Somewhere inside of him, in some deep unreachable place, the

Traveller knew he was unwell. That was why he didn't like doctors. He imagined they could see that dark spot on his heart, that black place where his rage kept his conscience prisoner, muted, sedated, anaesthetised, bound up by tangled images of children's torsos stacked in piles, flies picking over the meat, the blood sticky beneath his boots, the stench punching him in the —

'Fucking quit it,' he said to the mirror. He brought his fingers to his bad eye and rubbed it hard.

The bright, scorching pain blasted all thought away. He gritted his teeth and swallowed a scream. A warm, thick wetness rolled down his cheek. He wiped it with his sleeve, looked at the thin streaks of yellow on the material.

'Fuck,' he said.

He got hold of himself just in time to hear the coarse bark and clatter of a diesel engine starting up. Was it the cop? The Traveller listened to the engine grumble as he watched the gate beyond the van, blinking away the blurring in his right eye.

There it was, the Audi, the big cop's head just visible through the tinted glass. It pulled out into the traffic and disappeared from view.

The Traveller inhaled cool air through his nose, let it out through his mouth. The rage was barely contained, like a blister beneath his skin, ready to burst. It would be bad for Patsy Toner.

35

Lennon shook as he drove. As soon as he pulled onto the Sydenham bypass, he regretted it. His chest heaved and hammered, his palms slicked the Audi's leather steering wheel. He needed to pull over, get his head clear. Without thinking, he took the Bridge End exit and headed south.

Images and sensations flickered across his mind, but he couldn't grasp them. As the old Sirocco Works factory site, now an expanse of wasteland, passed on his right, he turned left. Republican murals everywhere, fallen martyrs twenty feet high to tell both locals and passers-by who owned these streets. He met the peace wall, the most inappropriately named of constructions, a barrier of brick and wire standing thirty feet high, slicing the community across its belly. He followed it as far as he could before dead ends and junctions forced him to a quiet street where no one walked. He pulled to the kerb, the Audi's tyres crunching on litter and broken glass.

As the engine died, he looked around him. The peace wall stood to his right, to the west, making the houses feel like barracks in a prison camp. Coats of red, white and blue paint had chipped and faded from the paving stones. The remaining rags of a Union Jack fluttered from a flag pole. The red-brick buildings had shuttered windows and doors, their eyes and mouths sealed shut by steel, blinded and muted by . . . what?

Lennon looked up and down the road, and then he realised. This was just one of many abandoned streets, deserted by fleeing residents who could no longer stand the running battles, the showers of bricks and bottles, the petrol bombs setting light to their roofs. One by one, on each side of the peace wall, the families moved out, piling mattresses and good tables and old mirrors that once belonged to grandmothers into hastily borrowed vans or trailers.

Did anyone live here now? He searched for signs of someone, anyone, making a life on this street. Not a soul. Less than a mile away, millions were being pumped into brownfield sites, building apartments, shopping centres, technology parks. Just across the river, property was changing hands for prices never imagined only a few years before. One-bedroom flats sold for a quarter of a million, snapped up by investors looking to make a killing out of Belfast's peace boom, desperate to get rich before the bubble burst as it surely would. And here, not ten minutes away, stood two rows of empty houses with generations of memories rotting away along with the mortar and woodwork, all because small-minded thugs couldn't see beyond the world of *Them* and *Us*.

Nausea gripped Lennon's stomach, turned and kneaded it. He pushed the car's door open and leaned out, breathing hard, swallowing bile.

'Jesus,' he said. His voice sounded hollow in this lost place.

Lennon spat on the pavement. The day's warmth faded fast. The air cooled his skin. He smelled smoke, a fire burning somewhere, old wood and tyres.

Patsy Toner said Marie and Ellen were there.

In the middle of the killing, on an old farm near Middletown, Marie McKenna and Lennon's daughter. They had survived, fled the country, but what had they seen? What had Ellen seen? He coughed and spat.

He tried to replay the conversation, to put the events in order. Once Toner had got going, he had recited them in a kind of monotone, as if he'd recounted the story to himself so many times the words had lost all meaning. A madman, a killer, cutting down Paul McGinty's faction, body upon body. At times Lennon had wanted to grab him, shake him, tell him to stop.

Lennon knew some of the names: Vincie Caffola was pure thug, Father Eammon Coulter an apologist for murderers, Brian Anderson a disgraced cop — the papers were full of stories of the backhanders he'd taken, the colleagues he'd sold out, after his killing. And Paul McGinty was the worst type of politician, just two steps from the gutter. A gangster who fancied himself as a statesman, a working-class hero, rather than the money-grubbing, power-hungry parasite he really was. Politics was simply a way to put a respectable face on his greed.

And Toner had confirmed it: it all started with Michael McKenna, Marie McKenna's uncle.

Marie had kept her background from Lennon when they first met, but she couldn't hide it for long. She had told him over dinner, tried to play it like it was nothing, as if her father and uncle's past had nothing to do with her present. But she was smarter than that. He could see it in her face as she spoke. She knew what it could mean for Lennon and his career, associating with the niece of a known paramilitary godfather, the daughter of his brother and lackey. She knew he would be compromised, his loyalty suspect, particularly given his own background.

The look on her face said: Here's your get-out. Leave now, with your dignity intact, no harm done, no foul.

Lennon stuck with her. Looking back, he sometimes wondered why, but really, he knew. He was getting tired, his early thirties nudging his mid-thirties, forty looming on the horizon. He'd started to feel old when he trawled the bars, the women looking younger and younger until they seemed mere girls, and the pursuit grew uglier by the night.

When things began to unravel, his great mistake was to tell Wendy about it. She had never given him a chance when they were both single, but when she saw him in a real relationship with another woman, saw that he could make it work, that changed. Her friendly interest in his love life, her fond wishes for his happiness, turned to flirting and questions he wasn't entirely comfortable with. When he told her how Marie's nesting instinct had started to grind on him, how he no longer felt in control of

212

his own life, Wendy's eyes glittered. She began to sit closer, her thigh brushing against his more often, her hand resting on his forearm for longer.

Night after night, as he lay listening to Marie's shallow breathing, he fought to keep his mind away from the sensation of Wendy's hand on his skin, to stop imagining the softness of her lips. He questioned himself in the sleepless hours. *Is this what I want? Is this, a life with Marie, what I really want?* The same answer came to him every time.

It's what I've got.

Lennon and Marie made love once more before it ended. He had been adrift for days, unable to tell her what kept him from sleep, even though she knew something was badly wrong. That evening they lay together, his head on her breast, desperately hoping her warm flesh would soothe him into reason. They moved together slowly, easily, just as they had done hundreds of times before. Her hands found him as he kissed her, pushing aside fabric. He slipped off her nightdress as she writhed beneath him. He entered her and they established the calm rhythm of familiarity. As his climax approached he tried not to imagine Wendy's body moving like that, her eyes closed, her mouth open to him. He buried his face in Marie's shoulder to block it out.

They said nothing, lying there, holding each other. When they separated he saw she was crying. With his fingertip he traced the path the tears had taken.

'What?' he asked.

'Nothing,' she said. 'We proved the point, didn't we?'

'What point?'

She got out of bed and wrapped herself in her dressing gown. 'That we can go through the motions when we have to.'

He watched her leave for the bathroom and felt suddenly ashamed to be naked.

★　★　★

It had been a grey day, cold outside, half-hearted raindrops on the window. Six weeks gone, she told him. Maybe this would bring them back together, she said. Maybe this would heal the rift that had grown between them. He had smiled and took her in his arms, told her everything would be all right, even as the panic bloomed in his gut.

He could no more be a father than he could a surgeon or a priest. He would fail. He would let his child down, just like his own father had. Still, he held Marie close, his soul crumbling as he lied to her.

★　★　★

Lennon stirred and remembered where he was. A breeze leaked in through the Audi's open door, cool air exploring a deserted street. Something snagged his attention, a movement at the periphery of his vision. He turned his head and saw an old Peugeot 306 pull in to the kerb in front of his car. Its engine grunted and wheezed, struggling to cope with the power forced upon it by boy-racer modifications. Its suspension had been lowered, alloy wheels and low-profile tyres fitted. Its rear windows were blacked out and a dark band obscured almost half of the front windscreen. Lennon could make out three forms inside, all wearing Rangers football shirts.

He considered easing his legs back into the Audi, pulling his door shut. His anger wouldn't let him. He watched the three of them climb out of the Peugeot. They wore trainers and tracksuit bottoms, just like the boy whose body Lennon had inspected in a backyard less than a mile from this spot. But that might as well have been a different planet; in life, that boy was as alien to these youths as prey is to a spider, even though they dressed and spoke the same. Just different coloured shirts, that was all.

The driver was the leader. Lennon watched him closest of all.

''Bout ya,' the driver said.

His friends flanked the Audi, eyeing it as they passed on either side.

Lennon said nothing.

'You lost?' the driver asked.

'No,' Lennon said.

'What you doing here?'

'Nothing much,' Lennon said.

The driver's friends reached the Audi's rear. One of them leaned on the boot, ran his hands along the back, looking for the release to open it.

'Where you from?' the driver asked.

'Somewhere else,' Lennon said. 'Tell your

mate to take his hands off my car or I'll break his fucking face.'

'What?'

'You heard me.'

The driver snorted. 'Here, Darren? C'mere!'

Lennon let one hand slip inside his jacket, released the catch.

Darren lumbered around from the back of the Audi. He was tall and heavy-set, with red cheeks beneath pig-like eyes and a blond crew cut. 'What?'

The driver pointed at Lennon. 'He says he's going to break your face if you don't leave his motor alone.'

Darren put a hand on the Audi's roof and leaned down to Lennon, his breath smelling of the cheap fortified wine all these toe-rags drank. 'You what?'

'Get your dirty hands off my car or I'll kick your face in,' Lennon said. 'You and your mates. Now fuck off.'

'*Your* car?' Darren asked. He pulled a knife from his pocket. 'This is *my* car. Now get the fuck out of it.'

In one smooth motion, Lennon seized Darren's wrist with his left hand and pressed the Glock 17 beneath his chin, the Glock 17 that had been in his right hand since the driver had first called his friend over.

'Drop the knife, you stupid fat fucker,' Lennon said.

Warm liquid splashed on Lennon's ankles as a dark stain spread on Darren's tracksuit bottoms. The knife clanked on the kerb and disappeared

216

beneath the Audi. The driver sprinted for the Peugeot. The third youth called after him, 'What? What's wrong?'

The Peugeot's overburdened engine coughed into life, and its tyres screeched as they fought to put the power down on the road. It roared away from the kerb, barely missing the Audi. Lennon followed it with his eyes until it disappeared around the corner.

Darren cried. The other youth came closer, saw the pistol, and ran like hell.

'Just you and me, then, Darren,' Lennon said.

Darren whimpered. He smelled of stale sweat and fresh urine.

'You and your mates,' Lennon said. 'I suppose you'd call yourselves Loyalists, right?'

Darren didn't answer. Lennon pressed the Glock's muzzle harder into the loose flesh beneath his chin.

'Answer me.'

'Yeah,' Darren said.

'Funny, that,' Lennon said. 'Your mates don't seem too loyal. Tell me, who are *you* loyal to?'

Darren's nose dripped snot on Lennon's sleeve. Lennon pushed the muzzle deeper into his flesh until the pressure against his windpipe made the stocky kid cough.

'Answer me.'

'Don't know,' Darren said, his voice a watery croak.

'Are you loyal to your friends? Your family? Your neighbours?'

'Don't know,' Darren said.

'Shit-bags like you,' Lennon said. 'You steal off

your own people, you intimidate them, you keep them quiet with your threats and all this bullyboy shit. You don't give a fuck about anything but trying to be the big men, lining your pockets, leeching off your own community. And you can call yourselves Loyalists because the arse-wipes who should be keeping you in line haven't got the brains or the balls to do it. And people wonder why the Republicans ran rings around your lot all these years.'

'Please,' Darren whined.

'Please what?'

'Please don't shoot me.'

Pity and contempt and anger fought one another in Lennon's gut. 'Give me one good reason.'

Darren's mouth opened and closed as he searched for something that could save his life. 'I'm . . . I'm sorry,' he said, his face contorting like a child desperate to escape punishment.

'Sorry for what?' Lennon asked.

'Don't know,' Darren said.

Lennon's laughter died in his mouth, dry like paper. 'Cunts like you made sure there was no one left around here to go to the cops, to speak up. No one sees anything, no one hears anything. You know what that means?'

Darren shook his head as best he could. His trembling grew to a crescendo, his weight pressing harder against Lennon's grip. His legs would go soon, Lennon could sense it.

'It means I could blow what little brains you have all over that wall, and no fucker would know a thing about it. Nobody to hear it, nobody to see it. And do you think your mates would stick their necks out and go to the cops?'

Darren sniffed a line of snot back up his nose. 'No,' he said. His weight shifted forward, and Lennon pushed him back.

'Get the fuck out of here.'

Darren stumbled backwards until he hit the wall. He stared at Lennon, his chest heaving, his eyes wide.

'Go on, fuck off,' Lennon said as he tucked the Glock away.

Darren retreated, shambling at first, then gathering speed. When he was ten feet away, he put his head down and sprinted as fast as his bulk would allow. He didn't get far before he tripped and landed face first on the pavement. Lennon grimaced as the boy puked. Darren picked himself up and lurched off again.

'Arsehole,' Lennon whispered to himself as the boy rounded the corner. 'Fucking stupid arsehole.'

He couldn't be sure if he meant himself or Darren.

36

The Traveller shut off the taps when the water reached the overflow. Its surface rippled as the last drops hit. He dipped his hand below the surface. Cold. He stood up from the edge of the bathtub and turned out the light. There was just enough room behind the door for him to stand unseen.

How long could he stand in one place? The longest had been almost four hours, in the corner of an accountant's office. He didn't even have to touch the poor fucker; the accountant keeled over, his heart stopped dead in his chest, at the sight of the Traveller rushing at him from out of the shadow. Easy kill, but the waiting had been a bastard.

Could he wait more than four hours, standing still? He thought so. He rarely got bored. He wasn't much of a thinker, but still, his mind could amuse itself for a long, long time. He could remember people he'd known, some he'd fucked, some he'd killed. He could think of Sofia and the baby he planned to give her.

Instead, he thought about Gerry Fegan. The Bull had shown him a photograph. Fegan was thin and wiry, like the Traveller, with a hard, pointed face. He wondered how many Fegan had killed. There were the twelve he'd been put away for, and then that spree a few months ago. How many had that been? Four in the city, then two on the farm near Middletown — a British agent and the politician Paul McGinty. That made eighteen. The Traveller had killed twice as many, and more.

Was he afraid of Fegan? Probably, but that was no bad thing. Orla O'Kane blustered about her father being scared of no man, except the great Gerry Fegan, but the Traveller knew it was just that: bluster. The man who feared nothing was the man looking to get himself killed. It was what you did with your fear that really counted. The Traveller turned his to anger and hate, things he could use to get the job done. And the job was more important than anything.

The Traveller closed his eyes, steadied his breathing, and waited.

* * *

An hour, maybe a little more, passed before he heard the bleep of the keycard in the slot, followed by the clunk of the lock opening. He listened hard, pictured Patsy Toner entering and closing the door behind him.

The little lawyer breathed hard as he crossed the room, his feet dragging on the cheap carpet. The Traveller heard the rustling of fabric as he removed clothing, probably his jacket, then the thumps of his shoes being kicked off. The mattress groaned. A lighter sparked, air was sucked in and blown out. A few moments later, the Traveller caught the bitter stink of a cigarette. Then sobbing, dry and pitiful, the sound of the wounded and dying. The Traveller knew it well.

221

A deep, wet sniff, and then a cough. The creak of weight lifting from the mattress, the padding of socked feet on carpet.

The bathroom light clicked on, and the Traveller squinted. From behind the open door, he heard the toilet lid lift, and Toner's fly opening. He'd let the poor shite finish pissing before he moved, let him get his cock put away.

'C'mon, c'mon, c'mon,' Toner whispered to himself before he was rewarded with the thunder of water on water. He sighed, the sound of it hollow against the bathroom's tiles. The Traveller smelled a sour blend of alcohol and tobacco. He listened to the last drops, then the rustling of fabric, the fly closing, and the toilet flush.

Then a pause, followed by, 'What the fuck?'

The Traveller gently, quietly pushed the door back.

Patsy Toner stared down at the bathtub full of water, his drunken eyes blinking as if it would make sense if he only tried a little harder. He turned his head and he saw the Traveller watching.

'No,' Patsy Toner said, his voice so small it was almost lost beneath the noise of the cistern filling.

The Traveller let the anger and hate take control, let it push him forward, took his speed from it. Toner barely had time to raise his hands and grab the breath for a scream that never came. It died in his throat as the Traveller slammed his forehead into the mirror above the bath, leaving a bloody star on the cracked surface. Pieces of reflective glass dropped into the water, turning through the swirls of red.

Toner's legs left him, and the Traveller let the lawyer's weight pull him head first into the water. He gripped the back of Toner's neck with one hand, his wrist with the other.

Nothing happened for a while, just spidery threads of crimson spreading out and dissolving among the bubbles.

Then Toner jerked.

Then Toner bucked.

Then Toner screamed beneath the water.

37

'Bonjou, Gerry,' Pyè said.

Fegan put his half-eaten slice of toast back on the plate. Pyè slid into the booth beside him. The Doyles' driver took a stool at the counter. It was early; only two others ate in the diner. A waitress dozed at a table.

'You a bad man.' Pyè wagged a finger at Fegan. 'Real bad man. Ou moun fou, a crazy motherfucker. Doyles, they tell me all evil shit you do. You malad, in head.' Pyè tapped his temple with his forefinger.

Fegan wiped his mouth with a napkin. 'So what now?'

'You come with mwen,' Pyè said. 'Go see Doyles. They waiting in machin la.' He jerked his thumb at the car idling outside, its windows darkened.

Pyè slid out of the booth and put his hand on Fegan's shoulder. 'Come, Gerry.'

Fegan put the napkin on his plate and pushed it away. 'I'll kill you all if I have to,' he said.

Pyè smiled. 'Maybe,' he said. 'Maybe not. Come.'

Fegan followed him out to the car, the driver coming behind. Pyè stopped and put a hand on Fegan's chest. He slipped his hands around Fegan's torso, feeling under his arms and behind his back.

'I'm not armed,' Fegan said. He'd left the gun

224

he'd seized in the alleyway back at the motel.

'Mwen look anyways,' Pyè said.

He crouched and ran his hands up and down Fegan's legs before dipping into his pockets. He found a wallet first, and then the mobile phone.

'Don't,' Fegan said.

'Don't what?'

'My phone,' Fegan said. 'I need it.'

Pyè laughed. 'You need anyen, Gerry.'

'What?'

'You need nothing.' Pyè dropped the phone to the ground. It bounced and rattled. Its screen fractured.

'Don't,' Fegan said.

Pyè raised his foot, ready to bring it down on the phone. Fegan formed his knuckles into a sharp line and stabbed at his Adam's apple. Pyè fell against the car and crumpled to the ground, coughing, his eyes wide.

'I said don't.'

Pyè blinked and gasped as he tried to get his feet under him. A thick-fingered hand grabbed Fegan's shoulder, tried to turn him around. Fegan grabbed the wrist with his left hand, turned inside the big man's reach, felt the nose crunch against his elbow, a warm spatter on his face as the blood came. Two more blows and the driver went down, cracked the back of his head on the ground.

Fegan turned back to Pyè. The Haitian gasped as his trachea swelled from the blow, his feet scrambling for purchase.

'Stay down,' Fegan said.

Pyè reached behind his back, grasping for

something. He got one foot under him, began to rise. Fegan's foot connected with his jaw, and Pyè sprawled in the gutter between the car and the pavement, a pistol clattering at his side.

Fegan picked up his phone, turned it in his hands, looked at the cracked screen, put it in his pocket along with his wallet. He reached for the gun, a semi-automatic. He aimed at the darkened rear window. 'Open it,' he said.

Nothing.

Fegan stepped closer and tapped the glass with the pistol's muzzle. 'Open it,' he said.

The vague forms of two men sat still inside.

Fegan struck the glass with the butt of the gun. It held. Two more blows and it shattered, fragments peppering the two men inside.

Frankie and Packie Doyle stared back at Fegan, their hands raised.

'Leave me alone,' Fegan said. 'If you come after me again, I'll kill you both. Do you understand?'

The Doyles sat frozen.

Fegan pressed the muzzle against Packie Doyle's cheek. 'Do you understand?'

Packie nodded. Frankie said, 'Yes.'

'Get Pyè to a hospital,' Fegan said. 'He might die. Do you understand?'

Frankie nodded. Packie said, 'Yes.'

'Good,' Fegan said. He tucked the pistol into his pocket alongside the phone as he walked away.

38

'Get out of here,' DCI Gordon said.

'No,' Lennon said. 'I want to examine the scene.'

'Scene?' Gordon said, blocking the doorway. 'There's no scene. It was an accident. He was drunk, he slipped and cracked his head open.'

Hotel guests hovered in the corridor, watching the comings and goings of paramedics and police.

'Someone tried to kill him two days ago,' Lennon said.

'Rubbish,' Gordon said. 'A woman was assaulted in his building. It had nothing to do with him. A coincidence.'

'Someone came to get him. He told me,' Lennon said. 'He saw them.'

'He told you?'

'Yesterday.'

'Where?'

'Here,' Lennon said. 'Downstairs, in the beer garden. He called my mobile, said he needed to talk to me. He was scared shitless.'

'Was he drinking?'

'Yes.'

'There you are, then,' Gordon said. 'He was drunk, slipped, that's all there is to it.'

Lennon stared at Gordon, tried to read the lines of his face. 'You know that's not true.'

'Easy, son.'

'You know there's more to it,' Lennon said. 'We know there was a threat against him, that he

227

was scared of someone. You can't pretend — '

'Shut up,' Gordon said.

'You can't — '

'Shut your mouth.' Gordon grabbed Lennon's sleeve and pulled him along the corridor until they reached a quiet corner by the fire exit. He put a hand on Lennon's chest and pressed him against the wall.

'Now, listen to me, son, your career depends on it.' Gordon looked along the corridor for eavesdroppers, then back to Lennon. 'Mr Toner was of interest to Special Branch. When someone is of interest to Special Branch, they call the shots. Their officers have already inspected the scene and declared it an accident. And you know what that means?'

'What?'

'That means it was an accident. No matter what you think, no matter what I think, it was an accident. End of story.'

'For Christ's sake, I can't — '

'Leave it alone, son,' Gordon said, prodding Lennon's chest with his finger. 'What in the name of God were you doing talking to Toner in the first place? First you were harassing that landlord on Wellesley Avenue, then — '

'I wasn't harassing anyone, I just — '

Gordon pushed him, hard. 'Shut your bloody mouth. You're on thin ice here as it is. Don't make it any worse. Keep quiet about talking to Toner. Don't mention it to anyone. If Dan Hewitt or anyone else in Special Branch gets wind of it, you'll be out on your arse. You don't mess about with those boys, you don't get in their way, and

228

you don't step on their toes. Do you hear me?'

Lennon breathed deep to quash his anger.

Gordon said, 'Do you hear me?'

Lennon closed his eyes, clenched his fists. He opened his eyes again and stared hard at Gordon. 'I hear you.'

'Good.' Gordon stepped back and straightened his tie. 'Now listen, you need to head back to Ladas Drive. There's real work to do, no more of this pissing about.'

'What sort of work?'

'I need you to prep an interview for me.'

'An interview? Who?'

'The other kid,' Gordon said. 'I got the call just before you arrived.'

'What other kid?'

'He handed himself in this morning,' Gordon said, smiling. 'The other kid who was at Declan Quigley's house the night he was killed. The one we've been looking for. I need you to pull together all the notes, all the photographs, everything we've got on the Quigley killing. I want pictures of his mate with his neck broken, that knife in his hand. I'll be done here in an hour, and I want it all waiting for me when I interview him. I want to wave those photos under his nose, scare the living daylights out of him. I want a confession before the end of the day. So, what are you waiting for? Get going.'

★   ★   ★

Lennon put pages and photos together into piles on Gordon's desk, the pictures on one side, the

229

notes on the other. The photograph of Brendan Houlihan lay on top, the boy staring back at him with dead eyes. His hand lay at his side, tucked beneath his thigh, a blade just visible between his fingers and the fabric of his tracksuit bottoms. The dirt on his other side, where it shouldn't have been.

'Too easy,' Lennon said.

He stood there, his eyes closed, running it over in his head. No, it was a stupid idea, he'd be in deep shit. He lifted the desk phone anyway, dialled the duty officer.

'Is the kid in the interview room yet?' he asked.

'Yes,' the duty officer said. 'The solicitor just arrived to look after him. They're ready to go as soon as DCI Gordon gets back.'

'No,' Lennon said. 'DCI Gordon just called me.'

'Did he? I didn't put him — '

'On my mobile. He's been held up. I've to go ahead with the interview.'

The duty officer remained silent for a few seconds, then said, 'And?'

'And that's all.' Lennon fought the quiver in his voice. 'I'm doing the interview.'

'Knock yourself out,' the duty officer said, and the line clicked dead in Lennon's ear.

* * *

Colm Devine, eighteen, pale and terrified. He fiddled with the discarded cellophane wrapping from the cassette tape he'd just inspected in an

230

effort to hide the trembling. He failed. Edwin Speers, the duty solicitor, sat beside him. He looked bored.

Lennon peeled the cellophane from the second cassette case, took the tape from the box, and inserted it in the recorder. He hit record, and the twin decks whirred.

Devine stared at the tabletop as Lennon went through the formalities of rights and warnings required for an interview under caution. The solicitor picked dirt from beneath his fingernails.

Lennon took a pen, ready to make notes. 'You know why you're here, Colm.'

Devine croaked, tried again. 'Yeah,' he said.

'Then you know how serious this is.'

'Yeah,' Devine said.

'You were a friend of Brendan Houlihan, who was found dead at the scene of a murder of another man, Declan Quigley, three nights ago.'

'Yeah,' Devine said.

'Were you with Brendan Houlihan on the night he died?'

Devine hesitated. Speers put a hand on his skinny forearm. 'No comment,' Devine said.

Lennon glanced at the solicitor.

'When was the last time you saw Brendan Houlihan?'

'No comment,' Devine said.

'Were you with a group of youths who were involved in a fight at the intersection of the Lower Ormeau Road and Donegall Pass on the night Brendan Houlihan died?'

'No comment,' Devine said.

Lennon put the pen down. 'Colm, did Mr

231

Speers here tell you to say 'no comment' to everything?'

Devine swallowed. 'No comment.'

Lennon stared hard at Speers. 'I'm guessing he did. Do you know why he did that?'

Speers coughed and fidgeted.

'He did that because he's the duty solicitor. A duty solicitor is only here to fill that chair and hopefully keep you from doing something stupid. In reality, he knows if you wind up in front of a judge, it'll be with a different solicitor, someone who actually knows what they're doing, who actually cares about your rights.'

Speers stiffened. 'Here, now — '

'When you're in court, you'll look as guilty as sin because you clammed up now. Mr Speers wants out of here so he can go for lunch, or a round of golf, or whatever he has to do that's more interesting than babysitting you. If you sit there and say 'no comment' to everything, he's on his way quicker and you think you haven't said anything to incriminate yourself.'

Speers wagged a finger. 'Listen, I won't sit here and — '

'Problem is, Colm, that thing I said earlier about not saying something you later rely on in court? That's the truth. You sit here now and say nothing but 'no comment', it makes you look guilty. I'll think you're hiding something, and so will a judge, and so will a jury. This isn't shoplifting we're talking about, Colm. It's not stealing a car, or even punching some poor bastard in the mouth outside a pub. We're talking about murder, here. We're talking about a life sentence.'

Speers stood up. 'Detective Inspector Lennon, I must ob — '

'Thirteen, fourteen years, minimum. You'll be in your thirties by the time you get out.'

A high whine came from Devine's throat.

'And it'll be hard time. It won't be a young offenders' place, no holiday camp like you've been in before. It'll be Maghaberry. You know who Declan Quigley was mixed up with? Their boys in Maghaberry won't let that go. You'll be lucky to — '

Speers stood and slapped the table. 'Don't you dare threaten my cl — '

'You'll be lucky to make it halfway through the sentence. So stop telling me 'no comment', for Christ's sake. Tell me what happened that night. This is your last chance to get out of this, Colm. Stop messing around and tell me or you'll wind up in — '

'I never done it!' Tears sprang from Devine's eyes.

Lennon sat back. 'Then tell me,' he said.

Devine's shoulders hitched as he sobbed. Speers sat down and put an arm around them. 'You don't have to say anything,' he said. He stared back at Lennon. 'You have the right to be silent, no matter what the officer says.'

Lennon said, 'Tell me, Colm.'

Devine sniffed and wiped his nose on his sleeve. 'Brendan was my mate. Since we were wee lads. We went to school together. We were supposed to go to Ibiza next year. He'd just got a job. He was going to pay for me and everything.

It's not fair. It was just a fight with the Huns, that's all.'

Lennon sat forward, lowered his voice. 'Tell me what happened.'

'We were just chucking stones and bottles, the usual stuff. The Huns was throwing them back.'

'By 'Huns' you mean Protestant youths from Donegall Pass.'

'Aye,' Devine said. 'No one got hurt, like. No one even got hit. Then the peelers came, and we ran. Me and Brendan got split up from everyone else and the car came after us. We went into this alley. We could hear the cops coming behind us. We were trying gates to see if any of them wasn't locked. We got to this one near the far end and it was open. Brendan went in front of me and it was dark, I could see nothing. Then I heard him falling, a crack like he hit his head. Then I skidded, it was all slippy, and I landed on my back. Then something heavy was on me and I couldn't breathe.'

Devine shuddered as a fresh wave of tears came. 'Oh God,' he said, his voice a thin wisp of air.

Speers sat silent, staring into space.

Lennon said, 'Take your time.'

Devine sniffed back the tears. 'Next thing I know I'm lying there and my head's busting, and I'm freezing cold. I could hear this screaming coming from somewhere, like a madwoman. Then it stopped. All of a sudden, like. It took me a while to get up, I was dizzy. I felt around for Brendan. It was still pitch black. I found his

234

shoes, and I felt up his leg. He was shivering, I remember that.'

'And?' Lennon asked.

'And I looked up,' Devine said, his eyes far away. 'Someone was there, at the back door. I don't know if he could see me, but I could see him. Just the shape of him. I couldn't see his face.'

Lennon waited. 'And?'

'And I ran.'

Devine's eyes came back to the present. He looked at Lennon. Before he could say anything more, the interview-room door burst inward, followed by a red-faced DCI Gordon.

'Terminate this interview,' he barked. 'Now.'

* * *

Gordon flicked the tape player off and leaned back in his chair. 'So?'

Lennon sat with his head in his hands, knowing it was useless. He said it anyway. 'So, I don't think Brendan Houlihan or Colm Devine killed Declan Quigley. I think someone else was there. I think he was there to kill Quigley. I think Houlihan and Devine were just in the wrong place at the wrong time. I think he disabled the two youths and carried out the murder. I think he killed Brendan Houlihan and planted the knife on him. I think he would've killed Colm Devine too, if he'd had the chance.'

'You're telling me you believe this kid's story?' Gordon asked.

'Yes, I believe it,' Lennon said. 'And I believe

235

the same man who killed Declan Quigley and Brendan Houlihan also killed Patsy Toner last night.'

Lennon listened to Gordon's breathing for endless seconds. Eventually he took his hands away from his eyes to see Gordon staring back at him. Gordon pressed the eject button, removed the tape, and tossed it into the wastepaper bin.

'You look tired, Detective Inspector Lennon.'

'I *am* tired,' Lennon said. 'You know what it cost me to be a cop? My family haven't spoken to me in more than fifteen years. Not one of my sisters. I only get to see my mother because she's too far gone to remember why she cut me off in the first place. I walked away from my family because I thought it was the right thing to do. I saw the misery the paramilitaries and the thugs who operated under their protection caused in my community. The cops could do nothing about it because the people hated them even more. I thought if I joined up I could change that. Even if it was just a little, maybe I could make it better.'

'What's your point?' Gordon asked.

'My point is . . . ' Lennon shook his head. 'There is no point. Not any more.'

Gordon leaned forward, his hands crossed in front of him. His grey eyes gave nothing away. 'Detective Inspector Lennon, you are no longer a member of my Major Investigation Team. I will speak with CI Uprichard about your reassignment. In the meantime, I suggest you take leave, effective immediately, while I consult with CI Uprichard about your conduct in recent days, and any disciplinary action that may be necessary. Do you understand?'

Lennon stood. 'I understand.' He walked to the door.

'I told you to leave it, son,' Gordon called after him. 'I did everything I could for you, but you wouldn't let it lie.'

Gordon's voice faded as Lennon marched down the corridor. He reached his own office and closed the door. He stood at the centre of the room, silent, his fists clenched, deciding on his next move: he went looking for Dan Hewitt.

39

The Traveller lay on the bed, the phone against his ear. A half-hearted rain shower pattered against the window. Horns blared below on University Street.

'Good job on Toner,' Orla said. 'Pity you fucked up on Quigley.'

The Traveller sat up, ignoring the protests of his shoulder. 'How do you mean?'

'There was another kid there. He turned himself in this morning. He told them there was another man there. He saw you.'

The Traveller thought fast. 'I never saw another kid,' he lied.

'Don't bullshit me. You knew he was there, and he got away.'

'He never got a proper look at me,' the Traveller said.

'Doesn't matter,' Orla said. 'He told the cops there was someone else there. It means they could be looking for you.'

The Traveller stood and went to the window. A car overtook a cyclist, cutting too close, almost causing the rider to fall. Smokers stood outside an old house that had been converted into offices, hunching their shoulders against the rain. 'So what now?' he asked.

'What now?' Orla's voice hardened. 'What now is we clean up your mess for you. We have a friend who can take care of the kid for you, make sure he has an accident in his cell tonight. But first, you have a job to finish.'

'The woman and the kid?'

'That's right,' Orla said. 'Her and the wee girl are on a flight home. She'll be in Belfast in an hour. You know what to do.'

Orla hung up.

The Traveller went to his bag and dug the file out from under the loose jumble of clothes. The key was taped inside the cover.

40

Lennon found Hewitt in the car park behind the main building, huddled between two Land Rovers, a phone pressed to his ear. Lost in his conversation, he didn't see Lennon coming.

'No,' Hewitt said. 'No, no way ... I know ... I know that ... I can figure it out, trust me ... I know ... I know ... I can't do that ... Jesus!' Hewitt almost dropped the phone when he saw Lennon. 'Listen, I'll call you back.' He put the phone away. 'Shit, Jack, you scared me.'

'What's going on?' Lennon asked.

'What do you mean?'

Lennon pushed him against the Land Rover. 'What the fuck is going on?'

'Easy, Jack.'

'Tell me what's going on.' Lennon pushed him again.

Hewitt held his hands up. 'I don't know what you mean.' He smiled. 'Tell me what you want to know, and I'll tell you if I can.'

'Declan Quigley and Patsy Toner,' Lennon said. 'Kevin Malloy before them.'

'Patsy Toner slipped and hit his head when he was piss drunk and fell into a bathtub. It was an accident.'

'You and me both know that's not true,' Lennon said.

'Declan Quigley got knifed in a burglary that

240

went wrong. One suspect is dead and the other's in custody.'

'Bullshit.' Lennon pushed him one more time. 'I interviewed that kid. He saw someone else there.'

'Oh, come on, Jack. You know what those wee shit-bags are like. They couldn't tell the truth if their lives depended on it.'

Lennon stepped back. 'I know about Gerry Fegan.'

Hewitt couldn't hide the surprise. Too late, his face hardened again. 'Who?'

'No more lies,' Lennon said. 'Not now. I know about Gerry Fegan, the shit-storm he started in Belfast and finished in Middletown. I know about Michael McKenna and Vincie Caffola. I know about Paul McGinty. I know Marie McKenna and my daughter were there. I know someone is tying up loose ends.'

Hewitt's Adam's apple bobbed above his collar. 'Fuck me, Jack, you've some imagination.'

'Don't,' Lennon said, putting a finger on Hewitt's chest. 'I'm warning you, don't laugh this off. Tell me what's going on. Right now.'

Hewitt squeezed past him. 'I don't have time for this. You're losing it, Jack. Everyone's talking about it. You should've got out five years ago when you had the chance.'

Lennon grabbed his wrist. 'Don't walk away from me.'

Hewitt looked down at Lennon's hand, then up to meet his gaze. 'Let go of me, Jack. You'd do well to remember I'm still your superior officer.'

Lennon pulled him close. 'You used to be my friend.'

'True.' Hewitt's lips curled in a facsimile of a smile. 'But you can be a hard man to like.'

'Look, I don't give a shit about what happened to McGinty and his cronies. Declan Quigley and Patsy Toner were both scumbags. We're no worse off without them. But Marie and Ellen. They never hurt anybody. I just want them to be safe. That's all. Please, Dan. Help me.'

Hewitt closed his eyes for a moment. He sighed and opened them again.

'Please, Dan.'

'All right,' Hewitt said. 'I'll give you one thing. I don't know anything about any Gerry Fegan. What happened with McGinty's faction was a feud. The inquiry found as much. There's no conspiracy here, Jack. Now, if I give you this one thing, promise me you'll stop this nonsense.'

'Tell me,' Lennon said, squeezing Hewitt's wrist tighter.

'Promise, Jack. Promise me you'll leave it alone. Will you do that?'

'All right,' Lennon said. He released Hewitt's wrist.

Hewitt smoothed his jacket and straightened his tie. 'Marie McKenna and your daughter are on their way home.' He looked at his watch. 'Her father's been ill. She's coming back to see him. They'll be flying in from Birmingham, landing at the City Airport. If you're quick you'll meet them off the plane. They land any — '

Lennon ran.

41

The Traveller sat alone in the darkened room. It was cold, smelled of disuse, like the houses of dead people. As he waited he ran his eyes across the different surfaces, imagining the life that had once been here.

Dust hazed a television set in the corner. A colouring book and various pencils and pens lay on the table beneath the window. A dead pot plant lay on its side at the foot of the fireplace, loose compost spilt across the hearth.

He mopped his eye with a tissue, winced at the sting. It burned, throbbing in time with his shoulder. He'd rinsed the eye with water before coming over to the woman's flat. His vision in that eye faded, blurring until he had to blink hard to clear it. His left arm had stiffened. That little fucker Toner had twisted in the bathtub, wrenching the shoulder and aggravating the wound.

His phone rang.

'Change of plan,' Orla O'Kane said. 'The woman and the kid will have company.'

'Who?'

'That cop,' Orla said. 'He's going to meet them at the City Airport. Get over there and keep a watch on them. He's too smart to take her to the flat. My guess is the woman will want to go see her father at the hospital.'

'And what do you want me to do with the cop?'

'He knows too much. You'll have to take care of him as well. You'll be doing a friend of ours a favour. You'll get a bonus for your trouble.'

'Bonus?' The Traveller's eye dribbled as he smiled. 'Don't need a bonus. It'll be my pleasure.'

42

Lennon searched the crowd gathered around the baggage carousel. He checked the video screen above it yet again to make sure it said Birmingham. People stood shoulder to shoulder, jostling with each other to get a good view of the conveyor belt even though it hadn't started to turn yet.

A buzzer sounded, and the crowd tightened. Lennon used his height to scan the heads, looking for a flash of blonde.

There, on the other side of the carousel. She stood taller than any of the women around her, the length and paleness of her almost alien. Strips of grey streaked her blonde hair now; her eyes had darkened.

And there was Ellen. The yellow of her hair stood out against the black of her mother's clothing. A naked plastic doll hung from her fingers, the kind of doll little girls dressed in grown-up clothes, with long limbs and an impossibly small waist. Ellen sniffed and rubbed her nose on her sleeve. Marie scolded her and bent down with a tissue. She pressed it to the child's nose, and Ellen's eyes screwed shut as she blew.

Lennon worked his way through the shoulders and bags and trolleys. He kept Marie in his sight as he rounded the carousel. People pushed and shoved as they went for their luggage. He pushed back until he found her stuffing tissues into her handbag.

He stood for a moment, wondering what to say. Her name was all he could think of. 'Marie,' he said.

She lifted her head, her face blank. Frozen there, she stared at him. Ellen hugged her mother's thigh.

Marie asked, 'What are you doing here?'

* * *

It took some time to persuade her to come with him instead of getting a taxi. Even as they approached his car, she protested. He insisted and loaded her suitcases into the boot.

'At least tell me what this is about,' Marie said as she strapped Ellen into the back seat.

Lennon held the passenger door open for her. 'Get in and I'll tell you.'

Marie held his gaze as she ducked her head in and sat down. He closed the door and walked around to the driver's side. A small passenger jet roared along the runway beyond the fence. Lennon watched it leap skywards before he climbed into the driver's seat.

'I know about Gerry Fegan,' he said for the second time in an hour.

Marie didn't react.

'I know what happened, that it wasn't a feud. I know you and Ellen were there on the farm near Middletown.'

Marie examined the lines and veins of her hands.

246

'Declan Quigley, McGinty's driver, was killed this week.'

'I know,' Marie said, staring straight ahead. 'I read it on the BBC News website. They said it was a burglary gone wrong.'

'Patsy Toner was found dead this morning,' Lennon said. He watched her for any sign of a reaction. There was none. 'He drowned in a bathtub in a hotel not half a mile away from here. The official version is he was drunk. He slipped and hit his head.'

'The official version?'

'And Kevin Malloy was killed just outside Dundalk a few days ago. His wife too.'

'Kevin Malloy? You mean — '

'Yes, one of Bull O'Kane's thugs.'

Her hands went to her mouth and her eyes brimmed. She sniffed hard, brought herself under control.

'I don't understand,' she said. 'They told me it was safe to come home. I've been trying for the last two weeks to get them to let me come home. My father had a stroke. He's in the Royal. They said he could have another one any time. I wanted to see him while I still could. I've been sitting in that bloody awful flat in Birmingham, just waiting for word.'

'Word from who?' Lennon asked.

'It's always come through the Northern Ireland Office. An allowance for me and Ellen, word on my parents, that sort of thing. It was them told me about the stroke a fortnight back. Then they called two days ago, said someone would be in touch from MI5. Ten minutes later,

I got another call. They said the situation was safe now. I could come home.'

She stared hard at Lennon. 'Is it safe?'

'No,' he said.

Ellen giggled and whispered something to herself in the back seat as she moved the doll's arms and legs into a walking pose.

'So what's going on?' Marie asked, her face betraying no fear.

'I think someone's in Belfast cleaning up the mess. I think he killed Kevin Malloy, Declan Quigley and Patsy Toner. I think he also killed a kid called Brendan Houlihan and set it up to look like it was him who got Quigley.'

'And you think they'll come after me?'

'Maybe,' Lennon said. He thought about it for a second. 'Probably.'

'Christ,' Marie said. She looked tired. 'I thought it was all over with.'

'You should have called me,' Lennon said. 'When Fegan was hanging around. I could've done something.'

'I never wanted your help,' she said.

Ellen laughed out loud. Lennon looked up at the rear-view mirror. Ellen turned to the empty seat beside her, brought her finger to her lips, shush.

'My daughter was in danger,' Lennon said.

'She's never been a daughter to you.'

'Because you never allowed her to be.'

Marie went to reply, but stopped herself. She covered her eyes and sighed. 'There's no point in arguing about that now,' she said. 'Are you taking me to your station? I want to see my father first.'

248

'I'm not taking you to the station,' Lennon said.

'Why not?'

'Because I don't trust my colleagues.'

'Why not?' Marie asked.

'My bosses know what's going on as well as I do,' Lennon said. 'But they're ignoring it, trying to sweep it away. I don't know who the orders are coming from, but I'm pretty certain you'll be safer away from them.'

'Then where do we go?' Marie asked.

'You can stay at my place till I figure this out,' Lennon said. 'There's room.'

'No,' Marie said. 'I don't want anything from you.'

'Look, this isn't the time for holding grudges. Ellen's safety is more important than anything that happened between you and me.'

He looked up at the mirror again. Ellen leaned to her side, cupped her hand around her mouth, and whispered.

'Who's she talking to?' Lennon asked.

'She has imaginary friends. People only she can see. She's been like that since . . .'

When Marie couldn't finish the sentence, Lennon said, 'What did she see?'

Marie didn't answer the question. Instead, she said, 'We went to a psychologist when we were in Birmingham, the NIO paid for it. Didn't do her any good. She has nightmares. They've been getting worse.'

Lennon watched her in the mirror. The thought of the child in fear made his stomach turn watery under the weight of his heart. 'What

249

does she dream about?'

'Fire,' Marie said. Her voice shook. Her eyes fluttered and brimmed again. 'She dreams she's burning in a fire. The way she screams, it kills me. I can't sleep for fear of her screaming waking me. I thought maybe if I brought her home, to the places she knows, maybe it would help. And now this.'

She leaned forward, her face buried in her hands, and wept in silence while Lennon watched, unable to do anything to soothe her.

When the sobbing ebbed away, Marie straightened and sniffed. 'I'm sorry,' she said. 'I haven't had anyone to talk to for months. It's been hard.'

'I know,' Lennon said. 'Listen, I'm going to fix this. I'm going to make you safe. You and Ellen both.'

'I don't know if you can,' Marie said. 'But maybe . . . '

Lennon waited. 'Maybe what?'

She shook her head, as if chasing an idea away. 'Nothing,' she said. 'Take us to the Royal first, then I'll find somewhere to stay.'

'Come to my place. Please.'

'No, I don't want to. Besides, if someone's looking for me, they'll know to go there, won't they?'

He had to concede. 'Possibly.'

'Take me to the Royal to see my father. Then we'll go to a hotel.' She allowed him a smile, but with no kindness or warmth behind it. 'You can stand guard at the door if you want.'

He thought about it for a few seconds and

realised she was right. 'No,' he said, 'no hotel. I know a place in Carrickfergus. It belongs to a friend of mine. It'll be safer than any hotel.'

He fired the ignition and set off for the Royal Victoria Hospital, fifteen minutes away if the traffic was kind.

43

Fegan knew it was useless, but he tried again anyway. The phone refused to come to life no matter how hard or how many times he pressed the button. The screen was cracked and the casing loose.

He brought it to his ear and shook it. Something heavy rattled inside. He could hear its movement above the rumble of traffic from the New Jersey Turnpike.

The Doyles had bundled Pyè into the back of the car and sped off from the diner, leaving their driver lying on the sidewalk. Fegan was confident they would leave him alone for the time being. Packie and Frankie had both looked terrified. But they wouldn't stay scared for long. Fegan needed to move.

He placed the phone on the motel-room dressing table. The dreams had been bad during the night, fire and screaming. He had woken soaked with sweat, his heart racing, his lungs burning for oxygen. Even now, hours later, he saw the flames every time he closed his eyes.

A jet roared overhead as it approached Newark Airport. Fegan took two items from his bag and laid them next to the broken phone: a roll of hundred-dollar bills, totalling just less than three thousand, and an Irish passport in the name of Patrick Feeney. From his window he could see the lights of an airplane as it took off.

'I'm going home soon,' Fegan said, his voice hollow in the miserable room.

He started packing.

44

The place felt more like an airport than a hospital, all glass and open spaces. Even a sculpture of a snake clinging to a pillar outside the entrance, for Christ's sake. The Traveller moved among the halt and the lame, avoiding their glances. Women in dressing gowns wandered aimlessly, coffee in hand, some clutching cigarette packets and lighters. Doctors who looked like children walked in pairs and threes.

No matter how clean it was, no matter how new, the smell of sickness still underlay everything. The Traveller hated hospitals almost as much as he hated the medical profession. Hospitals were churches of the dead and dying, and doctors were the thieves who robbed the corpses, even those corpses that still breathed.

One of the thieves approached.

'Are you looking for A&E?' she asked, a bright young girl with a white overcoat and pens in her pocket.

'No,' the Traveller said, turning a circle as he scanned the reception area.

'Oh.' She stepped away. 'Sorry. It's just your eye looks — '

'My eye's fine. Where do you keep the stroke victims?'

'Depends,' she said. 'When was the patient admitted?'

'Don't know.'

'I mean, they could be in ICU, or in Admissions, or on a ward, or — '

'I'll find him myself,' the Traveller said.

As he walked away, he heard, 'Well, fuck you, then.'

He turned back to the girl, but she was already striding away, her head down, her arms churning.

'Cunt,' he said to her back.

45

Lennon recognised Bernie McKenna, Marie's aunt, hovering over the bed, fussing about the motionless form, adjusting pillows and straightening sheets. Bernie stiffened as Marie approached, but did not look up. Ellen clung to her mother's fingers, her doll dangling from the other hand.

'So you're back, then,' Bernie said, her stare fixed on the bed.

Marie faced her across the bed. 'How is he?'

'How does he look?' Bernie smoothed the sheets and spared Marie a glance. 'Poor cratur doesn't know where he is. You'd have been better going to see your mother. It'd do her more good than him.'

Bernie looked up from the grey sliver of a man once more and saw Lennon. Her eyes narrowed as she searched her memory for his face; her jaw hardened when she found it.

'Jesus, you brought him here?'

'He gave us a lift.'

'I don't care what he gave you. You shouldn't have brought him here. Has he not caused you enough trouble?'

'I'll take a walk,' Lennon said. When Marie looked to him, he said, 'I won't go far.'

He backed away from the bed and looked around the bay. Old men gazed back, their eyes vacant, IV lines and oxygen masks hanging from them. Lennon shivered and went to the corridor. He leaned his back against the wall, keeping the women and the little girl in his vision.

They would be safe here, he was sure of that.

46

The Traveller watched the cop through the swinging doors as nurses and visitors brushed past him. He couldn't see the woman and the kid from here, but he could tell they held the cop's gaze.

Maybe this was the place to act, maybe it wasn't. A lot of people around. Sometimes that was a good thing. People are generally cowards. They'll keep their heads down if they can help it, not get involved.

Either way, he had time. All the time in the world.

47

Ellen clutched the doll to her chest and smiled at the air above her grandfather's bed. Lennon wondered what she saw there between the slanted shafts of light and the shadows. She opened her mouth and spoke, but Lennon couldn't hear her from his position at the other side of the corridor.

Marie and Bernie turned their heads to her. Bernie's brow creased while Marie showed nothing but a kind of surrendered fatigue. She put a hand on her daughter's cheek, said something, and her shoulders sagged at the answer. Marie's father watched them both with watery eyes that showed no understanding.

Ellen said something, pouted at her mother's response, said it louder. Marie closed her eyes and breathed deep. She stood, took Ellen's hand, and marched her over to Lennon.

'Please, take her for a walk, will you?' Marie said.

'What's wrong?' Lennon asked.

Marie looked down at their daughter. 'She's being a bold girl. Telling fibs. In front of Auntie Bernie, too.' She levelled her gaze at Lennon, her eyes shadowed with weariness. 'I'm sorry, it's just too much. Not when I have to see my father like that. Not when I have to face Bernie.'

Lennon straightened, lifting his shoulders from the wall. 'Do you trust me with her?'

'I don't have much choice,' Marie said, placing Ellen's hand in Lennon's. 'She's safer with you than anyone else. I mean, you've got a fucking gun, haven't you?'

Ellen stretched her hand up towards her mother's mouth, but couldn't reach. 'You said a bad word.'

Marie seemed to fold in on herself, a tired laugh breaking from her. 'I know, darling. I'm sorry.'

'I'll take her,' Lennon said. 'If she'll come with me.'

Marie hunkered down, took a tissue from her sleeve and dabbed at Ellen's face. 'You'll go with Jack, won't you, love? Maybe he'll take you to the shop downstairs. Get you some sweeties.'

Ellen leaned close to her mother, whispered in her ear, 'Who is he?'

Marie lifted her head, glanced up at Lennon, the sorrow laid naked across her face. She gathered Ellen close. 'An old friend of Mummy's. He'll look after you.'

Lennon swallowed a sour taste.

Marie untangled herself from her daughter, looked her in the eye. 'I'll be right here, okay? I'm not going anywhere. I just need to talk to Auntie Bernie for a wee while. Jack will bring you right back up once he's got you some sweeties, okay?'

Ellen stared at the floor, her doll clasped tight. 'Okay.'

'Okay,' Marie said. She stood upright, touched Lennon's arm. 'Just give me twenty minutes, all right?'

'All right,' Lennon said. 'She'll be fine.'

Worry crept over Marie's features.

'She'll be fine,' Lennon said again, firm enough to almost believe it himself.

Marie nodded, ran her fingers through Ellen's hair, and left the two of them in the corridor. Lennon and his daughter watched her leave. Ellen's fingers twitched against his.

'Okay,' Lennon said, moving along the corridor towing Ellen behind him. 'What kind of sweets do you want?'

'Don't know,' Ellen said.

'Chocolate?' he asked. 'Maltesers? Minstrels? Mars bars?'

She followed, her tiny hand lost in his. 'Don't know.'

'What about Skittles? Or Opal Fruits? No, they don't call them Opal Fruits any more.'

'Don't know,' she said as they reached the swinging doors.

'Or ice cream?' Lennon asked. 'God help us if you don't like ice cream.'

They walked through to the elevator bank. Ellen rubbed her nose. Lennon caught an odour on the air, something lurking between the hospital's sickness and disinfectant smells. Something goatish, a low tang of sweat, like the wards in the mental hospital Lennon had worked in when he was a student.

He exhaled, expelled the odour, and pressed the button to call the lift. Ellen's fingers felt small between his, cold and slippery. He looked down at her. She held her doll to her lips, whispered to it, said a word that might have been 'Gerry.'

48

Fegan sat down hard on the edge of the bed, his breath abandoning him. Waves of trembling rolled through him, from his feet to his fingers, churning his stomach as they passed.

His gut clenched and he threw himself from the bed. He staggered to the bathroom, shouldered the door open, leaned over the toilet bowl. The spasms brought him to his knees.

Between swallows of air and bitter retches, he said, 'Ellen.'

49

The Traveller watched them from the other side of the lobby, using a pillar for cover. The cop fished change from his pocket, struggling with his one free hand, the other clasping the child's. A juice box and a tube of Smarties sat on the counter. The change handed over, the cop gathered the sweets and drink and led the girl out of the shop. He looked upstairs to the second level then leaned down to the child. The girl nodded and allowed the cop to lead her upwards.

The Traveller eased out from behind the pillar, keeping them in his vision for as long as he could. He took a tissue from his pocket, dabbed at his eye, hissed at the pain. Passers-by looked at him, their mouths turned down in distaste. He ignored them.

50

Lennon chose a table by the ceiling-high windows and set down his paper cup full of tea, steam rising from the hole in the lid. Ellen sat opposite him while he pierced the juice box with the little straw. He placed it in front of her then prised the plastic cap from the tube of Smarties. She watched his fingers work as he spread a napkin on the table and tipped a few brightly coloured sweets onto the paper.

'There you go,' he said.

'Thank you,' Ellen said in the stiff manner of a child well instructed in politeness.

Lennon raised the cup to his lips and sipped hot sweet tea through the lid's mouthpiece. He did not see this new drinking technology as an advance in civilisation. It made him feel like a toddler with a sippy cup.

Ellen moved the sweets around the napkin with her fingertips, but did not bring any to her mouth. The doll lay naked alongside the juice box like a passed-out junkie.

Lennon flinched at the association. Ellen reached for the doll and arranged it in a sitting position. She looked up at Lennon as if asking if that was better. He went to say yes, but caught himself. He blinked hard to dislodge the foolish notion from his mind.

'So, did you like Birmingham?' Lennon asked.

Ellen looked down and shook her head.

'Why not?'

'Too big,' Ellen said. She put her hands over her ears. 'Too noisy.'

'You like home better?'

Ellen dropped her hands and nodded.

'Are you glad to be back?'

Ellen shrugged.

'It's home. Do you like home?'

'S'okay,' Ellen said.

'You don't know who I am,' Lennon said. It was a statement, not a question to test the child.

'You're Jack,' Ellen said, her face brightening a little for remembering the detail. 'Mummy said.'

'Did your mummy ever mention me?'

'Uh-uh,' Ellen said, shaking her head. She took a sip of juice, then a Smartie. She chewed with her mouth primly closed. She took another from the napkin and popped it in her mouth, again sealing her lips shut.

'You have very good manners,' Lennon said.

Ellen nodded. 'Mm-hmm.'

'Your mummy taught you well.'

Ellen smiled.

Lennon's throat tightened. He coughed and said, 'Well, eat up. Then we'll go back upstairs.'

Ellen drew on the straw, her gaze fixed somewhere behind Lennon. He looked over his shoulder, seeing only people moving between tables, their trays clutched shakily in front of them. Curved walls screened the area off, decorated with spoons and forks arranged to resemble shoals of fish against the blue-green paint.

'What are you looking at?' he asked.

265

'People,' Ellen said.

'What people?'

'All different people.' She put the juice box back on the tabletop. 'There's bad people here.'

'You mean sick people?' Lennon asked. 'There's lots of sick people. Most of them will get better, though.'

Ellen picked up the juice box and drained it. She popped the lid back onto the tube of Smarties and tucked the sweets into her coat pocket. 'For later,' she said.

Lennon took another swig of tea, but it soured his stomach. He took Ellen's empty juice box from the table and stood, gripping the litter in one hand. 'Come on,' he said.

Ellen gripped his fingers and followed him towards the litter bin beyond the curved walls, over by the kitchen. Lennon struggled to find a way through the people crushing around the till.

A cleaner tipped a tray of refuse into the bin as he and Ellen drew near. The cleaner dropped the lid and stepped aside. Lennon depressed the foot lever to open the bin. The lid didn't budge. He tried to lift it with the hand that gripped the tray. It didn't budge. People jostled as they tried to reach the till. Lennon suppressed a curse as shoulders nudged and shoved him. The cup slipped across the tray, and Lennon released Ellen's fingers long enough to save it from spilling. He finally lifted the bin lid and dumped the rubbish inside. That done, he added his tray to the stack nearby and reached back for Ellen's hand.

He found cold air.

Lennon spun to where Ellen had stood no more than moments ago. His stomach dropped through the floor.

51

The child came to him. The Traveller simply stood and watched her approach from his position behind the curved wall. All the time she had sat eating her sweets with the big cop opposite her, she kept looking the Traveller's way. More than once he found himself unable to return her stare, her eyes so bright and knowing. Like she could see the ugly things in his head, swirling and snapping at one another.

And here she came, her doll hanging loose by her side. The naked plastic body made echoes of some buried memory sound behind his eyes. He blinked them away, and a burst of pain like hot needles forced his teeth together.

'Hello,' she said. 'What do you want?'

The Traveller stared down at her, unsure how to answer the question. He looked back towards the cop who turned in a circle, horror breaking on his face.

'Do you know Gerry?' the girl asked.

The Traveller licked his upper lip. 'Yeah,' he said. He took her hand. 'Come on.'

They were halfway down the curving flight of stairs, ducking between patients and staff, when a voice called, 'Ellen.' It was weak, frightened. If the child heard, she didn't react.

The Traveller quickened his step, the girl dragging on his hand. 'This way,' he said as they reached the ground floor. The Quiet Room stood to their right, facing the shop he'd watched them in a few minutes before.

'Ellen!'

Louder now, not quite panic yet, but an angry edge.

The girl resisted, turned to look for the voice that called her name. The Traveller pulled harder. He scanned the shifting crowd for concerned onlookers as they passed the information desk. No one paid attention, so he marched to the Quiet Room, ignored the flare of pain as he shouldered the door open. Low lighting, a hush in the air despite the room being empty but for him and the child. The door swung closed, sealing them in.

Ellen tried to pull her fingers away from his, but he held firm. His breath sounded alien in this dim and silent place. He realised he didn't know what to do next.

Sweat prickled his skin and he swallowed against the dryness in his mouth. The child had come to him, sought him out. Stupid. He'd never been stupid in his life. He couldn't afford to be. Rash, yes, but never stupid. Not like this. All because the little girl came to him.

A strange and horrible idea burst in his mind. It took hold, bright and unyielding as only the truth can be. He looked down at the child. She smiled back up at him and all doubt was gone.

He had not captured her.

She had captured him.

52

Lennon forced the panic back down to his gut, willed himself to be calm even amongst the nausea and trembling. He turned another circle, picking over every detail, looking behind and through the people. He called her name again. Some glanced up from their trays of food, others ignored him.

The cleaner slipped past, and he grabbed her sleeve.

She spun, pulled her arm away. 'What do you think you're — '

'Have you seen her?'

'What?' Her face turned from anger to confusion and back again. 'Seen who?'

'The little girl.' Lennon grabbed her shoulders. 'She was with me just now. By the bin. You were putting some rubbish in. She's about five or six, blonde hair.'

Her expression softened. 'No, I never saw her. Have you lost her?'

Lennon turned another circle, searching, the panic climbing back up to his throat.

The woman pulled on his shoulder. 'You'd best go down to reception. They'll announce it on the speakers. She'll be all right, don't you — '

He walked away, calling, 'Ellen? Ellen!'

The tide of people on the stairs pushed against him as he descended to the ground floor. He moved faster, ignoring their complaints as he shoved them aside.

'Ellen!'

A security guard left his post at the exit and approached. 'You all right there, big fella?' he asked.

'My daughter,' Lennon said, continuing to turn and search. 'She's gone.'

'Well don't worry, we'll get an announcement out. Kids are always getting bored and wandering — '

Lennon gripped the guard's shirt collar. 'You don't understand. Someone might have taken her.'

'All right, all right.' He prised Lennon's fingers away. 'No need to be putting your hands on me, sir. We'll get it sorted, but just keep the head, okay?'

'Call the police, Grosvenor Road is closest. Tell them DCI Lennon needs urgent assistance. Tell them a child's in trouble.'

'You're a peeler?' the guard asked.

Lennon grabbed his tie, brought the guard's nose to his. 'Just fucking call them!'

53

'You can't get away,' the child said.

'I know,' the Traveller said.

He examined the door for a way to lock it, but there was none. He turned a circle, looking for another exit, but there was none. The quiet pressed hard against his temples, the dimly lit walls butting against his vision, the low rows of seats advancing towards him.

'Jesus fucking bastard of a — '

The girl tugged at his hand. 'You said a bad word.'

The Traveller pulled his hand away from hers. 'I know,' he said. 'Why did you do that?'

She sat down on one of the benches, arranged the doll in a standing pose on her lap. 'Do what?'

'Come to me,' he said. 'Why'd you do that?'

'To say hello.' She walked the doll back and forth along the bench.

Maybe he could just walk out and leave her here. Maybe he could slip out of the main doors, past the bloody snake on the pillar, and run. And maybe not. 'Christ,' he said.

'Do you know Gerry?'

'You asked me that already,' he said. Standing here fretting was doing no good, so he sat down beside her. 'I said yes, didn't I?'

'Do you really know him?'

He wrung his hands together, trying to force his mind into action. 'No, I don't. Why are you so bloody worried whether I know Gerry Fegan or not? Why would I know him, for Christ's sake?'

The girl leaned close until her shoulder pressed against his arm. He inched away.

'You've got friends like him,' she whispered.

'What?' He turned to see her hard blue eyes.

'Secret friends,' she said.

He laughed, but it died in his throat.

Her gaze did not waver. 'Lots and lots of them,' she said.

'What are you talking about?' He stood, wiped his sweating palms on his jeans.

She brought a finger to her lips, shush, and gave him a conspiratorial smile.

'What are you talking about, 'friends'?'

She grinned, then, and giggled. 'It's a secret.'

'Jesus,' the Traveller said, making for the door. 'Fuck this for a game of soldiers, I'm getting out. Don't follow me.'

He was halfway to the door when she sang, 'Gerry's going to get you.'

The Traveller stopped, turned on his heel. He considered calling her a liar, but the certainty on her face caused a ripple of doubt in his mind.

A cool draught licked the back of his neck.

'Can I help you with anything?' a voice asked.

Slow, easy, he swivelled to see a middle-aged woman wearing a sweater and a minister's collar closing the door behind her. She smiled the tepid, condescending smile of the clergy. He put his palm to the side of her head and shoved. She staggered shoulder-first into the wall, the shock

273

on her face the last thing he saw before he wrenched the door open and bolted outside, her scream the last thing he heard before it all went to shit.

54

Lennon heard the scream first, saw the pistol second. People scattered, falling over each other, limbs outstretched. He grabbed for his Glock, tried to keep the thin man's blurred shape in his vision as it wove through the panicked crowd.

'Stop!' he shouted as he levelled the Glock.

The security guard dropped the telephone and clambered over the reception desk. He tried to grab the fleeing form, but it turned. A boom, and the guard dropped, a hole torn in his shoulder.

Some threw themselves down, some huddled against any solid surface they could find, and others ran. The thin man found a path through them before Lennon could aim.

'Get down!' he shouted, knowing the terrified herd would not heed him. He caught the thin man's silhouette against the glass of the exit doors. 'Stop! Police!' he shouted.

Lennon took two steps towards the glass, then stopped, his fear coming back to him. 'Ellen?' he called to the confusion of bodies. Then he saw her in the arms of a woman, a chaplain, by the Quiet Room. He ran to them, pulled Ellen close and kissed her forehead.

'Don't move from here,' Lennon said to the chaplain. 'Keep her safe till I come back.'

He ran for the exit.

55

The Traveller slammed into the side of the ambulance and staggered back, dazed. The Desert Eagle slipped from his fingers and clattered across pavement and tarmac. He almost lost the gun beneath the ambulance, grabbed it before it went under the wheel, and threw his body towards the covered walkway.

The barrier that had risen to let the ambulance through dropped back into position. He hit it gut first, and his momentum carried his torso over, the earth spinning around him until the ground hit his back hard enough to drive every bit of breath from his lungs.

He rolled to his side, got back to his knees, then pushed away again. His lungs screamed for oxygen as he hauled the air in with desperate gulps, but he kept moving even as the black sparks danced across his vision.

Hard, quick footsteps slapping against concrete somewhere behind. A voice ordering him to stop. He spun, fired blind at whoever followed, kept running. Where to? He didn't know. His mind lurched as it tried to function amid the adrenalin's phosphorescent burn.

The car park.

If he could get there, lose himself among the rows upon rows of vehicles, maybe in the shadows of the lower level . . .

The footsteps faster now, closer. 'Stop!' the voice called.

A gunshot cracked, aimed overhead. A warning. The Traveller ignored it, willed his legs to move faster as he ducked under the shelter of the walkway, pedestrians leaping from his path as he tried to use them for cover. Up ahead, the steps down to the lower level with a pay station at the top of them. If he could get that far, he'd be safe.

He ran from the shelter of the walkway, dodged a car, kept his eyes on the stairway as it came closer. An old man was studying the pay station, coins in his hand, confusion on his face. He turned to see the Traveller barrelling towards him.

The Traveller pushed him out of the way, scattering coins across the concrete, a curse taking the last of his breath. He didn't see the nurse until there was no avoiding her. His chin connected with her forehead and the ground disappeared from under him.

56

Lennon saw them go down, the thin man and the nurse tumbling from the top step. He crossed the road from the walkway to the pay station, Glock up and ready.

The old man glanced up as he retrieved coins from the concrete. 'Bloody lunatic,' he muttered.

Lennon went to the lip of the top step. The nurse sprawled on her back, half a dozen steps down the upper flight. She blinked at the sky and moaned, a trickle of blood drawing a bright red line across her forehead.

A sputtering curse came from the landing below where the steps doubled back on themselves. The thin man sat with his back propped against the railings, the big gun almost within his reach. He pulled his feet back, trying to get them under him. He pitched forward, his hand falling close to the pistol's grip.

Lennon charged, taking two steps at a time, until he hit the landing. He let his weight carry him forward, slamming the thin man against the railing. A wounded cry and he slumped on the concrete.

Lennon rolled him onto his back and straddled his chest. He grabbed the big pistol with his left hand, keeping the Glock pressed against the thin man's cheek with the other. He eased back and stood, his aim still on the man's head.

'Sit up,' he said.

The man obeyed and cradled his left hand in his right. 'Jesus, I think you broke my wrist, you dirty fucker.'

'Against the railing,' Lennon said. 'Now.'

The man struggled into position, keeping his left hand tight to his stomach, and rested his back against the blue metal. Lennon studied his face, the swelling on his eyelid, the stiffness in his movement.

'I've seen you before,' Lennon said.

'Maybe,' the man said.

The big pistol was heavy in Lennon's left hand. A Desert Eagle, the sort of thing American gun nuts loved for its size and noise. He shoved it into his waistband. 'Who are you?' he asked.

The man laughed and wiped his eye on his sleeve. 'Many a fella's wanted to know that.'

'Who are you?' Lennon repeated. He took a step closer and steadied his Glock with both hands.

'Barry Murphy,' the man said.

'Is that your real name?'

'No, but it'll do for you.'

The accent was southern, more country than city. His left wrist had begun to swell in his lap. A bloodied tear ran from his right eye.

'You're a fucking mess,' Lennon said.

The man, Murphy, snorted. 'Yeah, well, it's been a rough few days. Lucky for you I'm not at my best.'

'What are you doing here?'

Murphy sniffed hard and spat on the concrete. Blood streaked the saliva and phlegm. 'Just doing a job,' he said.

'What was the job?'

'Look, shouldn't you arrest me or something? We're drawing a crowd here.'

In his peripheral vision, Lennon could see people gathering. He heard someone tend to the nurse behind him on the steps. He blocked it all out and kept his attention on the man before him.

'I'll arrest you all right,' he said. 'But not until you tell me what you're doing here.'

Murphy held his hands out, wrists together. 'Fucking arrest me,' he said.

'Why?' Lennon asked, hunkering down. 'Is there someone inside that's going to help you if I bring you in?'

Murphy smiled, his face a grotesque caricature of sweetness. 'As me ma used to say, that's for me to know and you to find out.'

'Is it Dan Hewitt?'

'Who?'

'Dan Hewitt. Special Branch. He told me Marie was flying in today, told me to meet her at the airport. He knew I'd probably bring her here. Did he tell you to be here waiting for us?'

'Don't know any Dan Hewitt.'

'What about Gordon? DCI Roger Gordon.'

Murphy shrugged. 'I don't know any cops up here in the Black North.'

Lennon moved closer, levelled the Glock at Murphy's forehead. He ignored the gasps from above. 'Then who sent you here?'

Murphy smiled up at him. 'Arrest me.'

'Who sent you to kill Declan Quigley and Patsy Toner?'

Murphy's smile broadened. 'Arrest me, you Prod fucker.' The shift on Lennon's face gave him away. 'You're not a Prod? Jesus, a Catholic cop. Not even one of the new recruits. How long you been on the job?'

'None of your business,' Lennon said.

'C'mon, how long? Ten years? Fifteen?'

'I'm not — '

'Before it was okay for Fenians to join up, anyway. Jesus, you must've been popular all over. I'm surprised you didn't get your fucking brains blown out years ago by one side or the other. What'd your family make of it?'

'Shut your mouth,' Lennon said.

'Touch a nerve there, did I?'

Lennon swallowed and pressed the pistol against Murphy's temple. 'Enough.'

Murphy grinned and another blood-streaked tear ran down his cheek. 'What, you going to shoot me? Eh? You going to pull that trigger and spray my brains all over the steps with this crowd watching?'

'Don't push me.'

'Like fuck you will,' Murphy said. 'Now fucking arrest me, you stupid cunt.'

Lennon sighed. 'Give me your hands,' he said.

Murphy held up his hands again, wrists together. Lennon grabbed the swollen one and twisted. Murphy screamed. Then he laughed. Lennon applied more pressure. Murphy screamed again.

'Tell me who sent you here,' Lennon said.

'Fuck you,' Murphy said between gasps. 'Arrest me.'

281

Lennon twisted again. Murphy screamed and kicked at the concrete.

'Who sent you here?'

Murphy spat in Lennon's face. It tasted of blood. Lennon slammed the Glock's butt into Murphy's temple.

Quiet, then, all around.

★ ★ ★

Lennon found them in the Quiet Room with the chaplain. Marie held Ellen on her lap. Her mobile phone beeped as she thumbed it off.

'Who were you calling?' he asked.

'No one,' she said. 'What happened? Are you okay? Who was that?'

The chaplain excused herself and left them alone

'I'm all right,' he said. 'He's in custody. You're safe now.'

'Safe?' Anger flashed in her eyes and she bared her teeth. 'From who, for Christ's sake? From what? From you?'

Lennon sat down beside her. 'Marie, I — '

'You were supposed to keep our daughter safe. How could you let that . . . bastard . . . '

The words trailed into sobs.

Lennon went to put a hand on her shoulder, but thought better of it. He stood and said, 'They'll want a statement.'

57

The motel had a small coffee shop attached. Fegan had wanted to stay out of sight, but hunger got the better of him. He sat at a table in the back corner where he could watch the door.

'What'll it be?' a waitress asked.

He studied the menu. Sandwiches mostly, all with cheese. He didn't like cheese. Why did Americans put cheese on everything?

He pointed at the menu. 'That one,' he said. 'Turkey. But no cheese.'

'Cook only works to lunchtime,' the waitress said. 'Sandwiches are all made up. Cheese is already on 'em.'

'All right,' he said. 'And water.'

From here he could see the afternoon traffic on the New Jersey Turnpike and the airport beyond, the control tower reaching towards the fading sun. Cutlery rattled as jets passed overhead, either ascending from or descending to Newark's three runways.

While Fegan waited for his sandwich, he took the phone out of his pocket. He set it on the table and stared at the screen as if that would make it spring to life. It hadn't hit the ground that hard, surely it couldn't be completely destroyed. He turned it over, examined the casing, tried the power button again.

A boy at the next table watched. 'Is it broke?' the kid asked.

'I don't know,' Fegan said. 'I think it might be.'

The boy's mother looked up from her limp salad. She gave Fegan a suspicious stare. He dropped his gaze back to the phone.

'Did you drop it?' the boy asked.

'Yeah,' Fegan lied.

'Let me see,' the kid said. 'I can fix stuff.'

Fegan looked back to the mother. 'Can he?'

She hesitated before nodding. 'Aaron likes to fix things. Anything you can take apart, he can put it back together.'

The waitress brought his sandwich on a plate with a glass of water. Fegan handed the phone to Aaron. While the boy held the phone to the light, Fegan set about removing the cheese from his sandwich.

'The casing's loose,' Aaron said.

Fegan took a bite. The bread was stale.

The boy popped the phone's back off and a rectangular block dropped to the table. 'See? The battery wasn't in right. It must've got knocked out when you dropped it.'

Aaron picked up the block and slotted it in. He aligned the rear casing and popped it home, then grinned and handed it back. 'Bet it works now,' he said.

Fegan thumbed the power button, and the screen lit up. 'You fixed it,' he said.

'Told you I could,' Aaron said.

'He told you,' the mother said with a proud smile. She had freckles on her cheeks.

'So he did,' Fegan said. He returned her smile.

'I'm Grace,' she said. 'What's your name?'

'Paddy Feeney,' Fegan said.

The phone vibrated in his hand. Fegan's stomach clenched like a fist. The screen showed a text message. It said, 'You have one new voicemail.'

'Are you okay?' the woman asked.

Fegan went to answer her, but realised he hadn't been breathing. He coughed.

'Drink some water,' she said.

'I need to go,' Fegan said.

'Oh,' she said, her smile falling away. 'Well, it was nice meeting you.'

Fegan nodded. He stood, looked down at the boy. 'Thank you,' he said, and headed for the door.

'You're welcome,' the boy called after him.

'Hey!' The waitress stopped Fegan at the door. 'You going to pay for that sandwich?'

Fegan took a bill from his pocket and pressed it into her hand. He squeezed past her and out onto the parking lot. Another jet screamed overhead.

'Hey!' the waitress shouted over the plane's roar. 'This is a hundred!'

Fegan ignored her and climbed the flight of steps to the top floor. He ran to his room, unlocked the door, locked it behind him again. He called the number to retrieve the message.

A metallic voice said, 'We're sorry. The service you are trying to access is unavailable when overseas. If you would like to enable outgoing international calls, please talk to one of our operators by dialling — '

Fegan hung up. 'Jesus,' he said.

Marie had called. No one else knew the number. There could only be one reason.

He put the phone in his pocket and took the roll of money from the dresser along with the Irish passport. What if it didn't get him past security? He'd have to take that risk. He lifted his bag, hoisted it across his shoulder.

The outside air cooled the sweat that had broken on his brow and sent cold fingers down his spine. He could wait for a cab, but twenty minutes on foot would take him to the airport. He knew there was an evening flight to Belfast, just a few hours from now, then six and a half more on the plane. He'd be home by the morning.

Fegan hoped it wouldn't be too late.

58

The Traveller's vision turned crimson for a moment before the nurse pressed a damp cotton pad against his eye. A searing hot ball of pain burned for a few seconds and eased to a small point of fire beneath the pad.

'Looks like a little bit of wood,' the nurse said. He heard a metallic clank as she placed the tweezers in a tray. 'It might have scratched the cornea too, and the eyelid's quite badly infected. When the bleeding stops we'll flush it out and get a little bit of antibiotic ointment on it.'

He couldn't see them, but he could feel the presence of the two uniformed cops guarding him. Big fuckers, faces like stone. The kind of arseholes who wanted to be cops just so they could push people around.

Handcuffs bound his right wrist to the trolley. A narrow bed with a thin mattress. The noise of the A&E ward's busywork whisked and rattled outside the bay. His left hand lay on a pillow. The wrist throbbed, but not with the deep, hard pain you get with a break. Sprained, more likely, and that cop Lennon hadn't helped it any. It pulsed in time with the sickly ache that sat lodged behind his eyes. They'd X-rayed his head and his wrist, and then put four stitches in his temple. That bastard cop had hit him just below the spot they'd pulled the chunk of Kevlar from all those years ago, opening the scar, and it had bled like hell. Now they waited for a doctor to have a look at the images.

The nurse had changed the dressing on his shoulder. When she asked how it happened, he said he'd fallen on a knitting needle. The nurse had blinked and looked away. She was a pretty thing, all right. Easier on the eye than the two cops, anyway.

She took the cotton away from his eye and dabbed around it with a clean piece. His vision cleared. The plastic curtain swished back and the doctor entered carrying a red folder.

Lennon stood beyond the bay, staring. The Traveller raised his head and grinned at him. Lennon shifted his weight, bristled.

'Lie back,' the doctor said.

'Fuck off,' the Traveller said. He pushed up on his left elbow, ignoring the screaming in his wrist. 'You and me. We'll settle it between the two of us.'

Lennon walked away.

'That Marie one's not bad looking,' the Traveller called. 'I'll let you watch me fuck her before we finish things.'

The nurse scowled.

The cop's footsteps receded, and the Traveller shouted after them, 'How's that, eh? You hear me?'

'Lie back,' the doctor said. 'Please.'

'Go fuck yourself,' the Traveller said.

One of the cops pushed past the doctor and put a hand on the Traveller's chest. He shoved hard and the Traveller's back slammed against the thin mattress, knocking the wind out of him.

The Traveller breathed deep then spat in the cop's face.

The cop made a fist, raised it.

'Come on,' the Traveller said. 'I dare you, you cunt.'

The cop shook his head and slowly lowered his fist. 'Either you stay down, or I'll make you stay down,' he said. 'And I won't be gentle about it.'

The Traveller laughed. He smiled and relaxed as the doctor took his hand, tuned out what he was saying. He ignored the pain as the quack manoeuvred the joint, pushing it this way and that. The Traveller didn't make a sound, just stared at the ceiling.

59

Roscoe Patterson waited at the door to the apartment, arms folded across his chest. Tattoos of Ulster flags and fiery skulls decorated the skin. He nodded as they approached. Lennon carried Marie's suitcase, and she carried a sleeping Ellen.

Roscoe handed Lennon the key. 'I tidied the place,' he said with a wink.

'Thank you,' Lennon said. 'No one knows she's here, right?'

'Not a soul,' Roscoe said. He slapped Lennon's shoulder. 'Look after yourself, big lad.'

'Who is he?' Marie asked once the lift doors closed on Roscoe.

'A friend,' Lennon said as he unlocked the apartment.

'He doesn't look like a nice man,' she said.

'He's not,' Lennon said. He carried the suitcase inside. 'He's a scumbag. But he's an honest scumbag, and that's good enough for me.'

Marie followed. 'Do you trust him?'

'I don't trust anybody,' Lennon said. He flicked lights on as he made his way towards the bedroom. True to his word, Roscoe had hidden the handcuffs and vibrators, the bowlful of condoms, the pornographic pictures on the walls. Lennon put the suitcase on the bed.

Marie hesitated in the hallway.

'You should get some sleep,' he said.

290

'So should you,' she said. 'Couch looks comfortable.'

⋆ ⋆ ⋆

Lennon drifted in and out of the world. His body ached for rest, but his mind raced. Every time his thoughts got caught in the quicksand at the edge of sleep they would break loose again, wild and darting.

DCI Gordon had taken his statement while Dan Hewitt and CI Uprichard stood in opposite corners. Hewitt had been pale and distant. Gordon had been gruff and matter-of-fact. Lennon told them he believed the man he had captured was responsible for the deaths of Kevin Malloy, Declan Quigley, Brendan Houlihan and Patsy Toner. Lennon watched them both as he spoke, but neither Hewitt nor Gordon reacted.

Hewitt and Uprichard left the room, but Gordon remained, when Lennon gave another statement to some pen-pusher from the Police Ombudsman's office. Gordon said nothing, stared straight ahead, when Lennon said he believed elements within the security forces had been protecting the arrested man.

When the statements were done, and the pen-pusher had packed up and left, Gordon put his hand on Lennon's shoulder.

'That's dangerous talk, son,' he said.

'It's the truth,' Lennon said.

'The truth is a slippery thing,' Gordon said. 'Watch your back, son, that's all I'm saying.'

Marie and Ellen had been waiting for him in

reception when he emerged at two the following morning. Marie had given her statement to a sergeant. There hadn't been much to say, there or on the journey to Roscoe's apartment in Carrickfergus; she'd seen nothing.

Daylight found the crack in the living room curtains. Seagulls screeched over the marina outside the window. Fatigue saturated Lennon's mind. He drifted.

★   ★   ★

Lennon dreamed of the women he'd known, the women he'd lied to, the women he'd let down. He passed among them, tried to speak to them. They turned away. They would not listen. His mother stood at the centre of them clutching a tattered shirt. As he drew close he saw the blood on it. Liam's shirt, the one he'd died in.

His mother said something, her words lost beneath the growing clamour of the women.

What? he tried to ask, but his lips and tongue were too leaden to form the word. He tried again, a dry croak this time. 'What?'

She opened her mouth, the sound eaten by a new noise, a high chiming.

'What?' he asked again.

She smiled as she faded into darkness and said, 'Answer the phone.'

★   ★   ★

Lennon sat upright, his head buzzing, his heart hammering. 'Jesus.'

That high chiming again. He scanned the room looking for it. Marie's shoulder bag lay on the glass coffee table, its mouth agape. Something glowed inside. Lennon leaned forward on the couch and reached inside the bag. The phone vibrated in his hand. He thumbed the green button and brought it to his ear.

'Hello?' he said, breathless.

A pause. 'Where's Marie?'

'Who's this?'

A loudspeaker made an echoing announcement somewhere. 'I want Marie,' the caller said.

'She can't come to the phone,' Lennon said.

'Where is she?'

'I can't tell you that. Who are you?'

Another pause. 'Is she safe? Is Ellen safe?'

'They're both safe. Who is this?'

'Where are they?'

'Are you . . . are you Gerry Fegan?'

Quiet for seconds, only bustle and echoes, then, 'I'll kill anyone who touches them. Keep them safe till I find them.'

'Stay away,' Lennon said. 'Don't come near them, do you hear me? Stay away from my daughter.'

'You're that cop she told me about,' Fegan said. 'You walked out on them.'

'That's nothing to — '

'Keep them safe.'

Lennon heard a click, and the phone died.

'Who was that?' Marie asked from the doorway.

60

Fegan slipped the phone back into his pocket and leaned against the toilet cubicle wall. That cop had Marie and Ellen. He was the girl's father. Maybe he could protect them. But he couldn't know the kind of men who wanted to hurt them. Fegan knew because he was that kind of man.

He picked up his bag and let himself out of the stall. No one had looked twice at his passport on either side of the Atlantic. He had tried to sleep during the flight, but the fear of the dreams of burning kept him awake, his legs and arms aching in the cramped seat.

As soon as he'd landed and cleared immigration, he found the nearest private spot to retrieve the voicemail. He dialled the number Marie had left. The call had led to nothing but more worry. He had to find Marie and Ellen, make them safe. The only place he could think to start was at her flat on Eglantine Avenue. He went to the bureau de change and traded the last of his dollars for pounds.

The morning sky was grey and heavy when he went outside to wait for the bus into the city. Marie and Ellen were somewhere under that same sky. So were the men who wanted to harm them. Fegan would find them first. Anything else was unthinkable.

61

They fed him tea and toast. The tea was cold and the toast soggy. The Traveller's head hurt like a fucker. The best they could give him was paracetamol. Waste of time, but he swallowed the tablets anyway.

The strapping on his left wrist made it stiff and clumsy. He laid it on the tabletop. The skin between the fingers itched. A wad of cotton and gauze was taped over his right eye, the eyelid hot and slick beneath it. A cop stared at him from across the table, all business. Gordon, he said his name was. Another cop stood in the corner and said nothing. He was pale and sweaty like he had the shits.

Gordon spoke to the tape recorder. 'For the record, the suspect who identifies himself as Barry Murphy has declined legal representation.' Gordon spoke to the Traveller. 'Now, Mr Murphy, we have checked with our colleagues in the Garda Síochána, and they tell us there is indeed a Finbar Murphy living at the Galway address you provided. They asked the county records office to email us an image of his driving licence.'

Gordon turned over a sheet of paper. A standard European Union licence was printed on it. It carried a picture of a red-haired man with jug ears and a prominent overbite.

'Jesus,' the Traveller said. 'Looks like he should

be playing a banjo in front of a log cabin in Alabama or somewhere.'

Gordon didn't return the Traveller's smile. 'So you agree that the man pictured on this licence, a licence registered under the name and address you provided to us, is not you?'

The Traveller shrugged. 'Doesn't look like it.'

'Care to tell me your real name?'

'Thomas O'Neill,' the Traveller said.

'And your address?'

The Traveller gave the cop the Wicklow address he'd memorised.

Gordon ripped the sheet from his notepad and went to the door of the interview room. He handed the paper to someone outside and returned to his seat.

'Should I expect that name and address to check out,' Gordon said, 'or have you provided more false information?'

'You never know,' the Traveller said.

'Your fingerprints don't match any record we have access to,' Gordon said. 'It'll be some days before the DNA swab we took comes back, but am I correct in expecting that to shed no light on you, either?'

'Stranger things have happened,' the Traveller said.

'Quite,' Gordon said. 'What were you doing at the Royal Victoria Hospital yesterday afternoon?'

'No comment,' the Traveller said.

'What did you want with the little girl?'

'No comment.'

'When Detective Inspector Lennon arrested you, you were in possession of a firearm, namely an Israel Military Industries Desert Eagle .44 calibre semi-automatic pistol. An unusual weapon in this part of the world. Did you bring this weapon across the border, or did you acquire it in the North?'

'No comment.'

'Not the most articulate individual, are you?'

'Me?' the Traveller said, grinning. 'I'm articulate as fuck. But all the same, no comment.'

62

'Tell me about Gerry Fegan,' Lennon said.

Marie sat opposite him in the living room while Ellen lay on the floor, drawing. 'What do you want to know?'

'Why you got mixed up with someone like him.'

'Someone like him,' she echoed. 'I didn't know what he was when I met him. It was at Uncle Michael's wake. He looked so lost.'

'He killed your uncle.'

Lennon watched his daughter as she drew a slender figure, sticks for arms and legs.

'I know that now,' Marie said. 'I'd heard of him. I knew he'd been inside, that he had a reputation. But I've known men like that all my life. I didn't think he was any different. I didn't know there were so many.'

'So many what?'

'Dead.'

Ellen drew dark lines for hair around the figure's head, then sad eyes and a soft smile.

'But he was so kind,' Marie continued. 'So gentle. And he was ready to give his life for Ellen and me.'

'He's a killer,' Lennon said.

'I know,' she said. 'He's a monster. He's insane. And he'd do anything to protect us.'

'So would I,' Lennon said.

In the stick-woman's arm, a baby with a small

round head, and tiny hands grasping at its mother's breast.

'Jack, you left us,' Marie said. Her eyes were cold. 'The time to protect us was when I had Ellen inside me. But you ran away from us when we needed you most.'

'I've missed you so much,' he said. 'I've missed Ellen.'

Marie gave a laugh like cracked ice. 'Jesus, don't go all sentimental on me, Jack. It doesn't suit you.'

Ellen began another figure beside the stick-woman. Slender again, but taller.

'It's true,' Lennon said. 'As soon as I left, I regretted it.'

'Only because she ditched you a week later.'

'That's not fair.'

'It's perfectly fair,' she said, her face hardening. 'What's it called? When you regret a sin only because you've been punished. Yes, that's it. Imperfect contrition.'

'I was punished, all right. You know, she tried to bring a sexual harassment charge against me. She told them I'd been pestering her, calling her up, following her, said I wanted to marry her. It was bullshit, of course. She just couldn't stand being in the same building as me, so she tried to get me fired. And she almost succeeded. It was a bad time. The way people looked at me in the corridors, especially the women, like I was filth. They offered me a deal, said if I resigned, they'd settle with her. She'd have got a payout, and I'd have been looking for a new job. The way things were it didn't seem like that bad a deal. I almost took it.'

'So why didn't you?' Marie asked.

'I remembered what it had cost me to be a cop in the first place. How much I'd thrown away just by joining up. I'd be damned if I'd let that crazy — ' He swallowed and glanced at Ellen. 'I wouldn't let her drive me out of my job just because she couldn't face up to what she'd done.'

'Face up to what she'd done? God, that's rich.'

Lennon ignored the jibe. He hesitated, wondered if he should tell her. 'I've watched you, sometimes. You and Ellen.'

'You followed us?'

'No,' he said. 'Yes. Not followed, exactly. I just wanted to see my daughter. You've never allowed me to know her.'

'You never deserved to know her.'

The new figure beside the stick-woman and her baby was a man. His face was not round like the woman's, but long and pointed. Ellen's tongue poked out as she concentrated on the lines that made up his body and legs.

'She's my daughter,' Lennon said.

'You've no — '

'She's my daughter,' Lennon said. 'I'm her father. I have a right to know her. She has a right to know me.'

'Rights,' Marie said. She stood and went to the window overlooking the marina. 'Don't talk to me about rights. You left me to raise a child on my own because you didn't have the guts to be a father. You gave up any right to her six years ago.'

Lennon followed her to the window. Sailing-boat masts swayed below. Seagulls pitched and swooped. 'You're using her to punish me. You always have.'

She looked back over her shoulder. Her face showed no emotion. She said, 'And I always will.'

Lennon couldn't hold her gaze, so he looked down at Ellen's picture. The stick-man had a pistol in his hand. He hunkered down beside her and put a finger on the figure.

'Who's that, sweetheart?' he asked.

'Gerry,' Ellen said.

He pointed to the other figure. 'And that?'

'That's the secret lady.'

'What does Gerry have a gun for?'

'To scare the baddies away.' She drew stick-Gerry's mouth as a thin, straight line.

'What baddies does he need to scare away?'

'Dunno,' Ellen said.

'Isn't Gerry a baddie?' Lennon asked.

Ellen put her pencil down and gave him a serious look. 'No, he's nice. He's coming to help us.'

'No, love,' Lennon said. 'He doesn't know where we are.'

'Yes, he does,' Ellen said. She picked up her pencil again. 'He'll be here soon.'

63

Gerry Fegan didn't slow his pace as he approached Marie McKenna's flat on Eglantine Avenue. A female cop leaned on a patrol car eating chips from a polystyrene tray. A bottle of Coca-Cola sat on the car roof. Another cop emerged from the house. He threw a stuffed bin liner onto the car's back seat and closed the door. He tried to filch a chip from the woman cop's tray. She pulled it away, but not before he snagged a few. He grinned at her as he chewed them.

Fegan was less than twenty yards away, on the other side of the avenue, when a young man came out of the house. He looked like a student. He exchanged a few words with the cops before heading towards the Malone Road, walking in the same direction as Fegan. Going to the university, or maybe the Student Union building.

Fegan lifted his pace to match the boy's. The cops were too busy arguing over their chips to notice him. What had happened there? The cop he'd talked to on the phone said Marie and Ellen were safe, and Fegan believed him. But for how long? If someone had tried to harm them, then they would try again. He quickened his steps to close the distance between him and the boy. By the time they reached the corner of Eglantine Avenue and the Malone Road, Fegan was just steps behind him.

'What was all that about?' Fegan called, his voice light and friendly.

The boy slowed and looked back. 'What?'

'Back there,' Fegan said as he drew level with the boy. 'The cops outside that house you came out of. Was there trouble?'

Unease creased the boy's forehead. He looked around him. The Malone Road teemed with life. Fegan kept his hands in his pockets, his voice friendly. He tried a smile. 'Just curious,' he said.

The boy kept walking. 'The woman who used to live there,' he said, 'she had some trouble yesterday. Something at the hospital.'

'What sort of trouble?' Fegan asked, keeping in step with him.

'I only heard what was on the news,' the boy said. 'Someone tried to snatch her daughter. Then the police came today to get some of her stuff.'

'Are they all right? The little girl, is she okay?'

'Far as I know.'

'Did they say where she is now?'

'No.'

'Is she with that cop?'

The boy stopped. He looked north towards the university, then back along the Malone Road. 'What cop? Listen, who are you?'

Fegan's cheeks grew hot. 'No one. I was having something to eat in the café at the other end of the road. The waitress said there'd been trouble. I was just curious.'

The boy started walking, but kept his gaze on Fegan. 'I don't know where she is. It's nothing to do with me. Look, why don't you ask those cops?

303

I need to go. I'm late for class.'

Fegan watched the boy walk away, caution and desperation fighting within him. He followed. 'Were they hurt?'

The boy quickened his pace. 'I don't know. I don't think so. Look, I really need to go.'

'What about — '

'I told you, I don't know anything about it.'

Fegan slowed, let the boy leave him behind. 'Thanks,' he called after him.

The boy looked over his shoulder once, but said nothing. He broke into a run when he reached the traffic lights at the end of the road.

64

The pale cop let himself into the Traveller's cell, closed the door behind him, and stood there, sweating. The Traveller lay on the thin mattress, one hand behind his head, the other resting on his stomach. The skin itched beneath the strapping.

'Do you know who I am?' the cop asked.

The Traveller could make no sense of the tag that dangled from the cop's breast pocket. 'No,' he said. 'Should I?'

'No, you shouldn't.'

The Traveller sniffed. 'Fair play, then.'

The cop stepped closer. 'You've been a good boy so far,' he said. 'You've kept your mouth shut.'

The Traveller went to sit up. 'I'm not — '

'Be quiet and listen.'

The Traveller eased himself back down.

'We have a mutual friend,' the cop said. 'He is very displeased. He considered arranging for you to have an accident in this cell. Maybe you couldn't cope with the fear, the guilt and finally being caught. You're not on suicide watch, so it could happen quite easily. Nobody would be watching you. Nobody would expect it.'

The Traveller picked at loose threads of elasticated bandage. 'Tell our mutual friend to make his threats in person, if he's got the balls.'

The cop moved closer still and leaned

forward. 'Don't play the big man with me, you piece of shit, or you'll be swinging by your neck before midnight.'

The Traveller sat up. The cop stood back and paled a shade closer to white. He pulled a small canister from his trouser pocket and shook it.

'You stay there or I'll spray you.'

The Traveller smiled. 'You'll have to explain why you had that. You shouldn't carry CS spray unless you're on the beat.'

'I'm in a cell with a suspect known to be violent. It's a sensible precaution.'

The Traveller stood. 'You've only got one eye to aim at, so you better aim good.'

'Sit down,' the cop said, the canister held in front of him.

The Traveller grinned. 'Fuck you, you black — '

The spray hit like hot needles in his one good eye. He sucked in air to scream, but the burning swamped his throat and nostrils. The scream came out as a strangled hiss. A hand on his chest pushed him back. He sat down hard. Even though he knew better, his sleeve went to his eye.

'Don't rub it,' the cop said. 'You'll only make it worse. Let your eye water to flush it out.'

'Bastard fucking shit-eating cunt of a whore.' He would have cursed more, cursed the cop to hell and back, but his throat closed against the burning. He coughed and spat as every part of his head and chest that could excrete a fluid kicked into action.

'Shut up and listen,' the cop said.

The Traveller hissed through his teeth. He

306

stamped his feet on the floor.

'You listening? I'll get you a wet cloth just as soon as you've listened to me. Are you listening?'

The Traveller stilled himself. He nodded, his eyes screwed shut.

'Good,' the cop said. The Traveller could barely make out his shape in the fiery blur as he hunkered down. 'Now, our mutual friend is a very generous man. That's why you're not going to have any accidents in your cell tonight, just so long as you do as I say. There's a way to make things right. A way to get your little project back on track, and help me out of a fix at the same time. Now, have I got your attention?'

The Traveller exhaled through his nose, felt the snot bubble and dribble across his lips. 'Talk,' he said.

65

'He's giving me nothing,' DCI Gordon said.

Lennon watched Ellen play from the kitchenette. He cradled the phone between his shoulder and his ear. Gordon sounded tired. 'Fingerprints throw anything up?' Lennon asked.

'Not a thing,' Gordon said. 'DNA swabs have been sent off, but I'm not holding my breath. Every name and address he's given us has checked out to a real person, a male around his age. He must've rhymed off a dozen. He had them all memorised. He's wearing cheap clothes from Dunnes and Primark, all new. His wallet had nothing but cash, sterling and euro, and a keycard for a hotel on University Street. We're trying to get consent for a search of the room from management. Shouldn't be long. I may need you to handle that.'

'No,' Lennon said. 'I can't leave Marie and Ellen.'

'Where are they?' Gordon asked. 'Where are you, for that matter?'

'I can't tell you. I won't until we know who he is, and who sent him.'

'I understand,' Gordon said. 'We have him now and they're safe, but I understand. I'll see if I can get someone else to search the hotel room, but I'd rather it was you.'

'I thought I was on leave,' Lennon said. 'By your orders, no less.'

'Well, things have changed. I'm not hopeful a search will turn anything up, mind you. A man as careful as this wouldn't leave anything around for a cleaning lady to find.'

'What about his car?' Lennon asked.

'We found a Mercedes estate in the hospital car park and towed it to Ladas Drive. It's still being pulled apart, but all we've got so far is empty water bottles, stained tissues and assorted litter. It's got Meath plates, but the Garda Síochána tell us they belong to a Merc that was written off five years ago.'

'No weapons?'

'Just the Desert Eagle he had on him and a spare clip,' Gordon said.

'That's all?'

'That's the lot.'

Lennon thought about it. 'He might have a stash somewhere in Belfast. A place or a friend he can store things with.'

'Possibly,' Gordon said. 'I'll give him another go, try that line on him. I'll let you know if it turns anything up.'

'One more thing,' Lennon said before Gordon could hang up.

'What?'

'Dan Hewitt.'

'What about him?' Lennon asked.

'Has he been involved, done any questioning?'

Gordon went quiet.

'Has Dan Hewitt been involved?'

'He sat in on my interviews,' Gordon said. 'And he went to the suspect's cell to double-check one of the names he gave. The

309

suspect became aggressive, and DCI Hewitt had to use CS spray to subdue him. What's on your mind?'

'I don't trust him,' Lennon said.

'DCI Hewitt is your superior officer,' Gordon said. 'It's not for you to trust him or otherwise. He's also Special Branch, which places him somewhere between me and God Almighty in the pecking order as far as you're concerned. We'll have no more talk of that, understood?'

'Just be careful around him,' Lennon said.

'No more, I said.'

Lennon listened to Gordon's breathing. Somehow he got the feeling Gordon agreed with him, but couldn't say it out loud. 'All right,' Lennon said. 'Forget I mentioned anything.'

'I already have,' Gordon said. 'I'll keep in touch.'

Lennon slipped the phone into his pocket and walked into the living area. Marie lay dozing on the leather couch, a blanket pulled to her chin. She hadn't slept much the night before, and it showed on her face. In fact, the dark under her eyes said she and good sleep had been estranged for some months.

He lowered himself into the armchair as quietly as he could, wincing as the leather creaked. Ellen looked up from her play and smiled. She had drawn more figures and carefully torn around their outlines. Now she arranged them in different positions depending on their roles in the drama she was acting out on the floor.

'Is that your mummy?' Lennon asked, pointing

310

to one of the figures.

'Mm-hmm,' Ellen said.

'And is that you?'

'Mm-hmm.'

'You didn't make one of me?'

Ellen shook her head.

'Why not?'

'Don't know,' Ellen said.

'But you made one of Gerry Fegan.'

'Mm-hmm.'

'Do you like Gerry?'

Ellen smiled. 'Mm-hmm.'

'Do you like me?'

Ellen frowned. 'Don't know.'

'You might do,' Lennon said. 'If you give me a chance.'

Ellen wiped her nose on her sleeve, sniffed, and said nothing.

'I used to be good at drawing,' Lennon said. 'When I was a wee boy. I never kept it up, but I was pretty good. I won prizes.'

'What did you win?'

'A cup one time, and a badge another time,' he said. 'One time I won a book token.'

Ellen tidied her torn-out figures into a pile that signalled she was done with them. She took the notepad and pencil and handed them to Lennon. 'Draw me a picture,' she said.

Lennon took the pad and pencil. 'What of?'

Ellen knotted her fingers together as she thought about it. 'Me,' she said.

Lennon selected the black pencil from her small collection. Remembering the lessons from art class a quarter-century before, he drew an inverted egg, then segmented it to place the eyes and mouth.

Ellen stood at his side, leaning on the armrest. She giggled. 'That's not me.'

'Just wait,' Lennon said. He pencilled in the ovals for the eyes, the soft undulation of the mouth, the nose so like her mother's. He defined her cheekbones with short strokes, then longer wavy lines for the hair. 'See?'

Ellen gave a small laugh, then covered her mouth as if she had let a secret slip.

Lennon took the yellow pencil from the floor. It was blunt, but it would do. He wound it through the darker lines to make the gold strands of her hair. When had he last drawn anything? Not since he'd been at school. He held the pad at arm's length and examined his work. It wasn't bad, considering. He showed it to Ellen.

'There, see?' he said. 'It's you.'

Ellen smiled and took the pad from his fingers. She dropped to the floor, lay on her belly, and selected the orange pencil. She sketched orange daggers radiating from her face until her portrait looked like a sun in a dull white sky.

'What's that?' Lennon asked.

'Fire,' Ellen said. 'It burns.'

'What fire? Did you see a fire?'

Ellen chose the red pencil next. She filled in the spaces between the orange daggers. 'When I have bad dreams. It burns. Then I wake up and it doesn't burn any more.'

'Do the dreams scare you?'

Ellen put her pencil down and hid her eyes

312

with her hands. She dropped her head so that her breathing sounded strange against the floor.

'I'm sorry,' Lennon said. 'It's all right. You don't have to tell me. They're only dreams. They can't hurt anybody.'

'That's what I've told her,' Marie said.

Lennon's heart skipped. 'You're awake.'

Marie stretched, her long arms reaching to forever. 'I don't think she believes me.' She extended her hands towards Ellen. 'C'mere, darling.'

Ellen sniffed and abandoned her pencils and paper on the floor. Marie held the blanket up. A puff of warm air and faded perfume brushed Lennon's senses. Ellen climbed onto the couch and burrowed in next to her mother. Marie engulfed her in the blanket, wrapped it tight around her, pulled her in. The warmth turned to chill, the perfume dissipated, and Lennon wondered if he'd only imagined them.

'What time is it?' Marie asked.

Lennon looked at his watch. 'Just gone five.'

'You don't have to stay with us,' Marie said. 'Nobody knows we're here, do they? Nobody but that man. The door looks like it's good and strong. We'll be fine.'

'I should stay,' Lennon said.

'What if I don't want you to?'

'I'll stay anyway.'

'Christ.' Marie closed her eyes. 'Is that all I am to anybody these days? A fucking damsel in distress?'

Ellen's head popped out of the blanket. 'That's a bad word, Mummy.'

313

'I know, sweetheart. I'm sorry.'

Satisfied, Ellen burrowed back down again.

'Was she worth it?' Marie asked. 'That woman. Was she worth what it cost you?'

'No,' Lennon said without hesitation.

'Then why?'

Tendrils of fear and need spread out from Lennon's heart. He had played out this conversation a thousand times in his mind. He considered his words. 'Because I was a coward,' he said.

Marie lifted her head. 'Good answer,' she said. 'Go on.'

'I was a child. I wasn't ready for . . . that. Being grown up, sharing things, not putting myself first all the time. I was scared. Wendy gave me an escape route, and I took it. When I look back, I realise that's all she ever was to me: an easy way out. A coward's way out. I don't know, maybe we weren't meant to be together. Maybe it was never going to work out. Maybe I just wasn't ready. Whatever it was, I could've done the right thing, but I didn't. You didn't deserve what I did to you, and neither did Ellen. If it means anything, I *am* sorry.'

Marie stared at some point miles above Lennon's shoulder. She stayed that way for minutes, her breath soft in the surrounding quiet, Ellen's softer still as it deepened towards sleep.

'It isn't looking good for my father,' Marie said. 'They said it's just a matter of time before another stroke comes, and that'll be that. He hadn't spoken to me since I took up with you.

314

Most of my family haven't. We both paid a price for you being a cop.

'I was feeding my father ice cream in the hospital, and he was watching me. I don't know if he really saw me, but I wondered what he thought. I realised I don't really know him. My own father, I'm sitting by that bed grieving for him, and I don't really know who he is any more.'

A tear escaped Marie's eye, crept silently across her cheek to drop onto Ellen's hair.

'You can see her if you want,' Marie said. 'When this is over, when we get settled. If you wanted to see Ellen, I wouldn't mind. If you want.'

'I'd like that,' Lennon said. 'Thank you.'

'S'okay,' Marie said. 'Just don't let her down. Ever.'

'I won't,' Lennon said. 'I swear.'

Marie closed her eyes and nestled deeper into the couch, gathering Ellen closer. When their breathing fell into step, and Marie's eyelids fluttered with dreaming, Lennon stood and went out to the hall. He entered the bathroom and closed the door behind him. He locked it and turned on the tap.

For the first time in sixteen years, hiding behind the sound of running water, Jack Lennon wept.

66

No one noticed Fegan as he entered McKenna's bar on the Springfield Road. It was early yet and only a few drinkers sat staring at pints of Guinness or glasses of whiskey. Tom the barman filled chill cabinets with bottled beer and cider, the clink of glass on glass piercing the gloom. His head was just visible as he crouched behind the bar.

This was where it had all begun, just a few months ago. Michael McKenna had placed a hand on Fegan's shoulder and set his own death in motion. Had that not happened, if McKenna hadn't sought him out that night, Fegan wondered if he might never have started this terrible journey. Perhaps the twelve would still have been following him, hiding in the shadows, emerging to torment him when sleep was all he wanted.

Fegan walked further into the pub, seeking the dark places. No one sat at the bar. He watched Tom work for a while before slowly, quietly approaching. Tom stood upright, an empty crate hanging loose at his side. He turned, saw Fegan, froze.

'Hello, Tom,' Fegan said.

Tom stared, his mouth hanging open.

'I want a word,' Fegan said.

Tom's eyes darted around the bar before coming back to Fegan.

Fegan nodded to the door behind the bar. 'In the back,' he said.

Tom didn't move.

Fegan walked to the side of the bar, lifted the hinged top and walked through.

'What do you want, Gerry?' Tom asked, his voice like sand on paper.

'Just a talk,' Fegan said. He indicated the door. 'It won't take long. Then I'll leave you alone.'

Tom backed up until he reached the door, the crate still in his hand. Fegan scanned the dark corners of the pub. No one watched. They both entered the back room, a small space with a sink and a microwave oven, boxes of crisps and peanuts stacked in the corners. Fegan took a stool and placed it at the centre of the linoleum-covered floor.

'Sit down,' he said.

Tom dropped the crate and did as he was told. 'I need a smoke,' he said.

Fegan nodded.

Tom took a packet of Silk Cut and a lighter from his shirt's breast pocket. He put a cigarette between his lips. His hands shook too hard to get the lighter to catch. Fegan took it from him and thumbed the wheel. The flame sparked into life. He held it to the end of the cigarette. It danced in the flame. Tom sucked hard, coughed when the tobacco caught, blew the flame out.

Fegan set the lighter on the worktop. 'You know why I came back?'

Tom shook his head, took a drag on the cigarette.

'Somebody tried to take Marie McKenna's

317

daughter yesterday,' Fegan said. 'I need to know who it is.'

Tom coughed again. 'I don't know anything about it. She's been gone for months, her and the wee girl. She cleared out after . . . you know.'

'She came back yesterday,' Fegan said. 'Someone tried to snatch Ellen at the hospital. It said on the news someone was arrested. It didn't say who. You know everything that goes on. People talk to you. Now you talk to me.'

'I don't know anything, Gerry, I swear to God.'

Fegan bent down so he was at eye level with Tom. 'You know better than to lie to me.'

'I didn't know she was coming back,' Tom said. 'I saw that thing on the news last night, but I never knew it was her and the wee girl.'

'Where'd she been?'

'Away somewhere, nobody knows where. After that business with her uncle and all, she took off.'

'What about that cop?'

Tom flinched. 'What cop?'

'The one she used to live with,' Fegan said. 'He's the wee girl's father.'

'Yeah, I know who you mean,' Tom said. 'What about him?'

Fegan straightened and looked down at Tom. The barman could barely hold onto the cigarette. He had started sweating when Fegan mentioned the cop.

'He's been around here, hasn't he?'

Tom opened his mouth ready to say something, but changed his mind. His shoulders slumped and he nodded.

'What did he want?'

'He was asking the same as you, about Marie McKenna and the kid, where they were. I told him the same as I told you: I know nothing about it.'

'What does he look like?'

'Big fella, broad-shouldered. Dirty blond hair. Dresses well.'

Fegan studied Tom as he sucked hard on the cigarette. 'There's more,' he said. 'Tell me.'

'He asked about what happened with Michael McKenna and that business in Middletown. About the feud. Then he asked about Patsy Toner.'

'And you told him nothing.'

'That's right.'

Fegan's gut told him to keep pressing. 'There's more,' he said.

'No, that's all,' Tom said. He brought the cigarette to his lips.

Fegan reached out and took the cigarette from Tom's mouth. He dropped it to the floor and crushed it beneath his heel. 'There's more,' he said.

'No, Gerry, that's — '

'Don't,' Fegan said. He stepped closer to Tom, forcing the barman to crane his neck to look up at him. 'Don't lie to me.'

Tom sighed. It turned to a whine in his throat, then a cough in his chest. 'There was another fella came round. I didn't like the look of him. He had a bad eye, infected or something. He was asking about Patsy Toner. Couple of days later,

Patsy Toner drowns in a hotel bathtub.'

'You think he was the one tried to take Ellen yesterday?'

'Wouldn't surprise me,' Tom said.

'What was he like?'

'Dark hair, cut short. Medium height, sort of thin, but built tough. All knuckles and muscles and veins, you know? Southern accent, maybe like a gyppo.'

'A traveller?'

'Maybe. Thing is, there was something about him, the way he carried himself, the look in his eye. He was like . . . '

'Like what?' Fegan asked.

'You,' Tom said. 'He was like you.'

67

'Where's the other fella?' the Traveller asked, his eyes still raw.

'I have asked my colleague to sit this one out,' Gordon said.

'Why's that, then?'

Gordon arranged his pen and notepad on the table between them. 'Because his presence was required elsewhere,' he said. 'Let's proceed, shall we?'

The Traveller smiled. 'Ready when you are.'

Gordon did not return the smile. 'I'm curious as to what contacts you might have in Belfast.'

'No comment.'

'We've recovered only one weapon, and two clips of ammunition, during your arrest and subsequent searches. We suspect another party may be hiding items for you somewhere in the city.'

'No comment.'

'We'll shortly have permission to search your hotel room. Are we likely to find anything incriminating there?'

'No comment.'

'If you cooperate with us now, tell us what we might find there, and where we might find it, that will be taken into consideration in our recommendations to the Public Prosecution Service.'

'No comment.'

Gordon hit the stop button on the twin-deck tape recorder. He stood and came around the table. He perched on the edge, folded his arms across his chest, and looked down at the Traveller. 'I miss the old days,' he said.

'That right?' the Traveller said.

'That's right,' Gordon said. 'The days before the Police Ombudsman and the Human Rights Commission. Back then we could be a little more . . . well . . . vigorous in our interrogations. We used to do all sorts, and nobody minded. I put away a lot of scumbags in my time, most of them based on confessions. You should've been around then, seen where that 'no comment' nonsense got you. I'm a Christian, you know.'

'Good for you,' the Traveller said.

'Yes, it *is* good for me. The missus converted me. I used to be a drinker. She soon sorted that out, got me going to church, got me right with the man upstairs. That was back in, oh, '79 or '80. And I'll tell you the funny thing: beating the likes of you senseless, knocking your teeth down your throat, that never bothered me. It never conflicted with my Christian beliefs.'

'That was handy,' the Traveller said.

'It was indeed, son. You see, I hold my beliefs very dear. I live and breathe by them. But when it comes to someone like you, or any of those toe-rags I put away back then, my beliefs cease to apply. Because you're an animal. The good Lord above has no more regard for you than for a pig in a slaughterhouse, and neither do I.'

The Traveller feigned offence. 'Here, now, there's no — '

'Shut your mouth.' Gordon leaned close. 'We don't do things the way we used to. I never saw it as torture, just rigorous interrogation. But the bleeding hearts and the politicians took a different view, so that's that. But it's not too late to turn the clock back. You're already looking pretty rough, so I wouldn't have to worry about leaving too many marks. Now you start talking to me, son, or you'll be getting a lesson in the police procedures of yesteryear. Understood?'

The Traveller said nothing.

Gordon gripped the Traveller's face in one meaty hand. 'Understood?'

The Traveller shrugged.

Gordon took his hand away, wiped it on his trouser leg. 'Right, then,' he said. 'Let's get back to it.'

He returned to his seat and started the tape recorder.

'Now,' he said, taking his pen in hand. 'Who is your contact in Belfast?'

The Traveller grinned. 'No comment,' he said.

Before Gordon could react, the door opened and the pale cop stepped in. The Traveller kept his stinging eyes fixed straight ahead. The pale cop approached Gordon, bent down, whispered in his ear.

Gordon stopped the tape recorder, coughed, and followed the pale cop out of the room.

The Traveller ran his tongue across his upper lip and smiled.

68

'Shit,' Lennon said.

'I'm sorry, there's no one else,' Gordon said.

'I'd rather stay here.'

'Nobody knows where 'here' is,' Gordon said. 'You won't even tell me, so how could anybody else know? Look, I need an officer of your experience on scene for the search. The hotel management are waiting. The only other officer I could send in is Dan Hewitt.'

'No,' Lennon said. 'I'll do it. I'll be there in half an hour.'

'Good lad,' Gordon said.

Lennon went into the living room and sat down on the couch beside Marie. Ellen dozed in her lap as late-night music videos played silently on Roscoe's huge television. 'I've been called away,' he said. 'But I'll stay if you want me to.'

'Go,' Marie said. 'I don't need a guard dog.'

'You'll be safe,' Lennon said. 'Roscoe has this place done up like Fort Knox. The door's got two locks and a chain. It's rock solid. Besides, no one knows you're here.'

'That Roscoe knows,' she said.

'I trust him.'

'I don't,' Marie said.

Lennon took the Glock from its holster. He held it out to her. 'Here.'

Marie stared at the gun. 'No,' she said.

'Take it,' he said. 'It'll make you feel better.'

'I very much doubt that,' she said.

'It'll make *me* feel better.'

'I wouldn't know what to do with it.'

'It's easy,' Lennon said. 'You just pull this back to chamber a round. Then you point it and pull the trigger.'

'I don't want it,' Marie said.

'Take it.' He held it in front of her. When she didn't take it, he stood and crossed the room. He reached up and placed it on a shelf, too high for Ellen to reach. 'It's there if you need it,' he said. 'But you won't.'

Marie didn't answer, just watched him from the couch as she rocked their sleeping daughter.

'I'll be an hour, two at most,' he said. 'I'll be back. I promise.'

69

The sound of heavy boots slapping the tiled floor jerked the Traveller from his doze. His body ached from lying on the thin mattress. He sat upright in the dark, sniffed, and wiped his one uncovered eye. He listened.

Running men and hard voices. Not panic, but some sort of emergency. One voice called for a doctor. Another called for a knife. The Traveller stood and walked to the metal door. He pressed his ear against it.

He heard, 'Stupid fucker.'

He heard, 'His trousers.'

He heard, 'Hanged himself.'

The Traveller smiled. He walked to the toilet, unzipped, and emptied his bladder. He tucked himself away and zipped up. He breathed deep, steadied himself, faced the door, and waited.

Perhaps ten minutes passed as more footsteps hammered along the corridor beyond the door. They all seemed to be travelling the same direction, past his cell, deeper into the custody suite. The footsteps died away, leaving only urgent voices in another part of the building.

The Traveller imagined the pale cop on the other side of the door, waiting for his moment. When Hewitt told him the plan, the Traveller didn't think he'd go through with it. But, by the sounds of things, he had.

The door clanked and creaked as a bolt moved

aside. The Traveller smiled. He squinted as light from the corridor flooded the cell. Hewitt stood in the doorway. The Traveller struggled to make out his features in silhouette, but he could see the cop was sweating, his eyes dull.

'You did it, then,' the Traveller said.

'Yes,' Hewitt said.

'Didn't think you had it in you.'

'Neither did I.'

The Traveller smiled. 'First one's the hardest.'

'There'll never be a second,' the cop said.

'You sure of that?'

Hewitt stood silent for a moment before stepping into the cell and closing the door behind him. It sealed them together in the dull glow from the nightlight. 'We haven't much time,' he said. 'Everyone's with the kid. The CCTV is down for the whole custody suite. You've got four, five minutes at most.'

The cop took a roll of cash from his pocket and handed it to the Traveller, along with a set of car keys. 'It's an old Volkswagen Passat, parked on the far side of the playing fields. Once you're out the gates, turn right then cut straight across the rugby pitch, it'll be at the other side. Keep out of sight till you're there.'

'Don't worry, I will,' he said.

'And here,' Hewitt said. He undid the catch on his holster, drew the Glock 17, and held it out butt-first.

The Traveller reached for the gun and tucked it into his jacket pocket. They'd taken his belt, so his jeans hung loose from his hips. 'I'll be off, then,' he said.

'Wait.' The cop gripped his sleeve.

The Traveller turned to see him in the dimness.

'It needs to look right,' Hewitt said, his voice wavering and cracking.

'All right,' the Traveller said. He slammed his forearm into Hewitt's face.

The cop stumbled back silently, blood spurting from his flattened nose. He slid down the wall, his jacket whispering on the painted concrete, his legs spreading out in front of him.

The Traveller patted Hewitt's pockets until he found the can of CS spray. 'Is he paying you well?' he asked.

Hewitt stared back at him with clouded eyes. The Traveller gave him a sharp slap, sending a fresh spray of blood across the floor. The cop blinked at him.

'Is the Bull paying you well for this?'

Hewitt coughed and moaned. 'Well enough,' he said, the words gurgling in his throat.

'Don't scream,' the Traveller said. He shook the can.

'No,' the cop said.

'You said it had to look real,' the Traveller said. 'You scream, and you're more fucked than me.'

'No.'

The Traveller covered his own mouth with his lapel, and aimed. He let Hewitt have it. The cop opened his mouth and leaked air. He inhaled, then convulsed as the CS attacked his chest and throat. He collapsed on his side, coughing.

'Nice working with you,' the Traveller said as he dropped the can and stood. He went to the door and listened. He heard nothing above Hewitt's gasping and spluttering. His own throat stung, and his good eye watered. He ripped the dressing from the other and blinked as the cool air washed around it.

He opened the door and glanced up and down the corridor, his vision blurring and sharpening as it adjusted to the light. He shook his head and blinked, tried to clear it. Voices came from around the corner, where the kid's cell was. They'd have cut him down, tried to resuscitate him. The Traveller hoped Hewitt had done a decent job of it. He drew the Glock, exited the cell and closed the door behind him. He slid the bar across and locked Hewitt's whining behind the steel.

The Traveller moved quickly and quietly. Left took him to the booking desk, now deserted as all hands tried to save the kid. Left again took him to the corridor leading to the reception area. He froze as he turned the corner.

Gordon stood by the locked door. They stared at each other, ten feet between them.

Gordon mouthed some words.

'What?'

Point the gun, Gordon's lips said.

The Traveller did as he was told, and Gordon raised his arms. The cop stepped aside so the Traveller could see the keypad for the lock. The door's small window showed the exit beyond. A camera watched from its perch where the ceiling met the wall.

He understood. 'Put your number in and open it,' he said, crossing the distance between them.

Gordon did it without argument. The lock whirred and clunked.

'There's no one on the gate,' Gordon whispered in a voice so quiet the Traveller could barely hear him. 'You've got a clean run at it, so long as you're quick.'

The Traveller nodded, kept the Glock trained on Gordon.

'Hewitt said I'd be looked after,' Gordon whispered. 'He said your people would take care of me.'

'That's right,' the Traveller said.

He put the pistol to Gordon's temple, waited long enough to see the realisation in the cop's eyes, and pulled the trigger.

The Traveller stepped over Gordon's twitching legs, and went for the outer door. Beyond it, the gates stood open and unattended. The night air cooled his face as he ran.

He didn't stop running until he found the Volkswagen.

70

Lennon had called Gordon's direct line the moment he saw the splintered door frame, but got no reply. He had tried three more times since, then tried the station's front desk. Still nothing. He might have wondered why if not for the more urgent worry of the hotel room. He made another tour of it, circuiting the bed, the chair, the open-faced wardrobe, the small bathroom.

The staff had been as indifferent and professional as he expected. They'd had to wait for consent from the manager to be in compliance with the law, but he'd been at a training day across the water. He'd come straight from the airport and had taken Lennon and the hastily assembled team to the room personally. The manager had looked at the forced door, then at Lennon, and said, 'Well, at least I don't need to call the police.'

Now Lennon watched the team work, pointless as it was. He knew they'd have turned up nothing useful, even if the door hadn't been forced. The suspect was too smart to leave anything incriminating here. Lennon could only stand by and wait for Gordon to reply to his voicemail.

Fergal Connolly, a fresh-faced constable, worked through the contents of a holdall he'd found at the foot of the bed: cheap hoodies,

T-shirts and jeans, along with a selection of socks and underwear. Everything was still wrapped in carrier bags from Dunnes, Primark and Matalan. Their man had been disposing of his clothes as he went along.

'Clever bastard,' Lennon said.

The room was neat, at least it had been before the search team started on it. The suspect had chosen a decent hotel because he knew the staff would keep it spick and span. Lennon doubted if there'd even be a hair in the plughole.

He checked his mobile for the tenth time since he'd been here. No missed calls or messages. He knew Marie and Ellen would be fine, but still, he couldn't dislodge that sour weight from his gut.

Having run out of things to lift, turn over, open, or generally inspect, the three constables now ambled around the room like sheep in a pen. They'd start searching one another soon, Lennon thought.

He spoke to Connolly. 'Have one last tour of the place, then pack up and secure the door. I want one officer to stay here and make sure no one crosses the threshold, you understand? Meet me downstairs in fifteen minutes. I want a word with the desk staff before I go.'

Lennon walked to the elevator bank and hit the button. He looked up and down the corridor. He took the phone from his pocket again and found Marie's number. Should he call her? Maybe, hopefully, she was getting some sleep. Wouldn't do to wake her. But he'd be happier if he knew she and Ellen were okay. And Marie would probably be happier if she knew Lennon was concerned enough to check in with her. He hit the dial button.

Marie answered with a sigh. 'What?' she said.

'Just wanted to see how you were,' Lennon said.

'I was asleep,' she said. 'That's how I was. Now I'm awake. And so is Ellen.'

Lennon heard a ping, and one of the elevator doors slid open. He stepped inside and pressed G. Ellen's voice rustled against his ear, all yawns and grumbles. The doors closed, and Lennon felt that odd weightlessness.

'Sorry,' he said. 'Just wanted to make sure you were okay.'

'We're okay,' Marie said. 'We'd be better if we were still asleep.'

'Yeah,' Lennon said. 'I'm sorry.'

'So you said.'

The phone died. The elevator's doors opened onto the reception area. Only one of the receptionists had seen the suspect's comings and goings. Lennon beckoned her over to a pair of soft armchairs. Her badge said her name was Ania, and she spoke Polish, Lithuanian, Russian and English.

'I saw him only a few times,' she said, her words spoken with a careful and deliberate clarity, her accent softened by years of Belfast living. 'He never said hello. He always kept his head down and walked right past. But once . . . '

'Once what?' Lennon asked.

'On the floor, after he had walked past reception, there was something on the floor, like dirt or mud. It was very small, like a coin. I took

333

a tissue and went around the desk. When I wiped it up, it was red. It was blood.'

Her face remained devoid of emotion, as if she was telling him special room rates. Just a week or two ago, Lennon might have tried his luck with her. Now her hard good looks stirred nothing in him.

'What about today, has anyone unusual been here? We requested that no one be allowed near that room. Could anyone have got past reception without being noticed?'

'I saw no one,' she said. 'But people come and go all the time. They have meetings here, business people, salesmen.'

'Is there another way in? A way to get to the rooms without coming through reception?'

'There is an entrance from the car park,' she said. 'But the car park is locked, unless . . . '

'Unless what?'

'There is a camera overlooking the gate. They are not supposed to, but if a car pulls up, often whoever is on the desk will just press the button to open the gate without checking. The customers get annoyed if they have to get out of their cars and walk to reception, so it is easier just to let them in and out. I tell them not to do it, but they do it anyway.'

'So someone might have — '

Before Lennon could finish the question he heard the static crackle of a radio over his shoulder. He looked around to see Constable Connolly half running across the lobby towards him, his face sickly pale.

'What?' Lennon asked, standing.

Connolly skidded on the tiled floor. He found his balance and said, 'We need to go.'

'Why? What's wrong?'

Connolly looked like he might throw up. 'It's bad,' he said. 'Really bad.'

71

The Traveller pulled off the dual carriageway and into a small housing development, a fresh clean new-build. Big houses, four and five bedrooms, all with their own paved driveways, four-by-fours and estates parked on them. He entered a cul-de-sac and made his way to the turning circle at the end. The Volkswagen's ancient brakes whined as he stopped.

At least Hewitt had got him an automatic. Changing gears would have been hell on his throbbing wrist. He flexed his fingers against the elasticated bandage then rolled his shoulder to shift the ache that had settled there. It felt tight where the knitting needle had punctured his skin, as if the flesh constricted on the bone.

He opened the door and got out. A cat watched him from its place curled up on a welcome mat on one of the doorsteps. The Traveller quickly scanned the cul-de-sac, checking for lights or twitching curtains. Satisfied, he opened the boot. There, just as Hewitt had promised, his long kit bag, the kind of luggage cricketers carried bats and pads in. The plastic cable tie still sealed it closed. He was surprised Hewitt hadn't had a peek inside. The tie was only there to keep the hotel maids out. You'd never know its contents by feeling the outside. Blankets softened the shotgun's shape.

The Traveller took a moment to get his

bearings. Follow the Shore Road, Hewitt had said, keep going till you see the masts.

★ ★ ★

The lighting around the marina cast oranges and yellows over the moored boats. Some were small sailing craft; others were bigger vessels with powerful engines. The place stank of money. It figured the Loyalist would run his whores from here. The Traveller circled the building, looking for danger. He expected none, the Loyalist had been paid good money for the address and the keys the Traveller had found in the Volkswagen's glovebox, but still, he would be careful.

He kept the Browning tight against his side, its stock inside his jacket, the barrel pressed against his leg as he walked to the far side of the apartment block where the few permanent residents' cars sat protected by the street lights. Four of them in all, plus the Volkswagen he'd driven here in. Most of the apartments were weekend getaways or holiday lets. The Loyalist had said his place would be the only occupied flat on that floor. The building's entrance was a sheltered glass door. He tried one of the three keys he'd been given; it didn't work. He tried the second and was inside. A plain, clean reception area with a lift. He took the stairs instead, two steps at a time.

Six flights to the top floor. The Traveller peered through the glass in the door leading to the corridor. Soft lighting and no movement. He pulled the door as slowly as he could manage, but still it creaked. He froze as the sound reverberated in the stairwell. No other noise, no disturbance in the only slit of light beneath one of the four doors. He slipped through, keeping his hand on the door to soften its closing. He stepped quietly along the corridor, his shoes whispering on the thick carpet.

The flat was second on the right; he recognised the characters 4 and B. He watched the dim sliver of light below the door as he approached. No sound came from within, not even a television. He pressed his ear against the wood. Silence. He put his eye to the peephole. Nothing but distorted shadows. He stepped back and examined the door. Good hardwood, oak by the look of it, different from the other apartment doors. Fitted special, most likely.

The Traveller slipped the first key into the deadlock and turned it, wincing at the noise of the tumblers. The door loosened in its frame. He withdrew the key, and found the one for the cylinder lock at eye level. It slid home smooth and neat, turned easy, and the door opened. It met something solid and immovable after less than two inches. A rustle from inside, the mewling of a child, another voice shushing it. He pushed again with more force. The hard sound of a chain pulled tight.

A frightened whisper from within, the child crying briefly, the patters of socked feet on carpet. The Traveller shoved hard against the door with his uninjured shoulder. He might as well have pushed the wall. It was a good security chain, a proper locksmith's job, not the crap

338

you'd buy in some discount DIY warehouse. Doors slammed inside, followed by more whispering feet. He put his good eye to the narrow opening. Now the shadows moved.

'I've got a gun,' a woman's voice called.

'So have I,' he said. 'I bet mine's bigger.'

'I've called the police,' she said.

'That was quick.'

'I'm doing it now.'

'Can you work the gun and the phone at the same time?'

The Traveller lifted the Browning and stepped back. He pumped a shell into the chamber, steadied himself, and blew a chunk out of the door where he reckoned the chain was. He chambered another shell and blasted the same place again. Once the smoke cleared, he saw he hadn't done as much damage as he thought. He stepped closer and examined the hole. A good amount of wood had been torn away, but twisted steel bordered the small tear the shotgun had opened. He looked through.

A shaking hand held a pistol, the same kind of Glock that Hewitt had given him, pointing back from a doorway. He could just make out her shape slumped against the door frame and heard a hiss, a moan, a gasp. The pistol's muzzle flashed and he ducked away from the gap. No matter. The bullet hit the steel reinforcement at least a foot away from where his eye had been.

'Jesus, you should practise with that thing,' the Traveller said. 'You're a fucking terrible shot. Still, no need to call the cops now. I'm sure some of the neighbours has done the honours.'

'Go, then,' she said, her voice cracking.

'Don't think I will,' he said. 'Listen, open this thing up and I'll go easy on the wee girl. Can't say fairer than that.'

Another bang from inside, another slam like a fist against the door. Then he heard ragged weeping. 'All right,' he said. 'You had your chance.'

He examined the door frame, found where the chain was attached. He raised the shotgun, pumped a shell, and blasted the door twice, leaving mangled craters and twisted metal. He reloaded the shotgun, straining through the ringing in his ears for approaching sirens. Nothing but the child's squealing from deeper inside the apartment, though even that was mixed with the high whine the shotgun blast had left behind. The bastards at the cop shop had taken his good Vater earplugs.

A mobile phone rang somewhere inside, its high chime cutting through the whine.

The Traveller took a step back, then forward, raising his right leg so his foot carried his body's weight as it slammed against the door. It burst inwards and hit the wall. The Traveller peered through the smoke as he pumped the shotgun. The phone stopped ringing. He raised the shotgun when he saw the woman cowering in the living room's doorway.

She did not move as he entered. He drew nearer and saw the red pocks on her cheek. A brighter bloom of red above her right breast. She inhaled and coughed as she stared up at him, her eyes full of fear and hate.

340

Beyond her, in the living room, the mobile phone rang again. Its screen doused the room in a dull blue glow. It inched across the coffee table as it vibrated.

'Let me get that for you,' the Traveller said.

72

Lennon kept the phone pressed to his ear as the Audi's engine roared. He squeezed it tight with his shoulder as he changed gear, then brought his hand back to catch the phone just as it fell. The answering service again. He changed up, the car hitting sixty as he neared the junction of York Street and the Westlink. Lennon leaned on the horn as the lights turned red, barely slowing as the few late-night drivers braked hard to avoid his path. The Audi's traction control indicators blinked on the dashboard, the car struggling for grip as it made the turn onto the M2. The wheels hit the kerb on the far side hard, and Lennon heard a screech as the rear quarter grazed a lamp post before the car bounced back onto the road.

He redialled for the third time, whispering, 'Come on, come on, come on . . .'

No dial tone this time. Instead, it went straight to the answering service. Who was she talking to? Was she calling him back?

'Marie, if you get this, call me right now. Right now, you hear me?'

Lennon hung up. His eyes flitted between the phone and the road ahead as he looked up his station's number. The dial tone clicked and switched three times as the call was bounced around. The drama in the custody suite had left the phone unmanned. He would be routed to the nearest station. When he got an answer, he said, 'Put me through to Carrickfergus.'

73

Fegan paced the small guesthouse bedroom listening to the dial tone. His fear fed on itself, remade itself again and again, stronger with each reincarnation. He had tried to sleep, but a vision of fire, the smell of burning flesh and hair, and a child's screams had shaken him awake minutes ago. Sweat soaked the clothes he lay in. He had gone straight for the phone.

The dial tone ceased, replaced by steady breathing.

'Marie?' Fegan said, fear sharpening his voice.

'She can't come to the phone right now.'

A man's voice. The kind of voice Fegan knew too well. His head swam. He sat on the edge of the bed.

'Where is she?' he asked.

'She's right here,' the voice said. 'Her and the wee girl.'

'Who are you?' Fegan said.

A pause. 'Would that be the famous Gerry Fegan?'

'Don't touch them.'

'I've heard all about you,' the voice said. 'I've been dying to meet you in the flesh. Something tells me we'd get on like a house on fire.'

Fegan doubled over as his stomach cramped. 'I'll kill you if you touch them,' he said.

'Too late for that. I've got to be honest with you, Gerry. Marie's not looking her best.'

'I'll kill you,' Fegan said. 'I'll make it bad.'

'It's that cop you should go after. The kid's father. You know what the useless shite did?'

'I'll kill you,' Lennon said.

'He left the child and her mother in a whorehouse in Carrickfergus. Just upped and left them here all on their own. Jesus, you wouldn't do that to a dog.'

'I'll — '

'Yeah, you'll kill me, I heard you. Time's wasting, Gerry. Gotta go.'

The phone died.

'I'll kill you,' Fegan said to the lifeless plastic.

He stood and went to the window. His room took up half the first floor of a converted terraced house. The street below ached with quiet, the lights making shadows pool around the parked cars and garden walls. The occasional rumble of traffic came from Botanic Avenue, less than a hundred yards away. It had been an hour, maybe more, since the last train had passed along the track that ran behind the guesthouse. Fegan had always cherished quiet, but now it lay heavy on him, like a cold, damp blanket.

The man with the mocking voice had said Carrickfergus. Where in Carrickfergus?

A screech split the silence. It echoed along the street, touching Fegan's heart like an icy finger. He held his breath tight in his chest. It came again, a high animal cry, the sound of suffering. Fegan looked up and down the rows of houses, searching for the source.

Then he saw it. The animal came creeping between two cars, long snout to the ground. Its large pointed ears twitched, and it raised its head. It opened its jaws wide and screeched again, the sound tearing through the street and over the rooftops.

The fox sauntered out onto the road, following some scent that had caught its interest. It froze, tensed, lifted its lean body flexing beneath the fur. It stared hard at the window and quivered.

Fegan put a hand against the glass. The fox raised its snout to the black sky and screeched once more. It bared its teeth. Fegan couldn't hear through the glass, but he was sure the fox snarled and growled before it blossomed in flame. Fegan blinked and heard the engine of a car. Its headlights burned and reflected on the fox's pelt as it approached. The fox looked to the light, then back at Fegan, before it dashed into the shadows.

The car passed, the driver oblivious to the watching animals.

Somewhere in the distance, across the city, sirens rose. In the dark hollows beneath the window, the fox answered.

Carrickfergus. A whorehouse, he said.

Fegan pictured the office behind the reception desk downstairs. He'd seen keys on hooks through the open door. One of them had been a car key. Fegan left his room, quiet as air.

74

The woman and that creepy kid huddled silent in the back seat as the Traveller drove. He had gone north then west from Carrickfergus, rather than cutting through Belfast, then south from Templepatrick. He would avoid the motorway until he was across the border, and stay out of the bigger towns like Banbridge or Newry. A lost hour was a price worth paying to escape notice.

He wondered if the woman would make it that far. Now and again he heard her chest rattle before she coughed. He had given her wounds a quick look before they left. She had a couple of pellets embedded in her cheekbone, and more in her right shoulder. But it was the cluster above her breast she had to worry about. The Traveller reckoned some had punctured her ribcage, and maybe even her lung. He had patched her up with a towel as best he could, but she was probably bleeding inside. A hospital could fix it, he was sure. But they weren't going to a hospital. Maybe she'd make it to Drogheda, maybe she wouldn't. His only worries were how the kid would react if her mother died as they held each other, and how the Bull would react when he brought the two of them to his doorstep.

Maybe he should have done them in the apartment. Probably should. But there was something about the kid, the way she looked at him, like she knew all his secrets. Even the things he kept hidden from himself. Whatever it was, it stopped him from snapping the child's neck. He'd let the Bull deal with them.

The woman and child had served their purpose. They'd got Gerry Fegan to show himself. Let the Bull decide the next move. Maybe he'd let the cops have Fegan. He'd be easier dealt with if he was locked up. But where was the fun in that? Either way, the Bull could do what he wanted so long as he paid up.

The car was approaching the roundabout at Moira when the woman asked 'Where are you taking us?' Her voice was small but strong. Maybe she wasn't as bad as he'd thought. He glanced at her reflection in the rear-view mirror and saw her reading a road sign.

'To see a man,' he said.

'What man?'

'You'll see when we get there,' he said. He steered onto the long straight section of the roundabout. 'Now be quiet, love, there's a good girl.'

'Is it O'Kane?'

'I said be quiet.'

'The last man who brought us to him is dead now.'

As he exited the roundabout, the Traveller switched his attention between the village of Moira ahead and Marie McKenna's reflection in the mirror. 'That right?'

'Gerry Fegan killed him.'

The Traveller's tongue slicked his upper lip. 'Did he, now?'

348

'He'll kill you too.'

He watched the mirror as the little girl covered her ears and buried her face in her mother's bosom. Marie winced at the pain but did not push the child away.

'You think so?' the Traveller asked.

'I know so.'

The Traveller smiled at the mirror. He would have winked if he could've managed it. 'Well, I wouldn't be so sure about that.'

The lights of the main street slipped past for a minute or two and then faded behind them.

Marie laughed, then coughed, then laughed again.

'What's so funny?' he asked.

She produced a tissue and coughed into it. Her face went blank. 'What's so funny? Earlier today I told someone I didn't want to wind up a fucking damsel in distress again.'

The little girl took a hand away from her ear and placed it over her mother's mouth. 'You said a bad word,' she whispered.

'I know, darling,' Marie said against the child's fingers. 'I'm sorry.'

The girl, placated, covered her ears and buried her face again.

'Tell me about Gerry Fegan,' the Traveller said as they approached another village, smaller this time. Magheralin, he thought it was called, but he couldn't be sure seeing as he couldn't read the sign.

'He's a good man,' Marie said, 'despite what he's done.'

'A good man,' the Traveller repeated, turning

the words in his mouth, testing their weight. 'And I'm not?'

Marie coughed, groaned at the pain. When she caught her breath, she asked, 'What are you talking about?'

'From what I hear, he's an animal. A killer.' He watched her face as the lights of the village caused shadows to flow across it. 'Just like me. What makes him a good man? What makes me a bad man?'

The light disappeared from her face, leaving only the glint of her eyes in a silhouette. 'You have me and my child as hostages, and you have to ask that question?'

More village lights ahead, and beyond them, the town of Lurgan with its knotted streets and traffic lights and cops. He took a left down a narrow country road to avoid them. The world darkened.

'I've been looking forward to meeting Mr Gerry Fegan,' the Traveller said. He grinned at the mirror, even though he could no longer see the woman or the girl in the blackness. 'Might not happen now. Pity if it doesn't. It'd be fun, seeing what he's made of. From what I hear, it wouldn't be easy. He'd put up a good fight.'

He waited for a response. None came save for the rattle of Marie's chest.

'I'd enjoy that,' he said. 'He might be a mad bastard, but so am I. I never met a man I couldn't take, and I like a challenge, you know?'

The Traveller searched the mirror, found nothing. He couldn't even hear the woman's laboured breathing now.

'You can be sure of one thing, though. Your friend Gerry is going to suffer for his sins. Whether it's me or the cops do it, it'll be bad for him. He'll be hurting when he goes. He's pissed off too many people to get off easy. Only question is, how ba — '

Fiery pain tore at his scalp as small hands jerked his head back. A high scream pierced his left ear as the hands twisted and pulled. He reached back with his left hand, but the strapping wouldn't let his fingers find anything but strands of hair as the girl shouted and thrashed. The car bounced as it hit the verge, the steering wheel bucking in his good hand. The woman cried out, and the girl was thrown to the side, but she kept her grip and now the Traveller was screaming as his scalp ripped. His right hand left the wheel and darted behind him, desperate to swat the shrieking child away, and then the seat belt grabbed his chest, his head whipped forward and back again, and everything was black and still and silent, apart from an insistent chiming as a cold breeze blew in from somewhere far behind him.

75

Lennon waited alone in the kitchen. A constable from Carrickfergus lingered uselessly in the corridor outside the flat while a sergeant took statements from the residents on the floors below. Everyone who could be spared was at the scene of DCI Gordon's murder. The best the Carrickfergus station could do was send their one patrol car, which had been on traffic duty looking for drunk drivers, to the apartment block. Lennon got there before them and came straight up to find the door blown in and the place empty.

Worry and fear quarrelled within him like feral cats. He couldn't keep his mind in one place long enough to plan a course of action. He phoned the station again, looking for CI Uprichard. When the duty officer finally answered the call, he told Lennon yet again: Uprichard was too busy, just wait there, secure the scene until a team from D District could be assembled.

'I can't just wait here,' Lennon said. 'He has my daughter. The same man you had in custody three hours ago.'

'I understand that,' the duty officer said, 'but an officer has been murdered here. Everybody who can be contacted is being brought in. Besides, you know Carrickfergus is D District; we can only send men if it's an emergency. Otherwise you'll have to wait for a team from Lisburn.'

'Emergency?' Lennon said. 'What the fuck are you talking about? This is my daughter. The same man who killed Gordon has her.'

'But he doesn't have her there,' the duty officer said.

Lennon had no answer for that, no words to express his frustration.

'To do any good, you need a proper MIT and forensics to go over the apartment,' the duty officer continued. 'Forensics are tied up here for the time being, and Lisburn will get an MIT over there as soon as they can. I'm sorry, sir, that's the best I can do at the moment. Now, if you'll excuse me, it's bedlam here.'

Lennon hung up. He paced a single circle around the small kitchen and stopped at the sink. He ran the tap, splashed water on his face, dried himself on his sleeve. He walked out through the living room and into the hall. His Glock lay on the floor. It hadn't done Marie any good. He stooped and picked it up.

The constable shuffled his feet and coughed in the doorway. Wallace, his name was, and he watched Lennon with nervous deference. He didn't look like he'd been long on the job, most likely a probationer paired up with the older sergeant to learn the ropes.

'Should you lift that, Inspector?' His face dropped as Lennon gave him a hard look. 'I mean, it's evidence at the scene, isn't it?'

Lennon patted his shoulder as he stepped past him to the corridor. 'You'll go far, Constable Wallace,' he said.

The lift doors slid open and Sergeant Dodds

stepped out. He reviewed his notebook as he walked.

'Anything?' Lennon asked.

'Nothing useful,' Dodds said. 'Only three other flats occupied. All of them heard the gunfire, and two of them called 999. Everyone locked their doors and kept their heads down till they heard our siren. Nobody saw anything.'

Lennon had expected nothing more. 'All right,' he said. He walked towards the lift. 'An MIT from Lisburn will be here when they have the people gathered, and forensics when they can get away. Wallace, you stay here. Dodds, you wait downstairs at the entrance. Don't let anyone use the stairwell if you can help it.'

Dodds followed Lennon into the lift. 'And where are you going?'

'To see a man.'

'What man?'

'Just a man,' Lennon said. He prayed Roscoe Patterson was on drinking form tonight.

76

The Traveller put his shoulder to the door and pushed. It budged only an inch or two before the hedgerow pushed back. 'Fucking bastard arsehole,' he said. He slid the other way and struggled over the armrest, going head first. The gear stick caught him in the balls and he groaned. In a second or two, that sick, heavy ache would join the throb in his chest where the seat belt had crushed the air out of him. And his neck hurt too. That pain seemed to begin in his shoulders, creep up to the back of his skull, then trace a line up and over to his forehead.

He opened the passenger door and climbed out. He grabbed Marie's mobile phone and hit a button. The screen had cracked, but it still worked, casting a weak light. He used it as a makeshift torch so he could inspect the damage to the car. It wasn't as bad as he'd feared. The hedgerow had cushioned its impact with the embankment, and the old Volkswagen was built tough. He shone the light down at the tyres. The earth wasn't too wet; he should be able to reverse the car out of the tangle of green.

The light died as the phone went back into standby. The Traveller turned in a circle at the edge of the little country road. An orange glow hovered over Lurgan to the west. To the north he could make out the soft rumble of night-time traffic on the motorway, lorries hurrying to make the early ferries to Britain, or holidaymakers heading to one of the airports.

He listened hard for noises closer to the road, for the sound of feet creeping through the hedges and fields. Was that a wheeze and a rattle from across the way? The sound was so small, perhaps he only imagined it. He closed his eyes, held his breath, and listened harder. A cold, damp breeze washed across his face.

There, a child's soft cry, then a hoarse whisper.

The Traveller opened his eyes. He looked in the direction of the sounds. A light, maybe a window, glowed dim in the distance. A farmhouse, about half a mile away. He thumbed the phone again. He turned, crouched down, and used it to find Hewitt's Glock in the passenger footwell.

As he straightened, the pistol cold in his hand, a weariness came over him. He leaned on the car's roof and breathed deep. New pains signalled from all over his body. He wished he'd never entered the bar in Finglas. He wished he'd never taken the note from Davy Haughey, the one with Orla O'Kane's phone number on it. He wished he'd never accepted her invitation to that fucking convalescent home near Drogheda, the one where Bull O'Kane wallowed in his own hate and shit-smelling stink.

An insane notion flitted through his mind, one so ludicrous he couldn't help but examine it as it passed. Just get in the car, reverse out of the hedge, and drive away. Leave the woman and her kid to their fate out here. Whoever was in that house would take them in, see them right. The Traveller could go to one of the flats he kept in Dublin, Drogheda or Cork, gather up his passports, and disappear. He had money stashed in accounts in Ireland, Brazil, the Philippines and more places besides, enough to see him to his dying day if he was careful with it.

But what kind of life would that be, hiding under stones like a woodlouse? And then another thought came to him.

Gerry Fegan.

The Traveller wanted to know if he could take Gerry Fegan. He considered his condition, the injured shoulder, the sprained wrist, the stinging eye. He inhaled, igniting a fresh pain in his chest. Maybe add a cracked rib to that list. He'd be at a disadvantage, and that gave Fegan a fighting chance.

If the cops didn't get to Fegan first, the Traveller could have a go at him. May the best man win, and all that.

Alone, in the dark by the side of the road, the Traveller smiled to himself as he made his mind up. He turned towards the sound he was now sure he had heard and started walking. When the crunch of country road under his feet turned to the soft squelch of damp grass he thumbed the mobile and let its glow reach into the dark. He watched and listened.

Another rattling inhalation. He trained the light on its source. Eyes glittered there. He marched forward, and he heard, 'Go, go, go!'

A small shape sprang from the hedge and disappeared into the black. The woman tried to raise herself from the tangle of greenery, but stumbled. He was on her before she could move. She didn't have the strength to struggle, just lay limp beneath him, her breath shallow and stuttering.

'Easy now,' he said, letting her feel the cold of the Glock against her neck.

The Traveller put the phone into his pocket, then eased back and slipped an arm around her waist. He got to his feet, taking her with him. She shivered against his body as he held her close, the pistol's muzzle beneath her chin.

'Call the wee girl,' he whispered in her ear.

'No.'

'Call her.' He jabbed her chin with the muzzle and she whimpered.

'No,' she said. 'I won't.'

'All right then, I'll do it.'

'She won't come to you,' she said, shaking her head.

'Oh, she will.' He pulled Marie tight to him. 'A wee girl like that won't leave her mammy. Watch this.'

She inhaled to call out, but he sealed her mouth with his strapped-up hand.

'Ellen!' the Traveller called.

Marie tried to prise his hand away. He pressed it harder against her lips and her teeth nipped at the skin of his fingers, trying to get a hold. He twisted her neck around.

'Quit it,' he said, his mouth buried deep in her hair. 'Quit it or I'll break your neck.' He looked back out to the darkness. 'Ellen!'

The Traveller slipped the Glock into his

waistband and took out his phone. It lit up in his hand, and he held it out in front of the struggling mother.

'Your mammy needs you, Ellen. Come on back, now. You don't want to be out there in the dark, all on your own. There's bad things in the dark. Things that'll get you. Things with teeth. Things that sting.'

He stopped, listened. 'Come on, sweetheart. Your mammy needs you.'

A shadow moved out there in the layers of black. He saw a glint. Then she came running from the darkness, fell, picked herself up again, and threw herself at her mother. Ellen wrapped her arms around Marie's thighs, pressed her face to the warmth.

The Traveller said, 'Good girl.'

77

The door of the Red Fox Bar, off the Shankill, was locked, but lights shone inside. Lennon hammered with his fist until the pane of frosted glass rattled in its frame.

'We're closed,' a hoarse voice called from inside. A silhouette formed against the glass. 'Fuck off.'

The silhouette faded.

Lennon kicked the door.

The silhouette returned. 'I told you to fuck off, we're closed. Away to fuck or I'll come out there and kick your shite in.'

Lennon kicked the door again and again until the glass cracked.

'Right, you fucker,' the voice said.

The bolts sounded like two rifle shots as they opened at the top and bottom of the door. It swung inward, and a heavy-set man with a shaven head and tattoos on his neck filled the doorway. He wore spectacles that sat at an odd angle. Before he could take a step, Lennon drove a fist into the valley beneath his belly and shattered his nose with the other. The man stumbled into the bar, blood erupting from between his fingers as he clasped his hands to his face. His spectacles fell away, cracked and bent. He tripped over his own feet and landed on his back.

Lennon stepped over him and into the bar.

Three men were gathered around a table strewn with cards and cash, bottles and glasses. Two were on their feet, their hands out and ready for action.

Lennon drew his Glock and aimed at Roscoe Patterson's forehead, one hand supporting the other in a combat stance. Roscoe sat at the far side of the table, his face blank, staring back at Lennon. The two standing men drew pistols, both small-calibre toys, the kind of weapons jumped-up thugs would carry to make themselves look big.

'Put 'em away, boys,' Roscoe said. 'No need for playing silly buggers, is there, Jack?'

The two men obeyed.

'Get rid of them,' Lennon said.

'Jesus, you got Slant a good 'un,' Roscoe said. He threw his head back and laughed. 'Fucking stove his face in.' He smiled at Lennon. 'Know why we call him Slant?'

'I don't care, just get them out of here.'

Roscoe continued, 'We call him Slant 'cause when he gets pissed, his glasses sit at a slant. Fucking comical. The way you just pasted his nose all over his face, he'll never get them glasses to sit straight again.'

Lennon took a step closer and steadied his aim. 'Get rid of them. Now.'

Roscoe's smile broadened. His eyes dimmed. 'You heard the fella,' he said to his companions. 'Fuck off and take Slant with you.'

'You sure?' one of Roscoe's thugs asked.

'I'm sure,' Roscoe said. 'Jack's a smart fella. He'll not do anything stupid. Will you, Jack?'

'Just get them out of here,' Lennon said.

'Go on, boys.' Roscoe dismissed them with a wave.

They sauntered past Lennon, rolling their shoulders, keeping eye contact with him, trying to show they weren't intimidated by a stranger with a gun.

Lennon kept his eyes on Roscoe. He heard Slant moan and curse as his friends gathered him up. The door closed, and all was quiet save for Lennon's breathing. Sweat dripped from his eyebrows.

Roscoe said, 'That was bad form, Jack.'

Lennon didn't answer. He took a step closer, kept the pistol trained on Roscoe's forehead.

'Making a cunt of me like that,' Roscoe said, his hand beginning to shake on the tabletop. His lips thinned across his teeth. 'Any other fucker tried that, I'd break the bastard's neck. I'd take that gun and shove it so far up their arse they'd frigging choke on it. I'd put my fucking boot in their — '

'I'm not here to play games, Roscoe,' Lennon said. 'I know what you did. I'll put a bullet in your bigoted little brain and I won't give it a thought. You understand? No threats, no fucking around. I'll shoot you dead.'

Roscoe stood up. He leaned forward, his knuckles on the tabletop, the cards spreading beneath his weight. 'Watch your mouth, Jack. I've been good to you, you've been good to me. I wouldn't call us friends, like, but as taigs go, you've been a decent sort of a fella. But no one threatens me. No one makes a cunt of me in front of my boys. You're playing with your life, here, Jack. Don't go making — '

Lennon focused on the heart-shaped tattoo on the back of Roscoe's left hand. He squeezed the trigger. The bullet split the tabletop an inch from Roscoe's fingers. Roscoe pulled his hands away, but didn't make a sound. He stepped back from the table, shaking his head.

'Who did you go to?' Lennon asked. 'Who did you tell?'

Roscoe held his hands up and backed away. 'What are you talking about, Jack? I told no one about nothing. You're making a serious mistake here, mate.'

Lennon followed. He pushed the table aside, ignoring the crashing of bottles as it tipped over. Paper money and broken glass crunched beneath his feet. He holstered his pistol. He flexed his fingers. 'You told someone where Marie and Ellen were. You told someone where my daughter was. Now they've got them.'

Roscoe backed towards the bar. 'Fuck's sake, Jack, you're talking out your arse. I told you before, I'm no tout. I said nothing to no — '

Lennon caught Roscoe with an elbow to the jaw. Roscoe dropped like a sack of loose flesh. He rolled on his side, hands to his chin.

'He has my daughter,' Lennon said.

Roscoe squirmed on the floor. He spat blood on the grime-caked tiles.

'He has my daughter,' Lennon repeated. 'Do you understand?'

'My tongue,' Roscoe said, his words blunt. 'I bit my fucking tongue, you Fenian bastard.'

Lennon stood over Roscoe, one hand on the bar. 'Talk to me now or I'll kill you, I fucking swear.'

'Shove it up your taig arse, you cunt,' Roscoe hissed. He spat again, spattering the floor with crimson.

Lennon kicked him in the gut. Roscoe doubled up, curled into a ball, rolled so his back was to Lennon. Lennon aimed his foot at Roscoe's kidney, felt the flesh give under the force of it.

When the squealing was done, Lennon hunkered down and said, 'You passed on the information. You tell me now who you talked to. See, I don't give a fuck. Ellen is the only good thing I ever gave to the world. I talked to her today. For the first time in five years, I talked to my own daughter. She has no notion who I am, but it doesn't matter. I have a chance to make it right. I have a chance to get her back. And you sell her out to some piece of shit.'

Roscoe uncurled. He tried to haul himself away, but the pain creased his face. 'You're wrong. I never — '

'You sold her out to the other side. You, the big Loyalist, you sold a child to the Republicans. It's like Patsy Toner said. The collusion, it goes all ways, all directions. All the likes of you ever cared about was lining your own pockets. You didn't give a shit about any cause, did you? Just so long as you were making money.'

'You're losing it,' Roscoe said. 'You're fucking off your — '

Lennon drew his Glock and pressed the

muzzle to Roscoe's forehead. 'You've got one last chance,' Lennon said. 'Someone will have reported the gunshot. The moment I hear the sirens, I'll pull the trigger and blow your brains out. It'll be self-defence, a known career criminal against a cop. The Ombudsman's office won't care. No one's going to give a fuck about a piece of shit like you. Do you understand?'

Roscoe blinked at him, his nostrils flared.

'The only way you live is if you tell me who you talked to,' Lennon said. 'That's all there is. No other choices. Now tell me.'

Roscoe squeezed his eyes shut. 'Fuck,' he said. His face went slack, his eyelids fluttered. 'Dan Hewitt,' he said. 'That Special Branch fucker. He's the one you want. He's the one put the word out. He wanted to know what you were up to, if anyone saw you around, if you came at anyone looking favours. I called him up. Told him you wanted the flat.'

Roscoe opened his eyes and smiled. 'What? You think you're the only cop I'm mates with? Like you said: all ways, all directions.'

Lennon stood upright and holstered the Glock. 'You breathe a word of this, I'll tell anyone who'll listen that you're a tout.'

'Fuck you,' Roscoe said.

'You know what they do to touts,' Lennon said. 'You come near me, or anyone I know, I'll tell every last fucker in this city you're a tout. You won't be able to show your ugly face on the street. You understand me?'

'Fuck you,' Roscoe said.

Lennon kicked him hard in the groin. Roscoe

365

curled into a tight ball, blood dripping from his lips. He vomited onto the tiled floor.

The smell of it hit Lennon hard, and he went for the door, swallowing against his own bile until the night air cooled his skin.

He didn't see the tall man coming, only felt the hard hands on his throat before he hit the ground.

78

'Where are they?' Fegan asked, his face inches from the cop's.

Lennon struggled beneath him, his shoulders twisting as Fegan fought for balance.

'I don't know,' the cop said.

Fegan tightened his grip on Lennon's throat, tried to find the windpipe with his fingers. 'You should've kept them safe.'

The cop reached up, going for Fegan's eyes. Fegan pulled back, twisting his face away. His balance left him, and he lost his grip on Lennon's throat. Another push and his back hit the pavement, a heavy body on his, a Glock against his cheek.

'Gerry Fegan,' the cop said.

'Why did you leave them?' Fegan asked.

'I had to,' Lennon said, panting. 'No one knew where they were.'

'But he found them.'

The Glock pressed harder on Fegan's cheek. 'I fucking know he did,' Lennon said. 'They were sold out. *I* was sold out. Now get away from here or I'll blow your head off.'

'No,' Fegan said. He pushed up with his elbows, ignoring the pressure of the pistol's muzzle against his cheekbone. 'Not until I know where they are.'

'Why?' Lennon pushed him back down. 'You caused all this. They'd be safe if it wasn't for you.

You started this whole thing, you crazy bastard.'

'I know,' Fegan said, strength draining from his body into the cold ground. He closed his eyes. 'I know.'

The muzzle lifted from his cheek, and the other man's weight left his chest. He opened his eyes. The cop stood over him, the Glock still aimed at his forehead.

'How did you find me?' Lennon asked.

'I talked to the man who has them,' Fegan said. 'On Marie's phone. He said he was in Carrickfergus. I drove around till I saw a cop car. I knew that was it. Then I followed you.'

Lennon stood back and waved the pistol at the empty street. 'Get out of here. Go on, disappear, or I'll turn you in.'

Fegan sat up. 'I can't. Not till they're safe.'

'They'll never be safe while you're around,' Lennon said. 'Can't you see that? Christ, there's no time for this.'

The cop stepped over Fegan's legs and headed for the Audi.

'Where are they?' Fegan got to his feet. 'What did you find out in there?'

'Nothing that concerns you,' Lennon said as he opened the Audi's door. 'Just go and don't come back.'

'Tell me,' Fegan said, fighting the anger that swelled in his chest.

Lennon raised the pistol again. His hand shook. 'Get out of here or so help me I'll shoot you dead.'

Fegan went for the pub's door.

'Don't,' Lennon called after him.

Fegan turned to face him. 'Then tell me.'

'He doesn't know where they went,' Lennon said, his shoulders sagging. 'But he told me someone who might. The one who sold them out.'

'Who is it?'

'An old friend,' Lennon said. 'A cop.'

Fegan stepped closer. 'Take me to him.'

'No,' Lennon said. 'Christ, no. Are you crazy? What am I talking about, of course you're crazy.'

The cop holstered his weapon and lowered himself into the car. Fegan ran to it and grabbed the door before Lennon could pull it closed.

Lennon glowered up at him from the driver's seat. 'Let go.'

'Will he tell you where they are?' Fegan asked.

'I don't know,' Lennon said. 'Maybe. Maybe not. Let go of the door.'

Fegan leaned into the car, smelled the cop's sweat and fear. 'Take me to him.'

'Why?'

'Because he'll tell me.'

'If he won't tell me, why in God's name would he tell you?'

Fegan said, 'Because I'll ask harder.'

79

The Traveller drove the Volkswagen up to the gate of the convalescent home Bull O'Kane had taken over. A man emerged from the shadows and shone a torch into the car, picking out the woman and child.

The man tapped the window. The Traveller lowered it.

'Who the fuck are they?' the man asked.

The Traveller could just make out a dark jacket and jeans. Something bulged in the man's pocket. 'They're old friends of your boss,' he said. 'Now open up.'

The man scratched his stubbly chin for a few seconds before waving the torch at someone. The gate opened, the keeper unseen, and the Traveller drove through.

The old house stood black against the deep blue of the coming morning. It grew as the car approached. Headlights reflected on sash windows. Gravel crunched beneath the tyres. The Traveller's head throbbed with fatigue. He prayed the Bull would allow him an hour or two's sleep once he got the woman and child off his hands.

The handbrake creaked as he stopped at the front door. It stood open, Orla O'Kane's wide body silhouetted by the light inside. The Traveller got out of the car.

'What are you doing here?' she asked.

'Just paying a visit,' he said.

She stepped out onto the gravel. 'Is that . . . ?'

'Yeah.'

Orla moved close to the Traveller. 'What in the name of Christ did you bring them here for?'

'Your auld fella wanted Fegan drawn out, didn't he? I reckon these are the girls for the job, so I brought them for a visit.'

Orla shook her head. 'No. Not like this. Not here. He won't have it. He made that mistake before.'

'That's his lookout, isn't it?'

She poked his chest with a thick finger. 'Well, I'm making it yours. You better — '

The Traveller swiped her finger away. 'Look, I did my bit, and I got the shite knocked out of me for my troubles. Do you see the state of me? You can do whatever the fuck you want with these two, just make sure I get my money.'

Orla stared at him while the machine behind her eyes worked, lives lost or spared with each option she considered. Finally, she nodded and said, 'All right.' She looked back to the car. 'Are they intact?'

'The kid is. The woman's hurt.'

Orla approached the rear of the car and peered in. 'How bad?'

'Bad enough,' he said. 'Any nurses here?'

'No. They go home at night. Aren't due back on shift for an hour or so yet. Just me and a couple of boys to keep watch.'

'Pity,' he said. 'She needs looking at. I don't give her much time otherwise.'

'Doesn't matter,' Orla said. She opened the

371

door and hunkered down at eye level with the child. The hardness of her face eased as she reached for her. 'Hello, darling. What's your name?'

* * *

The Traveller sat Marie McKenna down on a chair outside the Bull's room. Orla kept the child in her arms, whispering to her, rocking her.

Marie reached up. Sweat beaded on her skin at the effort. 'Please,' she said, her voice thin like paper.

Orla hesitated, then lowered Ellen into her mother's lap. Marie's chest rattled as she wrapped her arms loose around the child. She watched the Traveller with dark eyes set in an ash-grey face. She coughed, spraying red droplets in the little girl's hair.

Orla knocked the door to the Bull's room. A grunt came from inside.

'Da?' she called.

'Wait,' the voice from inside said.

'Da? What's wrong?'

'Don't come — '

She pushed the door open. Bull O'Kane lay sprawled on the floor between his chair and his bed, sweating and breathing hard. He stared up at the Traveller.

'Da, what happened?'

The Bull's wild eyes flicked back to Orla. 'Come in and shut that fucking door.'

She rushed in and slammed the door in the Traveller's face.

'Fuck me,' the Traveller said.

The Bull had looked like a discarded shell lying there, so weak he couldn't even keep his feet. Groans and hisses came from inside the room, the sounds of a strong woman hoisting up a frail old man. Fucking pathetic, the Traveller thought.

He listened as the voices volleyed back and forth on the other side of the door, firm at first, then climbing in anger. Several minutes passed before the door opened again. Orla stepped past him, her face flushed, her lips thin. She indicated with a tilt of her head that he should enter.

'If you've any brains left,' Bull O'Kane said from his chair, 'you won't take me for weak.'

'Wouldn't dream of it,' the Traveller said. He gave the Bull his most serious countenance.

O'Kane watched him for a moment, breathing hard. He wiped his sleeve across his forehead. 'You don't look so good yourself.'

'I've been better,' the Traveller said. He flexed his shoulders, working the stiffness out of them. The skin itched beneath the strapping on his left wrist.

'Maybe that's what's making you so fucking stupid.'

The Traveller winked. 'There's no stupid people in this room.'

'Don't smart-arse me,' the Bull said, leaning forward. His hands trembled on the armrests. 'You're lucky I haven't had you shot. You know what's going to happen now?'

'Yeah, I do.' The Traveller stepped forward. 'You do whatever you want with the woman and

373

the kid. I get paid and be on my way.'

'No.' The Bull sagged back into his chair. 'What happens now is he comes after them.'

'Gerry Fegan?'

The Bull nodded slow, his gaze locked on the Traveller's.

'He doesn't know where they are,' the Traveller said.

'He'll find out. Then he'll come.'

The Traveller smiled. 'Then you can watch me break his neck. How's that?'

The Bull sat still, lost in thought. Eventually, he asked, 'You sure you can take him?'

'I'm sure.'

'If you're wrong, he'll kill us all.'

'I'm sure,' the Traveller said.

The Bull inhaled, held it, released it, made his decision. 'All right,' he said. 'Bring 'em in now, there's a good fella.'

80

Lennon's phone rang as he pulled up ten yards from Hewitt's house. He gestured to Fegan to be quiet and answered it.

'Where are you?' CI Uprichard asked.

'Following up on something,' Lennon said.

'Lisburn have been on the line,' Uprichard said. 'They have an MIT together. Officers are on their way to Carrickfergus now. They'll be pissed off if you're not there to meet them after calling them out.'

'I've got other things to do,' Lennon said. He hung up.

Fegan indicated the big house beyond the security gate. 'Who is he?'

'Detective Chief Inspector Dan Hewitt,' Lennon said. 'A friend of mine. Used to be, anyway. Special Branch.'

'Jesus,' Fegan said.

'Might as well be,' Lennon said. 'You know how it works. They're untouchable.'

'He sold you and Marie out,' Fegan said.

'That's right.'

'Fancy house,' Fegan said. 'Old. Four, five bedrooms. How much does a Special Branch cop make?'

'Not enough to afford a big house in this part of Belfast.' A movement caught Lennon's eye. 'Hang on.'

The electric gates swung open, and an

unmarked police car drove out. Lennon got out of his Audi, and Fegan followed. They crossed the distance to the gates by the time the cop car turned onto the Lisburn Road and just made it through before they closed. A security lamp, triggered by the cop car's exit, bathed the garden and driveway in harsh white light. Beyond the grand bay window's voile curtains, Hewitt drank from a glass while his wife Juliet stood over him. A large plaster covered the bridge of his nose, and Lennon could just make out the bruising around his reddened eyes.

'What happened to him?' Fegan asked.

'No idea,' Lennon said. 'Keep out of sight.'

Fegan lost himself in the shadows beneath the security light's reach.

Lennon hammered the door with his fist. Juliet came to the window and peeled back the voile. She stared for a second or two before turning her head to say something over her shoulder. Lennon hit the door again. Her hands waved and pointed as she argued with Hewitt before she disappeared. Lennon waited and listened.

When nothing happened Lennon slapped the wood with his palm three times. 'Open up, Dan,' he called.

The door opened six inches, and Juliet peered out. 'Jesus Christ, Jack, what do you think you're doing?' She wrapped her dressing gown tight around herself. Her eyes were red and brimming. 'You'll wake the kids up again. I've had enough tonight without you — '

Lennon pushed the door open and stepped past her.

Juliet grabbed his arm, but he shook her off.

'Dan!' she shouted. 'Dan, call someone. I can't have this. Not tonight, not on top of everything else.'

She saw Fegan emerge from the darkness. 'Who are you?' She turned back to Lennon. 'Jack, who is that?'

Lennon ignored her and entered the living room. Hewitt sat on the couch, hunched over an empty glass and a bottle of gin. He froze when he saw Fegan enter behind his old friend. His eyes darted from man to man.

Hewitt blinked, coughed, forced a smile that seemed to crack his face in two. 'Christ, Jack, you're keeping bad company these days.'

A can of Coke sat alongside the glass on the coffee table. While Lennon and Fegan watched, he poured two fingers of gin and emptied the remainder of the Coke on top of it. The sickly juniper smell cloyed at Lennon's nose and throat.

'It's late to come calling,' Hewitt said, his voice made hard and nasal by the plaster over his nose. Purple blotches spread out beneath his eyes, which were bloodshot and watery. 'What do you want?'

'What did he do with them?' Lennon asked.

Hewitt winced at the alcohol's burn. He swallowed, coughed, and put the glass back on the table. 'What are you talking about, Jack?'

Lennon approached the coffee table. 'I'm warning you, Dan. Don't fuck me around. Not this time.'

Hewitt looked up. 'Don't threaten me, Jack.

Not in my own home, not in front of my wife. I don't care what cavalry you brought with you.'

Lennon upended the table. Gin and Coca-Cola soaked the thick carpet. The bottle smashed against the hearth, scattering green glass.

Juliet spoke from behind. 'Dan, I'm calling 999.'

'Don't,' Hewitt said.

'Dan, I — '

'I said don't. Go and see to the kids. Keep them upstairs.'

'But — '

Hewitt stood. 'Just fucking do as I tell you.'

Lennon glanced over his shoulder to see the hurt on her face. She closed the door behind her.

Fegan studied them both, his countenance unreadable.

'I told you to leave it alone,' Hewitt said. Dried blood stained his shirt front. 'You wouldn't listen, would you?' He waved a finger at Fegan. 'Now you've got this animal involved. Jesus, I didn't think you could make it any worse, but you've proved me wrong.'

'I know Bull O'Kane has them,' Lennon said, staring hard at Hewitt. 'Tell me where.'

Hewitt put his hands on his hips. 'I'll tell you this much as a friend, even though you don't deserve it,' he said. 'They're safe. That's all I know.'

Lennon stepped forward, grinding glass into the carpet beneath his feet. 'Where are they? I'll hurt you if you don't tell me.'

Hewitt laughed. Lennon felt the alcohol-tainted breath on his face. He slapped Hewitt

378

hard across the cheek. Hewitt fell back onto the couch. He sat there, open-mouthed, then laughed again. This time the laughter had a fluttering edge, like something about to be taken away on the wind.

'After what I've seen tonight, you're going to have to try a lot harder than that if you and your friend here want to scare me.'

Lennon drew his Glock and aimed at Hewitt's chest.

'Christ, Jack, just get back in that car you can't afford, and go home to that flat you can't afford. The best thing you can do for Marie McKenna and your wee girl is stay out of it. It's not them he wants. He's just using them. Once he has the man he wants, he'll let them go.'

Hewitt tilted his head and said, 'Isn't that right, Gerry?'

Lennon looked back over his shoulder. Fegan stood still as a rock, his eyes blazing.

'I've told you too much already,' Hewitt said. His face hardened. 'Now go home before you make things any worse.'

Lennon lowered his aim to Hewitt's thigh. 'I'll do it, Dan. Tell me where they are.'

'You'll do what?' Hewitt asked. He laughed again. 'Don't act the big man, Jack. It doesn't suit you. It might fool those sluts you pull in the bars, but it doesn't work with me. You're fucking with the wrong people now. I promise you'll regret it.'

'What are they paying you?'

Hewitt smiled, creasing the bruises beneath his eyes. 'Watch your mouth, Jack. Now put the gun away. We both know you won't shoot a fellow police — '

Silent like a cat, Fegan snatched the Glock from Lennon's hand, squeezed the trigger, put a neat hole in Hewitt's thigh. Hewitt screamed and rolled onto his side, clutching his leg. Squeals and crying came from upstairs, followed by quick footsteps.

Lennon stepped back, his heart thundering, his stomach cold.

'Where are they?' Fegan asked.

'Bastard!' Hewitt roared into the cushions.

Feet on the stairs, hammering as they descended. 'Dan?' Juliet called.

Fegan hauled Hewitt from the couch and threw him to the floor. Hewitt screamed again as he rolled on the broken glass.

Fegan took aim again. 'I'll put another one in you.'

Hewitt hissed through his teeth. He stared hard at Lennon. 'You're finished. So help me God, I'll put you away myself.'

'Where are they?' Fegan asked.

'Fuck you!'

Juliet tumbled in. 'Jesus, Dan!'

Fegan spun, aimed at her. 'Get out.'

She retreated. 'Don't. Please don't hurt him any more.'

Hewitt grabbed Fegan's ankle, tried to haul himself up. Fegan whipped his leg away and swung it back to slam his foot into Hewitt's stomach. Hewitt folded in on himself, drawing bloody lines where his thigh brushed along the carpet.

'Where are they?' Fegan asked, taking aim again.

Hewitt squirmed. 'Fuck you.'

Fegan kicked his injured thigh. Hewitt screamed. When he was quiet again, Fegan asked, 'Where are they?'

Sweat dripped from Hewitt's forehead to the carpet. 'Fuck you.'

Fegan went to kick him again, but Lennon said, 'Wait.'

He stepped past Fegan and hunkered down beside Hewitt. 'Tell me now or I'll let Gerry here blow out your kneecap,' he said, his voice low in his chest. 'You've seen the punishment shootings, same as me. You know what it does. You've seen the kids the paramilitaries did this to. They're lucky if they ever walk again. Is it really worth it to you? Are they really paying you enough to live with what it'll do to you? Think hard, Dan. I'm only going to ask you once more. Where are they?'

'Fuck you,' Hewitt said, his eyes brimming.

Fegan crouched and pressed the Glock's muzzle against the back of Hewitt's knee.

Hewitt began to weep. 'Fuck — '

As Fegan's finger tightened on the trigger, a small voice said, 'Drogheda.'

Lennon and Fegan turned to see Juliet cowering against the door frame. 'Don't hurt him any more,' she said.

'Oh Christ,' Hewitt said. 'Christ, Juliet, you've killed me. O'Kane will come after me now.'

'I've had enough,' Juliet said. She spoke to Lennon, her eyes glistening, her voice calm and

381

even. 'I've had enough of it. He's hardly slept in weeks. When he does, he wakes up with nightmares. When he came home from the hospital, I knew he'd done something terrible. I could see it on his face. Now this. I can't take it any more, no matter what they pay him.'

Lennon stood upright. 'Did you kill that boy?' he asked Hewitt.

'Fuck you,' Hewitt said, his eyes pressed into his forearm. Juliet crumpled against the wall, drew her knees up to her chin. Her shoulders jerked as she sobbed.

'Where in Drogheda?' Lennon asked. He extended his open hand towards Fegan. Fegan stood and placed the Glock in Lennon's grip.

'He'll kill me,' Hewitt said.

'That's between you and him,' Lennon said. 'Where are they?'

'A convalescent home outside town,' Hewitt said. 'His daughter owns it. It's an old mansion by the river. Torrans House, it's called. I don't know how to get there.'

'I'll find it,' Lennon said. He heard a siren in the distance. 'Careful what you say to them. You've more secrets than I do.'

Hewitt rolled to his side and stared up at Lennon, hate and fear in his eyes. 'Just get out.'

Lennon holstered the pistol and walked to the door, Fegan close behind. Juliet buried her face in her hands.

'I'm sorry,' she said. 'I never thought . . . '

They left the room before she could find the words. Lennon stopped in the hall when he saw the two children watching them from between

382

the banisters. The sound of the siren drawing closer got him moving again. He felt their eyes on him even as he drove away, Fegan in the passenger seat, the house disappearing in his rear-view mirror as flashing lights danced across the brickwork.

Dawn came like a forgotten promise as they headed for the motorway.

81

The old servants' quarters smelled of damp and mice. Cold white fingers of light reached through the dirty window, touching the peeling wallpaper and aged furniture. Marie McKenna lay on the bed, her eyelids fluttering, her breath coming in bubbling wheezes. Ellen clung to her mother's hand.

Orla O'Kane lowered herself to sit on the bed beside them. She reached out to touch Ellen's cheek, but the little girl pulled away. Orla folded her hands in her lap.

'Why don't you let your mummy sleep a wee while?' she asked. 'I'm sure there's something nice to eat downstairs. Maybe even ice cream. Come on with me and we'll see what we can find.'

Ellen shook her head and pulled her mother's arm around her in a puppet embrace.

'Why not?' Orla asked.

'Don't want to.'

'All right.' She studied the girl's pale skin and blue eyes. 'You're a pretty wee thing, aren't you?'

Ellen buried her face in the crook of her mother's elbow.

Orla leaned over and whispered, 'What's the matter? You going shy on me?'

Ellen peeked out from behind the arm. 'No.'

'Then what's wrong?'

The little girl's gaze shifted to something over

384

Orla's shoulder, her eyes darkening like a summer sky swallowed by rain clouds. Orla turned her head and saw nothing but shadows. When she looked back down to Ellen, the blue had drained from her eyes leaving a hollow grey.

'Gerry's coming,' the child said.

Orla sat back. 'Is that right?'

Ellen nodded.

'And what's he coming here for?'

'To get me and Mummy.'

Orla stood, smoothed her jacket over her stomach and hips. 'I see,' she said. 'You'd better get some sleep, then.'

As Orla walked to the door, Ellen sat up and said, 'You should run away.'

Orla stopped with her fingers on the door handle. 'I'm an O'Kane, sweetheart. We run away from nobody.'

Ellen lay down and rested her head on her mother's breast, turning away from the room and its milky light.

'Nobody,' Orla said to the child's back.

She let herself out of the room, locked the door behind her, and descended the flight of stairs to the first floor. She found the Traveller there, leaning against the railing that overlooked the grand entrance hall. He watched her approach, a sly smirk on his lips. His swollen red eyelid seemed to wink at her as it twitched.

'What are you looking at?' she asked.

'You,' he said. 'Were you up visiting with the wee girl?'

'Just making sure they're all right.'

'What do you make of her?'

Orla shrugged. 'She's a child. A brave one.'

'There's something funny about her, though,' the Traveller said. 'Like she's looking through you. Like she knows things.'

'You're talking shite,' Orla said. She brushed past him, heading for her father's room.

'Am I?' he called after her. 'You look like you saw a ghost. What did she say to you?'

Orla stopped and turned on her heel. 'She said Gerry Fegan's coming.'

'Well, then,' the Traveller said. 'We'd best be ready for him.'

82

Lennon's phone rang again and again, the number always withheld. He ignored it as he drove. Embankments and bridges blurred. Would Hewitt squeal? Would he tell his bosses to catch Lennon and that lunatic Gerry Fegan? Or that the hole in his leg was put there by Lennon's personal protection weapon? Or would the fear of what Lennon knew about Hewitt keep him quiet? Lennon couldn't gamble either way. If Hewitt talked there could be roadblocks going up even as he drove. Here, across the border, the Gardai might be on the alert, searching for them. Then all would be lost. He had to move, get there before anyone had the chance to find them.

Fegan sat silent beside Lennon, his hands on his knees, his body stiff. The killer's breathing remained steady and even, no sign of worry or fear on his face.

'How do you live with it?' Lennon asked. 'People like you. People like that animal I caught at the hospital. How do you look at yourself in the mirror? How can you face yourself when you're alone?'

Fegan turned his eyes to the window and the landscape beyond. If Lennon's words meant anything to him, it didn't show on his face.

Lennon said, 'I think of the things I've done, the things I'm ashamed of. It makes me sick to my stomach. How can you stand to — '

'Stop talking,' Fegan said.

'How can you — '

'Stop,' Fegan said, his voice tight like a fist. He turned his eyes away from the window and back to Lennon.

Lennon swallowed his retort and stared at the road ahead. They continued in silence, the motorway stretching into the grey morning ahead.

The Audi's satnav gave directions in its soothing voice. A woman's voice, refined and calm, as if the world still turned. Lennon had stopped twice so far to throw up at the roadside, the fear too heavy for his stomach. His nostrils stung, his throat burned. Fegan had watched him with those cold eyes, making the act all the more emasculating.

The speedometer read eighty-five as they approached the last exit north of the Boyne. The satnav's disembodied voice told Lennon to turn off here for Torrans House. A convalescent home, a place for the elderly to recover from broken hips, a place for Bull O'Kane to nurse his ruptured gut and his devastated knee, injuries caused by Lennon's passenger. The other man would also be there, the southerner who talked like a traveller, but who Lennon suspected was not. Two monsters in one house, surrounding the only good thing he had ever done in this world.

And now Lennon ferried a third monster to this place. That idea forced bile up from his stomach once more, but he willed it to subside as he hit the slip road.

His foot barely touched the brake as he reached the roundabout. Lights flashed, tyres screeched and horns blared as he cut across the early traffic. They might as well have been moths against a window.

83

Orla O'Kane stood over her father's sleeping form. His throat rasped with every breath, a line of drool across his chin as if a snail had crawled from his mouth. A carapace of a man, skin laid loose over old bones and hate. No longer a giant of the soul, no longer a warhorse thirsty for the fight. Just an old man without the sense to know his true enemies. The giant vanquished.

She reached out and smoothed the wisps of white hair across his scalp. Love swelled in her until she feared it might burst from her breast. She took a tissue from her sleeve and dabbed at the drool.

Orla had lost count of the times she'd had to push that panicky feeling back down to her belly, the one that told her that her father had lost his grip on the world he had built for her, leaving it to career into the sun. It would burn up, along with everything she knew.

And no one would mourn its passing.

She thought of the little girl upstairs. The mother didn't have long. Even if someone got her to a hospital, the greyness of her skin said it was too late.

But the little girl.

Maybe, when it was over and done with, the Bull might allow the little girl to live. He was not a monster, after all. Orla knew this to be true. She had not been raised by an animal, surely?

No, she had not. When things were settled, the little girl would live. And the little girl would need a *place* to live. A home. Orla had a house in Malahide with a sea view and a beach not twenty yards away.

Maybe, Orla thought.

'I hope . . .'

She put her hand to her mouth when she realised she had spoken out loud. Her father stirred.

'Hmm?' He blinked at her, his eyes like fish mouths gasping in the air. 'What's wrong? What time is it?'

'Shush,' Orla said. 'It's early.'

'Then what the fuck are you waking me for?' He tried to push himself up on the bed, but his flailing moved only blankets and sheets. 'What's going on?'

Orla put a hand on his chest. She arranged pillows behind her father's head. 'Easy, now. Nothing's wrong. It's just the wee girl.'

As she hoisted him up to a sitting position, the Bull asked, 'What about her?'

'She said something.' Orla pulled the blankets up and smoothed them. 'Some nonsense about Gerry Fegan coming.'

The Bull's eyes narrowed. 'Nonsense? But worth coming in here and waking me up for.'

'Maybe she contacted him somehow,' Orla said. 'I don't trust that gyppo fella you hired. Christ knows what happened when he took them.'

'Quit with the maybes and the somehows,' the Bull said. 'Tell me what you think. Is Fegan coming?'

Orla looked her father hard in the eye. 'We have to assume so. If he's as dangerous as you say, we can't take any chances.'

The Bull stared at the far wall as he thought. 'Right,' he said. He reached for her hand, squeezed it. 'You're right. You're a good girl, you know. Better than any of the men I raised, if you can call them that.'

Orla pulled the blankets back while she tried to hide the tears welling in her eyes. 'Thank you,' she said. She pulled his legs off the edge of the bed and knelt to fetch his slippers.

'It's nearly over,' she said. 'Gerry Fegan will be dead soon, and it'll be over.'

The Bull's shoulders dropped as he exhaled.

'Thank Christ,' he said.

84

Lennon followed the satnav's directions west, then south. He and Fegan crossed the River Boyne via a small bridge, then cut west again. The car's navigation had deserted him at the last junction, leaving him only a one-track road to follow. Up ahead, between the high treetops, he saw the roof of a grand old building.

Sickness and hunger wrestled in Lennon's gut. His eyes dried with tiredness, his mind flaking with the rust of fatigue. He blinked hard and wound the window down. Cool damp air rushed in to meet him. He breathed it in deep.

The road curved south, mirroring the river's arc through the countryside. A rabbit sprinted across his path, its white tail bobbing madly until it disappeared into the undergrowth. He'd travelled little more than half a mile when he slowed to a stop.

'How do we do this?' Lennon asked.

Fegan shifted in the passenger seat. 'What do you mean?'

'I mean we're here,' Lennon said. 'How do we do this? Do we find a way in or what?'

Fegan opened the passenger door. 'You can do what you want. I'm going in.'

'Wait! You can't walk straight in there, for Christ's sake.'

'They know I'm coming,' Fegan said. 'No point in sneaking around.'

'How do they know?' Lennon called after him, but the door slammed closed before the question was out.

He watched Fegan walk along the road ahead, sunlight creeping through the branches above and glancing off his shoulders.

'Fucking madman,' Lennon said.

Would he get Marie and Ellen killed? Possibly, but what other options were there? He and Fegan had discussed precious little on the journey here, let alone what they were going to do when they arrived. Now Fegan disappeared around the bend up ahead.

Lennon drummed his fingers on the steering wheel as he worked through the possibilities, panic edging in from the outer limits of his consciousness.

Surely they would kill Fegan as soon as he showed his face at the gates?

Yes, so they'd be busy there. And who were 'they' exactly? Bull O'Kane's people, Lennon supposed. Henchmen, maybe that was the word. Lennon thought of the useless lumps of belly and muscle Roscoe Patterson kept around him. O'Kane's men would be of a different order, Lennon was certain. But they still had Fegan to deal with.

Lennon looked to his right, along the river shore, beyond the woods. Did he have a better idea?

'Nope,' Lennon said to himself.

He pulled the Audi into the treeline, felt it buck and jerk over the terrain until the nose pitched downwards. He saw moss and earth spewed into the air in his rear-view mirror. He shut off the engine and got out.

Lennon stood back and looked at the car, its radiator jammed into a gulley. It wasn't going anywhere without a tow rope.

'Christ,' he said.

He looked to the water beyond the trees, the Boyne making its way to the coast. No other way to go, Lennon started walking.

85

Fegan stopped and studied the shadows around the entrance to the estate. Leaves and branches stirred in the breeze, but no human form emerged. They were there, Fegan was sure of it. They probably watched him as he stared back. He set off again, his eyes and ears open, ready for any movement, any challenge. When he reached the gates, he stood still, his heels together, his hands at his sides, and waited.

It had been only a few months since he'd last travelled to meet Bull O'Kane. That time he had thought he was done with it, that he would never return to this island again. Fegan supposed he knew deep down he would have no peace until either he or O'Kane was gone. And neither Marie nor Ellen would be safe while O'Kane breathed and hated, so the choice was clear. Fegan had to finish the Bull here, in this place. He had no idea how he would accomplish such a task, but then he never consciously knew how to kill. He simply did, and that was all there was to it. So, he would get inside and find a way.

A man emerged from the trees by the gate and approached. He held a shotgun and a piece of paper which he examined as he drew close. Fegan recognised the image printed on it as the one the Doyles had shown him back in New York.

'You've aged,' the man said. 'Go on. Straight

up to the house. You'll be met at the door. Do whatever they tell you. No fucking about.'

The gates opened with a slow mechanical movement. Fegan started walking without speaking to the man. The road turned from rough tarmac to gravel as he passed through the gates. The stones crunched beneath his feet.

The trees thinned to reveal an open sweep of green leading to the three-storey mansion at the end of the driveway. Flower beds punctuated the neat lawns, and smaller gardens split away from the main grounds to form enclaves of shrubbery and rock. A waterless fountain sat at the centre of the semicircle of gravel that fronted the house. Fegan skirted it and watched the vast wooden doors open.

A broad woman in a trouser suit descended the steps. A man came behind her, dressed like the man at the gate in jeans and a khaki jacket. Something bulged beneath the muddy-green material, something very like a pistol.

The woman took a step closer. She had hard features, narrow eyes and thin lips. Make-up failed to mask a bruise on her cheek. Her mouth split in a joyless smile.

'We've been expecting you,' she said. 'Come with me.'

86

Orla O'Kane led Fegan through the entrance hall and into the drawing room. She indicated the man who followed them and said, 'This is Charlie Ronan, and he'll shoot you dead if you move one single inch. You understand?'

Fegan nodded as Ronan pulled the small pistol from his jacket pocket.

Orla regarded the great Gerry Fegan. Tall and thin, but strong, a face cut from flint.

'You look tired,' she said.

'Yeah,' Fegan said.

'How did you find this place?'

'A cop,' Fegan said. 'He told me everything.'

'A cop?' Orla asked. 'Which cop?'

'I don't remember his name,' Fegan said. 'Big house off the Lisburn Road.'

'Dan Hewitt,' Orla said.

'Maybe,' Fegan said.

'How did you get here?'

'Drove,' Fegan said.

'Where's your car?'

'I left it out the road a bit,' Fegan said, jerking a thumb over his shoulder. 'An Audi. I stole it in Lisburn. You can send your boys to look for it if you want.'

Orla looked him up and down, the whole of him, trying to find what it was about this sad thin man that haunted her father's dreams. Then her eyes locked with his, and something cold shifted inside her. She looked away.

'I won't be long,' she said, and left the room.

87

The Traveller dreamed of dismembered children, bodies stacked upon bodies, blank little eyes staring to heaven. He dreamed of crackling pyres and burning meat. He dreamed of the boy who'd come at him with an AK47 in one hand, a newspaper in the other, no more than thirteen or fourteen years old.

Three short bursts of his MP5 cut the boy dead. In his dream, the boy floated to the floor like a sheet of fabric, the AK47 falling to one side, the newspaper to the other. But a draught caught the newspaper and spun it in a slow circle, before carrying it to the Traveller's feet.

He looked down at the ragged paper. There, his own face staring up at him, the letters forming shapes that said 'soldier' and 'killed' in the headline, the words beneath the picture coming into focus, a name becoming clearer until —

Wake up.

— the letters formed into words, words he could understand if he really wanted to, for the first time since they'd taken the Kevlar from his head, if he had the will to face —

Come on, wake up.

— them, but he could not face them, yet he could not turn away from them, they burned —

'For fuck's sake, wake up, you lazy gyppo bast — '

400

Before he even knew he was awake, the Traveller was up from the bed, on his feet, the stocky man's windpipe pinched between his fingers. The man croaked and his eyes bulged. His face turned red then purple.

'What did you call me?' the Traveller asked as he blinked the sleep away.

O'Driscoll grabbed his wrist, tried to loosen his grip.

'What did you call me, you fat cunt?'

O'Driscoll gagged as his mouth opened and closed. He tried to dig his fingers in between the Traveller's. Strong and hard as they were, they found no purchase. As sleep fell away from the Traveller, the room around him closed in from the edges of his vision. The hospital bed he had lain down on what seemed like an age ago, the clean functional furnishings, the tiled floor. He released O'Driscoll's throat.

O'Driscoll fell to the floor, gasping and clutching at his neck.

'Breathe,' the Traveller said. 'Slow and deep. Come on, breathe.'

O'Driscoll hauled air in and coughed it out again. He rolled to his side, moaned, and spat on the tile.

'Dirty fucker,' the Traveller said.

O'Driscoll's colour crept back to his normal pasty white and his breathing settled. 'What'd you do that for?' he said between mouthfuls of air.

'I don't like people sneaking up on me,' the Traveller said.

'I was only waking you up,' O'Driscoll said,

hoisting himself into a seated position. 'They told me to come and tell you when that Fegan fella arrived.'

The Traveller's heart fluttered with something that might have been joy, or fear, or both. 'He's here?'

'Downstairs,' O'Driscoll said. 'The Bull wants you beside him when he's brought up.'

The Traveller hauled O'Driscoll up by his lapels. 'Jesus, why the fuck didn't you say so?'

O'Driscoll could only blink back at him, his mouth sagging open. The Traveller let go of the jacket and was out of the room before O'Driscoll landed in a heap on the floor. For a moment, as he marched down the corridor, an image of a boy with an AK47 and a newspaper in his hands flickered in the Traveller's mind, a stuttering snapshot of something he couldn't quite place.

88

Fegan stood silent in the drawing room, his hands loose at his sides. Ronan stared from the other side of the room, that same pistol held useless at his side.

Fegan knew five paces would take him across the space between them faster than the other man could react, and he'd have the gun off him before Ronan could think of pulling a trigger. But what then? Better to stand and wait.

They'd stood like this for ten minutes now; not a word had been spoken since he'd been led into the room. Fegan closed his eyes and let his mind rest. An image of a face in a newspaper burst brilliant in his consciousness, but was gone in an instant, along with the smell of burning flesh. Sweat broke on his forehead. His stomach reeled. A weight settled in his gut, dense, sickly and insistent. He swallowed. A chill rippled from his heart to his groin, then down through his thighs to his calves, and on into the soles of his feet. He shivered like a horse overjoyed with exertion.

When Fegan opened his eyes again he saw Orla O'Kane by the open door. Something moved across her face. Fegan recognised it instantly, like a brother lost but not forgotten. Fear, sweet and giving, the one emotion Fegan knew by sight.

'Come on,' she said, dropping her eyes from Fegan's gaze.

Ronan indicated that Fegan should follow Orla to the grand entrance hall. Fegan did as he was told, glad to be moving, glad to get it over with. The thug closed the door and came behind them as they crossed the hall to the staircase.

Fegan's heart quickened as he climbed. The stairs levelled to a gallery, then doubled back on themselves to form an atrium beneath a stained-glass ceiling. Morning light shone through it, making orange, green and red shapes on the walls. When Orla reached the first floor gallery she turned right into a corridor leading to the east wing. Ronan gripped Fegan's shoulder to steer him after her.

Half a dozen rooms branched off the corridor, but Orla kept walking to the double doors at the end. She threw them open in an ostentatious gesture and stepped inside. Fegan entered the room and was met by a low smell of human excrement. He stopped, but Ronan pushed him ahead. Fegan halted as the plastic sheeting rustled beneath his feet.

'Hello Gerry,' O'Kane said, his lips parting to form a jagged smile.

The Bull sat in a wheelchair, a blanket covering him from midriff to feet. The chair was high-backed with small wheels, the kind hospital porters used to ferry invalids along disinfectant-smelling corridors. The Bull's flesh hung loose from his face. His eyes gazed too bright from their darkened pits, his cheeks sunken and hollow. A small bubble of spit glistened at one corner of his mouth.

Two men flanked the chair. Fegan recognised

one of them, Ben O'Driscoll, who'd done a short stretch in the Maze during his own time there. He had fat hands and a pugilist's build, thick around the torso and broad at the shoulders. But the other man was something different, something altogether more dangerous. Medium height, wiry build, and dead eyes. A killer. Fegan smelled it on him through the haze of odours that tainted the air. He knew beyond doubt this was the man Tom the barman had told him about, the one who had prowled Belfast in recent days.

From its size, Fegan guessed this to be some kind of recreation room for the convalescent home's patients, but all the furniture had been hastily pushed to the walls. Formica-topped tables stood stacked alongside vinyl-coated chairs, overlooked by paintings of the Drogheda countryside. The floor was empty save for the six people gathered there on the plastic sheeting that covered the parquet flooring.

'Where's Marie and Ellen?' Fegan asked.

'Don't worry about them,' O'Kane said.

'Me for them,' Fegan said.

'That was the deal last time.' O'Kane nodded. He laughed then, high and fractured. 'Didn't work out that way, though, did it? It's not going to work out this time either.'

Orla went to her father. She took a tissue from her sleeve and wiped the spit from his mouth. He slapped her hand away.

'Da,' she said, leaning down to him. 'I don't want to watch this.'

'All right, love,' O'Kane said. 'You go on, take

a walk or something. I'll call you when it's done.'

Orla did not meet Fegan's gaze as she passed. He heard the double doors close behind him, followed by footsteps fading into echoes. Five in the room, now. He glanced back over his shoulder to see Ronan resting against the wall. Fegan noted their positions. The man at O'Kane's right hand, the killer, stepped forward.

'I'd like to introduce you to a friend of mine,' the Bull said. 'He's been dying to meet you.'

89

Lennon edged along the riverbank, mud sucking at his shoes. Swans watched from the shallows, while others waddled through the grass and ferns between the wall and the water. They hissed as he neared them, raising their heads and opening their wings. Lennon went to the wall and clung to it as he passed them.

A gate sealed an opening in the old stonework. It bordered a landscaped area that stretched down to the water. The ground had been levelled off, and benches and picnic tables arranged on the lawn. A life ring was suspended from a post on the short wooden pier. A small rowing boat sat on the dry slipway. The convalescent home's patients must have used this place to relax when the weather was good.

He went to the opening and peered through the gate. A wide path cut through well-tended gardens, leading up to the rear of the house. Shutters blinded many of the windows. A quiet hung over the place like a shroud. Lennon leaned close to the bars and scanned the grounds, looking for movement. He saw nothing but magpies squabbling over scraps near a door at the back of the house. It was small and functional, probably an old servants' entrance leading to kitchens, Lennon thought.

A fire escape had been built on to the western side of the house, ugly steel steps and platforms just visible at the corner.

To the right there was nothing but open ground that would leave him exposed if he went for the fire escape. He could just make out a copse to the left, the trees forming a buffer between the wall and the gardens. They ran up to the east of the house. If he could get over the gate he might be able to use them as cover, then sprint to the door where the magpies fought over morsels.

Thick tangles of barbed wire raised the gate's height by a foot or so. Lennon stood back and studied it. He could climb the gate, but the barbed wire would cut him to shreds. The wall stood a good ten feet tall; he had no hope of scaling it, unless . . .

Lennon walked to the landscaped area and crouched by one of the picnic tables. Nothing rooted it to the ground. He tested its weight. Heavy, but not immovable. He set his feet apart, gripped each edge of the table. It moved more easily than he expected, the damp grass providing a slick surface to pull across. A few minutes' effort had it against the stonework. He climbed up and eased his fingertips over the top of the wall. As he thought, shards of broken glass had been set in concrete. It was a lawsuit waiting to happen, any insurance company would balk at the idea in case some burglar would claim for the lacerations, but Lennon imagined Bull O'Kane had no such qualms.

He pulled his jacket off and folded it into a pillow. He stood on tiptoe, balanced on the table, and laid the jacket across the glass shards.

The swans watched with interest from the riverbank as Lennon took a deep breath and hauled himself upwards. He drew his knees up, wincing as the dulled points of glass dug into his kneecaps, then manoeuvred his legs out from under him. The glass tore through the jacket to grab at his thighs. He eased himself over the edge, one arm clinging to the top. Jagged glass ripped through the fabric and scraped at Lennon's forearm. He let go, and his weight dragged his arm across the point of glass.

Lennon fell towards a bank of dock leaves, tatters of shirtsleeve trailing behind him. He tumbled down through the greenery and slammed against a tree trunk. He stifled a cry as pain shrieked in his ribs. A tapered streak of red blossomed on Lennon's exposed skin, six inches long. He righted himself, his back against the tree trunk, and examined the wound. It wasn't that bad, just a scrape, lucky it hadn't been worse. He reached out and grabbed handfuls of the dock leaves, wiped the sheen of fresh, bright blood away with one handful, then pressed another to the cut.

His breath came in hard rasps as he listened for movement in the gardens beyond the trees. Nothing stirred, so Lennon dragged himself to his feet. He kept the wad of leaves pressed to his forearm as he advanced through the copse, far enough behind the treeline to stay hidden but close enough to the edge to see the house and the gardens beyond. The two magpies still battled over scraps in front of the kitchen door.

Lennon walked steady until he stood level with the house's eastern edge. Fifteen, maybe twenty yards separated him from the building. He looked south and saw the lawns sweep into the distance, a long driveway cutting through them. He dropped the bloodstained leaves, took a breath, counted to ten, and sprinted across the grass and gravel.

He pressed his back tight against the sandstone, between the corner and the first window. His chest tightened as he listened. Nothing moved, no voice of warning, no footsteps on gravel. Lennon exhaled, sparks firing behind his eyes. He crouched and edged along the wall, keeping his head below the windowsills. Small stones ground together beneath his feet. The back door stood just twelve yards ahead, eleven now, nine, six —

The magpies squawked and launched themselves towards the sky, blurs of black and white, the remains of a Chinese takeaway scattered behind them.

The back door opened, and a woman stepped out onto the gravel, her broad back blocking the early sun. She took a packet of cigarettes from her jacket pocket, plucked one from the row of filter-tips with her teeth. Her lighter sparked, and the flame sputtered long enough for the tobacco to catch. She drew hard on the cigarette. A cough erupted from her deep chest, and she covered her mouth as she hacked. The fit passed, and she turned to see Lennon's drawn Glock staring back at her. She dropped the cigarette to the gravel.

'Take me to Ellen,' Lennon said. 'Take me to Marie.'

Her mouth opened, but no sound came.

'Now,' Lennon said.

90

The Traveller stood between the Bull and Gerry Fegan. 'So you're the great Gerry Fegan,' he said. 'I've heard a lot about you, Mr Fegan. Let's see if you live up to your reputation, eh?'

'Who are you?' Fegan asked, his first words since entering the room.

'Now that's the million-dollar question, isn't it, Gerry? I've got lots of names, but none of them's real. People call me the Traveller.' He gave Fegan a grin. 'Pleased to meet you, big lad.'

Fegan did not respond.

The Traveller turned to the Bull. 'How do you want it done?' he asked.

The Bull raised his head. 'Hmm?'

The old bastard looked weak and confused, like a man who'd walked many miles to a place, then couldn't remember why he'd made the journey.

'How do you want it done?'

The Bull's face seemed to solidify, the strength bleeding back into it. 'Slow,' he said.

The Traveller nodded to O'Driscoll and Ronan. 'Get a hold of him.'

They went to Fegan's sides and took an arm each. Fegan didn't resist. He stared straight ahead, his face expressionless.

The Traveller kicked him hard in the groin. Fegan's legs folded under him, and O'Kane's men pulled him back up.

'Slow,' the Traveller said. He turned back to the Bull, took the knife from his pocket, and unfolded the blade. 'I could gut him. Bad way to go.'

'Aye, that'll do,' the Bull said. 'Don't rush it, though. Give him some time to think about it.' His gaze fixed on Fegan and his lip curled. 'Give him time to think about what he did to me. How he got my son killed, and my cousin.' His voice raised in pitch, breaths forced between the words, as he leaned forward. 'How I got shot in the gut because of him. How I'm in this fucking wheelchair because of him. How he made a cunt of me. Give him time to think about all that.'

The Bull collapsed back, his chest heaving. The Traveller thought of a wounded dog he'd seen as a child. It was a stray, hit by a car, and it had dragged itself to an alleyway behind his mother's house. It snarled and snapped at anyone who came near until he went and got a shovel. Three blows had silenced its howling.

'I had no fight with you,' Fegan said to the Bull. 'You could've left me alone. You brought it on yourself.'

'Aye, I could've left you alone,' the Bull said. 'But I didn't. I don't give a fiddler's fuck if you had a fight with me or not. I had a fight with you, and that's all there is to it. You got anything else to say before our friend here goes to work on you?'

'One thing.'

The Bull tilted his head and smiled. 'What's that, now?'

413

'Remember this: I'm going to kill you,' Fegan said.

The Bull threw his head back and laughed, high and grating. 'Christ Almighty,' he said. He nodded at the Traveller. 'All right, finish him.'

The Traveller stepped close to Fegan, close enough to smell his sweat. He rolled his left shoulder, that stiffness continuing to nag at him, his wrist still bound in the strapping. He stared into the madman's eyes, looking for some sign of fear. There was nothing, only a steady calm. He held the blade up to Fegan's left eye.

'Maybe I'll scoop it out of your skull,' the Traveller said. 'How does that sound?'

Fegan didn't react.

The Traveller pressed the blade's edge against Fegan's cheek, below his eye, until red beads appeared on his skin. Fegan's eyelid flickered. The Traveller drew the knife down towards the mouth, leaving a bright crimson trail behind it. Fegan's lips tightened.

'I'm disappointed,' the Traveller said as he leaned forward, his voice conspiratorial. 'People kept telling me about the great Gerry Fegan, how he was the scariest fucker ever came out of Belfast. And look at you.'

'Was it you who took them?' Fegan asked, looking the Traveller in the eye for the first time. Blood pooled at the outer edge of his mouth.

'The woman and the wee girl?'

'Yes,' Fegan said.

'That's right.'

'Did you hurt them?'

'The wee girl's all right,' the Traveller said.

'The woman's hurt, though. She wasn't looking too good last time I saw her. I don't fancy her chances. Sorry about that.'

Something moved behind Fegan's eyes, a decision made, before he looked back into the distance. 'Go ahead and do whatever you're going to do,' he said.

'Fair enough,' the Traveller said, and grabbed Fegan's right ear.

91

'Who are you?' the woman asked.

'I'm the fella with the gun,' Lennon said. 'Now who the fuck are you?'

Her eyes flitted between his and the door and back again. 'I'm Orla O'Kane.'

'Bull O'Kane's daughter?'

She nodded.

'You own this place?'

She nodded.

'Where are they?'

'Who?'

'Marie and Ellen,' Lennon said. He took one step closer, squared his aim on her forehead. 'Don't fuck me about. I'll blow your brains out, you understand? Tell me where they are.'

Her eyes brimmed. She pointed one trembling finger towards the door. 'Inside,' she said. 'Upstairs.'

'Take me to them.' He took another step. 'Now.'

A tear dripped from her eyelash. 'Don't kill me. Please.'

'Just take me to them,' Lennon said. 'I won't hurt you if you take me to them now.'

'It's nothing to do with me,' Orla said, her words spilling out faster as she spoke, her nose running, her face creasing. 'It's my da, the stuff he gets up to, I know nothing about it, I never knew he wanted to hurt anybody, I wouldn't have let him use my place if I knew — '

'Shut up,' Lennon said. Another step, and the Glock's muzzle quivered inches from her forehead. 'Just shut your mouth and take me to them.'

'All right,' she said. 'But don't do anything stupid.'

'Move,' he said. 'You go first.'

Orla walked towards the door, keeping her gaze on Lennon as he came behind. She tripped on the step and turned her head to look where she was going. The door stood open. She slipped through into the shadows.

Lennon followed her into some sort of entrance hall-cum-laundry room. A bank of industrial washing machines and dryers stood against the far wall. Mildew coated the ceiling above them, and the air had a damp, cloying smell. Water pooled on the floor around the equipment.

Orla headed for a door to the left. It led them to a room cast in aluminium and stainless steel. What had once been a traditional country house kitchen was now a catering business, deep-fryers, bath-sized sinks surrounded by mould, grimy hotplates and ovens big enough to fit a person in. That thought spurred Lennon on.

'Hurry up,' he said, jamming the pistol between her shoulder blades.

Orla moaned and quickened her pace around the grease-coated islands as she approached a swing door with grubby glass at its centre. When she was ten feet from it, her shuffling steps became a brisk stride, then a jog.

'Don't,' Lennon said, hurrying to catch her, reaching out to grab the fabric of her jacket, his balance lost to the chase.

She slapped his hand away and sprinted across the few feet to the door. He followed inches behind, the pistol an idle threat in his hand. She grabbed the door's edge, threw it back behind her, slamming it into Lennon's outstretched hands as he tried to take aim.

'Da!' she screamed again and again as Lennon pushed through the door to see her trip and land sprawling on the floor. 'Da!' again, 'Da!'

Lennon saw only the silhouette of the gunman, barely registering the shape in the corridor's dimness before he raised the Glock and fired.

92

The cracking of gunfire halted the Traveller's hand. He would never admit it, but he was relieved to have an excuse to break away from Fegan's stare. The madman hardly winced when the Traveller started cutting into his earlobe, the bulging of his jaw muscles and a film of sweat on his forehead the only outward sign of pain. The blood ran in a deep red rivulet down Fegan's neck to be soaked up by his clothing.

'Da!' A high shrieking came between the gunshots, Orla O'Kane's voice cutting through the clamour. 'Da! Da!'

'What the fuck is that?' Bull O'Kane asked.

The Traveller released Fegan's ear, the lobe still attached despite the half-inch incision. He spoke to O'Driscoll and Ronan. 'Keep hold of him,' he said. 'I'm going to take a look.'

'Wait,' Bull O'Kane said.

The Traveller ignored him and went to the double doors that led to the corridor and the stairs beyond, drawing the Glock from his waistband. He opened one a few inches and put his eye to the gap. Nothing.

'I said wait.' Fear edged the Bull's voice.

The Traveller leaned out into the corridor. He pictured the layout of the entrance hall below. A grand staircase rose up along the right-hand wall before turning back on itself to form the gallery that lay ahead of him. Three doors stood beneath that. The left led to a series of rooms that had been converted into offices and treatment bays. The middle concealed a lift that had been built into the house's structure, its sliding door cut neatly into the wood panelling. The right opened onto a corridor off which branched patient and staff dining rooms, and the kitchen. The voice and the gunshots came from somewhere down there. The Traveller turned back to O'Kane.

'I won't be long,' he said.

'Jesus, don't leave me here,' O'Kane said, his face paling. 'Not with him.' The Bull's sagging cheeks reddened at the admission of his fear. He couldn't hold the Traveller's gaze. 'Go on, then,' he said.

'I wasn't waiting for permission,' the Traveller said.

He stepped out into the corridor and let the door swing closed behind him. A dozen light footsteps brought him to the top of the stairs. He clung to the wall as he descended and turned at the bottom. A dozen more paces took him to the door on the right, the one that led to the kitchen and dining rooms. Two splintered holes had been torn in the wood. He flattened himself against the wall.

One, two, three more barks of gunfire, close to the door. Then a squeal and a cry, followed by a man's hoarse shout. Two more shots, this time echoing from deep in the corridor, then something heavy thrown hard against the door. It opened outwards as a man's body spilled through. He landed on his back, two holes in his camouflage jacket radiating dark stains. He

420

groaned and gasped and coughed and writhed.

Somewhere beyond the Traveller's vision, Orla O'Kane screamed, 'Jesus Christ! Don't, don't, don't — '

The Traveller brought his pistol up and swung into the open doorway, searching for a target. Shapes moved against the glaring light from the kitchen, one clambering to its feet, the other already upright. They melded together as the Traveller strained to separate one shadow from the other in the bitter smoke. The larger of them moved towards him, fast. He couldn't tell which arm belonged to which silhouetted body, or where the screams came from in the corridor's echoes. When he saw a gun amongst the blurring shapes the reptile part of his mind took over, steadied his own Glock, and tightened his finger on the trigger.

The corridor amplified the boom and smoke burned his stinging eye. The shape still came at him and his finger closed on the trigger again. The muzzle flash illuminated Orla O'Kane's terrified face for an instant as the bullet ripped a piece of her skull away.

Her body's momentum carried her forward, and the Traveller stepped aside to let it tumble on top of the dying man, her weight crushing the last of the fight out of him.

'Stupid fucking bitch,' the Traveller said.

He edged back to the doorway and peered into the darkness and light. The other figure had gone, either retreated into the kitchen, or into one of the other rooms leading off the corridor. He replayed the scene in his mind, saw the width of the man, his height. Instinct and logic combined to tell him it was the cop Lennon.

'Bastard cunt fucker,' the Traveller said.

He stepped into the gloom, the Glock up and ready. If anything moved he would shoot first and worry about who he shot later. Two doors to his right, one to the left at the end, and the kitchen next to it. He moved slow and easy, his breath even and steady, listening hard.

The Traveller tried the first door on his right. The handle didn't move. Locked tight. No way Lennon could have locked it from inside. He would have heard the footsteps in the corridor, the fumbling of the key in the lock. The Traveller kept moving. The second door's handle loosened at the pressure of his fingers. He leaned tight to the wall and depressed the handle as far as it would go. The world slowed as he inhaled, then accelerated as he let the air out of his lungs and kicked the door open.

He ducked, his bandaged left hand coming up to support the pistol in his right. The door swung inward, struck the wall, and juddered with the shock of it. Nothing moved inside as the Traveller stopped the door swinging back with his foot. Chairs stacked on tables, clusters of them in the darkness as shutters blocked out all but the thinnest blades of daylight. Old odours of fried meat and overcooked vegetables drifted on the air along with the dust motes. He hunkered down and studied the forest of table legs. No one lurked among them. A pair of swinging doors in the far corner presumably led back to the kitchen, but the Traveller felt in his gut that the room's stillness had not been disturbed for weeks. He straightened and backed out.

The door at the end of the corridor stood open, the kitchen beyond, its steely brightness dulled by grime. He walked towards it, ready to fire at any movement, but a new smell stopped him before he got that far. A sickly, chemical smell that tingled in his nostrils. He took three more steps and the smell deepened. But it did not come from the kitchen. The door to his left stood slightly ajar. He pushed it with the Glock's muzzle, and the smell of fuel, petrol or something like it, washed up from the narrow staircase on the other side.

The Traveller spied a box of matches on a work surface just inside the kitchen. He smiled as he reached for them.

93

Lennon holstered his pistol as he picked his way through the semi-darkness, avoiding the debris on the uneven floor. A few small windows up at ground level allowed thin light through their dirt-caked panes, but not enough for him to be sure of his footing. He'd already stumbled over a stack of cans, spilling something that smelled like petrol or white spirits. It had soaked into his trousers and begun to sting the skin on his shin and calf.

Arches led further into the cellar in all directions. Lennon had to hope there were more ways in and out. There, up ahead, he could make out a haze of light. He advanced towards it, ducking his head beneath an arch. Old furniture, cardboard boxes, papers and fabrics were stacked against every wall. The musty smell mingled with that of whatever he had spilled at the bottom of the stairs. Something wrapped around his ankle as he struggled through the gloom. He kicked it away, losing his balance in the process. The stacked chairs he grabbed collapsed under his weight, and he fell to the floor as they clattered around him.

Lennon lay still and listened. Small things scurried amongst the boxes, disturbed by his intrusion. Tiny clawed feet dashed across the back of his hand, a tail brushing his fingers, but he did not slap the creature away. Slowly, his breath held tight in his chest, he rolled over onto his back. He froze and watched a shape come closer, framed by the weak light from the windows. Lennon wondered if the other man could see him lying there amid the upended chairs. The noise would surely have drawn his attention.

The petrol smell grew stronger as the form dipped beneath the arch and closed in to where Lennon lay.

'I know you're there,' the shape said.

Lennon recognised the voice. His heart lurched.

'You should've shot me when you had the chance,' the shape said. 'They've got your woman and your girl upstairs. When I'm done with you, I'll have a go on them. The mother's not bad looking, even hurt as bad as she is. Tell you the truth, I don't know if she'll still be breathing by now.'

The silhouette swelled in Lennon's vision. 'Well, if she's not, it'll be a pity. I'll just have to content myself with the wee girl. I'll do her quick, though. No sense in stringing it out for a little 'un. Not her fault she's got a useless shite like you for a father. No, I'll go easy on her. But I won't go easy on you.'

An arm swept out. Liquid splashed around Lennon. The petrol smell invaded his nose and mouth, made his throat tighten. He pushed himself back, his elbows and heels fighting against curtain fabric.

'Ah, there you are,' the silhouette said. He tossed the can in Lennon's direction.

It clattered on the floor, throwing a streak of pungent liquid across his lower legs. Lennon scrabbled back, no longer caring about the noise, until his head and shoulders pressed against the cold brick wall. He pushed himself up on his feet and drew his Glock.

The silhouette dissolved into the darkness. 'I'm going to burn you, Jack. I'll watch you dance for a while. If you're lucky, I might put you out of your misery before it gets too bad. If you're lucky.'

Lennon aimed at the voice, trying to fix its position among the cellar's reverberations.

There, a spark in the black, the killer's face illuminated for an instant. Lennon's finger tightened on the trigger. The spark again, but this time the match caught, throwing its yellowy glow just far enough for the killer to see the pistol aimed at his forehead.

Lennon's Glock boomed as the killer ducked, the noise filling every corner and crack of the cellar. Lennon followed the match's fall with his eyes. The flame sputtered before it caught the vapours from the can. Lennon threw his body to the ground as the heat surged around him and the killer screamed.

94

O'Driscoll said, 'We should get you out of here.'

Fegan watched O'Kane chew his lip, possibilities flickering across the old man's face, his eyes darting around the room. The heat in Fegan's ear pulsed as warmth spread down his neck and over his shoulder. A hard line of pain ran along his cheek. He tasted the blood at the corner of his mouth.

'Maybe we should get you to your room,' O'Driscoll said. 'Out of harm's way, like. Just till yer man's sorted things out.'

O'Kane glowered. 'Don't talk to me like I'm a child, for fuck's sake. This is the one thing I want. This is all I want. Don't fucking chicken out on me now. Don't turn tail like every other bastard.'

O'Driscoll stepped away from Fegan, but kept a grip on his arm. 'But, Christ, anything could be happening. You pay me to watch out for you and that's what I'm doing. Now come on, we need to get you out of here and locked in your — '

'Every one of you fuckers is the same,' the Bull said, his voice cracking between high and low. 'Them bastards in the North, they left me hanging. Everyone else abandoned me. Now you're going to do the same?'

O'Driscoll held onto Fegan's sleeve as he took another step towards O'Kane. 'Jesus, no Bull, I just want to make sure you're safe, that's all. I'm not going anywhere.'

Fegan's instincts flew, measuring the strength of O'Driscoll's grip, the distance between the men, the angles of their bodies, their centres of balance. He registered these calculations only as impulses, flashes in his brain before the act. But the act did not come. He suppressed it, a deeper and more trusted instinct telling him it wasn't yet time to move.

O'Kane jabbed his thick forefinger at Fegan. 'I'm not going anywhere till that fucker's dead.'

'You want me to do him?' O'Driscoll asked.

'No.' O'Kane shook his head and met Fegan's stare. 'Bring him here.'

'There isn't time,' O'Driscoll said. 'We need to — '

O'Kane's face reddened. 'I said bring him here.'

The men led Fegan forward. He did not resist.

'On his knees,' O'Kane said.

O'Driscoll placed a hand on Fegan's shoulder and pushed down. When Fegan didn't submit, he kicked the back of his knee. Fegan went down hard, his kneecap cracking on the parquet flooring. The plastic sheeting rustled as the other knee followed.

O'Kane leaned forward in his wheelchair. 'You could've killed me back there in that barn near Middletown. You had me at your feet. I was helpless as a pup, and you had a gun in your hand. Why didn't you do it?'

'Because I had no reason,' Fegan said. 'I was merciful.'

'Merciful?' O'Kane shook his head. 'You're not making any more sense than you did back then, Gerry. Are the people still in your head? Are they still telling you what to do?'

'I left them back there,' Fegan said. 'When I killed McGinty.'

'McGinty was a cunt.' O'Kane stretched a hand towards O'Driscoll. O'Driscoll placed a small semi-automatic pistol in it. It looked like a Walther PPK to Fegan. 'Not too many missed that bastard after he died. I sure as fuck didn't. You know, the politicians wanted me to let it go. They wanted the mess cleaned up, fair enough, but they didn't see the sense in going after you. They said I should let it lie. But they don't know you. They don't know what you did to me. They don't know how I haven't slept a single night since then. I won't live another fucking day with you in the world.' He breathed hard as he pulled back the slide assembly to chamber a round. 'So I told them, I says, I'm going after Gerry Fegan and that's all there is to it.'

O'Kane pressed the Walther's muzzle against Fegan's forehead.

O'Driscoll shifted his feet, loosened his grip on Fegan's shoulder. 'Jesus, what's that? Do you smell that?'

Ronan said, 'Smell what?'

'Smoke,' O'Driscoll said. 'Something burning.'

O'Kane lowered the pistol. 'A fire?'

The image burst in Fegan's mind, the dream that had haunted first his sleeping hours, then his waking: the child eaten by flames.

429

His instincts aligned, a perfect sequence of movements and pressures and weights plotted in his mind before he was even aware of them, telling him now was the moment to act.

95

The Traveller clambered up the steps, choking on the smoke. He couldn't quite believe how the fire had taken hold, how it had eaten everything around him in seconds. He had kept low, a handkerchief to his nose and mouth as he fought his way back to the steps. One side of his face glowed with a heat of its own where the initial bloom of fire had licked at him. He had been burned before, he knew this time wasn't bad, but it had been close.

The cop was lost among the flames. The Traveller glanced behind him as he reached the top step. Smoke, black and thick, under-lit in orange and red, curled up the stairwell. No way the cop could get through that. He fell against the door and dropped to the floor, gulping at the air, as a rush of heat came behind him.

The Traveller coughed and retched as he crawled, his eyes streaming, his spit streaked with black when he ejected it from his mouth. He hauled himself to his feet and ran for the door leading back to the entrance hall. His sides ached with the coughing, and his head spun. The air out in the hall tasted sweet and clean. He closed the door tight behind him and leaned his back against it for a moment as he caught his breath. One last hacking cough to clear his chest, one last spit to clear his mouth, then he'd go to O'Kane, warn him to get out.

He pushed himself away from the door and towards the staircase. His chest heaved as he climbed to the gallery and the room where he'd left O'Kane and the bleeding Fegan. As he reached the summit, the first gunshot came, and the first cry of panic and pain.

96

Fegan had never found it difficult, and he'd never wondered why. He simply did, and usually that was all it took. When O'Kane's attention was off him, the Walther aimed somewhere over his shoulder, and O'Driscoll's grip had loosened, Fegan moved.

He got his hands under the wheelchair's leg-rests, and pulled up hard. O'Kane managed a shot as he pitched backwards, but it caught Ronan's upper chest. O'Driscoll tried to stop O'Kane's fall, sacrificing his own balance, and Fegan had his legs from under him with a sweep at his ankles, the slippery plastic sheeting denying him purchase.

O'Kane landed hard on his back and rolled with the chair as it yawed to the side. He cried out when his injured leg hit the floor, tangled in the blanket.

Fegan got to his feet before O'Driscoll could recover. O'Kane tried to haul himself across the floor to where the Walther had fallen. Fegan stepped around him and claimed the pistol for his own. A shot rang out and he felt the heat of the bullet scorching the air by his ear. He turned, slow and calm, aimed at Ronan's raised head as the other tried to lift his own gun again. The Walther bucked in Fegan's hand, and Ronan's head jerked back.

O'Driscoll scurried across the floor, making

for the pistol in Ronan's dead hand. Fegan put two in his back. O'Driscoll collapsed on top of Ronan's legs, his shoulders shuddering. Fegan took the gun from Ronan's hand and pushed it into his waistband. He went back to O'Kane.

The Bull stared up at him, bubbling spit running from the corner of his mouth. 'Bastard,' he said.

'Where are they?' Fegan asked.

'Fuck you.'

'Where are they?'

'Fuck you, go ahead and kill me.'

'No,' Fegan said. 'Not until you tell me where they are.'

'Fuck you.'

O'Kane's left leg, the one that had taken the bullet months before, lay outstretched on the floor, no bend at the knee. Fegan put his foot just above the joint, where the bullet had hit. He settled his weight on it.

O'Kane screamed.

'Where are they?'

'Fuck you,' O'Kane said.

As Fegan put his weight on O'Kane's knee once more, the sound of the double doors behind spun him around. The Walther was up and aimed before Fegan was conscious of the movement, his finger tight on the trigger before the Traveller could raise his own gun. Fegan had just enough time to register the scorched skin and singed hair before the Walther barked, the shot going wide as the Traveller ducked.

Fegan backed towards the door at the rear corner of the room as the Traveller recovered and took aim. A hard grip on Fegan's ankle took his balance and he stumbled as the Traveller fired. Fegan let his body fall, the bullet passing over him. He landed on his back, O'Kane still clinging to his ankle. Fegan kicked out, his foot connected with O'Kane's forehead, and the grip fell away.

The upended wheelchair lay between Fegan and the far door where the Traveller crouched. Fegan scurried on his back towards the corner, one hand raised, keeping the Walther trained on the door. The Traveller straightened for a moment, and Fegan fired. It went wide once more, Fegan was no good at more than a few feet, but the Traveller dropped low again.

Fegan kept pushing with his feet until his back hit the wall. He shifted to his side and reached up for the door handle. It swung away from him. He fired once more at the other door to keep the Traveller down, and the pistol's slide locked in place, its magazine empty. Fegan dropped it and scrambled to his feet and through to the room on the other side. He closed the door behind him and backed into the empty room, a small kitchen with a sink, giant kettles by a cooker, a fridge humming in the stillness. He took Ronan's pistol, a chrome-finished revolver, from his waistband and fixed its sight on the door.

Would the Traveller come after him that way, or would he circle around? Another door stood to his right. Fegan struggled to picture the building's layout in his mind. That door must lead to another room that would open further along the corridor. He crossed to it and tried the handle. The door opened into a smaller space with comfortable looking chairs arranged in circles, coffee tables between them in the darkness, wooden shutters sealing out all but a hint of daylight. Two more doors matched the placement in the room he'd just left, one leading to the corridor, the other to another room like this one. He had no choice but to try it, stay out of the corridor.

Fegan headed for the door, but something stopped him. He froze, his senses picking at the air. Smoke, not far away, heat on the breeze that somehow swept through the room, and a crackling and sighing. Thin black fingers reached out from above the door leading into the corridor.

'Ellen,' Fegan said.

97

The Traveller crossed the room to the wheelchair and set it upright, kicked the brake to lock the wheels. He crouched down by O'Kane and got his hands under the old man's arms. Christ, he was heavy, frail and wasted as he was. The Traveller got O'Kane to the chair, hoisted him up and into the seat.

'Go finish him,' the Bull said between gasps of air, sweat thick on his face, spit hanging from his lip.

'I'm getting you out of here first,' the Traveller said. 'There's a fire in the cellar. Won't be long till it spreads up here.'

O'Kane grabbed the Traveller's arm. 'I'm not going anywhere till Fegan's dead.' Spit prickled the Traveller's cheek. 'Now for Christ's sake do what I tell you and go and get the fucker.'

The Traveller pulled his arm away and grabbed the handles at the back of the chair. He released the brake and pushed it towards the door, but O'Kane twisted in the seat and swung a big fist at him.

'I told you to go after Fegan, for Christ's sake, now do it or I'll fucking kill you.' O'Kane's eyes brimmed. 'I can look after myself. There's a lift out there. I can get out if I need to. Just do what I paid you for.'

'Jesus.' The Traveller let go of the chair and stepped back. 'All right, you mad old bastard, whatever you want.'

A high wailing cut the air as the smoke alarms kicked in.

'The fire's spreading,' the Traveller said. 'If I can't get back to you, then you're on your own.'

The Bull breathed deep, seemed to gather himself. He wiped his forearm across his mouth and eyes. 'Don't worry about me,' he said. 'Just worry about Fegan. He'll probably go after the woman and the kid. Go to them, then he'll come to you.'

The Traveller drew his Glock and left the Bull in the recreation room. He headed for the old servants' quarters at the other end of the building, using his teeth to pull at the tape that secured the strapping on his wrist. The bandage peeled away. He flexed his fingers. It triggered a spasm in his wrist, but the pain was better than the restriction when he had to fight.

Black motes floated in the hazed air as he walked along the gallery, his Glock held out ahead of him. That same air seemed to disappear for a second or two, long enough for the Traveller to feel it pull at his lungs. The floor shuddered beneath his feet, and he felt rather than heard the pressure of the blast somewhere below. He fell to his knees as the door he'd closed just a few minutes ago was blown across the entrance hall. He rolled away from a wave of heat that rose up from below and flooded over him.

The walls reflected shifting and flickering oranges and reds, and smoke leaked up between the banisters. Heat prickled his throat and chest and stung his eyes.

'Fuck me,' the Traveller whispered as he clambered to his feet and got moving, aiming for the door at the far end of the hallway. Beyond it lay a small staircase that led to a series of tiny hallways and rooms that would once have housed maids and valets. He took his time, mindful of the shadows. He stopped halfway to blow a mixture of snot and soot out of his nose onto the carpet. He pictured the layout of the rooms beyond the door, recalling what he'd seen of them as he carried the woman up the stairs to Orla's room, the girl following, clinging to her mother's loose hand. There was a fire escape at the outer wall. If he could get Fegan, then fine. If he could get back to O'Kane, then all right, he would. If he could do neither, then to hell with Bull O'Kane and his money, he'd get the fuck out and leave them to burn like the cop in the cellar.

A thin dark blanket crept along the ceiling above him and the air grew hotter. The Traveller quickened his pace until he reached the door to the servants' quarters. He tested the brass doorknob for heat like he'd seen on television. It was cool. He took a breath, coughed, and threw the door open.

A wall of heat and black smoke knocked him to the floor. He landed on his back, blind and choking. The Glock had slipped from his fingers. He rolled onto his belly and felt the floor around him, seeking out the comfort of cold metal. He blinked hard, and his vision returned in a watery haze, but not enough to make out the pistol. His fingers brushed something solid as they swept along the floor, and he swung his hand back to find nothing. Had he knocked it away? No, he couldn't have, he'd hardly touched it.

'Fucking bast — '

Hard hands seized his collar, hauled him to his feet, and spun him around. He blinked again and again, trying to clear his eyes, until the stony ridges of a face came into focus, a face streaked red and black.

'Where are they?' Gerry Fegan said.

98

Fegan pushed him hard against the wall. A picture fell from its hook, the frame splitting as it hit the floor. The Traveller blinked back at him, tears cutting clear streaks through the black on his face.

'Where are they?' he asked again.

The Traveller wiped his eyes on his sleeve. He coughed and spat on the floor at Fegan's feet.

Fegan pushed him again. 'Where are they?'

The Traveller waved a hand at the door. 'Up there. Next floor up. I don't fancy their chances. The woman was half dead any — '

The heel of Fegan's hand rocked the Traveller's head back to smack against the wall. He staggered sideways but kept his footing. He brought a hand to his jaw. 'Jesus, the place is burning down around us and you want a fist fight? The Bull was right. You are a mad fucker.'

Fegan took the Traveller's Glock from his waistband. He aimed at the Traveller's forehead.

'Jesus, just go and get them while there's time,' the Traveller said as he raised his hands. 'It's up one flight, then the end of the hall, last on the left. The fire escape's right there. You might get the wee girl out if you go now. Christ, the stairwell's filling up, look at it, you might not make it.'

The moment Fegan chanced a look over his shoulder towards the door he knew he'd made a

441

mistake. The Traveller was on him with more speed than he'd ever seen, like a starved cat on its prey. He grabbed Fegan's wrist, forcing the pistol up, his momentum carrying both of them towards the smoke-filled doorway. Their feet tangled, and Fegan fell back, the Traveller's lean body landing on top of his.

The Glock bounced away across the carpet. The Traveller tried to scramble after it, but Fegan grabbed his shirt collar and hauled him back. A knee slammed into his groin, and Fegan convulsed, but didn't let go. He threw his weight to the side, rolling the Traveller's body away from his own, and followed, trying to straddle him. The Traveller bucked and twisted, not letting him take hold. He reached up and grabbed Fegan's throat with both hands. Instead of pulling away, Fegan let his weight press down on the arms until they quivered and buckled. His torso landed flat on the Traveller's chest, their eyes inches apart, the breath hot on Fegan's cheek as teeth snapped at his flesh.

Fegan cried out at the pain and the tearing sensation beneath his eye. He pushed himself up onto his knees. Smoke flooded his lungs, and the world shifted its balance, taking his own with it. He steadied himself against the wall, the Traveller still writhing beneath him. Fegan shook his head, tried to dislodge the heavy fog that had settled over his mind. He focused on the other man's face, brought his fists together to form a hammer, and smashed them down on the bridge of the Traveller's nose. It shattered against his hands, blood hot on his skin.

His vision blurred and swayed as the smoke clawed at the back of his throat. He pitched forward, jarring his elbow on the floor by the Traveller's head. The Traveller renewed his struggle, throwing his body from side to side. Fegan reached back to his waistband, searching for the revolver he'd stowed there. His hand closed on it, its metal chill reaching up through his arm to clear his mind. Fegan seized on that glint of clarity as he pulled the pistol free, used it to focus through the pain and black clouds. He brought the revolver around, tried to aim at the Traveller's forehead, but another wave washed over his consciousness. His upper body rocked forward from the waist, his spine seeming to give way. He saw the Traveller's hand too late as its heel shot upwards and connected with his jaw, slamming his teeth together, taking a piece of his tongue.

The world rotated around Fegan, first the floor and the Traveller's blood-streaked face rushing away from him, then the door, belching smoke up from the belly of the house, followed by the ceiling's blur as it raced past his vision. Red hung in the air as it all spun away from him, and somewhere in the fading light of his mind, he knew it was his own blood. The floor hit the back of his head, barely cushioned by the carpet.

Sparks and black dots peppered his vision, and through them, a grin surrounded by crimson, the Traveller, rising.

99

The Traveller untangled his legs from Fegan's, kicking the madman away. The Glock lay out of either man's reach. He raised himself up. Fegan watched from under drooping eyelids. The Traveller coughed, then doubled over, vomiting up the blood he'd swallowed. His head seemed to float, lighter than the rest of him. He knew he didn't have long, but he had to finish it. He had to see Fegan's life end.

The ceiling was lost now above a canopy of roiling darkness. Currents of hot air ferried black motes past his eyes. The Traveller tasted the burning through the blood and bile in his mouth. He swung his right foot into Fegan's groin. Fegan curled into a ball, his forearms across his stomach. The Traveller edged along the wall, using it for balance. When his feet were level with Fegan's eyes, he kicked hard. Fegan rolled away, spitting blood and a tooth.

The bright and beautiful joy of it flared in the Traveller's heart, sending waves of giddy happiness up to his brain. He stepped over Fegan's body, ignoring the clutching hands as he tried to rise, and drove a heel into his upturned face. It connected with Fegan's chin, and his body flopped back to the carpet.

Before he could follow the kick with another, a tidal wave through the centre of his brain sent the Traveller staggering sideways. His legs deserted him, and he landed on his side. He blinked, tried to clear his mind, but it was so hard, and he was so tired. Warmth enveloped him, pulled him down so his cheek rested on the carpet. His eyes closed for a few seconds, at first against his wishes, but soon he welcomed the darkness. It wouldn't be so bad to sleep here, to just let his eyes stay closed, let the warmth take him.

No.

Warm, like a soft bed on a winter morning.

No.

As he drifted, he saw Sofia and her round hips, her soft thighs, her belly swollen with the baby he'd resolved to give her.

No.

His eyes snapped open as a thunderbolt of pain cracked behind them. He screamed against it, filled his lungs with the precious clean air near the floor, and coughed. A spray of blood marked the carpet. As his vision cleared he saw the Glock just inches from his fingers. With every bit of strength left to him, he reached for it, took it in his grasp.

The Traveller forced his body up until he sat with his back against the wall. Fegan stirred, his chest rising and falling, his hands reaching up to grab at whatever phantoms circled him. The Traveller raised the Glock and blinked hard as he tried to align the sight on Fegan's head.

He drew in the clean air and held it in his lungs as he struggled to his feet. His legs quivered, but the wall held him upright until the

Glock picked out a point between Fegan's distant eyes.

The Traveller's finger tightened on the trigger, but a voice called to him from somewhere far away.

'What?'

The word emptied his lungs, forcing him to breathe the tainted air. His head immediately lightened, and he searched around him for the source of the intrusion.

There, by the door, the shape of a man, his blond hair blackened and burnt, pointing back at him. No, not pointing, aiming something —

Two hard punches to his shoulder, one after the other, and the floor slammed into his back. The ceiling looked like a churning river of black. Everywhere was silence, save for the faintest whistling in his ears. He tried to breathe in, but his lungs would not obey. His hands would not move to his chest to remove the weight and heat that had settled there.

100

Lennon stayed low, breathing as shallow as he dared. His eyes streamed and stung. He grabbed Fegan's collar and dragged him along the floor, managing a few feet before he had to stop, his lungs screaming.

Fegan rolled to his side and moaned. Lennon knelt down beside him.

'Can you get to your feet?' he asked.

Fegan blinked at him, his mouth open.

Lennon slapped his bloodied cheek. 'Listen, I need you to move. It's not far, just through the door.'

Fegan looked to the doorway, his face twisting as he tried to concentrate. His eyes cleared as he seemed to realise what Lennon wanted from him. He got to his hands and knees and crawled towards the door where smoke swirled in the battling air currents.

Lennon came alongside him, keeping his head down. He wedged a hand under Fegan's arm and pulled him to his feet. They staggered together, but Lennon steadied them. If he could just get Fegan to the fire escape, only fifteen feet away. He dragged Fegan after him, moving more by the momentum of their bodies than the will of their legs. The blackness swallowed them, billowing up from the stairwell, carried by the searing heat.

'Go,' Lennon said, his throat tightening

against the fumes. He pushed Fegan forward until he saw the light at the end of the corridor.

Fegan stumbled, landed on his knees. Lennon wrapped his arms around his torso and hoisted him up. He shoved him towards the open door and the fire escape's platform beyond.

Lennon tumbled through the door after Fegan, both men collapsing against the steel grating. Fegan gulped air. The gash beneath his left eye streamed red, the flesh around it swollen and puffy. More blood coated his neck, trickling and pulsing from his nearly severed earlobe. Lennon pulled himself up by the railing and breathed deep. He spat over the edge, fighting the swimming sensation that started in his head and ran down to his legs.

'Where are they?' Lennon asked.

Fegan retched and coughed.

Lennon hunkered down beside him. 'What did they do with them?'

Fegan turned his face to him. 'Upstairs,' he said, his speech slurred, his tongue red and swollen behind his teeth.

Lennon leaned back and looked at the platform above. 'Up there? In what room?'

A fresh wave of heat burst out of the door. Through the smoke, Lennon saw the flames advance.

'He told me the end of the corridor,' Fegan said. He coughed again and spat blood on the grating. 'In one of the old servants' rooms.'

Fegan got to his feet, using the railing to haul himself upright. He lurched towards the metal stairs and climbed. Lennon followed, pushed past him, taking two steps at a time despite the weakness in his legs. Fegan quickened his pace behind him, his feet slapping hard and clumsy on the steel steps.

Lennon reached the upper platform and went for the door. Like the fire exit below, it was old with plain glass panes set in a wooden frame. He smashed one of the panes with the pistol's butt and reached inside. The heat lapped at his hand as he fumbled at the lock. He pushed the door open and dropped low as a scorching black cloud billowed out.

Fegan reached the platform and staggered past Lennon into the darkness beyond the door.

Lennon followed him in. 'Which room?' he called after Fegan. The smoke attacked his chest, and he crouched down, coughing until his sides shrieked.

'Here,' Fegan said. He opened the nearest door, and fell through.

Lennon scrambled towards it. Through the black swirls he saw the shape of a man lying a few feet along the corridor, maybe a guard, either unconscious or dead. He crawled through the door and found Fegan hunched against the wall, his face blank and staring as his chest rose and fell. Tears mixed with the blood on his cheeks.

Marie McKenna sprawled on a bed, her sweater soaked red, her skin grey. Ellen lay on the floor beside Fegan, her eyes closed, her lips slightly parted.

'Christ,' Lennon said. 'Christ, no.'

He crawled towards Marie and took her hand.

The chill went to his core, the skin of her fingers dry and papery. Lennon's stomach turned on itself. He swallowed and forced his mind to focus, then reached over to Ellen, running the backs of his fingers across her cheek.

Still warm.

He pressed his ear to her chest. He tuned out everything, the crackling of the fire, the distant wailing of the smoke alarms, and listened. There, maybe, perhaps, a faint hint of a heartbeat.

He looked up at Fegan. 'I think — '

Fegan sat forward.

Lennon leaned down so his cheek was an inch from her mouth. The softest movement of air brushed his skin, sweet and warm.

'She's alive,' he said.

Fegan smiled. 'Take her. Get out.'

Lennon took Marie's hand one more time, squeezed the cold fingers between his, and whispered, 'I'm sorry.'

'Go,' Fegan said.

Lennon gathered the child in his arms and stood up. 'You can make it out. It's only a few feet.'

'I can't,' Fegan said. 'I'm tired. I want to sleep. That was all I ever wanted. To sleep.'

Lennon supported Ellen in one arm, and grabbed Fegan's collar with his free hand. Fegan brushed it away.

'No.' He coughed and gasped. 'For Christ's sake, get out and let me sleep.'

Lennon nodded and cradled Ellen. He turned and left Fegan in the room. The smoke in the corridor formed a solid wall now, and only a faint haze of light showed where the exit lay. He crouched as low as he could and made for it.

The floor rushed at him before he was aware of the grip on his ankle. He broke the fall with his forearms, pain shooting up from his elbows, and barely avoided crushing Ellen.

Big, hard hands grabbed at his legs, and Lennon couldn't tell if they were clawing to escape, or trying to drag him back. He kicked out, his foot connecting with something huge and immovable before the hands seized him again.

Lennon looked back as he struggled to free himself from their grip and saw Bull O'Kane's blackened face, his eyes wide and wild, his teeth bared.

The Bull screamed something as Lennon's foot slammed into his jaw.

101

Fegan couldn't be sure what got him moving. Had something shifted inside, telling him he wanted to live? Perhaps it was the fear of burning, though he knew the smoke would get him long before the flames. Whatever it was, it came with a burst of clarity, but something had preceded it. A shape in the swirling darkness, a woman with a baby in her arms, a woman with a soft, sad smile who had once shown him mercy. For a moment, he had thought she had come to welcome him to her place, wherever that was, but then she was gone and he wanted to move, tired as he was.

His legs carried him out to the corridor as his hands sought the walls for support. He went for the light, but stumbled over something hard and angular. The Bull's upended wheelchair, he realised as he untangled himself from it. As he crawled, he found a pair of legs, one stiff and unmoving, the other pushing at the floor.

Fegan saw the broad back and heavy shoulders, the meaty hands clasping at something. He threw himself on Bull O'Kane's back, snaked his arms around his huge chest, and pulled.

The old man screamed as Fegan dragged him deeper into the black. The smoke tore at Fegan's eyes and throat, but he kept pulling as O'Kane struggled. The clarity and strength that had come upon him in Marie's dying room began to slip away, and he pulled harder again, O'Kane's weight wrenching at his arms.

O'Kane reached up, tried to find Fegan's eyes. Instead, Fegan closed his teeth on the thick fingers and bit down. O'Kane squealed like a pig in an abattoir as the blood in Fegan's mouth mixed with his.

The heat grew until Fegan smelled burning hair and felt the skin on the back of his neck blister. Through the blackness he saw flames rise up from the stairwell behind him. He hauled O'Kane closer, fighting the rolling waves of fatigue and nausea, until he found the lip of the top step under his foot.

O'Kane cried out as he saw the fire below piercing the smoke to illuminate them both. He reached up, trying to get hold of the railing, but Fegan turned his weight towards the drop. With one last push, he threw O'Kane down towards the flames, but the Bull's fingers clasped at Fegan's clothes. The world turned and tumbled, wooden steps rushing up to batter Fegan's shoulders and ribs. His hand found the railing as O'Kane's bulk carried him on through the smoke to the burning pit below. The fire swallowed the Bull along with his screams until the only sound was its own roar.

Fegan willed his legs to move, his arms to drag him up the steps. He tried to breathe, but his ribs howled as they flexed, and he knew they were broken. Up above, through the smoke, there was light. He crawled towards it, pushing back against the pain until it evaporated. The light brightened as he climbed. How many steps had he fallen down? Surely not this many. The steps seemed to go on and on until he stopped counting them.

Still he climbed until the light was everywhere, and he had forgotten everything he'd ever known except a golden day in Belfast, not so long ago, when Ellen McKenna held his hand.

Fegan fell, hard wooden steps pressing against his cheek and his chest, soft as air. Sleep beckoned like warm arms. He listened, the whole wide world rushing past his ears.

In a strange and simple realisation, he knew his heart had stopped. The whistling in his ears swelled and lightning flashed across his vision. Faces formed in the black river that raged about him, some kind and loving, others frightened and hateful. His mother passed among them, and he remembered the rocks by the Portaferry shore, her spinning in circles while his hands clung to hers, lighter than air, his feet free of the earth as they both giggled, and he grew dizzy and frightened, but the laughter was bigger, and they spun and spun and spun for so long he thought they would spin for ever, but then the lightning came again and that was all.

Gerry Fegan met eternity with sun and salt air on his skin.

102

Lennon laid Ellen out on the grass, her pale face turned skyward. Somewhere in the distance, sirens wailed. He pinched her nose and covered her mouth with his. Her chest rose as he blew gently then fell as he took his mouth away. As he blew again he scrambled for the prayers his mother used to recite. This time Ellen coughed as the air escaped her. She gasped as she pulled more in, her back arching for a moment, then coughed again. Her eyelids fluttered but did not open. Her chest rose and fell of its own accord.

He put his ear to her heart and heard it beat, pressed his cheek to hers, let her warmth meld with his. The last of his strength faded, and he collapsed to the grass beside her. He rolled onto his back and took her hand. Her fingers twitched between his. Fire leapt from the mansion's upper windows. He knew grief lurked beneath the surface of his consciousness, but fatigue kept it submerged. It would have to wait.

Smoke curled up into the blue. Crows circled through it, cawing their alarm to one another. The sirens came closer, but he never heard them arrive.

103

He crawled, pain driving him on. Light ahead, just feet away. His lungs screamed. Heat everywhere. Just the will to live.

And the hate.

He reached forward, grabbed floor, pulled.

Hate.

Hate can carry a man far.

Far past the pain.

Even when the mind has gone, hate can carry the body forward.

Forward to the light.

The light is cool, clear.

Like a pool of clean water, waiting to soothe.

One more foot.

Six inches.

One more inch.

Air. Dear Christ, the air, so cool, so clean.

Falling now.

Oh God, the pain.

Pain, pain, go away, come again another day.

The Traveller screamed.

The Traveller breathed.

The Traveller laughed.

The Traveller crawled.

Epilogue

Ellen stared ahead, her hands wrapped together in her lap. She seemed so small on Lennon's big leather couch. He'd paid a stupid amount for it. No, he'd *borrowed* a stupid amount for it. Now it looked ridiculous, along with all the rest of the crap he had spent years gathering around himself.

He sat down opposite her.

'Susan will be here soon,' he said.

Ellen did not respond.

'She'll bring Lucy with her. You like Lucy.'

Ellen looked down at her hands. She made patterns with her fingers, as if communicating in some kind of sign language.

'I won't be long,' he said. 'Just a couple of hours. Then when I come back, we can watch a film. What's that one you like? The one with the fish.'

She folded her fingers together again and stared at a point behind Lennon. Her eyes followed something, as if tracking a person's movement across the room.

Today would be the last closed session of the inquiry. Dan Hewitt would take the stand and endorse Lennon's record. Lennon had felt not the slightest shred of guilt in blackmailing him. No one need ever know that the wound to Hewitt's leg had not been the result of an accidental discharge that occurred while cleaning his own personal protection weapon.

457

Uprichard had taken Lennon aside a few days back and assured him the discipline would be light. He would likely drop a rank, but they might let him keep his pay grade. Anything to avoid a fuss, the Chief Inspector had said, unable to keep eye contact.

The doorbell rang, pulling Lennon's attention back to the present. He went to the door and opened it for Susan, the divorcee from the floor above, and her daughter Lucy. Lucy carried a bag full of toys. As on other occasions when she'd visited, she would leave without some of them, even though Lennon had bought Ellen plenty of her own. She seemed to favour toys that had been played with, the more worn the better, as if old laughter clung to them, waiting for her to share.

'How is she?' Susan asked.

'Better,' Lennon said. 'Quiet, but better. She slept right through last night.'

Susan smiled. 'Good,' she said as Lennon led them back to the living room.

He stopped in the doorway, as did Susan. Lucy squeezed between them.

Ellen stood in the middle of the room, her hands reaching up to touch something, her voice low and soft as she spoke to the air. She dropped her hands to her sides and fell silent when she realised she was not alone.

Lennon went to her and crouched down. 'Who were you talking to, love?'

Ellen smiled for a second, mischief in her eyes, before her face went blank again. 'No one,' she said.

'Lucy's here,' Lennon said. 'Go and say hello, there's a good girl.'

She walked to her friend, her steps slow and deliberate. Lucy held the bag open for Ellen to inspect the contents, as if they were offerings.

Lennon bent down to kiss the top of Ellen's head. He had taken two steps away when she caught up with him and hugged his thigh, her head against his hip. She let go and returned to her friend Lucy. The two girls huddled together and whispered.

It saddened him to be away from her, but he had to leave, trust Ellen to his neighbour's keeping.

She was safe.

That was the most important fact in his world now, the one thing that made tomorrow better than yesterday, and he clung to it like a pillow in his sleep. His hand brushed Susan's as he left, and her fingers flexed against his, warm and firm.

Ellen was safe.

Lennon entered the lift, hit the button for the ground floor. It would be a hard day, questions upon questions, even if they skirted the hardest truths. But he'd get through it because he knew this one thing.

She was safe.

Acknowledgements

Once again, many people have helped in bringing this book to publication, and I'd like to thank just a few of them:

Nat Sobel, Judith Weber and all at Sobel Weber Associates for being the best agency a writer could hope for.

Caspian Dennis and all at Abner Stein Ltd for all their work on the home front.

Geoff Mulligan, Briony Everroad, Alison Hennessey, Kate Bland and all at CCV for their hard work and support.

Bronwen Hruska, Justin Hargett and Ailen Lujo at Soho Press for going many, many extra miles for me. And to the memory of Laura Hruska, who will be sadly missed.

Betsy Dornbusch, who continues to be a far better friend than I deserve, as well as Carlin, Alex and Gracie for welcoming me into their home.

Shona Snowden, whose insight always helps.

Juliet Grames for her excellent advice, and showing me a different side of New York, complete with karaoke.

David Torrans and all at No Alibis, Botanic Avenue, Belfast, for being the best bookshop on the face of the planet.

James Ellroy for dispelling the notion that you shouldn't meet your heroes, as well as all the other great authors I've met over the last couple of years. They are far too numerous to mention.

Craig Ferguson for giving me such a boost in the US, and for being very sweary.

Hilary Knight for her wonderful PR services.

Gerard Brennan, Declan Burke, and all the bloggers and online reviewers who have shown tremendous support since the very start. Again, they are far too numerous to mention by name, but you know who you are.

Ruth Dudley Edwards for being generally excellent.

Jo, for making everything better.

Finally, two books have helped enormously in writing this one. They are *Policing the Peace in Northern Ireland: Politics, Crime and Security after the Belfast Agreement* by Jon Moran (Manchester University Press) and *More Questions than Answers: Reflections on a Life in the RUC* by Kevin Sheehy (Gill & Macmillan).

THE TWELVE

Stuart Neville

Sooner or later, everybody pays — and the dead will set the price . . . Former paramilitary killer Gerry Fegan is haunted by his victims, twelve souls who shadow his every waking day and scream through every drunken night. Just as he reaches the edge of sanity they reveal their desire: vengeance on those who engineered their deaths. Greedy politicians, corrupt security forces, street thugs and bystanders who let it happen must all pay the price. As Fegan's vendetta threatens to derail Northern Ireland's peace process and destabilise its fledgling government, old comrades and enemies alike want him gone. Double agent David Campbell, with his own reasons for eliminating Fegan, takes the job. The secrets of a dirty war should stay buried, even if its ghosts do not.

DEADLOCK

Sean Black

Elite bodyguard Ryan Lock and his trusted friend, Ty Johnson, become convicted felons — sentenced to twenty years in Pelican Bay, California's notorious supermax prison . . . at least that's what the FBI and the United States Justice Department want everyone to believe. In reality, their mission, to keep one man alive for one week, is not straightforward. The inmate Frank 'Reaper' Hays, founding member of the white supremacist Aryan Brotherhood prison gang, is about to give evidence against members of his own gang for the brutal slaying of an undercover ATF agent and his family. And Hays refuses protective custody. In a world dominated by violent gangs, mistrust and constantly shifting alliances, Lock knows that he faces the toughest assignment of his career — just to stay alive . . .